PRAISE FOR CHARLIE N. HOLMBERG

KEEPER OF ENCHANTED ROOMS

"Filled with delightful period details and artfully shaded characters, this whimsical, thoughtful look at magic and its price is the perfect read for a cold fall night."

"Readers will be drawn in . . ."

T0044498

"This is Charlie at her best—intriguing mystery, creative magic systems, with plenty of romance to keep me turning the pages."

—Jeff Wheeler, *Wall Street Journal* bestselling author

STAR MOTHER

"In this stunning example of amazing worldbuilding, Holmberg (*Spellbreaker*) features incredible creatures, a love story, and twists no one could see coming. This beautiful novel will be enjoyed by fantasy and romance readers alike."

—*Library Journal*

THE SPELLBREAKER SERIES

"Those who enjoy gentle romance, cozy mysteries, or Victorian fantasy will love this first half of a duology. The cliff-hanger ending will keep readers breathless waiting for the second half."

—*Library Journal* (starred review)

"Powerful magic, indulgent Victoriana, and a slow-burn romance make this genre-bending romp utterly delightful."

—*Kirkus Reviews*

THE NUMINA SERIES

"[An] enthralling fantasy . . . The story is gripping from the start, with a surprising plot and a lush, beautifully realized setting. Holmberg knows just how to please fantasy fans."

—*Publishers Weekly*

THE PAPER MAGICIAN SERIES

"Charlie is a vibrant writer with an excellent voice and great world building. I thoroughly enjoyed *The Paper Magician*."

—Brandon Sanderson, author of *Mistborn* and *The Way of Kings*

"Harry Potter fans will likely enjoy this story for its glimpses of another structured magical world, and fans of Erin Morgenstern's *The Night Circus* will enjoy the whimsical romance element . . . So if you're looking for a story with some unique magic, romantic gestures, and the inherent darkness that accompanies power all steeped in a yet to be fully explored magical world, then this could be your next read."

—Amanda Lowery, *Thinking Out Loud*

THE WILL AND THE WILDS

"Holmberg ably builds her latest fantasy world, and her brisk narrative and the romance at its heart will please fans of her previous magical tales."

—*Booklist*

THE FIFTH DOLL

"*The Fifth Doll* is told in a charming, folklore-ish voice that's reminiscent of a good old-fashioned tale spun in front of the fireplace on a cold winter night. I particularly enjoyed the contrast of the small-town village atmosphere—full of simple townspeople with simple dreams and worries—set against the complex and eerie backdrop of the village that's not what it seems. The fact that there are motivations and forces shaping the lives of the villagers on a daily basis that they're completely unaware of adds layers and textures to the story and makes it a very interesting read."

—*San Francisco Book Review*

THE
HANGING CITY

ALSO BY CHARLIE N. HOLMBERG

The Whimbrel House Series

Keeper of Enchanted Rooms

Heir of Uncertain Magic

The Star Mother Series

Star Mother

Star Father

The Spellbreaker Series

Spellbreaker

Spellmaker

The Numina Series

Smoke and Summons

Myths and Mortals

Siege and Sacrifice

The Paper Magician Series

The Paper Magician

The Glass Magician

The Master Magician

The Plastic Magician

Other Novels

The Fifth Doll

Magic Bitter, Magic Sweet

Followed by Frost

Veins of Gold

The Will and the Wilds

You're My IT

Two-Damage My Heart

THE
HANGING
CITY

CHARLIE N. HOLMBERG

Published by 47North, Seattle

www.apub.com

Amazon, the Amazon logo, and 47North are trademarks of Amazon.com, Inc., or its affiliates.

ISBN-13: 9781662512162 (hardcover)
ISBN-13: 9781662508707 (paperback)
ISBN-13: 9781662508714 (digital)

Cover design and illustration by Micaela Alcaino

Printed in the United States of America

First edition

To Leah,
who has always supported me the way W10 x 12s
support a composite floor.
(She will think that's funny.)

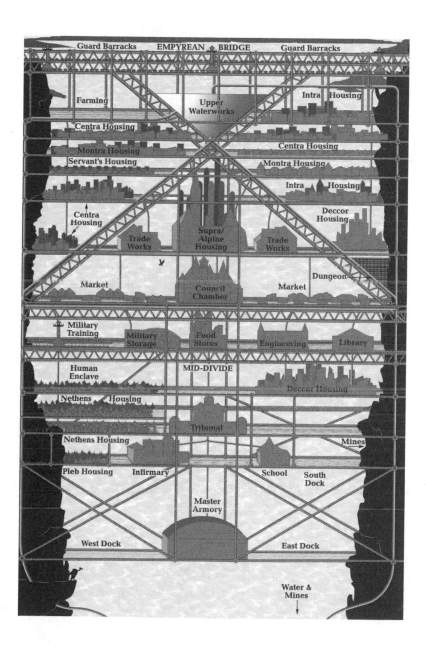

PROLOGUE

"Let me tell you about Paca's journey to Eterellis," the old bard says, sitting on a dried stump and drumming knobby fingers on his knees. Everyone gathers around, even the adults. I approach cautiously, still very much a newcomer in this township, even after two months. But I'm keenly fond of stories, and of learning anything this man knows that I do not.

Finnie, of an age with me at thirteen, nods encouragement. I kneel behind a cluster of children, the youngest ones shoving at each other for better seats.

One complains, "We know that story. Tell us another."

The bard feigns shock. "But there are so few stories to tell. They all dried up with the rain, and folk are so few and far between, no one has a chance to weave new tales."

I have stories, I think, but none of them have happy endings. Not yet. Out of habit, I look up at the emerging stars. The South Star burns brightly already; it is always the first to appear as the sun sets and never shifts from its position in the sky, ever shining the way to Eterellis, even after the city's death.

Another child groans.

"My version is special, little ones," the bard insists. "Listen carefully."

He sits up straighter, pulls a seven-string mandolin onto his lap, and plays a song that is simple in melody but complex in technique. My mother had an instrument like that. I was never allowed to touch it.

"Paca was a poor woodworker," he begins, "who wanted to marry the local lord's daughter. Mind you, back then wood was common and didn't have the value it has today, and lords were well known and powerful."

I think of my father and shiver.

"And so he wrote her a poem confessing his love, pleading for just over one year's time to make his fortune and win her hand."

The bard begins to sing.

My love is true, my heart is yours
You deserve much more than I am
Four hundred suns, and I will come
A wealthy and affluent man

"Then Paca set out to go where any man would to seek his fortune—the great kingdom of Eterellis. Where every building touched the sky and was made of topaz and marble. Jade lined the sidewalks, and the trees grew taller than the mountains."

I've imagined the dead human city many times, though the buildings were always white as sun-hot sand and the cobblestone gleamed silver. But before I can adjust the image, the bard continues.

"He traveled far over this land, crossing the rivers that once flowed and the forests that once stood. His rations grew thin, but he always managed to sell a carving or fix a wagon wheel when he grew desperate. And soon he came to the great crack of Mavaea, and the mighty Empyrean Bridge that spanned it."

His playing takes on a darker tone.

A canyon so deep, a canyon so wide
Monsters who feast upon flesh lurk inside
On his way to the glory of man
Crossing the bridge built by ten thousand hands

"But of course, as soon as he stepped onto the bridge—"

"The troll came out," interrupts the first child, his tone bored. His friends snicker.

"*Two* trolls came out." The bard sounds smug at the soft correction, and I smile to myself. He waits for his small audience to quiet before continuing. "Two trolls came out, their tusks sharp in their mouths, their bodies heavy and green as moss.

"The one on the right said, 'Human, give us all you have of worth if you want to cross the bridge. That is the toll of the trolls.'

"Paca, though afraid, held his ground. 'But if I do *not* give it to you, you will kill me where I stand and take it anyway.'

"The troll chuckled. 'I give my word that I will not.'

"Paca gestured to the troll on the left. 'But he has not made the same promise.'

"The two trolls looked at one another, smiling. The troll on the left said, 'But I may.'

"Now, Paca was very clever. He saw that these trolls were trying to be smart; he needed only be smarter than they. Or, in this case, more confusing." The bard touches the side of his nose and glances at the interrupting boy. "And so Paca said to the left troll, 'And then you will take all I have for yourself, and leave us both empty-handed.'

"Now the first troll narrowed his eyes, trying to follow Paca's logic. For of course the two trolls had come out together, and thus the earnings should be split fairly. The first troll argued with the second, saying he should not take it all for himself, and the second grew angry that the first would think him a thief. Their honor came into question, and then their seniority, and finally their strength, which made it a sore discussion indeed, for trolls value nothing more than their strength."

A quiet lad at the front raises his hand. "But we know how this goes. The trolls are so distracted that they do not see Paca draw his sword and kill the both of them. He crosses the bridge without trouble."

The bard shakes his head. "It is there you are wrong, for Paca was not a violent person. This tale happened in the days of the power of men, so he had little need to be. No, the trolls grew so enraptured with their argument that Paca snuck by unnoticed."

The boy snorts, but the bard is unhindered.

"Just as he was passing, Paca heard one of the trolls make an oath to the other, words he had never heard uttered before. An oath to promise trustworthiness and innocence. Paca could feel that the oath had power, and so he kept it in his heart and continued on his way.

"He went to Eterellis, and he found his fortune—*how* is another story for another day—and after four hundred days had passed, he made his way home, a richer man than he had ever been before. And when he stepped back on the bridge, two new trolls emerged atop it, again demanding all he had as toll.

"But this time Paca uttered the oath to the trolls, shocking them greatly. The trolls honored the power of his words and let him pass without trouble. Paca wended his way back home, where he met with his love's father and boasted of his success and indeed won the hand of the lord's daughter. And all his life he kept the troll oath sacred—"

"But why?" Danner, Finnie's oldest brother, four years my senior, asks. He stands at the edge of the firelight, his arms folded tightly across his chest. "Why would it matter? They're *trolls*."

The bard gives him a knowing look. "Not just *trolls*, my boy. They're your counterparts. There was nowhere for the trolls to go, so they built their city in the darkness descending from that very bridge. The humans drove them from the sun, until the sun searched for them so hard that the land became unbearable for living. The city still stands today."

A few people murmur to one another. Pairs of adults lean close. No one likes the idea of the endless drought being their fault. I glance to Finnie, but she has lost interest in the tale and draws patterns in the dust at her knees. Her father calls out, "Sing us a song."

But the bard responds, "That will be another bag." Everyone groans and begins to depart. A bag of amaranth flour, he means. A small one, barely larger than my fist, but food is too precious to be wasted on a song, especially when there are a few among us who sing well enough.

The bard puts away his mandolin and picks himself off the stump. I hesitate, but as the crowd clears, I approach him, wringing my fingers together.

"What was the oath?" I ask. I offer him a copper, though foodstuff is worth more. Still, I have a good handful of money taken from my father's house, hidden away in the room I share with Finnie.

The bard dips his head and accepts the coin. "It is but a story, lass."

"Then it is a story that leaves out the most important part," I argue.

He studies me, his pale eyes raking over my face. "It is told in many ways, Paca's journey to Eterellis. But the way I have heard is this: that Paca crept away from his would-be robbers, and as they argued, the second said to the first, 'By sun, earth, and shadow, and as Regret forms on my lips, I am of trollis and am bound by its words.'"

I mouth the strange oath. I don't understand its meaning, but it's beautiful, poetic in its own way. "Thank you," I offer.

The bard smiles before swinging his pack over his shoulder and starting for his bed.

I can't help but notice the sharpness of his teeth.

Chapter 1

The Empyrean Bridge is the most wondrous thing I've ever seen.

Despite my dry throat and empty waterskins, the blisters on my feet, and the sunburn stiffening my arms and shoulders, I marvel at it. It has not been used in a hundred years or more, not since the drought hit and wiped out Eterellis, the great human city far west of it. The bridge spans a canyon that cuts the world in two, a dark, jagged line stretching farther north and farther south than I can ever hope to see. Its workmanship is impeccable, more brilliant and beautiful than any other architecture I have ever beheld, beyond what I had pictured since hearing of its existence. The stories don't do it justice. Its many arches gleam white as sun-bleached sand. It's longer than any township, including my hometown of Lucarpo, the largest east of the canyon, 150 miles almost due east, if I've read the stars correctly. I know Lucarpo is the largest, because I've been to every human outcropping worth a mark on a map. I've visited them all, slept in their peoples' homes, worked in their dying fields, and run from their borders. Often because my father's men, or rumor of them, arrived. Other times, because others saw the darkness within me and hated me for it. I once wielded it like a vile sword against one of their own, who was equally as vile.

That, I do not regret. But I do miss Terysos more than any other township. Terysos is the reason I've sacrificed everything to travel here, to a place of rumor that might not even exist, all on the word of a wayward bard. All on the hope that the South Star shines not as a grave marker for Etcrellis, but as a guide, leading me to a place I might belong. Shining as a punctuation of the reading that a kind Cosmodian once gave me by my father's woodshed, planting the first seed of hope in the gloom of my soul.

If the bard's tale is true, then this is the one place my father will never look for me. If false, I will die here, overtaken by thirst. There is no other refuge.

Thick parapets gleam copper in the bright daylight across the bridge's full length, clear to the other lip of the canyon. The bridge spans the canyon's narrowest point, as far as I know, but surely it will take me half a day to cross it. I think back on the stories of Paca the woodworker and wonder how he got all the way to the end of this monstrosity without killing the trolls who stopped him.

My faith in the old bard wavers.

The bridge grows larger as I near, revealing detail work along its thick stone towers. The decking looks as brilliant as the parapets. If this is simply the bridge *leading* to Eterellis, then surely the ancient city itself is breathtaking, even in its death. It is said the drought started in that kingdom, its hold so great that nothing can live there, not even tarantulas or sagebrush.

I pause before the great architecture can fill my entire view, knowing I will not be able to run if I change my mind. I've traveled too long and too far. My rations are gone, and there is nowhere to replenish them, save for this place of myth and story.

Cagmar, the city of the trolls.

The gods made the stars, and through them made creatures in pairs: the fette and aerolass to rule the air, the merdan and gullop to rule the sea, and the humans and trolls to rule the earth. And so we did, before the earth changed and ruled us instead. According to the stories, in the time before, humans dominated, despite trolls being larger and stronger.

War-torn brutes. Angry. Animals. Merciless. In all the tales told at bed-side and campfire, trolls are always the enemy.

I could use the same words to describe my father. I know I should fear coming to Cagmar more than I do, but fear has been such a constant companion to me I hardly notice it anymore.

I take in the bridge. Legend doesn't matter. Now, the humans and the trolls have something in common. We are all trying to survive.

I check over my shoulder, scanning the heat-curled horizon for shadows or pursuers. But I have kept ahead of them, as I always have. I am utterly alone and without options. Even if the trolls are as terrible as stories say, if I can keep even one thread of agency, they will be better than what I left behind.

Pushing one sore foot ahead of the other, I swallow against an arid throat. My pale hair is loose and flows around me as a gust of hot wind passes—better for keeping off the sun this way. The Empyrean Bridge grows as I approach, looming and magnificent.

I have a weapon, if my words fail me, though I've never used it on a troll. If Cagmar is a myth . . . perhaps it would be better to jump from the bridge than to be captured. I do not want a slow death. Or perhaps there is a township on the other side of the canyon, not marked on my map, that would take me in, if dehydration doesn't claim me first.

Theories, theories, theories.

As I approach the canyon wall, I see darkness stretch below the bridge. The sun is descending but is not yet set. That darkness is not shadow but stone.

It does not look like a city, but I of all people know that looks can easily deceive. The dark mass is enormous, unlike any township I've ever beheld. It makes me think of a moth pupa.

Despite its majesty, the bridge is not as spectacular as it appears from a distance. It, too, has fallen to the elements. The centuries of drought. Rocks crack, wood splinters, iron rusts. Décor has chipped and worn. Yet the bearings still appear strong, as do the girders. As though they've been maintained.

Point one for the bard.

I offer a prayer as I stand before the bridge, only a pace from its first plank. I wonder if I am ready for death. I am almost thirsty enough to believe I am.

I wait to be attacked. To be robbed. I wait to see the beasts of legend. I stand at the edge of the broken path for several minutes, waiting, listening, tasting the air. Nothing happens. Neither bird nor cloud touches the sky. Not even a second breeze passes to stir the dust.

I step onto a thick wood plank. I expected it to creak beneath my weight, but it holds steady. A lock of hair sticks to the sweat along the side of my face. I don't peel it away. I'm surprised I have anything left to sweat.

Another step, and then another. Not a single creak nor echo. I cross the first plank, then the second. The third, down to the eighth. I see no sign of life, only a nearly endless path ahead.

Did the drought wipe out the trolls, too, leaving their shadowed city to hang in ruins? Is my last attempt at shelter to go unachieved?

Could I make it to Eterellis, and see the great ruins for myself, before my body withers and dies?

My steps become surer, my strength rallying as the sun dips, cooling the air a degree at a time. I count the planks as I pass them, wondering at the enormous trees they must have hailed from, when one—the twenty-sixth—groans beneath my weight. I slow, examining it. The wood neither bows nor splinters. I shift my weight, and the sound repeats, but farther to my right.

It is then I realize it has not creaked beneath *my* weight, but someone else's. Someone coming from *below*.

I step back, my breath coming quick. I search the bridge, scanning from one side to the other, when I hit something solid behind me.

Whirling around, I look up, up, *up* . . . into the face of a troll.

My heart drops to my stomach, while my stomach rushes to my throat. Again, my imagination has failed me.

The troll is immense and green as onion shoots. Hammered armor crosses his massive chest, leaving room for the natural spikes on his shoulders to protrude outward. His muscled forearms are covered with sheaves of fur, also cut to reveal a row of smaller bony spikes. Nubs of bone line the widest jaw I've ever beheld. His nose is short, and his green brow is so thick it hides half his eyes. His greasy hair forms a widow's peak, with yet more bony nubs sprouting on either side of it. Short tusks jut forward from wide, snarling lips. A thick belt of some sort of leather encompasses a middle six times thicker than my own.

I am six feet tall standing straight, but this creature towers over me. The top of my head comes to the base of his chest. He raises a spear, and his ears—like large human ears with the top curve sliced off—twitch.

With one muscular arm, he points the tip of the chipped spearhead at my throat.

The bridge creaks again. I spin, my hair catching on the spear, to see two, three, *four* trolls climbing up and over the sides of the bridge like spiders. Three green, one a sickly shade of gray. Two wield spears, two swords. All are made of thick, rippling muscle.

They form an armored circle around me that narrows and shrinks.

Fear bubbles within me, reacting to my own. It presses against my skin, eager to be released.

Before it overwhelms me, I peel my tongue from the roof of my mouth and screech the oath I repeated a thousand times on my journey here: "By sun, earth, and shadow, and as Regret forms on my lips, I am of trollis and am bound by its words!"

The blades stop. Heat pummels me like a hammer. Sweat slicks my skin. The air feels so arid, I struggle to breathe.

The first troll says, "You dare speak an oath to us?" His language is my own, but his accent is hard around the edges, otherly.

I dare to meet his gaze, pressing down my inner darkness. I don't understand the meaning of the words, but they're all I have. Fists clenched, I repeat, "By sun, earth, and shadow, and as Regret forms on my lips, I am of trollis and am bound by its words."

One of the trolls behind me spits. Another grumbles, "It is law."

The first troll growls, turns his spear around, and jabs its head into the wooden plank he stands on. He pulls a cloth from around his waist.

Large hands grab me, a hard knuckle grazing my arm.

The cloth, a bag, jerks over my head, smelling foul. But it is more than a sour smell, because my head starts to spin. I struggle to focus, only to feel weightless, the air punched out of my lungs.

All is black. When I come to, my hands are tied tightly behind me, and I bounce as though carried over a shoulder. A bony protrusion presses into my ribs. I try to squirm away from it, but the thick, muscled arms around my legs only tighten, holding me in place. The bag clings to the sweat of my temples. I try fruitlessly to spit out my own hair. Panic flashes cold across my skin, but I remind myself that although I'm being taken by trolls, they have not hurt me yet. That must mean something.

Still, I am carried for a long time, shaken as though descending stairs, then weightless again as though slowly falling down holes. The air around me cools significantly. No light peeks through my bag.

How far into their city have they carried me, and how will I ever find my way out?

By the time I'm roughly deposited on a smooth stone floor, I'm shaking, and not from the chill. My stomach threatens to upturn, my mouth is dry, and when the sack is yanked off my head, it takes me too long to orient myself. I stare down at the dark cobbled stone under my hands. I stare and stare, trying to make sense of it.

"She spoke the oath," a low voice says behind me. The first troll from the bridge.

"Another one?" spits a hard baritone. A beat passes. "I'm going to find this singing louse and rip his tongue out. Well, what is it?"

The words dance around me like drunk fairies.

A low woman's voice barks, "Oh, for Regret's sake, give her some water."

My thoughts catch on the use of that word, *regret*, but my mind pushes forward to the more crucial offering. *Water?*

My dry eyes struggle to blink clear. Something hits the stone beside me with a tinny ring. It takes a moment for me to recognize it as a pitcher of water.

A soft squeak escapes me as I grab it and drink, the water stale and metallic and wonderful. Some of it sloshes down the front of my dress. I drink until the pitcher is empty and my stomach aches.

"Thank you," I wheeze as I set the pitcher down.

I try again to survey the room. It's about three times the size of my father's sitting room in Lucarpo, with a higher ceiling and higher door-ways. It's lightly furnished, with wide swaths of fabric hanging from the ceiling and connecting to the walls, reminding me of a bed canopy. An enormous fur rug swallows the center of the floor—it comes from a monstrous creature I cannot name, for it is all one hide. I sit only a couple of paces from its edge. On its other side sit five elaborate chairs made of stone, each cushioned, each bearing a terrifying troll. Their skin varies in shades of gray and green. They all sport wide features, though the one on the farthest left throne is a little narrower than the others, with shorter tusks and longer hair—the woman who demanded I be given water. If they have the same bulges of strength as the trolls who brought me down here, it's hidden beneath their robes.

"Thank you," I repeat.

Her heavy brow lowers.

The troll in the center throne leans forward. He's the largest of the bunch, with enormously broad shoulders covered by a fur stole. His hair is short and slicked away from his face, emphasizing the bony nubs trailing back from his forehead. His tusks—or feasibly large lower canines—are massive.

"Do you even know the words you speak, human?" he asks. His is the baritone voice.

I nod slowly, though in truth, I can't possibly understand the oath based on a single story told when I was thirteen. Remembering myself, I reposition onto my knees and bow.

The troll snorts. "A polite human, at least."

"We've enough of their kind, Qequan," the troll to his right says. His voice is so low it reverberates through the stone. Qequan must be the name of the center troll. Judging by his position and size, I assume him to be the leader. The bass continues, speaking now to me. "Sniveling humans who can't work their own land come crawling across the desert to take what is ours. The trollis kingdom grew in the cracks of the earth to avoid your kind. And the moment Regret no longer favors you, you beg for help."

I shiver. I don't understand his meaning of *regret*, but his words are not untrue. Yet it seems wise not to respond.

Qequan frowns and studies me. I focus on the fur rug, for I know I will unabashedly stare at him otherwise. Sounding amused, he says, "She made the oath. Will you not honor it?"

The bass doesn't reply.

Louder, Qequan adds, "Ichlad makes a most excellent point. You sit before the council of Cagmar unharmed. We have fulfilled the words of our ancestors. You will now be escorted out."

"No, please." I prostrate myself. "I've come a long way to find shelter within your city. I can work. Anything you need." Silently I pray to the South Star. I need to know I chose correctly. I need the brightness that the Cosmodian promised me eight years ago, and I don't know where else to search for it.

One of the other trolls scoffs.

The woman says, "We do not make a point of housing refugees."

I lift my head. "Have so many come?"

She exchanges a glance with Qequan.

"Some come." She doesn't look at me. "Few have even the worth to clean our commodes."

I believe her. Very few humans would be as daring as I, coming to a place rumored to be riddled with war. The home of our ancestors' mortal enemies. The monsters of the canyon.

But monsters lurk among humans, too.

"Please," I press.

Qequan sets his elbow on his armrest and leans into his palm. The room is lit by austere sconces that cast his skin a dark olive. "What is your name." It's an order, not a question.

Calia Thellele slips through my mind like overused oil. But I have not uttered that name for seven years. "Lark, Master Qequan." Lark is the nickname my nursemaid gave me when I was small, claiming I sounded like the bird when I wailed. I have never heard one myself. Larks live by large bodies of water, and none of those exist around here.

His lip quirks. "I do not think I've ever been called *Master*."

At his side, Ichlad murmurs, "Do not let yourself be charmed by one of *them*."

The others seem to echo the displeasure, and I wonder what sort of stories have been told about my people at their bedsides. Are we painted as terrible and vicious, or weak and unseemly?

"Your skills?" Ichlad asks me.

I straighten but remain on my knees. "I can read."

The troll rolls his eyes, which stuns me. In every human township I've been to, I have been admired for my ability to read. It declares my usefulness more than anything else.

Are so many trolls literate as to demean the skill?

"I-I can read missives, books, maps, anything." I see my father's study around me and blink it away. "I'm familiar with political strategy. I can clean and cook—"

"Everyone can clean and cook," the woman snaps. "If you cannot prove yourself useful, you will be taken above."

I hear what she doesn't say. *Your oath will not work on us twice.*

15

The cool touch of panic crawls over me like lice. "I can also read music. Play the harp"—though I haven't touched one since before my womanhood—"and I can sing." *A little.*

Qequan glances to the others. "We have no need for musicians and librarians, little bird. Do not visit us again. And if you've *any* respect for sacred things, you will never utter that oath to another creature, do you understand me?"

They are casting me out.

They are *casting me out.*

A hand touches my shoulder, ready to drag me away. I start and turn, noticing four armored trolls behind me, by the large door I must have come through. One still holds the head sack.

No, no, *no.* If I leave Cagmar . . . there is nowhere else to *go.* Nowhere else to hide.

Your path will not be straight, but broken and looping, the Cosmodian's voice whispers in my ear. The prediction I've clung to since childhood.

"Please. I'll do even your filthiest jobs."

The troll grasps my arm and hauls me to my feet. Qequan's countenance is hard as stone. He looks away from me. The woman shakes her head. The troll drags me toward the door.

"I'm a fast learner!" I shout. "And I've good eyesight! I could scout for you!"

The troll on the far right chuckles. Another troll takes my other arm.

I don't know how to read this, Calia, her voice whispers.

My father will find me. He will punish me. And then he will use me, as he always did.

Use me.

Use me.

"*Wait!*" My voice echoes between stone walls. Ichlad startles. Even the guards hesitate.

Qequan's gaze slides back to me.

"I have one other skill. One you've never seen." My words rush and slide together until they're almost nonsensical. I can hardly believe I'm uttering them. Never in my life, *never*, have I willingly shared my secret. Never have I told a soul about my darkness. A few have seen it, felt it for themselves, but fear can always be explained away.

"You try my patience." Qequan's voice is a threat.

The guards release me. Rubbing my arm, I say, "It's a talent unique among my people." Stars bless that it's also unique among the trolls. "But it's a guarded one."

Qequan raises an eyebrow.

I step away from the guards. "I . . . I ask for as few witnesses as possible."

The trolls frown at me.

After a breath, Qequan says, "I will not deplete the council."

I glance to the guards.

"Nor my men."

I stand tall. Or try to. How would my father turn this to his benefit? He would play on the troll's pride. "Do you fear a human will harm you, Master Qequan?"

He smirks again. At least he has a sense of humor. Several seconds pass before he dips his head, and the four troll guards move away from me and out the door. It shuts heavily in their wake.

"If you're wasting our time . . . ," Ichlad begins.

I hold up my hands in surrender. "I am not. But I do have to demonstrate on someone."

The second troll from the right, who has been quiet, says, "And what is it you plan to *demonstrate*?" His tone is mocking, his accent thick.

I lower my hands. "I . . . I scare people."

Multiple chuckles reverberate across the thrones. Ichlad says, "You are human. You are fragile as the stem of a feather. You seek to incite terror in *us*?"

Even the smallest among them could likely snap my neck in the crook of an elbow. The gods built these creatures well.

If for some reason my darkness is not effective on trolls . . . then my fate remains what it was.

"Would . . ." My mouth dries again. "Would one of you volunteer?"

Qequan and Ichlad exchange a look. Qequan says, "I'm amused. You may try it on me."

He stands, and he is *enormous*. Over eight feet tall, surely. Taller than all the trolls in the room and on the bridge. He is broad and muscular, though his stomach is round and well fed. He is a troll who has seen battle; it's evident in his stance.

He crosses until he stands in the center of that large monster's pelt, then holds out his hands. "Do your worst, little bird."

"I'll have on your honor that I will not be harmed." If trolls have oaths, they must have honor.

He grins, showing me his teeth, emphasizing his tusks. "Of course."

I swallow. Men usually have two responses to fear—fight or flee. Qequan does not seem like one to flee.

Taking a deep breath, I adjust my stance, feet shoulder-width apart. I want to say I've never used my darkness like this, that it's always been a last resort, self-defense, anything. But I have. I've used it in calm, quiet rooms against those both bigger and smaller than myself. Sometimes with my father's hand on my shoulder, sometimes with his expectations pressed to my spine. I haven't been so calculated about it for a long time.

I brace myself, trying not to cringe. My ability is a double-edged sword. I cannot wield fire without getting burned, so to speak, though knowing that the fire isn't real helps me control the pain.

Qequan appears bored, so I dig down. My body is on edge, my mind bogged with worry, and so it comes up readily, a locust eager to feast. I pull it out of me, an invisible force, an unheard song that trickles through my veins and makes my heart race, my back sweat, my jaw clench. The physical manifestations hit first, then the mental ones. My own urge to flee, the tunneling of vision, the warping of time. If I push too hard, the fear goes straight to my heart and becomes my own blind panic, rampant and hungry and cold. I gauge it carefully. I need to stay myself, but I *need* Qequan to see me.

Steeling myself against the fright, I shove it at the troll.

His reaction is immediate.

His breath hitches. Eyes widen, whites glistening. He takes a step back as though pushed. His knees tremble.

And then he rips the hammer from his belt and rushes at me with a war cry that nearly breaks my eardrums.

I cut off the fear immediately, but he's still charging. I stumble back and fall onto the cold stone, natural terror surmounting me. I shriek, lift my arms to protect myself—

"Qequan!" Ichlad bellows.

Silence, save for heavy breathing that isn't mine. My heart hammers quarter seconds. Several pass. Carefully, I move my arms and peer out. Qequan is right there, nearly touching me, his hammer raised. Confusion crinkles his expression, his chest heaving like a bellows, just like mine. The faint sconce light glimmers off two rows of turquoise beads on his right sleeve.

He blinks. Heavy lines crease his brow. He lowers the hammer slowly, as though the joints of his shoulders were rusted. Steps back. Again. Looks at me as though I've turned into a snake. I swallow deep breaths, trying to find my calm.

Two of the other four council members, Ichlad and the woman, have risen from their seats. Several heartbeats pass before the former asks, "Are you with us?"

Qequan's body relaxes. He drags a large hand over his face and turns to them. "I am." He glances back at me.

I'm ready for him to call me a monster, to cast me out the way Finnie and her family did, the way Andru did. But as Qequan studies me, unabashed, the confusion melts into intrigue. That is, if I can even hope to read the expression of a troll.

"You didn't even move," he says.

I get my feet under me. "I-I don't have to."

"By will alone?"

Rolling my lips together, I nod.

He returns the hammer to his belt and strides across the room, wholly dignified, taking his place in the center throne. The woman and Ichlad follow suit. Once Qequan is comfortable, he says, "How?"

I walk forward until my toes touch the animal pelt. "I don't know. I've had it since I was a child."

The troll on the far right says, "She would prove excellent in interrogations."

Sweat beads down the center of my back. I hadn't considered *what* the trolls might use my horrid curse for. They wouldn't . . . They wouldn't make me torture people, would they? Because fear is a torture in and of itself. My father's favorite method.

Stars above, what have I done?

Qequan has not taken his eyes from me. "It works on anything?"

I try not to fidget. "I . . . I know it works on humans, and wolves. And apparently trolls."

He frowns, though I'm not sure why. "Then it would work on the creatures of the canyon."

The woman shifts to the edge of her seat. "You think she could frighten those beasts?" She sounds incredulous.

Qequan smooths his stole. "Would you like her to demonstrate on you, Agga, so you can gauge for yourself?"

For the first time since I arrived, Agga looks out of her element. Uncomfortable. And I hate that it's because of me. But I also need them to accept me. Help me. Hide me. And if they respect this currency . . . I will freely give it.

To Ichlad, Qequan says, "Choose one of our slayers to partner with her until she learns what she needs to know."

Ichlad considers me. "Will you allow her to wield a sword?" As though I'm not standing right there.

"She doesn't need to." Qequan smiles. "She *is* one."

Chapter 2

I wait for several hours in what must be a prison cell. It's small and cold, without a single light or window. I'm desperate for a window, to witness the passage of time, to see the stars and any advice they might have for me, for what little of them I understand. I've found strength in the night sky when I could find none in humankind, and so I seek out their light even here, locked away beneath the surface of the world.

On the well-worn floor is nothing but an old cot, where I sit, and a tin water bowl like one might give a dog, which I've already drained. The door is narrow and heavy, with a thin slider that can be accessed only from the outside. But the slider is open, letting in light from sconces in the hallway, so I don't worry *too* much.

As I lean against the cool wall, dozing, heavy footsteps approach. I start and listen. Three pairs of them, but two drop away, leaving only one pair to reach the door. She blocks the light, which makes her difficult to make out, but I do not miss that she is unhappy, for that expression is similar across all the gods' creatures.

She's over seven feet tall, with thick divots in her arms and shoulders marking every massive muscle and taut sinew. Her waist tapers above notably round hips. Her skin is a deep shade of green; dark-auburn hair is pulled away from her face, emphasizing a widow's peak; and bony studs gleam on her scalp. Ivory teeth bookend her lips and nearly reach her nostrils. Her eyes remind me of uncut topaz. I notice two turquoise beads on her sleeve, similar to Qequan's.

I stand, and she looks me over briefly, her frown deepening. "You're Lark."

I nod.

She grumbles something under her breath, then turns and leaves. I follow, quickening my steps to keep up with her long stride. When I'm at her heels, she says, "Don't know what use you'll be at the docks."

"Docks?" I repeat, ducking to avoid a sconce. "You have ships?"

She gives me an incredulous look. "No." She rubs the spot between her brows. "Regret knows what I did to deserve this."

That term, again. *Regret.* "I'm sorry, but what was your name?"

She drops her hand. "Unach."

It's a hard name, *oo-natch*, and my tongue resists when I repeat it. "And where are we going?"

Unach seems irritated even by my voice. "We're going to my quarters. The council has decided that you are somehow *worth* something, and I'm supposed to house you until they can find some other nook to shove you into."

I guess by her tone and choice of words that the council respected my request to keep my abilities secret, the last thing I'd begged of them before a guard escorted me to that cell.

Worth something. Even children know the trolls value strength above all else. I never considered myself weak, but I'm truly nothing next to the others I've met in size and bulk. All the food and exercise in the world would never get me close.

We start up narrow stairs, forcing me to walk directly behind Unach. At least we're leaving the prison.

"I'm a slayer," she continues. "I'll be teaching you the ropes. Literally."

Her accent is so heavy it sounds like her words barely make it past her lips. I don't know what she means by the "ropes," but I hesitate to ask. She mutters something I catch only half of, but I piece together the meaning. *Qequan has finally lost his mind.* And then what sounds like a curse about humans.

Unach searches through a bag at her side as we reach the top of the stairs, and she hands me a hard, lopsided, bright-pink circle, roughly the size of my hand. "Here."

I take it, the edges rough and flaky. "What is this?"

Her brow lowers. "What does it look like?" She rolls her eyes. "It's *food*, human." And she starts walking again.

I turn the disk over in my hands, hurrying to catch up. *This* is food? My stomach tightens and rumbles, so I raise it to my lips. It smells oddly floral and doesn't taste like much, slightly sweet with a mildly bitter aftertaste. But it's edible, so I chew and swallow, chew and swallow, until my jaw hurts.

We walk down a narrow corridor that isn't stonework like the council room or the prison, but solid stone, carved out of the cliffside itself. The corridor gives way to a short wood-and-metal box, which Unach steps into. There's a pulley inside, and after I join her, Unach tugs on the rope and lifts us up, her biceps bulging impressively. Her clothing appears to be mostly leather, with some fur, covering her shoulders but leaving her arms exposed, save for two leather straps that meet a leather cuff. Bony nubs, roughly the size of coins, protrude from her forearms. I wonder if she catches me staring, for when we reach the next level, she gives me a chiding look and walks even faster than before.

I hurry to follow her, nearly tripping over myself as I take in my surroundings. The short, narrow passageway opens into an atrium lit by sconces and other lights I can't identify. I assume that the dark holes in the ceiling are flues of some kind to let out smoke. Carefully mortared stonework, concrete, and metal beams are ever present, but here an artful array of iron and wood composes my surroundings, not unlike the architecture of a bridge.

A gleam of starlight falls through a large window ahead, and I look up, catching a glimpse of the constellation Swoop, the spoon. It's before midnight, then. My hands tighten on the disk in my hands. Swoop is the constellation of harvest and bounty. It seems to say, *See? I've fed you.*

Down toward the shadowed canyon below me, trolls call out to one another, but I can't understand them. The canyon distends from the city, impossibly deep and dark, but Unach allows me little time to gawk. I glance up and catch sight of one of the Empyrean Bridge's girders. We are well and truly below the bridge, then. I see nothing else through that sliver of a window, only the bulk of city above me, nearly as dark as the canyon below. Human settlements tend to spread out like an open hand, but Cagmar is long and deep, like a tooth.

My fascination is almost enough to quell my apprehension.

Up, up, up, I'm led, then down again. Unach pushes me through a winding tunnel, past a few watching eyes. No one asks what she's doing. I wonder whether it's because she's unfriendly, or if there's a different reason. We take another lift and walk a darker corridor before she finally slows at a door. Under the maze of beams and arches, Unach pulls out a heavy key, shoves it in the lock, and turns it.

"Don't touch anything," she says. "And stay out of the way. This is only temporary."

I don't think she cares for a response. I don't blame her for her rudeness. Aside from having a stranger cast upon her without warning, humans and trolls have a history. No human township would treat *her* kindly. Indeed, they'd likely kill her. I'm merely grateful *I'm* not dead.

The door opens, and I'm surprised at the apartment within. I was expecting something coldly constructed, like the rest of the city, but it looks rather . . . homey. A fireplace fits snug against the far wall, and two braziers smolder on either side of a decent-sized main room. They give it light, though little warmth, and the chill of Cagmar burrows into my skin, almost making my teeth chatter. Furs and woven rugs take up much of the floor, and an enormous, overstuffed pillow—to be used as a chair?—sits near the fireplace. On the other side of the room is a tall table and a narrow kitchen with a strange-looking sink, cabinets, and shelves. Everything is a little too large, made for the use of a troll. The room curves in the back, toward the left, to somewhere I can't see. Past the entrance to the small kitchen, there's a door on the left and a door on the right, both closed.

"You'll not have a room to yourself. There isn't the space." Unach shuts the door behind her. She sets her shoulder satchel on the table and strides to the far wall. "You'll sleep on a pallet there."

Trying not to feel small, I follow her and peek around the corner. A short, mortared hallway ends at a dark space with folding doors, little more than a closet. Within lies a bin of soiled laundry and a washtub.

I glance at the hard floor. I've slept on worse. And Unach had mentioned this was temporary. I can handle temporary.

"You'll contribute to housework and run your own errands," she continues, kicking a half-spent piece of coal into the fireplace. "And you'll cook for yourself."

I nod. I want to ask for water, but Unach is a taut band, ready to snap.

The door on the right—now my left—swings open, and a troll steps through. I guess him to be a few inches over seven feet, and the emerald shade of his skin is a little richer than Unach's. His dark hair is longer, too, corded and held back with a thick tie. His tusks are shorter and more slender, but his torso is notably wider. He wears clothes made of hide and a woven material I can't identify, but his arms are bare and, like the others', notably robust. "Unach, who are you—"

And then he notices me.

He doesn't react at first. At least, I think he doesn't. I'm hardly practiced at reading trolls. His eyes have the same topaz sheen as Unach's, though his take on a darker, more amber hue. They could almost pass as human. His heavy brow furrows. "Who is this?"

"Wayward human who convinced Qequan she'd do well as monster fodder."

I frown and meet the new troll's gaze, trying to act resilient. I'm still not used to the way they look, the way they talk, the way they regard me. "Unach is kindly showing me the ropes."

25

Unach snorts and folds her arms. "Next time a summons comes to my door, I'm not answering it." She rubs her head. "She has to stay here until they can accommodate her."

The male troll looks at her. "Can she not stay in the enclave?"

Enclave? My earlier interaction with the council confirmed that I am not the first human to seek shelter here. How many more live within the city?

"It's already overrun." Then, to me, Unach repeats, "Don't touch anything." She disappears through the other door, which I presume to be her bedroom. Unsure what to do in her absence, I offer a shallow bow to the other troll.

"I came looking for work," I explain. "I won't be a bother. I'm sorry to put you out."

He seems confused by this admission. "You'd do best to stay out of the way."

I guess I shouldn't expect much in the way of friendliness. But I'll take safety over friendliness any day.

Unach emerges from her room and chucks a blanket at me. Or rather, a badly skinned hide with a few holes where the knife cut too close to the fur. I'm not sure what animal it comes from. "Make up your pallet. It's late."

The space allotted to me isn't long enough for me to stretch out, but I'm in no position to complain. In truth, this is all very dreamlike, as though my mind has not come to terms with being *in* Cagmar, speaking to *trolls*. And I'm going to *stay* here. I notice a slit in the wall just above the short hallway. A window. It's grown utterly dark outside, so it blends in with the rest of the stone. If I stand on my toes, I can see a few distant stars that don't belong to any constellation. But surely they aren't without meaning. Cosmodian belief says that the gods watch us still, but they can communicate only through the night sky. Rich, poor, male, female—it doesn't matter. The gods made all of us. If only I had a teacher, or a book on the stars, I might be able to sort out what they are telling me now. Until then, I'm grateful for any slice of the sky, however meager.

All I can think to say is "Thank you." Then I glance between the two rooms. "You two are . . . siblings?"

Unach gives me a disgusted look. "What else would we be?" She heads into her room, closing the door firmly behind her.

Her brother frowns at me. Before I can inquire as to his name, he retires as well, and I'm surrounded by closed doors.

Chewing on my lower lip, I hold out the fur. It's about five feet long, a little short to cover me. I fold it in half lengthwise and set it against the hard floor in the hallway. Then I search about the fireplace coals. Surprisingly, I find a short stack of quarter logs and pull one free.

Unach's door opens suddenly, and I wonder if she'd had her ear pressed to it. "What are you doing?" Her peevish tone slices through the room.

I stiffen. "The fire—"

She glares at me.

Trolls must be more adapted to the cold, what with their . . . thickness. I quickly replace the log. Unach scrutinizes me, as if she's thinking about shoving me through that single, narrow window. I hurry to the fur and lie down, and she retreats once more.

I lie on the hide for some time as the braziers slowly fade. I'm used to camping on hard ground, but this floor makes my bones feel too sharp for my skin, even with the hide. The temperature drops, and the night looms. I roll up in the hide for warmth, but without its barrier, the frigid floor shocks my skin. I now understand the need for rugs.

Unach may not like it, but I grab the end of a small rug and pull it over for a mattress. It blocks out the cold, thankfully, though it does little in the way of cushioning. I could try to relight a brazier—but I fear to bring the wrath of a troll upon me. Fear of something *always* lurks in my thoughts or crawls beneath my skin. Fear has been my greatest companion since before I can remember. It has kept me alive, fuels me, protects me. In truth, I don't know what I would do without it.

Fear tells me that Unach is a barely contained bonfire. I'm not yet sure of her brother's temperament.

And so I lie here, shivering, my knees pulled to my chest, my arms folded tightly together, using my own hair as a pillow.

At least if I don't sleep, I won't dream of whatever monsters the council intends for me come morning.

I can't breathe. I can't—

I wake up to a hand around my mouth. It's large and calloused, and I know exactly who it belongs to when it jerks me free of my little pallet in the stable.

Screams build up in my throat as my father's men pull me back. It's early, too early. The cock hasn't crowed yet. Their hands grapple everywhere, holding down my flailing limbs, jerking me this way and that, carrying me out like a rabid dog into the blue-hued light.

"Ignore it! It's not real!" one hisses to another, and I spare only half a second of surprise that my father would tell them why I'm so valuable. But thieves must know what to expect when stealing something that can fight back.

But that fear is their own. Not mine.

I add to it, pushing the darkness out, escalating my own terror in the process.

The man holding my legs flinches, but the one covering my mouth drops me like I've bitten him and reels back.

All my screams escape me, surging through the township of Dorys like a murder of crows. The fear heightens my senses, strengthens my limbs. Pleads with me to flee, flee, flee.

"Shut her up!"

I push my fear harder.

Men drop me. I scramble across the dry ground, trying to orient myself. Cry out for help.

Something, perhaps a boot, hits the side of my head. The world spins. The blue light momentarily turns black.

That's the weakness of my power. I can instill terror into any man, but the minute I leave, so does the fear.

When my thoughts return to my throbbing head, I'm being manhandled again. One of my kidnappers grabs my breast—not in a sexual way, but in an effort to throw me onto the back of another's horse.

No, no, NO. I will NOT go back, I will not—

"Leave her be!"

The sound of Cando's voice—it's his stable I'm sleeping in—is such a relief and a horror that I nearly wet myself. Relief that someone has come for me. Horror at what these three men might do to him, for my father's men are armed and armored, and they ride horses, which are increasingly rare in these parts. Even Cando doesn't have a horse. He uses his stable for goats and storage.

I crane to see. Cando stands there in his underclothes, a pitchfork in his hand. Elisher, his neighbor, is also present and half-dressed, but he holds a makeshift club, a heavy staff with nails protruding from its tip. They eye the kidnappers warily.

I send out as much fear as I can, pushing it out like sweat, seizing all three brutes. I've only just learned how to do more than one at a time.

Two of them stiffen. The third drops me, and I hit the ground on my knees, splitting the skin of one. Sensing an advantage, Elisher moves forward and takes a swing at one, missing widely. These men aren't warriors.

And so I direct my attention to the horse. It whinnies and rears before charging east.

"No!" one of my father's men yelps, while the other draws his sword, ready to fight Cando. I shove terror into him, and he nearly drops the blade. He turns to me, but instead of a hard look, he appears like a child beneath a grizzly beard, likely grown during his search for me. Just a boy, alone and afraid.

Just like me.

I choke on fright, but I am merciless, and the men begin to shake and weep. The legs of one grow wet with urine, and they flee Cando and Elisher, two on horses, one on foot, taking off in the direction of the lost steed.

I push the fear as hard and far as I can, until I'm sobbing and can no longer hear their retreat beyond the squat township buildings. Cando lowers his pitchfork. "Are you all right, Lark?"

I'm slow to return to myself. Gritting my teeth, I have to convince myself not to run. Coerce my heartbeat to slow, my breaths to even out. Persuade my mind that that fear isn't real, though much of it is. But I'm not all right, for I know I must leave, because now my father's men know where I am, and they'll come back with reinforcements. An army these people could never hope to best. This is a small place with few people, as most townships are. Farmers and the desperate, not trained warriors. And I, a fifteen-year-old girl, can only do so much.

Had they hit my head first, before dragging me out of the stable, I wouldn't have been able to do anything, even scream. Next time, they won't make that mistake.

I wake from a fitful sleep with memories of Dorys dancing behind my eyelids. I'd hoped that I'd find the Cosmodian I'd met as a girl when I'd moved to the township, but she wasn't there. Still, the people of Dorys had been kind to me, until after that morning. Then they were suspicious. But humans are superstitious creatures. I don't know if I could have stayed, even had I tried. Dorys is probably the human settlement closest to Cagmar, about sixty or seventy miles northeast. It sits in the middle of human land, as though its founders had left the long-dried river in an attempt to reach the canyon and given up halfway. Dorys always makes me think of sagebrush. There was so much of it there.

Silver light seeps through the narrow window above me, a predawn sky high above where I slumber, cradled by canyon walls. I smile at it before rubbing sleep from my eyes. As I sit up, a second blanket, thick with fur and heavy, falls from my shoulders. I gape at it, having no recollection of it. Unach must have had a change of heart . . . or my shivering was loud enough to bother her. Either way, my heart fills at the sight of the blanket, for surely where there is kindness, there is hope for me.

I fold the blanket and leave it by Unach's door. I'm not sure what to do for breakfast. I have only what's in my small bag, which is little more than a change of clothes. Eyeing the two closed bedroom doors, I slip into the crammed closet and change quickly, my cold fingers struggling with the buttons of my dress. Stepping out, I braid my hair over my shoulder.

Fortunately, I don't have to wait long. I've just returned the rug to its place when Unach opens her door. She is perfectly put together and alert, her topaz eyes darting to the fireplace before looking over the floor. In this better light, I struggle to hide my awe of her. She stands over seven feet tall, equal to her brother. Her clothing reminds me of leather armor, and like the guardsmen on the bridge, she wears a thick belt around her middle, which emphasizes her small breasts. Her arms bear more muscle than any human man's, and every bony nub and spike on her is polished and white.

She is terrifying and magnificent and every bit a troll.

Eyeing me, she crosses the room to light a small fire, which she then places a pot over. She doesn't speak as she does this, or as she prepares something in the kitchen. When the water begins to bubble, she pulls a tin cup from the cupboard and fills it. "There's food for you in the cold storage box." She points to a cupboard in the floor. "It needs to last the whole day," she adds with a tone of warning, "which means you need to get your rations from the market. If they don't have any for you, it's the council's problem, not mine."

Relief calms my hunger. "Thank you." I head into the kitchen. It's small and cramped, and it's not hard to find the cold storage box recessed into the floor. Inside is some dried meat from an animal I'm not sure I want to identify, as well as some cucumbers and what looks like . . . flower petals? I grab the meat and close the box, taking a large bite and working it in my mouth.

31

When I return to the main room, Unach looks me up and down and sighs. "Makes no sense." She heads for the door, stops, and plants a hand on her hip. "Well? You expect me to wait for you?"

I blanch, grab my bag from my pallet, and hurry to Unach's side. Scoffing, she rips open the door and steps out into the dimly lit corridor. She walks with long and purposeful strides. We return to the lift from before, dropping to a different floor that opens up to a maze of tunnels that makes me think of an anthill.

Cagmar is much more alive at this hour; trolls crowd everywhere. While they come in an assortment of heights, shades, and sizes, they all dwarf me. Several give me strange looks as I hurry to keep up with Unach. Others pay me little mind, which means other humans *must* be here, else my presence would be more novel. When Unach takes a sharp turn, I bump into a dark-gray-skinned woman, who spits, "Clumsy louse," at me before continuing on her way.

The next corridor has a floor made of wooden slats on metal girders, and it brightens as we walk through it. It takes me a beat to realize that the light comes from the sun itself; the wall to my left suddenly opens up, revealing the steep cliffside of the canyon. It's covered with various loops and trellises, and hanging from them streams vegetation in all the colors of the rainbow. Vines, climbers, flowers—so many flowers, many the color of the strange disk Unach gave me to eat the night before. The smell consumes me, earthy and floral and lovely. Trolls hang from short bridges and trellises, watering, pollinating, or harvesting the plants. I'm utterly enthralled. My steps slow as I take in the impressive garden, grasping a handrail that separates it from the main path.

A strike from a shoulder sends me to the floor. The shock of the landing radiates up my tailbone. I look up to see a large troll looming over me. He is broad and gray skinned, with beefy arms folded across his chest. His jaw and chin are the widest I've seen yet, accented with large bone studs. His tusks are narrow and sharp, almost like fangs.

"Never seen food before, *human*?" He sneers at me. He stands aside from the flow of traffic. Did he go out of his way to collide with me? "If you think you'll get away with stealing it, you're a fool."

I grab the handrail and pull myself up. "N-Not at all. I'm already provided for." I bow my head and try to move around him, but he side-steps and blocks my path. A buzz of fear creeps up my spine.

He leans close. His hot breath smells of fish when he speaks. "You'd do better providing for the monsters below."

I gape and glance past the handrail. If I wanted to, I could jump past the lip of the opening and fall into that endless darkness. How long would it take for me to hit?

"Move it, Grodd."

A sigh escapes me. Unach's voice has never sounded so sweet.

Grodd turns and glares at Unach over his shoulder. He has several inches on her . . . and more of those turquoise beads, I notice. "What business is it of yours?" His tone is hard, but not entirely disrespectful. Meanwhile, several passing trolls duck their heads away, as though wanting to be unnoticed. I wonder at their deference.

"Council business," she answers flatly.

A smirk pulls on Grodd's lips. He turns his back to me, and I use the opportunity to slip into the corridor and loop around to Unach. He must see the lack of mirth on her face, for his smirk fades. "You jest."

She gives him a cold look without answering, then starts down the corridor again, and this time I stick to her heels like a pup. I glance over my shoulder once, to see Grodd watching me, his mouth pulled into a frown, his eyes dark.

Once we reach a quiet set of stairs, I ask, "Who was that?"

"A self-important Montra. Stay away from him." She descends, leaving no room for follow-up.

We walk for a while, always descending, passing all sorts of doors and rooms and atriums I want to know about. But Unach is a woman on a mission, and she does not give a tour, except to announce the south dock when we arrive. It opens just as the gardens did, but the mouth is much wider, the sun dimmer, and there are no guardrails. One other troll occupies the dock, a shorter troll—still a head taller than myself— thickly built and girded about with both animal skins and leather straps covered in various knives. His skin is bright as a blade of spring grass in the morning sun.

"What in the dark pits is this?" he asks when I follow Unach in.

"Council orders," she says blandly. She sounds tired and immediately goes to an open chest full of cords, ropes, and straps. "She's hunting with us." She points a thumb at the troll and introduces him as Troff.

Troff lets out a belly laugh that echoes through the dock, but when Unach doesn't join in, it piddles out to nothing. "You're serious." He studies me, his gaze narrow, skeptical. I've always been tall, especially for a woman, but under that gaze I feel a slip of a thing. A child.

"Yep. Don't ask me why." Unach pulls out a clump of straps and holds them toward me, as though measuring me. "Unless you want to explain?"

Both trolls stare at me. I simply shake my head. I revealed my secret to the council for self-preservation alone. I did not *want* anyone else to know. Indeed, the only time my horrid abilities have ever truly benefited me was in that council room.

Cold memories slide up my neck. I push them away.

Unach silently strides over and hands me a harness, then returns to the chest to grab another. Troff already wears his, and he studies me unabashedly while Unach suits up. I try to mimic her actions with the harness, but Troff's steady gaze makes me self-conscious. Finally, Unach comes over and untangles the thing, explaining in as few words as possible how to put it on. She assists me again, once everything is in place, only by grabbing a strap around my waist and yanking it, pulling so tight that it digs into my stomach.

"Thank you," I murmur, but she acts as though she didn't hear me.

Troff begins hooking ropes up to various pulleys along the walls and ceiling.

My stomach drops. "We're going over the side, aren't we?"

Unach rolls her eyes. "Where else do you think monsters live?"

I swallow, wondering what sorts of creatures inhabit this canyon. What sorts of creatures could be more terrifying than a troll.

I think of Grodd and shudder.

Unach shoves my shoulder and leads me to the end of the dock. For an awful second, I think she's going to push me over, but she doesn't, only points to the parts of the city we can see. She indicates a tunnel to the left. "That leads to the mines. East dock." It appears to be the lowest part of the city. "Master armory. Water harvesting. We passed the tribunal, school, and infirmary on our way here. We're on the southeast edge of Cagmar. You'll want to get familiar with it as we move around, so you don't get lost. If you stay with me"—she says it like it will be a chore—"you'll always work this dock. Otherwise you'll move to the east or west. How well can you climb?"

I haven't had ample opportunity. None of the townships on my map are near the mountains. "Well enough," I manage.

Unach sighs. "Troff, spot us."

The troll readies himself as Unach secures separate ropes to herself and to me. She opens a closet on the wall, revealing a score of weapons, mostly heavy blades. Unach is already armed; she keeps her weapons in her apartment. But she selects a few blades for me and hands them over. I strap them on, following the style she and Troff use. While I'm not trained, I've used a knife to defend myself before.

"So we scout the monsters, and kill them?" I ask.

"If they get too close," Troff answers, though he still looks at me with a confused expression. At least it's not one of malice. "Alarms outside the city scare off most. Sometimes we just scare them away. Hunt the smaller ones."

"For food?" I've eaten worse.

"Depends on the monster," Unach answers. "Some are poisonous." She steps toward the edge.

Troff adds, "We use their hides, their oil, some stuff for medicine. The large ones are too deadly to harvest."

Unach waves for me to join her. My heart rises into my throat when I look into the depths of the canyon. Supposedly a river flows down there, but all I can see is endless black. My voice borders on a whisper when I ask, "How many are large?"

"Most of them," Unach snaps before jumping over the ledge.

A gasp catches in my throat, but Unach has only dropped down to handholds bolted into the stone wall of the city. After ensuring that Troff is holding my rope, I carefully lower myself down after her. My arms strain, but I find footholds that bear most of my weight.

A cold wind rushes up, wet and smelling of mildew, as if the canyon itself breathes. Unach doesn't mind, so I try not to. I'm slow to follow her. I'm suitably strong, but my attention flits everywhere at once, scanning the sides of the city, the canyon walls, the gorge's depths. Looking for movement, for a shift in color, for anything. We climb, sidestep, climb, stopping occasionally at small, flat viewing stations carved out of rock. We pass by windows; Unach gives me little time to peer in, though the enormous drop below me mutes my curiosity.

My hand slips once, and I nearly let go. When I grasp the handhold again, I stay there for a long time, hugging the city like a long-lost lover.

"If you slip, you'll fall, but Troff will pull you back in." She gives me a narrow look before moving on. But in her eyes, I can almost read, *Though it would be better if he didn't.*

Chapter 3

Fortunately, Unach and I found no monsters during the long four hours of our watch. Two were spent hugging the outside of the city, two in the dock, myself with a spyglass, Unach manning the ropes for Troff, as I don't have the strength necessary to haul him up should his grip fail. He still regards me oddly when he gets back, like he's waiting for Unach to give up the joke any moment now. I don't blame him. I hardly look able to fight a beast of the depths. I do nothing to defend myself against the unspoken inquiries.

Unach opens the closet and gestures at me to return my weapons. "Never take them from the dock," she says coolly. "Humans aren't permitted to carry."

I'm hanging up my last knife when three trolls come onto the dock, two women and a man, all laughing. I step closer to the closet to shield myself from notice.

"Unach!" The woman on the right punches her in the shoulder. "I thought you'd be here. We're playing kow'tug in the rec and need another player."

"I'll play," Troff volunteers.

The woman laughs. "We'd have better chances with a human."

They all chuckle, even Unach. I stay tucked away.

Unach waves them off. "I'll meet you there. Just cleaning up." They exchange a few more words before leaving. She pulls off her harness and chucks it in the chest. Looks at Troff. "Kub's late again."

Troff shrugs. "Noon shift."

She turns toward me, her gaze narrowing. "Go to the market. We passed the road for it on the way down. It's below the trade works."

I hesitate. "Where . . . was the trade works?"

She frowns. "Outside the farm walls." Groans. "How good is your memory? I don't want to write this down."

"It's good—"

"Go to the market," she barrels on. "It's on the eighth level, down the way you came yesterday but through the west tunnel. Go to the food handlers and request rations for . . . What's your birth year?"

I blink. "945 . . ."

"Lark 945." She adjusts a leather bracer on her arm. A long strip is cut out of it for the bony nubs that protrude from her verdant skin. "While you're down there, get mine and Azmar's, too."

I nod, wanting any excuse to appease Unach.

She responds, "Unach 935 and Azmar 937."

It sounds like trolls use birth years instead of surnames. Which also means Unach is twenty-nine and Azmar is twenty-seven.

I light up. "You're Iter."

Unach hesitates. "What did you call me?" Her voice rings sharp as a saw blade.

"I-I." I force myself not to shy back. "Your birth year. It aligns with the planet Iter, the spider."

She gawks at me like I'm speaking another language.

Steadying myself, I say, "The planets in the cosmos, I mean. Among the stars. You and I are the same. Iter, the fifth planet. It . . . It represents strength and cunning."

Unach looks me up and down and snorts, as though finding the comparison laughable. I suppose it is. But there are different sorts of strength. A different strength for every person, if they know where to find it. The Cosmodians believe that the gods speak to us through the stars, and following the path of a birth planet helps us interpret their words. I don't share this, though.

"Azmar is Ura," I offer. The seventh planet, which can be seen only through a powerful spyglass.

"Unach!" the chatty female calls.

"Kesta!" Unach calls back in a mocking voice. Refocusing on me, she sighs. "You'll have to ask for a tradesman package as well. You'll get some pushback, I'm sure, but just say the council approved it, and the council will be very angry if they don't accommodate you. If they don't believe you, use my name."

I wonder what sort of weight the name *Unach 935* carries.

Knowing she's eager to leave, I speak quickly. "And there's an enclave here? Of humans?"

She looks at me as though the question is absurd. "How should I know? I don't associate with humans."

If she notes the insult in her words, she hardly cares to amend them.

Unach continues, "You'll also need to go to the Rooms Office and request servants' quarters. You might not get them; the city is only so big." Looking at the ceiling above us, she clucks her tongue. "I don't need you taking up space in my lodgings. Azmar takes up enough already."

I nod. *Rooms Office. Tradesman package. Unach 935, Azmar 937.*

She lists several more items to collect and errands to run, and I panic inwardly, sure I won't remember all of them, but I don't want to ask her to repeat herself, and I have nothing on which to write. I offer another nod, and Unach leaves with Kesta and the others.

I'm nervous to wind through Cagmar by myself, especially after my encounter with Grodd . . . but if more trolls are like Troff, it won't be so bad. And I'm used to being novel. When one moves from township to township, she is always the "new girl."

I start for the door. Pause. Turn back to Troff. "I . . . I'm so sorry, but how do I get to the farm walls, again?"

He cocks a brow, winding rope around his forearm. "Go up the lift and turn left for the school block. Follow the stairs past Deccor housing and the Mid-divide. Quickest way is to follow that toward Storage and then up the lift again."

I understand only a fraction of what he says. Before I pass through the doorway, he adds, "You have to default for the lifts."

I hesitate. "Default?"

He nods. "Trollis first."

Oh. "Thank you."

Like Unach, he regards my gratitude strangely. Do trolls not thank one another? I ponder the question as I head away from the docks. I remember walking a straight line when I come to the first fork . . . but I'd been so focused on not losing Unach a second time I get turned around quickly. Up a lift and . . . left, wasn't it?

I come to another fork. I can see a lift at the end of the tunnel to my left, though the passage is swarming with troll bodies. There's a set of stairs straight ahead. Didn't I take stairs with Unach? Either way, both would take me up . . . and were I to wait for every troll to go ahead of me at that lift, I might never get to the market.

I take the stairs. One troll, then another, comes down from above. I press myself to the wall to let them pass. Neither takes interest in me, though the second does inspect my clothing. I wonder if the tradesman package Unach instructed me to collect includes Cagmar regalia. Will I have to pay for it, or is the name and birth year adequate? Is there some sort of tab?

I follow a corridor, staying close to the rough wall, trying not to meet the glances of passing trolls. This corridor opens into a decent-sized atrium. I search for signs to point me in the right direction, but there are none. Unach and I had descended far enough for my ears to pop on the way to the south dock, so surely I need to go up.

I continue walking, subtly looking around like I know where I'm going. I find a pathway that looks familiar and follow it, but it gets so narrow toward the end that I think I must be mistaken, so I turn around and take another left, succeeding in locating another set of stairs. I pass a great crisscrossing of metalwork that looks similar in build to the

Empyrean Bridge. That must be the Mid-divide. Troff had said something about following it . . . Did he say which direction?

After debating the choice to keep climbing or follow the girders, I
choose the latter. In the distance I see a flash of tan and think it must be
a human, but it's gone just as quickly. I search as I walk; surely another
human would be understanding and tell me . . . where to go . . .

I stop walking when I realize I've entered a maze. Someone
nearly runs into the back of me and mutters as they go around. I
should keep moving . . . but I'm floundering. Multiple lifts, stairs,
corridors, doors . . . they're everywhere.

"Move!" growls a bald troll, bent with age. He hobbles around me,
whacking my calf with his walking staff as he passes. Gritting my teeth,
I follow him, then duck into the first passageway I reach, grateful the
throng here is somewhat less dense. I press my back into the wall and
take a deep breath.

Just ask someone. Someone who doesn't look busy. They can't all hate
humans, if we're allowed to live here. I did have to give up my greatest
secret to stay here, which doesn't bolster my courage.

What did Troff say? Follow the divider, and . . . something about
storage?

"Lark."

A voice sounds over my head, and I jump, whirling around to face
another troll. It takes me a heartbeat to recognize him, and relief floods
my limbs. "Azmar."

He regards me with what I can best describe as restrained curiosity.
"What are you doing here?"

"I . . ." I look around. "I don't know where 'here' is, precisely. Could
you tell me how to get to the market?"

He frowns. "Unach is foolish to assume you wouldn't get lost." No
animosity colors his voice; he says it merely as a fact. He reaches down
to a hefty belt around his hips and pulls from it a pencil and a piece
of paper—I'm impressed—and begins to walk away from me. I follow,

but he stops after a few paces, where the rocky wall gives way to smooth steel plates. He presses the paper there so he can write.

The council hadn't been impressed by my literacy. The citizens of Cagmar must have a good schooling system. Before coming here I'd expected only training fields, weight rooms, anything denoting strength and war and prowess. Though admittedly, my knowledge of trolls was limited to rumors and tall tales.

Azmar draws swift, straight lines, forming arches and triangles, rooms and what I suppose are roads. He labels them, though his handwriting is not nearly as neat as the sketch. I notice the absence of any of the turquoise beading I've seen on many of the other trolls. Indeed, Azmar lacks any sort of décor, unless one counts the pencil sticking out of the knot at the back of his head.

"You're here." He draws a sort of star near the center of the map. "The market is here." His low voice bears that peculiar troll lilt, but it isn't unfriendly. He adds two small triangles. "This is the food handlers, this is the Rooms Office, here's the supply center where you'll ask for your tradesman package."

I nod, though my attention slips from the map to him. His bicep is thicker than my thigh. He could kill me with a single strike, surely. And humans are not permitted to carry weapons! He tucks the pencil into his dark hair and hands the paper to me.

I study the map and relax. "Thank you. Truly." I don't understand parts of it, but I hope the drops and passageways will become clearer as I walk them. "How . . . will I pay for it? The supplies, I mean."

"On credit." He steps away from the wall. "They will know Unach, and you're obviously human."

I tilt my head. "Yes . . ."

He hooks his thumb into his outer belt. "Humans aren't trusted with currency."

Oh. I suppose that makes sense, if we're such low-class denizens.

Since he's being frank, I ask, "And Unach's name is enough?"

"Unach is Montra."

There is that word again. "She's . . . an official?"

Azmar frowns. "Montra is sixth caste. The food handlers and Rooms Office workers will be Deccor at best. That's third caste."

I blink, mulling over the information. Thinking of Grodd at the farm walls, the way other trolls steered clear of him and Unach both.

"There are eight castes," Azmar continues patiently. "Supra, Alpine, Montra, Centra, Intra, Deccor, Nethens, and Pleb. Humans have no caste. If you want to survive, you need to remember that. Stay out of the way."

That's the second time he's given me that warning. Troff said something similar. "And you and your sister are Montra."

"I am Centra."

One below. "But you're the same family . . ." Realizing I'm forgetting myself, I step back and bow my head. "I'm sorry, I should be on my way."

"Give deference to everyone you meet," he warns.

I glance at the map.

He points back the way I came. "If you go to the furthest lift, you'll get up more quickly."

I suck in a deep breath. "Okay. Thank you."

Unlike the others, Azmar nods to my thanks instead of behaving as though I'd spoken a foreign language. The easy gesture emboldens me. I can do this. I've gotten through worse, haven't I?

After memorizing my path, I tuck the map away and venture into the crowd, not bumping into a single troll along the way.

Had I started from Unach and Azmar's apartment, I would have found the market with more ease. It's the largest part of Cagmar I've seen thus far, with high, cavernous ceilings and wide roads lined with stone shops and stalls. It's busy, but an orderly sort of busy. As though everyone knows their place and which direction to walk. I try my best not to disrupt any of it.

What's especially strange in these crowds is how small I am. I came into my height in my teen years and am notably tall for a human woman. And yet even the shortest troll has a hand's length on me. Only the few, stout children I've spotted are shorter.

The stonework and supports surrounding me amplify the noise of the market, making it sound busier than it looks. I check Azmar's drawing, squinting at his handwriting. If he hadn't described it to me, I'd think this was written in another language, his writing is so . . . hasty. Was this the Rooms Office or the food handlers?

I walk forward, stepping out of the way of two enormous trolls. A bright-green troll woman hawks strings of beads ahead of me. An adolescent just taller than myself has a basket of some sort of fried food I can't identify. When he meets my gaze, he snarls. I quicken my step.

Voices louder than the rest catch my attention. I spy a hand-pulled cart on the edge of the cobbled road, three trolls beside it. One of them catches my attention in particular. I know I'm gawking at him, but I can't help it. He's unlike any other creature I've seen in this place.

He's short, and by short I mean a hand's width taller than myself. His skin is ashen, not gray or green, but something different altogether. His features definitely lean troll, but they lack the same thickness and width as those near him. His nose is longer, his widow's peak less severe.

I quickly realize the trolls near him—one dark as charcoal, the other green as a sapling—aren't friendly. I can't make out what they're saying, but the first spits at the ground as the second shoves the smaller troll's shoulder. "Just a . . . Nethens . . . fodder." I can't make out the rest. Laughing, they take up their cart and wheel it away.

The troll scowls and picks up a satchel from the ground. I think I recognize the name they used: *Nethens*, the second on Azmar's list of castes, though I could be wrong.

Perhaps it's my foolish gawking, or because I am a pale contrast to the city around me, but the troll's gaze finds me. He looks surprised.

We stare at one another for several seconds before I adjust my bag and continue forward, searching for the food handlers. But as I near, he speaks to me.

"You're the monster slayer."

I stop and turn back. "You know that?"

He eyes me from head to toe, slowly. I push away feelings of self-consciousness. "I overheard a few people talking about it."

I twist the strap of my bag in my hands. "Is it so strange?"

"Yes." He's incredulous that I even asked. "Humans are trade workers only. Monster slayers are Montra."

I hadn't realized . . . but that does make Troff's reaction more understandable. I shrug. "The council ordered it." Seeing that he has yet to scowl at me, I ask, "What's your name?"

"Perg."

"Lark." I offer a smile. "I'm staying with Unach."

He whistles. "I don't envy you."

"She's been kind." I study his face. His skin has slight hues of green, making me think of a human who's terribly ill. He is broad for a man, but not for a troll. His ears are rounder than a troll's, his hair a little thinner. His tusks look more like large teeth than anything else.

"Do I look so strange?" He wipes a hand down his face in a wholly insecure gesture.

I step back. "N-No! I'm sorry, I didn't mean to stare. I'm just . . . I'm not accustomed to your people yet."

"My people," he repeats. "Just as much your people, if you must know. That's why they treat me the way they do."

He looks past me, to the path the other trolls had taken upon my arrival.

My heart thumps in my chest. "You . . . You're part human?" Half? Was such a thing even possible?

Perg glowers, but he tips his head in the affirmative. I think I should apologize for the question . . . but he said it first, didn't he? Instead I try "It must be hard here."

He chuckled. "It would be hard anywhere."

I have to agree.

He shakes his head. "Why would you come here? They hate humans."

I wring the strap of my bag. "It hasn't been . . . terrible." Wishing to make a friend, I allow myself honesty. "I'm not well loved among my own kind. I thought I could try a new life here."

His expression is so incredulous that I laugh. He hesitates. "What was your name again?"

"Lark." After seven years, I don't even think twice about the name.

"Lark." On his lips, it's the strangest-sounding name I've ever heard. "Lark," he says again, then sighs. "Stay out of the way, Lark. You'll live longer."

Our amiableness lost, he pushes past me and heads down a side corridor. Only then do I notice a great war axe strapped to his back. I wonder where he's going, and what he plans to use it for.

Part human. But troll enough to carry a weapon, apparently. I peer around the marketplace, wondering if I'll see another like him, but every creature in sight is pure troll.

I ponder this as I follow Azmar's map and find a large building with what looks like a lamb shank and a potato painted on it. Several trolls stand in line. I stand behind the last one, but another arrives and butts me out of the way. Holding my tongue, I move behind him. The line moves fairly quickly, but two more trolls enter and push me aside without comment, taking my place. I remind myself that I am not in a township anymore and pull on my patience. I'm nearly to the front when another troll enters and, again, cuts in front of me.

I will never finish my errands at this rate. I study the newcomer. He's dressed in wovens, similar to what Perg wore, and I wonder if his caste is low. Allowing myself some courage, I mutter, "Unach 935 will be very angry if I do not retrieve her rations."

The troll turns and looks at me. Frowns.

But, to my relief, he steps back and allows me to retake my place. I let out a long breath and hurry to the counter. The troll managing it isn't surprised to see me. I place my order, as well as Azmar's and Unach's, and I receive three packages that I can barely carry. I imagine the small one, the length of my forearm, is mine. I'm impressed that my information is here so soon . . . but according to Perg, I'm becoming more well known than I ought to be.

I go to the Rooms Office. The troll there is less friendly and says nothing about accommodations, only scribbles down my name and returns to other work. I find the supply center, and after spending half an hour in a line, I receive a fourth package and another frown when I give thanks for it.

I juggle the packages to review Azmar's map, trying to sort my way back to his and Unach's apartment. I'm near the edge of the market when I see a wonderful sight. My pulse quickens. There *are* other humans here!

This is into the field of family, the Cosmodian's voice echoes in my head. *You will have one of your own.*

Every time I found a new township, this promise has come to mind, along with the hope that maybe *here* will be where I belong. *Here* will be my home. *Here* I'll find my family. A good family. Someone who loves me.

I think of this every time I've left as well. Chased or scared away. *Next time,* I think. *Next time, it will work out.* The broken road just stretches a little farther.

Maybe it can finally end in Cagmar.

The humans' clothing is similar to the trolls' in material but not in style. An older man wears a leathery vest and matching kneepads. Another man, a girl, and a woman wear knit fabrics in beige and gray. The woman, who looks to be about fifty, notices me and peers with drawn brows, almost as if she recognizes me, but try as I might, I cannot place her. She has a fallow complexion and graying auburn hair pulled back in a low tail. The others are on the paler side, which isn't surprising, given the general darkness of Cagmar.

After checking the way to ensure I won't cut off the path of any trolls, I pass quickly to them, smoothing my hair as I go, hoping to make a good impression. I'm taller than all of them, even the men, and I hunch down a bit. They regard me with interest, though the younger man frowns.

"Hello!" I say, maybe too cheerily. "You must be from the enclave?"

"We are," the older man says. His white hair pokes out from a cap as though trying to escape, and his thick white mustache curls at the ends. "And you're the newcomer."

They've heard of me. *A good sign!* "My name is Lark."

The girl chimes, "I said it was Lark."

My heart swells.

The woman says, "You said Loon, Tara."

I beam. "Which is very close."

"Is it true?" asks the younger man, who looks about my age. His isn't a remarkable face, but it might grow more handsome with familiarity. The way Andru's did.

I blink away that seed of memory before it can take root. "Is what true?" I think of Perg and lower my voice. "The monster . . . fighting?"

He nods. I nod.

He reels back like I slapped him. It shifts his hair, and I notice a bruise on his forehead, drooping down the side of his temple. It looks to be a day or two old. I hesitate, wondering if I should ask—

"Remarkable," says the older man. "I've never heard of such a thing."

The younger man shakes his head, letting his hair cover the mark.

Searching for a reason that isn't entirely false, I say, "I have good aim." At least, with my fear, I do. I need only to look at my victim . . .

A chill runs up my arms. I rub it away. I won't let fear destroy this chance. My last chance. I've nowhere to turn if Cagmar's people turn me away.

Family.

"Impossible," the younger man says.

"This is Colson," the woman intercedes, still studying my face. "I'm Ritha." She gestures to the older man. "Wiln. And Tara." The girl.

I greet each of them. They act comfortable with each other, familiar but unrelated, based on their looks. But there's more to friends, to family, than blood. "Are there many of us? In the enclave?"

"It's full," Colson retorts. "More than full."

Ritha shoots him a wearied look. "It's very small. Cagmar, the way it's built, it can only house so many people. It can only grow so much. They barely tolerate us, so our space is very small. I share a bed with Tara." She pats the girl on the shoulder. "That's why we were so surprised to hear about you!"

I hug myself. "Understandable. I didn't know they let in children. I had to . . . prove myself, to say the least."

"They don't," Ritha replies. "Tara was born here. We make sure she stays useful, running errands, doing behind-the-scenes work."

Tara chirps, "I'm going to be a scribe."

Ritha sets a hand on her shoulder. "Her handwriting is quite good."

Colson snorts, but I don't question him. Instead I ask, "Would they really exile a child?"

Ritha and Wiln exchange uncertain looks. A familiar fear cools the base of my belly. None of us is truly safe, then. I can only imagine they came here out of desperation as well. Even in the townships, the drought has made living hard.

I want to change the subject. "What is it you do?"

"I'm an herbalist. And a midwife." Ritha glances lovingly at Tara.

Wiln smiles, his white mustache stretching. "I'm a horologist."

I brighten. "A clockmaker?" I haven't known one since I left Lucarpo.

"A tinker as well. Keep that running." He gestures to a white-faced clock high on a nearby stone wall, which I hadn't noticed earlier.

"Do you . . ." I hesitate, trying to choose the best words. "Do you work with sundials at all? Or the stars?"

Wiln shakes his head. "Not for a very long time. Very little sunshine down here." He gestures toward the market's high ceiling of unending near-black rock, as if we're inside an obsidian egg, blocked entirely from the world beyond. "Why do you ask?"

Again, I hesitate. I've had little opportunity to talk about those deep desires within me, about the heavens that have molded themselves into a faith all my own. "I . . . I met a Cosmodian once. I thought her work was fascinating."

His brow tightens, and he rubs his chin with the pad of his thumb. "A worshipper of the stars? I thought they'd all died off. Makes me think . . . Well, I'll check on something."

Before I can ask what he means, Wiln looks expectedly at Colson, who says, "I work the mines."

I'm surprised. "They wouldn't accept me for labor alone."

Gaze narrowing, he reels back. "Pardon me for not being a scholar."

My gut clenches. "I didn't mean—"

"Colson has been here awhile," Ritha's voice soothes. "Even grown he can get into places the trolls can't."

"Or pick ore from their pebbles," he quips.

Wiln peeks at the clock again. "You'd best get on your way, Miss Lark. Work shift ends soon, and if you get caught up in the traffic, you'll never get where you're going."

I glance at the clock. It's nearly the third hour.

"Thank you. And . . . the enclave?"

"It's full." Colson's tone is even more bitter than before.

"Down," Ritha answers, pointing to a nearby tunnel. "Past military training, just below the divide on the west."

"Thank you. Even if I can't join . . . I would like to visit and know you better, if I might." I glance at Colson. "All of you."

He folds his arms and averts his stony gaze.

After taking my leave, I check Azmar's map before hurrying to get as far as I can before the shift changes. I make it up a lift and past the farming walls before it does, but so high in the city, I only need to duck out of the way for trolls a few times. I reach the apartment and am relieved to find it unlocked. Azmar was the last to leave today; he must either have thought ahead on my behalf or isn't concerned for security.

In the little corner allotted me, I sort through my packages, finding several floral disks in my foodstuff and a clean set of clothes in beige and white, just as the others wore. The clothes measure too wide but fit lengthwise. They can be adjusted with drawstrings, belts, and the needle and thread I have in my few personal belongings. I leave Azmar's and Unach's packages outside their doors. I don't want to presume I can enter their rooms.

I stretch out for an hour, munching on a floral disk, before Unach comes home. She says nothing about her excursion. "Your shifts will be longer in the future. Don't expect time to laze around."

To that I say, "Would you like me to cook dinner?"

She pauses, noticing the packages by the bedrooms. "Human food?" she questions with a down-turned lip.

"I can keep it simple. I'll look at what you have."

She considers me for a long moment before conceding. Feeling useful, I unwrap her and Azmar's rations, familiarize myself with the tiny kitchen, and start water boiling over the fire. I've got a stew simmering when Azmar returns. He looks tired. A splotch of ink stains his shirt and one of his hands.

Upon Unach's appraisal, he says, "The council wants the quarter section extended, but I don't see how it's possible without building up from the ground. Which is also impossible."

Unach shrugs. "You'll make it work."

Azmar frowns and peers toward me, where I sit stirring the pot. I take in the ink stains, the belt—which looks like it carries a ruler and some other tools—and think of the neat, precise lines of the map he'd drawn me. He doesn't look anything like the sniveling scholars and scribes so often called into my father's office.

"You're an engineer," I murmur.

Unach folds her arms. "And?"

And . . . I'm not sure. It didn't fit the idea of trolls painted in my mind. That they value only strength. That they're a war-hungry people. Yet they have higher education, which is hard to find amidst the townships—

"And," I say, stirring, "I think that is rather marvelous." And very much in alignment with Ura, the seventh planet.

Unach throws her head back and laughs. Azmar regards me with a closed expression.

She squares her shoulders. "I am a warrior. Azmar might keep the city up with nails and hammers, but I keep it up by slaying the monsters that would tear it down."

More to himself than anyone else, Azmar says, "Hardly nails and hammers."

Unach passes me a calculating glance. "Monster hunting is not a job for the weak. So tell me, Lark. What did you say to the council to convince them you're not?"

I try not to squirm under her gaze. Changing the subject, I ask Azmar, "Are you not also a warrior?" and pull the pot from the fire.

He takes a seat beside his sister. "We all undertake military training in our youth. It is required."

Unach scoffs. "She doesn't need to know."

"The more she knows, the better she will fare."

Unach considers that. I try to show my gratitude, but Azmar has lost any interest in me and instead pores over a sheaf of paper in his hands. I spoon the stew into bowls, keeping my own portion small and stowed away in the kitchen before serving them. Though he saw me stirring the pot, Azmar looks surprised at the offer and nods his thanks. Unach eats without comment. Before I head back for my own meal, I glance at the sheaf Azmar placed on the floor, looking over the careful charts and numbers, a smattering of equations at the bottom. He's calculating forces for what looks like a support system. It's rather brilliant.

"Does something concern you?" Azmar asks softly.

I meet his tired gaze and gesture toward the equations. "I could finish this for you, if you'd like."

His brows stitch together. "You know advanced figures?"

"Yes." My father was a horrid man, but he was a rich one. I had my share of tutors. *No use in having you stupid,* he once said.

Confusion wrinkles Azmar's forehead, but he acquiesces, and I take his papers and pencil with me into the kitchen, careful not to spill on his work. He has only a few calculations left, and it takes me a moment to remember the methods. I ran away when I was twelve, after all, and have not undertaken any schooling since. But I manage it by the time Azmar finishes his meal. I don't know how much time I've saved him, since he double-checks every single one of my calculations, but it prides me when he does not alter a single one, and he regards me, briefly, in his quiet way, before retiring to bed.

Chapter 4

Over the next week, I learn more about the trolls' complicated caste system and, to an extent, how to determine the caste of those I see. Weakness *is* despised among these people, who adapted themselves to war during the rule of the humans. Humans, because they can breed so much quicker, vastly outnumbered trolls, and even now, years after the drought crumbled the empire of my ancestors, Cagmar holds combat strength in the greatest esteem.

Supra is the highest case. All Supra are council members, meaning there are only five total. Qequan, who tested my fear and deemed me worthy to stay, heads the council, making him the most powerful troll in Cagmar.

Beneath them are the Alpines, composed of decorated warriors and military leaders. Beneath them is the sixth caste, Montra. Many of the monster slayers are Montra, Unach included. It's understandable why my place here confuses so many, as I'm a human and without caste. Unach knows I'm hiding something. Others, like Troff, assume the council simply wants an accident to take care of me.

Because engineering is so critical to the survival of Cagmar, many engineers claim the fifth caste, Centra. Azmar is Centra. During my carefully placed questions about the caste system, Unach let slip that Azmar contradicted his family's wishes by pursuing engineering, and he dropped a caste level because of it. His parents, grandparents, and so on were highly trained warriors. Why Azmar strayed from that path, I do not know, and yet I understand it. I'm not what my father wanted me to be, either.

Centra and the fourth caste—Intra—are composed of teachers, hunters, and strategists. Those in higher positions of employment, such as food handlers, make up the Deccor caste, and below that sit the Nethens, including Perg. Plebs, the weakest trolls and lowest caste, work in servitude. From what I've seen, they're treated little better than humans.

I internalized the hierarchy quickly. So many years at my father's side, whether negotiating land or war, taught me the importance of information, especially in the political sphere. I am the lowest of the low in Cagmar, but I will not be caught unaware.

Unach has decided to uncover my secrets by pushing me to my limits: making me stitch together my own armor, sharpen weapons, and mend rope and having me do drills in the docks. (Humans are not allowed in the training hall, or the "rec," as Unach's friend called it earlier.) She still speaks to me brusquely, like I am a burden, but I don't entirely mind. Unach is constant and predictable, and she often lends me that extra blanket at night, though always after I've fallen asleep. She hides a soft spot in her heart, I think, under all those layers of hardened muscle.

Unach tries to get under my skin by signing me up for two shifts, the first of which I must report to by the fourth morning hour, which thankfully passes without event. However, because of the shift in schedule, I manage to have time between shifts to visit the enclave. I wind up to the market, using Azmar's fading map, and find the tunnel Wiln pointed out to me before. It's a direct route, thankfully, and I soon find myself in a hallway similar to the one where Unach's apartment is, but many of the walls have been knocked away for more open space. Altogether, it's about the size of my father's house, if all three stories were laid out in a row. Two hundred feet long, made of stone and steel.

Colson had not been lying when he said it was full.

The enclave is even more packed than the main roads on shift changes. Humans bustle everywhere. It's impossible to walk the single path without brushing shoulders with them. All in all, I estimate fewer than one hundred of my kind, but in such a cramped space, their numbers seem monumental, and that doesn't include humans away at work.

There are no separate apartments, only tiny rooms made from hanging leather, rugs, and cloth—whatever is on hand. Some of them have been drawn aside, exposing pallets and beds. Everyone here must share. But all the draperies lend color to the enclave, and despite the dim light from sconces, it's the cheeriest-looking place in all of Cagmar, if not also the most disorderly. The entrance to the enclave has several blankets laid out with human-made goods for sale, likely only to other humans—others would be taken to the market, for I can't imagine someone like Unach coming here to shop. I get a few inquisitive glances as I pass through. Everyone would know everyone else here, and I'm a stranger.

Still, despite the bodies and the clutter and the fullness of it all, I want so badly to belong.

I find Wiln's spot among the chaos easily. I want to call it a shop, but poorly tanned leather composes its walls, upon which hang gears, tools, and clock pieces. It has no door and only a tiny three-legged table for him to work on. The entirety of it measures no larger than the closet in Unach and Azmar's apartment.

"Miss Lark!" Wiln waves when he sees me, and a thick monocle pops from one of his eyes and dangles from a tarnished chain fastened to his vest. His cheer spreads over me like a balm, soothing hurts I'd long learned to ignore. "What a surprise! You found us."

"It's been the easiest place to find yet." Someone rushes by, singing a song at the top of his lungs, while a woman chases him, wielding her shoe like a club. I laugh and watch them weave in and out of makeshift shops and homes, never once colliding into anything. I can tell they've been here for a long time.

"Will you be moving in?" Wiln asks, picking up the monocle and wiping it on his shirt.

"Not yet." I haven't heard anything from Housing. Unach, too, grows impatient with it. "Soon, I hope." I don't care where they fit me. I'll sleep under someone's bed, or standing in the corner. The idea makes me grin.

"Where is Ritha?" I ask.

Wiln shrugs. "Likely either distributing in the market or collecting off the walls. Cave walls, that is. Sometimes they let her venture to the surface to look for the plants she needs."

I run my finger over the sharp edges of a gear on the table. "Sometimes?"

"We're not slaves here. But they don't want us leaving once we come in. Darkness, monsters, and trolls aside, Cagmar flourishes where our townships do not." Wiln slides the monocle into a trouser pocket. "They don't want us sharing what we know with others. Could invoke war."

I can't think of a single township that could hold its own against the warrior-driven trolls of Cagmar, but then again, if they were to bind together . . .

My father would find a way to best them, if he set his mind to it. He is not a man who accepts failure.

Wiln snaps his fingers, the sound muffled by his gloves. "That's right, I wanted to lend you something." He turns to a shelf behind him, only as high as his knee. There are a few books and several sheaves of papers on it. He pulls out a particularly worn volume. Its front cover has been torn free, and water damage has crinkled and yellowed the pages.

He extends it to me, and I take it gingerly in both hands. "What is this?"

"An almanac."

My breath catches. My father had almanacs. I already know what lies within—

"It's old, but it dates the seasons, sunrise and sunset, the like," Wiln explains, unable to hear the whirring of my speeding thoughts. "Also includes the night, of course. Star charts and comets, if you're interested."

"Yes. Yes!" I hug the book to my chest. "Oh, yes, thank you! I'll copy everything I can out of it and return it to you." A passing human glances at me—I hadn't realized how loud I'd been speaking. "I'll take good care of it."

Wiln is about the same age my father would be, and when I realize that, a sudden image comes to me. Not of sitting, invisible and quiet, in a shadowy corner of the immaculate office of my father, Ottius Thellele, waiting for his gesture to shrivel a man, but of sitting on that little stool in front of me, handing Wiln the tools he needs to build or fix or invent, sharing quiet jokes and warm smiles. Hearing his advice and talking about almanacs. The very idea raises gooseflesh on my arms.

Wiln chuckles. "I'm sure you'll be kinder to it than I have." He spies someone over my shoulder. "Is it working?"

I step aside to see a man of about forty approaching with a pocket watch. "It was until I dropped it."

"Let me take a look." Wiln extends his hand, and I retreat, allowing him to work. I thumb through the almanac, finding a cluster of information on the heavens near the back. Anything I can learn from this, anything at all, I will cherish forever.

I should probably make my way back; there's little to explore here. But I don't get far before I hear my name.

"Lark."

It's cool and calm as autumn wind. I turn and see Colson leaning against one of the piles supporting the roof. A boy stands near him, likely in his later teens, though he's small in stature.

"Hello." Colson's chilly disposition douses my enthusiasm, and I hug the almanac a little closer.

He dips his head toward his companion. "This is Etewen. How are you finding Cagmar?"

Colson's question gives me hope that he's warming up to me. Not everyone accepts strangers as easily as Ritha and Wiln have. "Well enough. I still use a map to find my way around. And I'm getting the timing of the shift changes as well."

"Good." Colson folds his arms across his chest. "You'll need to know how to rearrange your tasks to avoid a whipping."

My spine turns cold. "Whipping?" I think of his bruised face days before, though the markings have nearly faded.

"I heard what Wiln said," he goes on. "We're not slaves, sure. But they have a task force 'specially for monitoring us. Keeping us in line. Make sure we're contributing. If we're not contributing to their liking, we're reminded of our place. They have prison cells here for a reason, though some trolls just like to remind you they're bigger than you."

I hadn't been told about this. I glance at Etewen. "Truly?"

"You think I'm lying?" Colson pushes off the pile.

"Grodd is the worst of them," Etewen murmurs. He shifts uncomfortably, like he's hurt, and I wonder if he's been beaten recently. The name on his lips makes my stomach sink.

"The big gray one?" I say. "Montra?"

Colson looks surprised. "So you've met him."

Only briefly, thank goodness. "Only in passing."

Colson considers me before shrugging. "It isn't all bad. On fifth days we congregate in the back of the schoolyard and catch up. Play a few games we remember from . . . before."

Etewen scratches his cheek.

I perk up. "Today is fifth day."

Colson offers a small smile. It makes him look so much more approachable, and I find myself relaxing. "It is, if you want to come. Some of the trolls don't like it, so we have to start late. Around the twenty-second hour."

I'm usually in bed by then, to ensure I'll get plenty of sleep for my shifts, but the longer I'm in Cagmar, the more I ache for a friend, a confidant. The more I wish for someone like Finnie or Andru. "I'll be there." I pull out my map and search for the school.

Etewen and Colson exchange a glance. "I guess you're still new," Colson says, and points east. "Four levels down that way, right of the *X*, which sits just below the Mid-divide. Eastmost side."

"I'll find it." I can't hide my grin. I'll be able to introduce myself to so many others, and possibly find comradery with Colson, since we're close in age. "Thank you. I'm excited to get to know you all."

He looks up, and I follow his gaze to a clock on the ceiling, its gears exposed. He curses. "I have to go. See you tonight." He pushes past the throng, making his way for the exit. Duty in the mines, no doubt.

To Etewen, I ask, "Will you be all right on your own?"

He shrugs, then winces. "I'll be fine."

Thinking of Grodd and this task force, I take the same path Colson did. I'd better get back. Make sure I know all my shifts for the week. Practice the drills Unach gave me. Perhaps the real reason she's worked me so hard is that she knows how crucial it is that I fulfill the role given to me. My appreciation for Unach is renewed, as is my excitement for tonight. I'll meet more people, learn more names, and reunite with my own kind.

Slowly and surely, Cagmar is becoming a place where I might actually belong.

Unach quizzes me as I fasten the belts of my harness.

"Gunchar." She doesn't meet my eyes as she cleans her nails with a knife.

I think back to my studies. "Bird, thirty-foot wingspan. Short beak. Deadliest weapons are its talons."

"And?" she presses.

"And . . . they nest high in the canyon and generally stay away from the bridge?"

"*And* their wings create gusts that can knock you off the wall." She grabs a rope and tosses it at me. I catch it with both arms. She's manning my line today. "Crag snake."

"Crag snakes live in the south—"

"North."

"North," I amend, then remember. "Near the mountains, but occasionally they travel down here if prey is scarce. Two heads, with sharp teeth. Blind. Poisonous. Inedible."

Unach nods, which is the most praise I can expect from her. I loop the rope through my harness, triple-checking the tightness of the knot. I'm still not comfortable climbing across the city and canyon walls, even with the handholds.

"Spreener."

"Also poisonous." I hand the rope back. I'm tall for a human woman, but I can't reach the pulleys on the ceiling of the south dock without help. Unach does so with an annoyed grunt. "Spiders with sharp beaks and tusks, hard outer armor. They . . ." I look upward, trying to remember. "They like crevices?"

Unach nods again. Kesta, the female troll with deep-gray skin and long dark hair, pushes off the wall, twisting Troff's rope in her hands. "Can we get going?" She glances to the door. "Kub's late, as always. I'm getting sleepy listening to her school lesson."

I try not to frown. "I'm ready."

A soft garble sounds in the distance. The others hear it as well. Unach's shoulders stiffen.

Kesta looks at me. "Next question. What was that?"

"Uh." I glance at Unach. "Tor rat?"

Troff snorts. "It's a lecker. Let's go."

Lecker. My mind spins as Troff climbs out of the dock. *Edible, large and agile. Lizard-like. Spiked tail?* I can't remember. Unach ties my ropes around her waist with an air of impatience, so I hurry to follow Troff, watching which handholds he grabs. I haven't yet encountered any canyon monsters, so knowing a lecker prowls nearby spins fear up my legs. But I'm familiar with fear. It's as much a part of me as my own blood, and I need to prove myself.

Pulling on a mask of bravery, I drop from the dock, grasp my first handhold, and hurry after Troff, who moves far more swiftly than I do. He's had more practice. Has more muscle as well. All the trolls are riddled with muscle, even the elderly and the few children I've seen.

Troff stops at the first lookout. I climb up after him, trying to keep my heavy breathing quiet. He pulls a spyglass from his belt and peers into the canyon. I squint and search. Far to the south, a shadow moves.

"There." I point. Troff confirms with a grunt. We watch the shadow silently for two full minutes before it shifts into the light. Before I can take a breath, it vanishes into the darkness. "It's huge," I whisper.

Troff laughs, readying a sling to scare it away, should it come closer. "That's only a juvenile."

A shiver courses down my back. "Truly?"

He raises an eyebrow at me, a shade of distaste passing over his face. "Yes, truly. Are you scared, little human?"

I bury my fear deep inside my gut.

"Yes," I admit. "But I would be a bad slayer if I weren't."

I have only a couple of hours after my second shift to read the almanac before meeting up with Colson and the others, and I don't waste a second of it. Crouching by Unach's hearth, I hold the old book sideways, pinching it carefully, as several pages have come unglued from their spine. I read through the entire section on stars, wondering if Azmar would lend me paper to copy down everything verbatim later, including the star charts. I learn that the constellations Ufreya, the queen, and Sankan, the oak tree, cross paths every twelve years. Some read it as an omen for fertility, others as a sign of war, thinking that the queen will take boughs from the tree to fashion weapons. The almanac is very old indeed, for its list of sightings of this phenomenon ends at 796, and the year is 964. I do the math and realize that the constellations will cross again this year, and I wonder if I'll be able to witness it.

Time rolls forward, and I know I need to leave or else be late. I kiss the almanac and stow it under my pallet. I'm to meet new friends tonight, carve out a little niche for myself in this heavy city made of stone. I think again of the reading that the Cosmodian—a servant to the stars—gave me when I was eleven. She'd come for my mother, who wasn't religious; none of my family was. But she found star-reading intriguing, a rare treat for the household. For whatever reason, she'd forbidden me to be present, despite including my two half siblings. This wasn't a surprise. She had never favored me. But the Cosmodian, whose name I never learned, had seen me crying by the woodshed where my parents wouldn't hear. My mother hated tears almost as much as my father did, and I hadn't the strength for a beating.

The Cosmodian took pity upon me. Asked me my birthdate and year, traced the lines on my palms. I've repeated her words many times since, so as to never forget them.

"You are strong, Calia," she says with a grin, looking into my eyes. "So strong that others fear you."

"I know."

She's surprised by that response. She taps a line on my hand, then opens up her ledger of star charts. "You are of Iter, the spider. Spiders are often feared, but unjustly so. They will fear you for your strength, my child."

Such an idea has never, in all my eleven years, crossed my mind.

The Cosmodian frowns. "Your path will not be straight, but broken and looping. Yet there is a purpose in all things, and this path will lead you to your purpose." She lifts her ledger and tilts it toward the moonlight. "Your stars extend here, and here." She points to the first. "This is the field of family. You will have one of your own someday."

A family of my own. Another thing I have never envisioned. I could be a mother and do all the things I wished my own could do. I could choose a good father, someone unlike Ottius in every way. I could have a babe on my arm that might love me the way my siblings didn't.

"And this." She traces the second set of stars, then pauses, her lips curving low. I can't make out the stars she touches; they're bisected by too many lines on the paper. Lines that, ironically, make me think of a spiderweb. *"Hmm. I don't know how to read this, Calia. But I think your future will be bright, and wholly unexpected."*

That prediction had come to mind every time I arrived at a new township, met new people. *Will this be my family? Are any of these the bright end to this broken road?*

Now I wanted nothing more than to understand what she meant. To read the stars the way she had. To unlock the skies.

Tonight was another opportunity.

I don't think I'll be in trouble, leaving the apartment. I've been in Cagmar for nine days, and not once has anyone mentioned a curfew. Unach hardly cares what I do so long as I show up for work and keep my things to the little corner allotted me. So an hour after the sun sets beyond the narrow window above my pallet, I plait my hair over my shoulder, put on the clothing I arrived in, and slip out into the corridors.

Everything in Cagmar is dim. Windows to let in natural sunlight are few and far between, and most exist only to vent the smoke from sconces, lamps, and torches. But at night it's especially dark. About half of the lights are put out to preserve fuel. But it's still bright enough for me to pick my way around.

The city doesn't sleep. I can hear blacksmiths' hammers as I approach the trade works, just above the marketplace. A few Deccor guards scurry about, but being out at night is not a crime, so I pay them little attention. Pleb workers sweep the streets and carry deliveries. I wait for them to cross before hurrying in the direction Colson pointed out to me, my eagerness driving away the day's exhaustion. The tunnel I take ends in a narrow staircase, and my knees hurt by the time I descend past the Mid-divide. There's a lot of housing here, smaller apartments and shacks in poorer repair than Unach's. I see one of the great barriers that form the *X*, so I follow it down a ways to what must be the school, since it has a designated stone yard, presumably for recreation. I've always gone around this section of the city, so all of it is new to me. But I'm willing to get lost, retrace my steps, and look generally foolish, in order to share a night with my kind. It's been a long time since I was part of a group. A long time since I played games. My heart is so full, my nerves so quick, I feel I might burst.

I don't hear anything, but humans would likely aim to be quiet in a troll city, so I follow the stone wall of the great building around, searching for the familiar beige clothing against the darkness. The yard itself isn't lit, but lights from nearby roads and districts shine down like close stars, casting everything in a sort of orange glow. It reminds me of bonfires back in Dina. In my mind's eye, I see Andru's laughing face as we clasped hands and spun until vertigo swept us off our feet. For the moment, the memory doesn't sting, as it so often does. Soon I'll have new memories to replace the old. Good things to bandage the bad.

I reach the back of the school and see no one, then wonder if I've arrived too early.

"There she is."

Colson's voice. Relieved, I turn.

Just as a fist connects with my cheek.

I stumble back and lose my footing, falling to my hip. My shaking hand rushes up to my face, where pain slowly sets in. Blood trickles from my nose. Blinking, I'm just able to make out Colson above me, and Etewen behind him—along with two other men. One of them helps me up, only to throw me against the stone wall.

My heart lodges in my throat, and for the briefest instant, I am in my father's house again. I fight the instinct to curl into a ball and guard my head.

"Do you have *any* idea," Colson says, his breath hot on my face, "what it's like for us down here? We work long hours, have our valuables taken from us, scrimp and barter for everything we have. And you just dance in here and play Montra? While the rest of us get beaten, just like this"—he slams knuckles into my breast—"by the bloody task force?"

I swallow, gripping his wrist to pull him off, trying to claw through the web of confusion engulfing me. "I-I didn't assign myself—"

A fist hits my mouth, and I'm not able to get the words out. A knee thrusts into my stomach and knocks the wind from me. I drop to the pavement. I gasp, my thoughts muddled, trying to find my bearings. A trap? Was the meeting a lie?

The memory of bonfires fizzles into black coals.

Fear coils up my middle, itching to be released. But I don't want them to fear me. I don't want them to go home to the enclave and tell everyone what I am. I don't want to lose my chance of having a home here. They . . . They're my last chance.

I have nowhere else to go.

A boot to my hip sends me sprawling. "You make a mockery of us." Colson's voice.

I hiss as I'm lifted by my hair. *Fear*—

A blow lands at my kidney, another in my stomach. Bile rushes up my throat and burns my mouth.

Don't you dare *use it on me!* my father screamed as his open hand burned across my cheek. *I know what it is! Don't you* dare*!*

Fear slips from me, like a wild animal on a tether, jerked free. My bones chill as the man holding my hair drops me, wheeling back as though I'm one of the monsters from the chasm.

But then Colson's hands squeeze my throat. I claw at him, trying to breathe. My fingernails cut into the skin of his hands, but he doesn't relent. I barely feel the following blows to my legs as the others barrage me.

Do what they want, think what they want, but I won't let them kill me.

My fear explodes outward, a great boulder dropped into a lake. My body mirrors the sensations of horror I invoke so strongly that my heart threatens to split in two. Colson releases me, and I drop to the ground, gasping. My assailants step back as if I were a viper.

Fight or flee. These cowards choose the latter. They run back the way I came, trampling my shredded hope underfoot.

I kneel there, doubled over, every blow making itself known slowly, achingly. Tears run down the sides of my nose. Odd. I never cried when my father beat me. He hated tears.

I hear heavy footsteps and shudder. Perhaps I didn't scare them off after all. Perhaps the human task force heard of this meeting, and Grodd has come to deal out his own discipline.

The steps slow. "Lark?"

That voice. How do I know that voice?

Holding my throat, wheezing, I look up and blink, peering through the darkness. A tall figure stands over me, not quite troll, not quite human. Perg?

I feel his strong hands on my elbows, just as the dim lights of the schoolyard wink out.

Danner's palm presses against my mouth.

I startle awake, tasting the salt of his hand. It burns against a small cut at the corner of my lip.

Something's wrong. I wait for Danner to tell me what, but he doesn't speak, only climbs into the bed, crushing his sister, Finnie—but Finnie isn't there. She fell asleep by the fire.

The moon shines full and bright, washing out the stars, casting the tiny room Finnie and I share in shades of blue and steel. I try to push Danner's hand away, to ask what's wrong, but he presses it down so hard my teeth cut the inside of my lips. The house sleeps; everything is quiet. Danner, four years my senior, slips under the cover.

I don't realize he shut the door until his hand grabs my breast. I'm only fourteen. A year ago, I didn't have a breast to grab. Tendrils of fear awaken in me, curling like hungry worms. Like the curse knew, before I did, what was going to happen. That I was going to lose all of them.

Finnie's parents were my parents. Finnie was my sister. Danner was my brother. They were supposed to be my family. The Cosmodian had promised me a family of my own.

I push at Danner, stalling him, but he's stronger and heavier than I am. "It won't hurt," his hot whispers promise. "Shh," he coos, like I'm a baby. "They won't know."

Tears come, but still Danner doesn't move his hand from my mouth. His other slides up my nightdress. I push again, I plead, the sounds dying against his palm.

When the fear flies out of me, almost of its own accord, Danner flies with it. He leaps back from the bed like it's made of hot embers instead of cotton-wrapped hay. He screams, loud enough to wake the house.

He sputters truths mixed with lies. "Monster," he says. Truth. "Tried to kill me," he says. Lie.

But he is their son, her brother. They are family, and I am not. And so I flee with everything I can carry, everything I can grab as Finnie's father rains blows on my back.

My road breaks a little more.

That was Terysos. The Cosmodian had not been in that township, either.

I'm murkily aware of strong arms encircling me against a wide chest. Voices spin in senseless orbits. A light blooms nearby.

My body burns, bruises pulsing and radiating from my head to my ankles.

"What do you mean, *found her*?" Unach's voice snaps like a whip.

"By the school where I live, with the humans." Perg's voice sounds close. It reverberates in his chest.

I blink. I'm in Unach's apartment. Did he carry me all the way here?

"She's awake." Azmar's baritone cuts through the muddled sounds. "Lay her here."

My feet hit a doorjamb as Perg carries me into a dark room and lays me on something . . . not soft, but softer than the stone floor. A light follows. It illuminates Perg's face, which hovers over me. It may be a trick of the shadows, but he looks remarkably human in this light.

I try to speak, but soreness pinches my throat. My voice comes out in a rasp. My mind returns to me, painting the schoolyard on the back of my eyelids. I gasp. It feels as though someone hammers a wooden shim into my chest, just above my sternum. I reach for it, but there's nothing there.

Perg clasps my hand. "Don't worry, Lark. We'll get you a healer."

Unach snorts. "Who will come for a human this time at night? Why was she even out of the apartment?"

"I don't think the injuries are life threatening," murmurs Azmar.

"Ritha." Perg steps back. I turn my head to follow him, wincing at how stiff my neck is. "She's in the enclave. She knows some healing."

Unach grumbles; I feel it through the mattress. "Go, then."

Perg ducks out of sight, and I close my eyes once more.

I wake up to a sharp pain in my hip. My eyes flutter open. Two large candles flicker near my head. The ceiling arches. Wooden supports. A bed, too large. Walls modestly adorned. A side table with an old tome and a stack of papers on it.

I'm in Azmar's room.

Looking down, I see a human woman—Ritha—pressing something against my hip. Her dark gaze meets mine.

"It will help with the bruising," she says, and I realize she's applied a poultice.

Tears blur my vision, but I blink them away. *Ritha wasn't there.* She wasn't one of the humans who hated me. She's safe. "Thank you."

She leans back, pulling the blankets up to my ribs. My body is a spattering of aches and pains. I lift a hand to touch the swell of my cheek. A cut splits my lip as well.

"When you're ready, drink that." Ritha tilts her head toward the side table. A cup of something rests behind Azmar's papers.

I swallow to wet my throat, and ask, "Do you hate me, too?"

She frowns. "Why would I hate you, Lark?"

"They hate me," I whisper, forcing each heavy word over my tongue.

"They are fools."

I close my eyes. Somehow, it makes the pain worse. I cling to Ritha's words for stability. *Ritha is here. Ritha will help me. It's not over yet.*

"Lark." Ritha's soft voice is a caress. "What is your last name?"

I blink against blurry vision. *Thellele.* "I don't have one."

She purses her lips and studies me, but she accepts the lie.

I think our conversation finished. Ritha's thoughts have obviously led her somewhere else, and she doesn't talk for several minutes. Then, as she's gathering her things, she says, "Rest for a day. It's not so bad."

I shift on the bed, wincing at the bruises. *Not so bad.* Nothing broken. I remember how this goes. My father never broke anything. I was too useful to be broken.

"I'm sorry they did this to you." Ritha pulls a tattered bag over her shoulder. "But, Lark"—she looks at me pointedly and lowers her voice—"it's not them you should fear."

She glances toward the door.

"Unach and Azmar have been kind to me," I rasp, though I'm not sure she meant them.

Ritha excuses herself without another word, and I fall back into oblivion.

Chapter 5

I can't gauge the time without a window; I can only guess at its passing by the melting of the candles. When the wicks nearly drown in their own pools, I force myself to sit up and groan against two dozen aches. But Ritha was right; they're not so bad. They will fade in time and with movement.

I pray she is wrong about the trolls. But just in case, I want to vacate Azmar's room as swiftly as possible.

I slide off the too-high bed onto the floor, then nearly collapse as pain zings up my left leg. I gasp and spit loose hair from my mouth. I steady myself and pull up my skirt and look at the damage. A purpling bruise the size of my open hand forms there, hot and hard. It will darken over the next day. I don't think Ritha saw that one, for the one on my hip, which she treated, is not nearly as dark.

I search for a mirror but find none. Likely for the better. Though it hurts to raise my arms, I rebraid my hair and fix my clothes, trying to look presentable. Then, leaning against the wall, I make my way out into the main room.

Unach crouches by the fire, where water boils, running a sharpening stone over the long, curved blade of a sword.

I need to be useful. Taking a deep breath, I hobble for the broom. Unach looks up and barks a laugh. "I don't know what's more funny," her low voice resonates, "the fact that your face looks like a marmot liver or that you're trying to sweep."

I manage the smallest smile I can without opening the cut on my lip.

She stands, reminding me of her size. Had it been trolls, even just one troll, behind the school last night, I would not be breathing this morning. She slides the great sword into a sheath hanging off her hip.

Does she use that weapon only for monsters?

"Fortunately, you've been approved for housing." Unach places her hands on her hips without another word uttered about my appearance, my injuries, or my beating. When it happened in my father's house, no one spoke of it, either, but it's not shame that drives Unach. Being a warrior, she might be used to such bludgeoning blows. I find her lack of pity oddly reassuring. "Technically it's servants' housing, but you take what you can get."

"Good." It will be beneficial to Unach, and I won't have to try to make myself comfortable on the floor anymore. "Where?"

"Only one level down." She strides over and hands me an iron key. "Come. I'll give you the day off. Waste of effort to have you bleed out internally."

I force back another smile. *Soft spot.*

Then I think of the gleam in Colson's eyes and clench my teeth to banish the image away.

Passing me, Unach picks up the heavy fur blanket I rolled up on my pallet last night. The almanac drops out. She examines it, loses interest quickly, and shoves it into the blanket roll before tossing the lot to me. I barely move fast enough to catch it.

"Azmar insists he doesn't need it anymore, so you might as well take it." She shrugs.

That causes me to pause. I hold the soft fur tightly against me. Azmar? So he'd laid the blanket upon me when I was shivering in the dark?

Unach doesn't give me time to ponder. She strides for the door, and I hobble after her, using the broom as a crutch. She waits a moment, then rolls her eyes. "Regret's breath," she mutters, then steps toward me and swoops me into her arms.

Gasping at the pain of her forearm against my thigh, I say, "I can walk."

"I don't have all day." Unach steps into the corridor and takes the lift down a single floor.

Wishing to get my mind off my bruises, I ask, "Wh-Why does everyone say that? 'Regret'?"

She looks at me incredulously. "Not much for religion, I take it."

My lips part. "I . . ." I have always considered myself a believer, especially after meeting the Cosmodian. I piece together everything I know of the trolls and Cagmar. "We . . . Our gods do not have names."

Unach snorts. "The only god who listens to the trollis is Regret. He is the only one who cares for the world's castaways." She steps off the lift as another troll heads our way. "Now hush." Her words are sharp, but not unkind. So I stay quiet, avoiding the curious eyes of the passing troll, knowing that my being carried construes weakness. I mull over the idea of Regret as a deity. In the past . . . it's easy to label the trolls as castaways. To deny it would be to deny Cagmar's existence: a great city built beneath the earth, away from the reach of human hands. But now, with the drought, the playing field has leveled. Or even, finally, granted the trolls the gods' favor.

I wonder what the names of the other gods are, or if they'd even want us to know.

Near the end of the stone corridor stand several wooden doors, thinner and narrower than Unach's, and closer together. She stops at the second one and sets me down none too gently.

Inside is a cramped space with a troll-sized cot and an empty crate. No water pump, wash basin, fireplace, or cold storage. But to my delight, another one of those skinny, horizontal windows splits the rock. Tendrils of distant sunlight slice through it.

"Lie down," Unach snaps. "I'm not covering all your shifts, hear?"

"Unach?"

She frowns. "What?"

"What does the sun, earth, and shadow have to do with Regret?"

Her frown fades as a sudden soberness overtakes her. "You mean the oath."

I nod. *By sun, earth, and shadow, and as Regret forms on my lips, I am of trollis and am bound by its words.*

"It's old folklore, really." Her voice lowers. "It isn't anything we believe or practice, but tradition . . ." She swipes a hand through the air between us. "The gods made the sun, and then they made the earth. But the earth blocked out the light and created shadow. And from the shadow came the trollis." With a half-hearted shrug, she adds, "I suppose it's not too inaccurate, given where we live."

"You've always lived in Cagmar?"

She nods.

Her honesty warms me. "Thank you. For that, and for helping me with my shifts."

She leans away from me, uncomfortable with my gratitude. Without another word, she turns back for the corridor and shuts the door behind her.

I rest as long as I can before my mind grows antsy. I reread the almanac, studying the star charts, wishing I could compare them to tonight's sky. I've nothing else to read, and no one to converse with. I am grateful for the rest, but this blessed space begins to close in on me. I miss sunlight, starlight. Carefully peeling my aching body from the bed, I stumble toward the door. I am stiff and sore, but not wholly incapable. I wait at the lift a long time, allowing troll after troll to pass by. I pull my hair around to the swollen side of my face to hide it. I know how these people view weakness.

When the lift is finally free, I step inside and, setting my jaw, pull the rope to lift me to Unach's level. My shoulder strains with the effort, but my few belongings remain in her apartment, as does the medicine Ritha left me.

Masking my limp as well as I can, I approach the door and raise my hand to knock, but Unach's angry voice causes me to hesitate.

"—no surprise there."

I hear Azmar respond softly, but it's too quiet for me to understand.

Unach snorts. "It's far within my rights. He can writhe and scream all he wants. One less human is nothing to complain about."

A chill courses down my spine. After trying the handle and finding it unlocked, I push the heavy door open and nearly fall to my knees as a stabbing sensation in my leg causes me to lose my balance. Only my grip on the door handle keeps me upright.

Unach's gaze burns like hot embers on my face. She stands near the table, her thick arms folded across her wide chest. Azmar sits on a chair, hunched over, his elbows on his knees.

Righting myself, I push the door closed. "Who are you talking about?"

Unach's brow tightens. "I told you to rest."

"I am much rested and obliged to make your dinner," I protest, noticing that there are no dishes, or even a fire, to suggest they've had their supper.

Unach shifts her weight onto one foot. "His name is Colson. I had an investigation done, and Perg validated. He's to be cast to the darkness."

My joints freeze. "Cast to the darkness?"

"Over the edge," Azmar murmurs, "into the depths of the canyon."

Mouth agape, I would slide to the floor if I trusted my legs to push me up again. I lean against the wall instead. "Please don't have him killed."

Unach stares at me, incredulous. Surprise warps Azmar's features.

I push off the wall and cross to Unach, knowing I overstep my bounds. I try not to limp, to show as much warrior prowess as I can muster. I square my shoulders and put on a brave face, despite the bruises that mottle it. "I beg you to spare him. It was a misunderstanding."

Unach's fury is palpable. "He would have killed *you*."

No, he wouldn't have. Even without my ability, even without Perg, I do not think he would have. Though I might be in far worse shape than I am now.

All I ever wanted was a place where I could be accepted and not feared. I do not want Colson to die. I do not want the few others of my kind in this dark city to despise me, like so many others have.

"It's me he hurt," I try, mentally scrolling through every persuasive tactic my father taught me, even if it was unknowingly, "and I forgive him."

Unach barks a mirthless laugh. "He has committed a crime, and he will pay the price."

"Please, Unach." I raise my clasped hands and stumble, unable to hide my wincing. "If he were a troll, would you not consider—"

"That," she interrupts, her voice dark as cinders, "is too far."

"But—"

"Go." She turns her back to me. "Rest, before I beat you myself."

My lip and hands tremble. My situation is so precarious I dare not argue with her further. Were this my father's house, I would use my hateful talent, bending Unach as though she were the human and I the troll. But I have no desire to cow her. I've never wanted to cow anyone, despite all the times I have.

"As you wish," I whisper, and hand to the wall, I limp back into the corridor, alone.

For all my struggle yesterday, I still didn't manage to retrieve my things, so I brave Unach's temper in the morning and knock on the door before her shift starts. She wrenches it open violently, her hair damp, clothed but without her leather armor. Before I can explain my presence, she releases the door and walks away, as much of an invitation as I'll get from her.

Water heats over a dying fire. I cross the apartment to my pallet and kneel down, rubbing my back. After setting my bag aside, I roll up the blanket, then find one of my shirts hanging in the little laundering closet. Blanket under my arm, bag over my shoulder, I stir the fire with a poker, coercing the flames.

When I turn around, Unach and Azmar are staring at me. For lumbering giants, they're certainly light on their feet.

Unach grumbles. "You're not ready. Go back to bed."

Realizing I'm hunched like an old woman, I straighten. "I really am fine." It warms me that she notices. That she cares.

Bristling, she snaps, "I said go to—"

"I need to be useful, don't I?" I keep my voice calm, but it's the truth. "I know about the task force. I'll manage."

Unach's green lips pinch together.

"She can help me in Engineering today."

Both Unach and I turn toward Azmar.

He offers a half-hearted shrug. "She's good with math, and we're struggling with designing the council's extension. She can sit on a stool."

Unach guffaws. "And you'll, what, carry her over your shoulder the whole way down? I'd love to see that."

Despite my embarrassment, I pinch down a smile. I envy the way Unach and Azmar speak to each other. So candidly. There's a depth behind every remark, gesture, and glance. A depth that makes me wish I'd tried harder with my own siblings, though my parents kept us separated.

I could have tried harder.

"I-I can walk." I'm fairly certain I can, if I use the lifts and not the stairs or ladders. "Thank you." Admittedly, I've been curious about Engineering. This may be a silver lining to my predicament.

Azmar gives his sister a look I can't identify and heads into the small kitchen nook.

Frowning, Unach looks over the mess of the floor. "At least eat something so you're not a burden."

I smile, but it fades. "Unach, how do I get water? And cook?"

"You'll have to get water from the market. And your food has to be precooked." She must notice my down-turned face, for she groans. "Ugh. If only to prevent *me* from having to carry it for you while you're being delicate, you can use the pump up here. And the fire, but only if you cook for us, too." Then, as an afterthought, "And clean."

Relief cools me. "Thank you. I don't mind at all."

She fishes around in her pocket and slaps a key onto the table.

I dare say the gruff Montra is starting to like me.

I don't say a word about it.

With Azmar as my escort, I don't have to defer to most other trolls in the corridors or on the lifts—it seems the higher castes have fewer members, while the lower have many. If not for my slowness, we would have made good time to the market. Azmar doesn't complain, though. He walks beside me, which signals to the other trolls that I'm with him and don't need to move aside. I'm grateful for it.

While waiting for a lift, I see my distorted reflection in a metal plate supporting the shaft. Two bruises on my face have merged into one, resembling the body of a spider, which ironically recalls Iter, the fifth planet. The larger one on my cheek, deep purple where it passes over my cheekbone, overshadows the smaller one next to my mouth, which isn't quite so discolored. In my father's house, I could use powder to hide the marks, but here I just use my hair. Thus far, I haven't seen anything in the way of troll cosmetics.

We take the lift down, Azmar working the rope, and cut through the corner of the marketplace. We're halfway across when I notice Perg pulling a small wagon. Excitement blooms in my chest.

"Azmar." I grasp his forearm to stop him, then immediately release it, unsure if such an action breaks protocol. When I have his attention, I gesture to Perg. "Could I speak with him a few minutes? Please? He's the one who found me."

Azmar's topaz eyes look toward Perg before lifting to the clock. "I know. Can you find your way?"

I pull the map from my pocket. "Always do."

His lip makes the slightest quirk, though for how serious he is, I might have imagined it. "Be careful."

I nod. He hesitates, glances to Perg, then continues down to Engineering.

Crossing the road, I call out, "Perg!"

He stops and looks to either side, and I chuckle at his confusion. I hurry, gritting my teeth each time I step with my left foot. He must catch the movement from his periphery, for he turns abruptly toward me. To my delight, he grins.

"Lark." His grin fades as he takes in my face. "You're still not well."

"Not well looking, perhaps, but well enough." I take a second to catch my breath.

He glances at my leg. "Well enough," he repeats. "I'm sorry for what they did."

The memory takes me aback—that and his concern for me. I glance at his wagon. "Where are you going?"

"I'm a stone layer." He says it like it's the most menial and unimportant job in Cagmar. "Taking this down to Deccor housing."

"That isn't near Engineering, is it?"

He tilts his head. "Close. Why are you . . . Oh, Azmar."

I start walking, and Perg follows, kindly slowing his step to keep pace with me. "I'm taking a rest from physical labors and helping him today."

Perg's eyes are a very human shade of hazel, but they regard me suspiciously. "You can read?"

"And write, and do arithmetic." Growing up, I'd never realized what a privilege that was.

"But you're human." He winces. "I mean, not that all humans should be . . . Well, they are—"

"It's all right."

Perg releases an audible sigh at my dismissal. He shifts the handle of the wagon to his other hand as we walk. "I'm glad you're all right, anyway."

I smile at him, and he turns away, avoiding my gaze. We walk in silence a ways, though it isn't an uncomfortable one. A few trolls throw hard looks my way, but as I reach the corridor leading to the lower levels, I realize more than half of them are for Perg.

It's one thing to be human, but is it worse to be both? Yet Perg is not the *lowest* caste, only near so.

Thinking of his past honesty, I say, "Might I ask you . . . a personal question?"

Perg runs a thumb over his pronounced canines. "Who were my parents and why did they have the audacity to create me?"

I trip at his words. "I . . . well, I would not ask it so . . . bluntly." Heat rises in my cheeks, making my bruises throb.

A sad yet mischievous half smirk, all too human, stretches his face. "My mother was trollis, actually. Most assume it's the other way around. But it's no love story, if that's what you're hoping for." The smile fades, flattening his expression. "I don't know everything. Some drunken revelry, mistakes, and there I was. Half human, without a bloodstone pairing."

"I'm . . . sorry." I'm unsure how to respond. "Bloodstone pairing?"

"Trollis trade bloodstones to mate."

I stare up at him, considering. "Is marriage so easy?"

He lifts an eyebrow. "It's . . . Oh, you mean the human custom."

No marriage, then. "Yes."

He considers. "I suppose it's similar. Never been to the world above. They'd hate me more than the trollis do." He runs his hand over the less prominent nubs of his forehead, into his hair. "We get bloodstones once we finish military training, but . . ." He shrugs.

I reach out and touch his wrist, just below the bony protrusions there. He slows noticeably, and the weight of his wagon bumps him forward a step. His looks to my hand, then to my face, then back again.

Seeing his discomfort, I pull away. "They wouldn't hate you."

He scoffs. "You're playing pretend, then, Lark."

He's right. "*I* don't hate you."

He doesn't look at me. The ensuing silence is awkward, and I shuffle, trying not to think of the pulsing in my hip, especially when I have to step closer to Perg to let a Montra pass by.

"You don't owe me a life debt," Perg says, so quietly I can barely hear him over the wagon's wheels.

"I liked you before that," I admit.

His head snaps toward me. A weak laugh escapes him, and he points down a corridor to our right. "Down that way is Engineering. Don't get in the way. It won't go well for you. They might expect you're a troublemaker, because . . ." He gestures with his chin to my bruises.

I dip my head in thanks. "How long will you be laying stones?" I need to rest after the day's work, but I desperately want to water this seedling of friendship.

"Too long. Afterward I go to the military grounds. You wouldn't be welcomed there, even with Unach's blessing."

"Military grounds? To train?" He doesn't look young enough to be under the mandatory training Azmar mentioned.

His features grow stony. "To practice. There are few ways to improve your rank in Cagmar. One is through bloodstone trade, another through education. The last is through combat."

I lick my lips. "To become a warrior?"

"To beat one." He flexes his hand as though the hilt of a sword rests in it, while the other touches a small blue bead on his sleeve. "I did, once. Someday, I will again. Then they'll see."

My lips part. The idea perplexes me. Someone like Azmar, an engineer, is Centra, and yet if a Pleb or Nethens was born a little bigger, or trained a little smarter, and bested him in a feat of strength . . . then that troll would be Centra? Or Montra, or even Alpine or Supra? By that logic, a foolish or cruel troll could potentially rule all of Cagmar, merely because of his strength.

"And," I feel a little awkward asking, "you've tried to elevate your status through trading?"

Perg's complexion pinkens. "I don't have a bloodstone, Lark."

I pause. "But you completed military training—"

"They didn't give me one." He shrugs stiffly. "Guess they don't want me spreading any humanness around." He lifts his head, and his expression darkens.

I choke on a mix of condolences, wondering if any of them could possibly be of worth to him. Turning to follow his gaze, I'm surprised to see Colson coming up from the tunnel leading to Engineering. He has a bandage around his neck and up the side of his face, parallel to his hairline. As though someone had taken a knife to him. A sick feeling churns at the sight of it, but the shock is stronger.

Colson is alive.

I gawk at him. His gaze meets mine, but he turns away sharply and increases his speed, hurrying from my sight. Behind me, Perg growls.

"Better he was dead."

I turn toward him, incredulous. "But he was supposed to be. Unach said."

Perg shrugs and pulls the wagon forward. "His punishment was deferred to the task force. Awfully merciful, especially considering Grodd has to approve it." He rubs his chin. "Grodd, he's—"

"I know him." I shake my head, relieved yet confused. "I thought they would push Colson into the canyon."

"Usually they do." Perg steps away from me. "From what I heard, Azmar spoke on his behalf."

Azmar?

I look down the dark tunnel leading to Engineering. Azmar had been present when I pled to Unach. Had he agreed with me? Had my words moved him, even when his sister had been deaf to them? Or was he simply sympathetic to humans? He hadn't seemed pleased when Unach brought me home.

I look for Perg, questions dancing across my tongue, but he's already several paces ahead of me, heading toward his job. I'd hate to make him late.

Mulling over this revelation, I cross to the tunnel, pressing one hand against its cool stonework for support. Minutes later, the light of Engineering engulfs me.

Chapter 6

Cagmar is a precarious city. It hangs from a human-built bridge, wedged between the steep, never-ending walls of a great canyon. As a whole, it is just enough. Just enough space to sleep, just enough space to walk, just enough space to breathe. So when I enter the massive cavity that holds Engineering, I gape at its high roof and wide tables, its breadth and openness. Its shape reflects its name, for a complex network of beams and columns and brick and stone composes ceiling, floor, and walls, all fitting together in a patchwork nearly as fascinating as the night sky.

A sky, I realize, that I have not worshipped for some time. I've spent more nights lying out beneath that vast blanket of stars than not, and while I now have a roof over my head, I find myself missing it.

The clinking of hammers and other tools fills the air, though I cannot see where physical workmanship takes place. The cavity is notably warmer, which means fire burns nearby, possibly several fires. The trolls must smelt their own metal. Do they do it in Engineering, or somewhere close by?

I take only two steps inside before the largest troll I've ever seen, a stationed guard I hadn't noticed, turns and growls at me. His gray skin has a blue tinge to it. He appears even better fed than Qequan, and his thick limbs lend tremendously to his size. His nose and lips are enormous, his tusks small. The bony protrusions on his forearms, shoulders, and shins extend long as daggers.

I step back, the ache in my thigh and hip reminding me of my own fragility.

He hefts a wicked-looking hammer and points it at me. "Out, human!"

"Down, Sleet." Azmar's coolness pierces through the tension like a pike through an iced-over pond. I dare look away from the massive troll to see Azmar striding toward us from the left. "She's here to assist me."

Sleet scowls. "A human to assist you? Ha!"

Azmar gestures for me to follow him.

But Sleet shifts and blocks my path with the shaft of his hammer. "This is your sister's pet. No humans here."

Unruffled, Azmar folds his arms, emphasizing his thick muscles and heavy veins. Though he has to tilt his head back to meet Sleet's gaze, it somehow appears that he looks down on him.

I wait for Azmar to say something sharp, perhaps about Sleet's caste, but he doesn't. Merely looks. And Sleet, amazingly, lowers his hammer. Grumbling something under his breath, he stalks away from me and retakes his post.

I am utterly dumbfounded. But Azmar gestures for me to follow, so I do, as quickly as my sore body will allow. We walk past several of the long tables where an array of trolls sit, men and women, gray and green, large and less large. Most don't notice me, as they're focused on their own work, hunched over with pencils and charcoal and quills. I glimpse a hallway down to a blacksmith bellows. There is another blacksmith in the trade works, but this one must work only on city construction.

Several high tables, almost like desks, occupy the far side of the room. Azmar stops at the first, then, seeing the second unoccupied, takes the chair from it and sits it at the corner of his own. With a subtle gesture, he beckons me to sit.

The stool seat is nearly five feet off the ground. My injuries protest as I lift myself up, but I don't ask for help, though Azmar scrutinizes me as though ready to offer it.

Paper and a couple of slates litter his desk, while little tin cups organize his writing utensils. Several rulers, along with two leather books, press against the corner.

"What caste is he?" I whisper, tilting my head toward Sleet.

Azmar doesn't look over. "Deccor."

"But he's *huge*."

Azmar meets my eyes, making me feel foolish. I rush to explain. "He would do well in the caste tournament, wouldn't he? Why is he only a Deccor?"

"His challenge to a higher caste has to be accepted, either by previous agreement or stance of challenge," he explains. "Wise trollis do not accept challenges they cannot win."

"What is 'stance of challenge'?"

He arranges a few of the papers. "When a victor in a battle remains on the field to take on new opponents, to increase their pips." He touches his shirt, where those small blue stones would be, if he had any.

"So winning two fights in a row gets them a higher caste, and then a higher rank within that caste."

A brief nod. "How is your geometry?"

Doubt creeps into me. "I can determine the area of a triangle . . ."

He appears neither disappointed nor surprised. After grabbing some chalk and one of the slates, he begins jotting down equations in handwriting that is becoming more and more legible to me. I'm surprised how small his numbers are, given the size of his hands.

He offers me the slate, followed by a piece of parchment full of dimensional shapes and material weights. "Calculate the tributary area and multiply it by the appropriate weights—the sections should say what material is used. Put the results on the right."

I marvel at the numbers and letters and compare them to his drawings.

He asks, "Do you understand?"

"Oh yes." I set the slate down. "I'm just . . . It really is rather intriguing." I grab a pencil and start plugging in the figures. I can feel Azmar's gaze as I do the first equation, but he soon returns to his own work. My arithmetic skills gradually return to me, and I can't help but smile. I haven't had a chance to use them in a long time. The joy of mental work is sweeter than wine.

When Azmar returns his attention to me, I ask, "What is all of this for?"

"Calculating load." He takes the first page from me and glances over my writing. He appears pleased. "The council wants an extension behind the slayers' armory, regardless of our insistence that it isn't wise."

"Why isn't it?"

He sets the paper down and picks up another. "Because of the lack of weight distribution along the canyon wall at that point. There's too much load."

"The load is what the addition will hold?"

He regards me with those dark-harvest-gold eyes, as though unsure of my question. To clarify, I say, "I'm curious. I . . . I love to learn." Time with my tutors was always my favorite, partially because it meant time away from everyone else. "This all fascinates me."

He runs a hand back over his corded hair. It's bound at the nape of his neck and falls to the small of his back. "There is the dead load, which is the weight of the addition itself, the components of the structure—the steel, flooring, façade, piping, everything. The live load is what moves around inside of it: people, furniture, supplies. If not calculated correctly, the addition could crumble, possibly taking pieces of the city with it." He sighs. "I do not think it wise to add there. It would be better to build outward from the Empyrean Bridge. Make additional connections to the canyon wall."

"Then why don't you?"

"Because the council insists we keep Cagmar as clandestine as possible, despite enemy threats being practically moot." He looks at me then, and his brows draw together. "What?"

I realize I am smiling at him and quickly school my features. "Nothing. I mean, I'm sorry. That's frustrating. It's just . . . this is the most you've ever spoken to me."

To my relief, his lip ticks up. "Do not take it personally. Unach was always better with words."

"Yes, she throws them and twists them and bullies them into doing whatever she wants." Chuckling, I start on the next set of calculations, but my conversation with Perg rises to the top of my thoughts. "Might I . . . ask a question? Not about this?" I wave my hand over the papers.

He glimpses me before continuing his work. "I do not promise to answer."

"Did you speak on behalf of Colson?"

He's tracing a line with a ruler when I ask, and his pencil stops. Three heartbeats pass. He finishes the line. "I did."

"Thank you. Truly."

He shuffles the papers together. "I would not have done so were you not adamantly against his punishment. I believe you had more say in the matter than anyone else, human or not."

My whole person feels a little lighter, my injuries far from my mind. "That is very kind of you to say, troll or not."

"It is fair, not kind." He straightens, towering over me. "I should also inform you that while I'm sure it's a term you've grown up with, the word *troll* is a derogatory one."

All my good feelings coalesce and rain cold in my stomach. "I-It is? I'm so sorry! I didn't know!"

He shrugs, unaffected. "We prefer *trollis*. That's what we are."

"Of course you do." I turn away, embarrassed. I lean hard into my hand to hide my face while I focus on the numbers. My work goes notably slower, my thoughts refusing to be corralled. I finish and sheepishly hand the last of the papers to Azmar. He tucks it in the back of his stack.

"I believe," he begins softly, "that error, made in ignorance, is forgivable."

I dare to peek through my fingers at him. "You're not angry?"

"I never was." Gathering his papers, he says, "Come."

He turns from the desk and walks toward the back of Engineering. I follow him, hissing through my teeth when I jump off the stool and jar my leg. Azmar doesn't comment, only waits for me to catch up.

We near the hallway leading to the blacksmith. "If it isn't too much to ask," I try, limping a little more now, "I would love to know anything else. Anything I'm saying wrong, greetings I should or shouldn't be using—"

"You're faring well."

"But not just that," I insist as we turn down the hallway. The heat increases to a pleasant, summery temperature. I step behind Azmar to show deference to a troll—trollis—coming the opposite way, then hobble after Azmar. "All of it. How your society works. The city. Engineering. The canyon, the food and where it comes from. The farms. I want to learn everything."

He pauses halfway between the blacksmith and a sizable lift. Looks down at me. He's a full foot and a half taller than I am, yet his looming isn't intimidating in the slightest. Not as it had been with Sleet or Grodd.

"You don't plan to request leave, then?"

"I can do that?"

"I'm not sure." Azmar rolls the papers in his hands. If he discards any of them, I'll snatch them up so I can make copies of Wiln's almanacs in the unused spaces. "Most humans who come here do so in desperation. But given recent events . . ." He glances at the bruised side of my face.

I shake my head. "In truth, there's nowhere else I'd want to go."

He nods, finding the weak explanation perfectly acceptable. "I'll see what I can do."

And like that, hope reignites, just as the blacksmith's bellows light their coals.

We start for the lift. "Where does this lead?"

"Down." The large lift appears less used and has a grating in front of it that Azmar pulls aside. "This will take us near the south dock. I want to survey the area again. I don't trust these measurements."

He steps onto the lift. I follow and lean against its far wall. The lift's ropes are thicker than others I've seen. When Azmar begins pulling them, the lift moves slowly. His arms bulge with the weight of it, and tension settles into his jaw. How heavy is the lift?

"Do you want help?"

He shakes his head. "Almost there."

The lift touches down a moment later. Azmar shakes out his arms before stepping out. We walk a short way before I recognize where we are. We're just under the south dock. I usually pass overhead to go to my shift.

A wisp of fresh, mildew-scented air tousles my hair. The light of the distant, setting sun reflects off stone. I breathe deeply and waver as nostalgia strikes me, yearning for an open sky and all its stars, the chirp of hidden crickets, the smell of dry earth.

Azmar walks nearly to the edge of the floor, where a ladder descends even lower. I carefully follow down after him, testing the strength in each of my legs. When I reach the bottom floor, I'm technically below Cagmar, standing on a ledge of the canyon wall itself. It's about ten feet wide and fifteen feet long. Not too dissimilar from a viewing point.

As Azmar pulls out a coil of measuring tape from his belt, the platform quakes. Softly, like it's snoring, but Azmar freezes, his entire body tense.

Another shake, this one a little harder. Somewhere above us, the voices of trollis burst like blisters, interrupted by the distant sound of a horn. A hard word escapes Azmar's lips, and though I've never heard it before, it has the sharpness of a curse.

My gut sinks. Fear tickles the base of my spine, the arches of my feet. I know what it is, what is has to be, but still I ask, "What?"

Azmar shoves the measuring tape into his belt. "We need to leave. Now."

He's right. He doesn't need to answer.

The cliff shakes again.

Monster.

Chapter 7

Azmar hurries for the ladder, but he waits for me at the base of it. I move quickly, my injuries forgotten, and start climbing. "The center of the city is safest," he says behind me. "Centra take shelter in food storage. Hurry."

"*You're* Centra," I say, but I keep climbing, hand over hand, until I reach the stony lip of the next floor. It shakes again, and again, evenly. Like footsteps. I pull myself up, gasping when stone presses a bruise on my thigh. I start for the lift.

"No lifts during an attack. They're not safe." Azmar's focus darts around, and he gestures west. "Stairs."

I start to run in the direction he pointed, but the ground shakes and trips me. I fall hard on one knee and grimace. The little bit of sunlight we had vanishes. I look toward the open canyon and see something blocking the cliffside. Something dark and slithering.

Azmar grabs my arm and hauls me to my feet, retreating until we hit a wall. His grip doesn't relent. He watches the moving body, jaw set. We're close enough that I can hear his heartbeat. For all his demeanor of calm, it's racing.

One finger touches his mouth, urging me to be quiet.

I watch the slick body pass. It reminds me of a snake, but its movements jerk, delineating legs. It must be enormous. *Only a juvenile,* Troff said.

My fingers tremble of their own accord. Forming my hands into fists, I focus on the monster and push my fear across the platform and into its black skin.

The monster and I jerk at the same time. My body instinctively pushes back into the rock as terror seizes it, and the monster's movements come to a complete halt. I hiss through my teeth. *It's only fear. It isn't real. It's only fear. It will pass.*

Fight or flee.

I can't tell which the monster chooses, but it bolts away, clamoring over the city's west wall, making it shake with the effort. I have a cold feeling that beasts such as this do not scare easily.

I pull from Azmar's grip. "I need to go to the dock." I limp for the stairs.

Azmar's long strides catch me quickly. "Leave it to the Montra." His hand on my back hurries me up the stairs. The shaking of the monster's climb reverberates through them.

"I need to go." Fear has burrowed itself into familiar places in my chest and the base of my skull. I crest the stairwell and spy another set of stairs ahead. The south docks are immediately to my right.

"Lark." He grabs my shoulder, pulling me to the stairs. To safety. "You don't need to prove yourself here."

I dig in my heels. "I can *help*."

So often I have not been able to.

Azmar studies me, his eyes shifting between each of mine. He's probably looking at my bruises and doubting me. *I* would doubt me. If I couldn't fight back my own kind, how can I fight off a monster?

Seeing him waver, I press, "The council assigned me to Unach for a reason."

His head turns toward the stairs.

"She's out there." Unach's on shift right now. I touch the hand still gripping my shoulder. "Let me help her. Please, trust me."

Azmar presses his lips together, emphasizing the short tusks on either end of them. The city shakes beneath our feet. He says nothing, only steers me toward the south dock. Elation and fear swirl together in my middle, so tightly I'm dizzy with them.

I run onto the south dock. Four trollis already man the others' ropes. I hurry to the chest and find the smallest harness, stepping into it and clipping it in place with practiced ease. Azmar is at the closet, pulling out belts and sheaths and knives. The ground shakes again. He hands one belt to me, then takes the liberty of securing another over my shoulder. I grab a rope, and he takes the other end.

"I'll spot you." He ties his end around his waist and looks at me directly. "Be careful."

He doubts me. I can read it in his face, his posture. But he's giving me a chance. It's all I could possibly ask of him.

With my rope secure, I step off the dock onto the footholds. I grip the handholds tightly with my clammy hands and climb. The bruises on my legs and back fire in protest, but the higher I climb, the more numb they become. The four other monster slayers' ropes lead upward, following a wet trail. Slime?

I reach for a higher handhold and grasp it, but as I pull myself up, I scrape my bruised hip. A startled cry escapes me. Gritting my teeth, I push strength into my limbs, imagining my arms are as thick as Azmar's. Imagining I'm safe in a lift. Reminding myself that if I fall, he'll hold the rope. Azmar will not drop me.

The city shakes in regular bursts under my hands, forcing me to hold steady and press my body into the outer wall. The monster runs. A strange sound, like a mix between a crow and a cat, tears through the air. The slime gets thicker. The ropes of my colleagues shift.

I groan through my teeth as I pull myself up a steep part of the wall, trying to keep my weight on the footholds. My head raises just high enough above the next lip that I can see the monster in its entirety. It's *enormous*, at least fifty feet long. Its skin is black and porous, its limbs thick and ending in reptilian feet with massive claws. Its eyes are so dark I can barely tell them from its black skin, its head the shape of a spade. A sharp beak glistens around its mouth. I recognize it from my studies: *lecker*.

I spot Unach. The city slopes in such a way that she only needs one handhold, and she's looped her rope through it so she has better mobility. She's immediately below the monster's shoulder and slashes at it with her great curved sword. Every time the beast dances away, the city shakes. I readjust my hold, fear making my hands even slicker. Troff sidesteps near the monster's tail and slashes it with his own blade, spilling black blood. The other two shuffle on the other side.

I grip the lip of the city and haul myself up, hissing against my bruises and the sweat dripping into my eyes. A gust of hot wind rips past me, as though trying to peel me from the city. I grip tighter and pray to the stars to hold me there.

When I look up again, I see what the others do not: a second monster, dark and sleek like the first, coming up the canyon wall, slow and silent. If the monster can jump, it will be on them in seconds.

Fear bursts from my heart and powers my arms. I haul myself onto the lip and press myself to the city wall. I'm able to stand here, but one good shake, one strong gust, and I'll topple over. I wedge my foot into a crevice where the walls connect and grab a handhold over my head.

The second monster leaps.

I push everything I have at it. Every goose bump, every shudder, every clatter of teeth. My hurt, my pain, the terror that both fuels and stiffens me. Every memory of fear I can muster, and I have many.

I lock my gaze on the beast and terrify it, and in the process my knees buckle and my vision darkens. My body heaves with the fright, but I squeeze the handhold until the skin over my knuckles splits. I know fear. Unadulterated fear, without a wielder, cannot hurt me.

Here, I am the wielder. I am the weapon.

The monster screeches, alerting the slayers, if not the entire city, to its presence. It wrenches in midair and lands on its side atop the city, then rolls down toward me.

Shrieking, I duck low, wedging my toes into the crevice. The monster's body bounces, jarring the wall, and flies over my head into the canyon below. The first monster screeches and scurries in the same direction, blood dribbling from its neck. Unach must have gotten in a blow when its companion distracted it.

All of Cagmar quakes as the creature pads down its side, leaps to a cliff wall, and flees into the shadows.

My bones quiver. My blood feels thick as honey, but I have enough wits about me to reach into the belt around my hips and yank out a sling before the slayers' attention shifts from the monsters to me. Carefully, knees weak, I stand, still gripping that single handhold. I meet Unach's startled gaze and hold up the sling.

"Lucky sh-shot," I stutter. My heart thumps so swiftly I can't tell one beat from the next. But it will subside. Fear always does.

I drop down, sitting on the lip of the city, giving my spent body a moment of reprieve. But in truth, I want to make myself less visible.

I don't want to see the stinging suspicion etching lines in Unach's face.

Chapter 8

Unach is unharmed. She was born a Montra, but she deserves every bit of the title.

It's late. Very late. The sun sets before I finish climbing down to the dock. I sit there for a long time, cold and weary. Unach and the others say nothing, only pull off their harnesses and set about their normal tasks, as though we'd just had a regular evening of scouting.

Azmar looks more curious than suspicious as he listens to the story of what happened, regarding me nearly the entire time.

Unach glances my way. "Did it with a sling. Never seen her use one before."

I manage to shrug. "Haven't had a reason to."

Azmar offers to carry me home, but my body still buzzes with uncomfortable energy, so I walk.

When we reach it, Unach controls the lift and deliberately passes my floor. A silent invitation—or, more likely, a demand.

She lights the fire in her apartment and starts boiling water for that spicy drink she and Azmar like. I settle on the floor near the flames to warm myself. That, and I don't want to get too comfortable with their few pieces of furniture. I'm *earning* my place, yes, but I do not yet feel I have won it. I settle on the floor by the fire, relaxing as the heat soothes away the near-constant gooseflesh that Cagmar's chill breathes onto my skin. Azmar flops down on an overlarge pillow across the room, laying his head back and rubbing his eyes. Unach slips into the kitchen, returning with a single mug. Grabbing one of two wooden chairs, she drags it toward the corner where my pallet used to be and sets the mug on it.

To my dismay, she then pulls a sling and a hard bead of iron from her pocket, which she brings to me.

"Do it again." It isn't a request.

Keeping my face smooth, I play innocent. "Do what?"

Unach drops both sling and bead into my lap. "Hit the cup off the chair."

Azmar lifts his head.

"I . . . I'll break it," I protest.

"I don't care. I'll glue it back together." She grasps my upper arm and hauls me to my feet, then jerks her chin toward the opposite wall. "Let me see you hit it. It's not far. Should be easy, right?"

My mouth dries. In truth, I've never used a sling in my life. I'm not sure I can get the iron bead close to its target, let alone hit it. And I'm certain Unach knows it.

"Lucky shot, Unach," I press, tensing.

Unach's fists rest on her hips. "Just do it, Lark."

I pull the sling through my hands, my heartbeat picking up again.

"Unach." Azmar's voice slides under the building tension. "We're all exhausted."

"It's one shot," she argues.

Azmar sits up and rests his elbows on his knees. The long cords of his hair spill over his shoulders. "Based on your own account, Unach, she saved your life."

Unach frowns.

He tips his chin toward the cup. "We shouldn't waste resources. Leave her be." He meets my gaze. "Go down and rest, Lark. You need it."

I self-consciously touch the largest of the bruises on my face, wishing Azmar could read the immense gratitude I have for his intervention.

I start for the door—I have food in my apartment—when Unach settles onto the rug and says, "Rare that they breach."

I pause. "They broke through the wall?"

Unach grunts. "Deccor housing. At least the deck will be reconstructed to a higher standard."

Fear, my familiar friend, trickles back into my blood.

Hadn't Perg been working in Deccor housing?

Azmar sniffs. "If the joists we'd asked for had been approved, there would have been no structural damage, at least."

Unach waves off his concern with a flick of her hand. "I've every confidence in you."

"Were there casualties?" I murmur.

Both siblings glance my way. "Not among the slayers," Unach says.

"But in the city?"

"We won't know until morning." Azmar's brow lowers. "What's wrong?"

I lick my lips. "Perg was working in Deccor housing today."

"The half-breed?" Unach asks, then laughs. When neither of us joins her, she sobers. "I'm sure he's fine. He's survived worse."

I wonder what she means by that, then remember Perg's other task for the day—training to fight for a higher caste. Maybe he made it to the training hall before the attack.

"You're right. He's probably fine." I smooth my unease as best as I can before glancing at Azmar. "At least with the breach, you won't have to work on the addition right away."

His lip quirks at that, and it pleases me that my attempt at humor struck home. Then I dip away, silently stepping into the cool outer hallway. This late, there's no competition for the lift, and I make it to my room quickly. I'm tired, but it's a sleepiness deep in my bones that doesn't quite touch my skin. Taking a floral cake from my rations, I lie down on my cot. The quiet of the place eases the clutter of my thoughts and saps out the stress of the day's events.

I rest for some time and whisper prayers of gratitude, for Azmar's resiliency and kindness, for Colson's being spared, for my and Unach's safe return. But as I stare out my slip of a window, thoughts of Perg nag at me again. What if he hadn't been evacuated before the monster broke through Deccor housing? What if another trollis enacted a cruel joke and locked him away somewhere, leaving him as fodder for the beast?

Would the gods be so cruel as to take away my friend so soon after allowing me to call him that?

Needing to know for myself, I slip out of my narrow quarters and head toward the lift. The night I spent sneaking about the city pulses fresh in my mind and body, but I don't think I can sleep without confirming Perg's well-being. Perg said I wouldn't be allowed on the training grounds, but with nearly all the trollis recovering from the attack, there might not be anyone nearby to complain—at least, none of the human task force, or so I hope. I'll stay away from the enclave, just to be safe.

If I can just *see* Perg, or find some evidence to attest to his welfare, I'll be happy to fall asleep and leave the rest alone.

I pass through a corner of the market, trying to make myself small and unseen, noticing the same subdued activity as the night I snuck off to the schoolyard. No humans out. More importantly, no Grodd. I glance about for witnesses as I head down the corridor that I'm sure leads to the training ground, but the only trollis nearby are tucked away in an alcove behind a shop, thoroughly exploring one another's mouths. I blush and hurry on my way.

Clearly trollis express affection the same way humans do. And their tusks don't get in the way, either.

The corridor widens abruptly, and it ends in a doorway, unlike the other city cavities I've visited. It's unlocked, and I peek inside.

I thought Engineering was immense, but it's nothing compared to these training grounds, which confirms where the trollis place merit.

It's enormous and layered—I can see a second and third floor above me. They don't meet the wall overhead, but end short of it, with guardrails to section it off. There are more doors and several sparring arenas. Much to my luck and relief, I see a familiar face in the very first one.

I close the door quietly behind me. Perg is shirtless, save for two leather straps across his torso, similar to what the noncombat guards wear. In the yellow lighting of the lamps, his skin looks more tan than green. Remarkably human. I wonder what his father looked like.

He swings a long-handled war axe with practiced grace in a series of memorized movements that repeat after every eighth swing. He is utterly remarkable with it, so much so that his movements look like a dance.

I wait, to avoid startling him. When he lowers the axe, his shoulders heaving with effort, I whisper, "Perg!"

He whirls around, sweat glistening on his face and chest. Confusion scrunches his features. "Lark?"

I wave a little awkwardly. "I know I shouldn't be here, but . . . the monster attacked Deccor housing. I wanted to make sure you'd gotten out."

His brow relaxes, and I almost think a little pink lights his cheeks, though with their trollis tint, it's hard to discern. "I . . . did." He lowers the axe head to the ground. "I'm surprised you remembered where I'd be."

I shrug. "I asked earlier, because I cared." After glancing over my shoulder, I take a few steps toward him. "Perg, I know you're a Nethens and I'm only a human—"

He laughs. "You say *Nethens* like it's some great feat." His humor evaporates, and he knocks the axe handle between his hands. "It's not."

"Regardless." I splay my hands before me as though I have something to offer him. "You've been kind to me when others were not. I was hoping we could be friends."

He raises a brow. "Friends."

I lower my hands. "I wouldn't . . . tell anyone."

"It's not that." He shakes his head. "It's just . . . well, no one's ever made the offer before. Not so forthrightly, at least. Even the Plebs don't care for me."

Feeling bold, I say, "I care for you. Or I will, if you'll let me."

The expression on his face, though it lasts only half a breath, is so pained and vulnerable that I feel tears come. Something so childlike swims through it, so innocent.

"I would like that, Lark."

I smile. "Good. I don't mean to interrupt you. I should get some rest for tomorrow."

"Perhaps I'll see you in the marketplace."

I nod. "Perhaps."

Lighter on my feet, I turn back for the doors. I've nearly reached them when Perg calls, "Lark."

I hesitate.

Letting the axe handle fall to the floor, he crosses over to me. He is immensely wide and tall, and yet his size fails in comparison to a full-blooded trollis. He reaches to his belt and pulls a sheathed dagger from it. It's a reasonable size for human hands.

"Here." He hands it to me. "I don't want to worry about you, either."

Stunned, I take the gift. The craftmanship is unelaborate but solid. I owned a small knife before coming to Cagmar, but the guards who captured me on the bridge must have taken it, for I haven't seen it since then.

"Humans aren't allowed to carry these," I whisper.

"Then don't let anyone see you with it."

I clutch the dagger to my chest. I wonder, if Perg knew what I really was, whether he'd be so ready to befriend me. Or arm me. "Thank you." I pause. "Perg, what's your birth year?"

He tilts his head. "941, why?"

"Merces, the wren. Adaptable, quick, persistent. It suits you."

He raises an eyebrow. "What are you jabbering about?"

I shake my head. "Nothing. Good luck."

He returns to his axe.

I hurry back to my small room, making sure to hide the dagger beneath my skirt before I reach the marketplace.

Chapter 9

Over the next two weeks, I heal and find a comfortable groove among the city. I adjust to an official work schedule and time my errands in the marketplace so I'll be as out of the way as possible for Unach and Azmar, though I enjoy their company. I run Unach's errands between shifts and learn several trollis dishes, which I cook to her satisfaction. I watch how Unach sharpens and polishes her weapons, which in turn teaches me to care both for the south-dock weaponry and for the dagger Perg gave me.

I see Perg often, sometimes late at night when he's training, sometimes when our paths cross in town, though I spend most of my daylight hours at the south dock or crawling the outside of the city. I learn the plumbing and even fix a leak in Unach's apartment on my own. I'd love to visit one of the waterworks to see how it all functions. There are two of them: the smaller lies near the top of the city and distributes water via gravity through pipes. The larger caps the very base of Cagmar, where water is collected, stored, and purified. According to Azmar, the water fetchers have the most dangerous job in the entire city, for while Unach battles monsters irregularly, they work in fear of them every day. Cagmar is massive, but it comes nowhere close to reaching the river at the bottom of the canyon, so the water fetchers must leave the safety of the city to ensure its survival.

All of them are Plebs.

I've dropped off a leather girdle of Unach's for repair in the market-place when I see Ritha's familiar face pulling a heavy wagon of foodstuff. For a fleeting moment, I imagine myself walking behind her, pushing the cart as she pulls, going about our daily chores together. What would my life have been like if she had raised me?

I hurry across the street and approach her carefully, earning her attention with a light tug on her sleeve.

Ritha turns, her expression immediately softening. "Lark. You're looking well."

"Much thanks to you. How are you?"

She tucks auburn hair behind her ear. "I do not have a lot of time to dally, if that's what you mean."

"I'll walk with you," I offer. "Is Colson doing well? He was hurt, last I saw him."

She blinks surprise at me. "Yes, he's just fine. He got a good beating for what he did."

I hunch, suddenly feeling too overbearing in my height, for I'm a good half a foot taller than Ritha. "I'm sorry. I didn't mean for that to happen."

Her forehead wrinkles. "He deserved much more! I heard what happened. You saved his life."

"Azmar did."

She shakes her head in silent disagreement.

"And Etewen?"

"Fine as can be."

We walk in silence for several paces. "Ritha, can humans compete to rise in the caste system?"

She chuckles. "Oh, Lark, your head is full of stars. No, we can't. Even if we could, how would we best a troll? Even the half human would crush the strongest of us."

"Perg wouldn't do that."

"He would in the caste tournament."

We halt as a group of high-ranking trollis pass by. I search for Unach and Azmar among them, but they're not there. We cross once the way is clear again.

"I suppose you're right." I pause. "You know . . . they're called trollis, not trolls."

She glances at me. "I'm aware."

"*Troll* is a disparaging term . . ."

Ritha slows and studies me. "You're quite attached to them, aren't you?"

My face warms. "I only mean to be fair. Perg, Azmar, Unach . . . they're kind to me."

She watches me a little longer, her eyes discerning in a way that makes me feel vulnerable. "Where are you from, Lark? Which township?"

The question catches me off guard. I had been asked my name and spoken a new one, but no one cared where I hailed from. I'm not sure how familiar the trollis are with human townships. I cannot imagine any harm in being honest, so I answer truthfully. "Lucarpo, originally. But I traveled a lot before coming here."

Ritha's expression grows distant and thoughtful. We reach the lift.

"Thank you, Lark." She pulls the wagon onto the lift quickly, while it's available. "Stay safe."

"I will." If I can befriend Perg, Azmar, and Unach, then I can befriend others. Show them the goodness of humans. Even persuade them to treat my people more fairly.

I turn from the lift and almost immediately meet the eyes of a trollis across the way. He is large, gray, and incredibly broad—enough to make someone like Perg look malnourished. He blends in with the stone behind him, so it takes me a beat to recognize him.

Grodd. Leader of the human task force. The one who dealt out Colson's beating.

I wonder, had he been at the school that night, whether he'd have bothered to stop mine.

He folds his meaty arms and stares at me, and though at least twenty yards separate us, I feel as though I stand beside him. I consider lowering my gaze and moving away, showing deference even from this distance, and yet I find I cannot. Not because Grodd's glare fascinates me, but because it disgusts me. I see pride in every inch of his stance and hate coloring every inch of his skin.

And so I stare back, lifting my chin, my heart pounding in my chest. Only when a group of trollis walking up from one of the tunnels comes between us do I retreat where he can't see. In part so that he doesn't know where I'm going. In part because I don't want him to know I looked away first.

I climb the levels faster than usual, and reach Unach's apartment out of breath. I beam at the narrow window on the far wall and the sunlight sneaking through it. I want to curl up where it meets the floor, but my brief conversation with Ritha is fresh on my mind, and the desire to prove myself is stronger than ever.

I picked up Unach's and Azmar's rations again and now organize them in the narrow cupboards. I'm filling up a pitcher of water to take to the fire when the door to that small washroom opens and Azmar steps out. He startles me, for I'd thought myself alone. He and Unach both usually work at this hour.

I nearly tip over the pitcher when I see him. He is entirely unclothed, save for a short towel around his hips. Water drips from his thick hair down his chest. His bare chest.

And though I know he is a trollis, I find myself gaping at him, for his torso is not very different from a human man's, save that it is remarkably well sculpted. All of him is.

The rush of heat to my face warns me that I am staring. My head whips back to my work so quickly that I pull a muscle in my neck. "S-Sorry. I-I didn't think you'd be home."

I don't dare look at him to determine his expression, but his voice is even. "I had to aid with smelting today, to help with the rebuild. It's dirty work."

I swallow, wishing my face would cool. "I thought to make a root stew tonight." I speak too quickly and force my tongue to slow. "Use up the rest of last week's rations." Unach always eats the meat first.

Azmar's steps move away, to where his clothes lie on a drying rack just inside that little room. I peek up again. Muscles from, I presume, years of military training and . . . smelting assistance . . . stretch across his wide back. His wet hair hangs heavy against his spine, unbound, and a few drops of water patter to the floor. A hand's-length scar shifts under his right shoulder blade, straight and silver. I wonder if he's spent time on the surface, to have such a wound.

But when he turns again, I notice something I didn't before—another silvery scar, this one just as straight but much longer and thicker. It looks to be opposite the first, like he was run straight through with a sword, similar in size to the one Unach carries.

This time I know I'm caught staring, for when I lift my eyes, Azmar regards me with something I can't quite put my finger on. Restrained curiosity? Confusion?

I clear my throat. "I'll . . . start cooking." My voice rasps, quieter than I'd meant it to be.

He nods and strides to his room. "Thank you."

Azmar and Perg are the only trollis who thank me for anything. In the past few days, Azmar has even begun saying please.

I glance after him, wondering at the scar, for I know from Perg that trollis don't ever use battle-ready weapons against one another, except in a caste tournament, and I'm fairly certain Azmar has never participated in one. It feels like an invasion of privacy to ask him, and I know Unach won't tell me. The question alone would irritate her.

I finish filling the pitcher, set it aside, then replace the vegetables in the cold box with the new ones from the market. Azmar doesn't come back out until I've cut up the last of them, a new sheaf of paper in his hand, pencil tucked behind his ear.

Despite the fact that he is fully clothed, my face heats once more.

The following day heralds the caste tournament.

According to Unach, it happens every quarter, and there are always challenges. The caste tournament is the best way a trollis has to improve his or her standing in the complicated caste system. All a trollis has to do is defeat a higher-ranked person in personal combat, and their castes switch. A Pleb can even challenge a Supra, not that it's ever done. There's a reason the Supras sit at the top of the chain. That, and challenged opponents are not required to accept. When they do, it's usually out of pride or esteem. The turquoise beads I've seen on other trollis' sleeves indicate caste tournaments won, and they can be used to settle arguments among trollis of the same rank.

"Suppose two Montras reach a lift at one time," Unach explained to me. "One wants to go up, one to go down. But the first has two beads, and the second none. The lesser must defer."

I am not one for bloodshed, but I want to support Perg, who has trained so hard to improve his standing. He struggles to find trollis willing to fight him, not because he's terrifying, but because he's half-human and they consider it disgraceful. His last tournament was two years ago, and he failed to win. A year before that, he'd beaten a Nethens. His mother had been Deccor, but because of his father, Perg had been born a Pleb.

The council holds the tournaments on the Empyrean Bridge itself, the only time that the trollis come up into the light collectively. My favorite thing about my occupation is that I get to go outside and see slivers of sunlight, but admittedly, it's much nicer to do so when I'm not clinging for my life to iron handholds. Up here the sky stretches full, bright, and hot, burning away the canyon's chill. The world seems too big and flat from the bridge, broken only by the uneven bumps of distant mountains to the north. I unbind my hair to shield my skin from the resilient sun, but I welcome the sting of its heat.

I walk with Unach and Azmar part of the way, but I have to defer to all trollis in the narrow corridors, so I quickly lag behind. Caste designates seating as well, so I'm not able to sit with anyone I know. Unach has participated in the caste tournament twice, both times challenged by lower-ranking trollis. She won both contests. My earlier assumption proved correct; Azmar has never participated, and I find myself inspired by that. For a man—trollis—raised in a militant society, he's never once taken the bait to harm another for his own benefit.

At least, not in the tournaments.

I try not to think about his scar.

Bodies pack the bridge and its surroundings. I see no other humans in attendance, so trying to find a seat that doesn't break any laws proves tricky. Admittedly, it crossed my mind to help Perg out. He has an unfair disadvantage against full-blooded trollis, and using my ability to whisper trepidation to his opponent could even the playing field. But the council might suspect foul play, and I can't risk getting kicked out of Cagmar. Or worse, hurting Perg. If he were caught cheating, he might lose the Nethens title he worked so hard to earn.

I remind myself that I should have faith in him. And I do. A few silent prayers to the stars rise from my thoughts as I weave through straggling trollis.

I search for the Plebs, who fill tall seats on the east end of the bridge, some on the canyon lip itself. I cannot sit *with* them, so I linger where I won't get in trouble, searching for the best vantage point. Fortunately, I've honed my climbing skills over the last month, and I find a place under one of the bridge's arches.

The first challenge is between an Alpine and a Supra. Both trollis are *enormous*, easily eight feet tall and as thick as the columns in the training room. The Alpine wields a heavy sword and a club; the Supra, who gets cheers from the audience, hefts a spear and a long-handled axe.

I recognize him from the council: Ichlad, who was the most adamant about ejecting me from the city. He looks so much more vibrant, more dangerous, in the sunlight.

The sun glints off the trollis' weapons, emphasizing their sharp edges. I second-guess my coming here; I don't have the stomach for true violence. I hold my breath as the combat begins and find myself often looking away.

I will stay for Perg's battle, cheer for him, and then slip back into the city.

Bluish trollis blood spills on the bridge, but the fight lasts only a minute or two. The Alpine surrenders, raising empty hands and naming the Supra the winner. Both are able to walk away.

A Montra and an Alpine claim the next match, and the Alpine wins. The next is the same, only the Montra wins and the Alpine has to be dragged away by medics. He will survive, but the memories of my bruises—recent and long past—come to life as I watch.

I turn away from several of the contests. The lower-caste trollis are more desperate, their tactics more gruesome. No sense of chivalry exists between combatants—indeed, I cannot decipher any rules at all. One fight unravels with such violence that I plug my ears, and when I dare to look, both trollis have fallen. I'm not sure who will be named the victor, or whether there even is one.

I'm taking deep breaths to calm my roiling stomach when the announcer finally calls Perg. I stand and crane my neck, watching as he strides onto the bridge, his chin high and shoulders square. My heart twists at the sounds of laughter rippling through the crowd. A few trollis even jeer and spit names at him. Perg ignores them.

Please, gods, stars, give him this win. Give him a rank so he can feel loved.

A Deccor steps forward to meet him, and my knees threaten to buckle. The trollis is nearly the size of that first Supra. His stomach juts out like a pregnant woman's, but his arms ripple with muscle. His neck is as thick as his head, and his tusks are enormous, though the point of one has been severed. His shaved head gleams in the sunlight, and his hand bears a wicked sword, similar to Unach's.

I peer up into the stands and search for her, but she's lost among waves of gray and green. Azmar as well.

Nearby, the Plebs start whispering. Trollis currency consists of uncut gems of various sizes, and a few exchange hands as bets are placed. If I had one, I would put it on Perg's name, in the hope that he would feel my support.

I supplicate the heavens one more time. *Please let him live.*

The fight starts suddenly. I blink, and the two trollis lock in combat. The height difference between Perg and his foe measures the same as between Azmar and myself. I can only assume that is why the Deccor agreed to fight a half human; he will obviously win, and have an extra bead to bolster his rank.

But Perg is focused. I'm too far away to read his expression, but his determination permeates the hot air. His swift footwork helps him dodge the Deccor's blows, but he's yet to return a single one. The battle goes like this for some time, longer, I think, than the other bouts. Perg keeps the Deccor turning and eventually starts blocking the blows instead of evading them.

Because he's moving in closer, inch by inch. And I don't think the Deccor realizes it.

Perg shifts suddenly to the right, and his axe strikes the Deccor's arm. I gasp, my hands flying to my mouth. The larger trollis drops his sword and stumbles back to cradle the injury. I can't tell how bad it is, but I can imagine. If the trollis is *lucky*, that blade would have stopped at the bone.

The Deccor roars and charges, but his feet shamble from all the spinning. Perg ducks in and strikes again as he passes, to the side, I think; the Deccor's enormous body blocks my view. The larger trollis falls prone, and Perg leaps onto his back, axe head pressed to the Deccor's neck.

Yet the Deccor does not surrender. He rolls, sending Perg sprawling, but he's not fast enough to retrieve a weapon. I look away when Perg brings the axe down with both hands, and a gasp echoes through the crowd.

Clenching my jaw, I peer back. I believe the Deccor still lives, but he's unable to stand. Silence holds its breath. Medics come out to the arena.

A few boos burst from the audience. Behind me, many of the Plebs cheer—maybe they bet on Perg after all. The officiator comes out to declare Perg the winner, and the crowd erupts with a mix of pleasure and disdain.

I can see Perg's grin from my cramped spot. He's done it—he's a Deccor, the third rank in the caste system. Cry as the crowd may, he's rightfully earned it.

I applaud. But the sound of the crowd cuts out sharply. Perg hasn't left the bridge. Someone shouts, but I can't hear what.

Hoping to go unnoticed, I worm my way closer to the action, slipping between arches, then through clusters of trollis sitting and standing. Most are too intent on the arena to notice me. Others, I hope, will merely think I'm delivering a message to one of my betters.

"—and allow such monstrosity?" a bold, familiar voice bellows. I step around a trollis woman, and my stomach sinks as I recognize Grodd standing before the crowed, his arms raised. "He should not even be allowed the tournament! He is an abomination!"

About half of the crowd reacts in low, angry voices. Angry at Grodd or at Perg, I'm not sure, but my skin tingles as I watch. Nothing good can come of this.

Grodd marches forward and disappears into the crowd, and for a moment I think the complaints will end, but he returns swiftly, dragging a smaller trollis woman with him. Judging by her dress, she's a Pleb.

He hands the shaking woman a sword and steps back, his arms spread wide.

Someone from the highest seats, near what I assume is the council, shouts, "A tournament cannot be entered unwillingly."

"Oh, she's willing," Grodd bellows back. He looks at the Pleb. I'm not so far as to miss the malicious gleam in his eye.

Will he kill the woman out of anger? Does she mean something to Perg? Yet Perg looks as confused as I feel. What—

The woman lunges for Grodd, and Grodd allows her to strike him across the face with the flat of her sword. He falls dramatically to the ground.

The crowd gasps. I don't breathe. I don't understand.

Grodd, still supine, motions to someone, and the officiator hesitantly comes out to announce the Pleb the winner.

Another gasp sounds around me. Cold seizes my fingers. I press them into my neck.

Grodd, a *Montra*, just willingly gave his title to a Pleb. He exchanged one of the highest ranks for the lowest.

Why?

"Oh stars," I whisper.

Taking the sword from the Pleb—the new Montra, who seems utterly stunned—Grodd turns for Perg.

No. He's going to fight Perg. Strip him of his new Deccor status and make him a Pleb. And while Grodd isn't nearly the size of Perg's first opponent, he waits like a viper, cruel and tense. And Perg is tired.

I rush to the nearest trollis, a gray woman, and say, "But Perg has to agree!"

She looks at me, surprised—I imagine she's Intra and I'm overstepping my bounds—but shock must sway her to speak with me. "No, he's still standing on the battlefield. He can still be confronted if he remains. It's a stance of challenge."

Stance of challenge. Azmar explained that to me. Strength oozes from my legs. "But Grodd came too quickly. Perg wasn't challenging anyone! He was confused . . ."

The Intra gives me an odd look, and I excuse myself before I get in trouble. I turn back for the arena as Grodd advances on Perg. Perg grips the long handle of his axe with both hands. He bares his teeth, bends his knees. Perhaps he can win this.

But Grodd is Montra, or at least he was, and Perg just gave everything he had to beat a Deccor. He's exhausted. I'm not sure if he can turn down a fight when, in the trollis' eyes, he initiated the stance of challenge.

No one was calling out Grodd's manipulation of it.

"I'm so sorry, Perg," I whisper. No one hears me.

Grodd roars when he strikes. Perg blocks with the shaft of his axe, but the strong blow forces him back. Flashes of sunlight gleam on Grodd's savage blade as he swings, driving Perg back, and back again. Perg loses his stance as the blade slices open his arm, and he falters when it opens up his trousers above the knee, his blueish blood flowing freely.

I shove my knuckle into my mouth to keep from biting my tongue. *Just surrender, Perg!*

Perg tries to strike back, but his swing goes wide. Grodd moves in and shoves the hilt of his sword painfully into Perg's gut. When Perg bends over from the blow, Grodd twists and swings high, his blade slicing clean across Perg's collar, part of his neck, and his face.

I scream, but it's drowned out by the sound of the murmuring crowd, all morbidly fascinated with the fight.

Perg drops to one knee. His blood spatters the ground. He spits and glares hatefully at Grodd. He lifts a hand to surrender, but before he can raise it fully, Grodd attacks again.

Cold seizes my entire body. Grodd hits, strikes, cuts, kicks. Over and over. He's already won, but he doesn't stop. Doesn't let up. Perg's face swells. A well-placed foot to his knee bends it backward, and he topples.

Still Grodd does not relent. The medics don't rush forward. No one calls him off.

They value strength above all else.

Perg is going to die.

I push through the bodies, even shoving a trollis as I rush toward the battlefield. Perg struggles to get up, to get his hand in the air. Grodd whirls and sends his heel into the side of Perg's head.

"Stop!" I scream, waving my arms to gain notice. "Stop, he's already won!"

Gasps and groans sound from the audience, but no one moves.

And then I'm charging the battle, my feet pounding the bridge, my heart thrumming in my head. I'm rushing toward Perg's fallen form, over bloodstained planks, right toward Grodd. I can barely hear the audience jeering and complaining over the wind rushing in my ears, punctuated by my thundering pulse.

Grodd lifts his sword for a killing blow, then pauses, noticing me. A smile twitches his mouth.

Perg dropped his axe several feet away, and I grab it. It's alarmingly heavy, but with both hands I'm able to point its top pike at Grodd.

Silence overtakes the onlookers.

"You're killing him!" I shout.

Grodd laughs. "Two for one." He steps toward me.

I hold the axe forward and release *everything*. All the fear swirling inside me. Fear for myself, fear for Perg, fear of retribution for my actions. Fear of the monsters that attack Cagmar. Fear of the forever depths of the canyon. Memories of my father's hard words and harder hands. Danner, the mobs, the wild beasts. My capture on the bridge. All of it.

I shove it from my body, through that axe, and out, so suddenly that I scream. Only the shaft of the axe, so long it presses into the ground, keeps me from crumbling under the weight of my own terror.

Grodd drops his sword. His eyes widen until they're more white than green. He stumbles back, shaking. Liquid floods his trousers as he scrambles to get away, like a child confronted with a bedtime demon. Lamblike mewls escape his throat. Tears spill, and gooseflesh prickles his arms.

Mimicked terror tightens my limbs, but as Grodd scrambles, I unclasp stiff fingers from the axe handle and rush to Perg's side, fear from my curse and fear for my friend mingling into one painful rhythm within my chest. He's barely breathing. His face is unrecognizable. His blood clings everywhere, warm and blue and tacky.

I look up. "Help! Someone help him!"

The entire crowd goes silent. Gaping. Staring at me.

I broke my rule. I had to.

Tears flood my vision. "He's *dying*!" I shout. "Someone help!"

Bodies shift in the stands straight ahead, and I nearly sob as Azmar rushes down the narrow stairs toward us, removing his vest as he runs.

Finally one of the medics follows. Then another. Then someone I don't recognize from the crowd.

I don't know where Grodd is, but I don't care. Azmar drops beside me. He looks over Perg's injuries before meeting my eyes.

I see his confusion and awe. "Please," I whisper.

He blinks, focusing on Perg. He tears the vest in half and tourniquets the deepest wounds. Then the medics and the others arrive, stanching and bandaging what they can. A stretcher appears. They slide Perg onto it.

Not one trollis in the crowd takes their eyes off me, and over their heads, I meet the serpentine and unyielding glare of Qequan.

Chapter 10

I sit by the fire in Unach and Azmar's apartment, absentmindedly peeling a large sweet potato over a dented bucket. My hair brushes the floor, falling around me like a protective curtain. I've always kept it long for that reason. It gives me a place to hide.

A knock sounds at the door.

"I'll shove fire ants up your backside if you even *try* that lock!" Unach barks. Tense silence fills the room. I don't hear whoever it is depart, but there's no second knock.

"Sorry," I murmur, focusing on the sweet potato.

"I'll do it to you, too, if you say that again," she snaps. She leans against the door frame to her bedroom and runs both hands down her face. Azmar, sitting nearby, looks thoughtful, leaning over a ledger, pencil in hand. He hasn't written anything in an hour.

It's been nearly a full day since the caste tournament. Since I broke my one rule and blatantly used my ability in front of the entire city of Cagmar. It was a fight to get Perg taken to the infirmary, but it was a bigger fight to get myself away from the questions, the stares, the grabbing hands. Unach came down from the stands and guarded me from the front, while Azmar stood at my back. They marched me immediately up here, and I haven't stepped outside their apartment since. A blessing, given that Unach assailed me with her own barrage of inquiries and theories. She's considered everything from me whispering blackmail and threats that only Grodd could hear, to using human hypnotism or wielding the urine of a spreener—a canyon monster.

I refuse to confirm or deny anything. And it hurts.

I'm surprised I'm not in that cell again, and that Qequan hasn't called upon me. He saw. They all *saw*.

Curious trollis come by, wanting to know. Wanting to ask. Wanting to stare at me like I'm an animal caged for their entertainment.

They're not the only ones.

"Just *tell* me, Lark," Unach presses.

I peel the sweet potato.

Unach growls. "You're killing me. You're honestly killing me."

After taking a deep breath, I say, "I suppose Grodd just saw something he didn't like." I have no idea if my victims see anything when I inflict fear upon them. I'm fairly certain they just feel inexplicably afraid, just like I do. "Maybe he's never fought a human."

Unach dismisses the explanation with a snort. "All trollis have fought humans."

I glance up at her, but my attention shifts to Azmar, who looks notably uncomfortable. He drops his pencil and rubs his temples in circular motions.

I think of the scars on his torso and wonder.

"Raids, mostly," Unach goes on. "Though those have become less and less common. Your kind keeps scattering, moving farther and farther away. For a species that can pop out a child in less than a year, your numbers sure aren't improving."

"Unach." Azmar sounds tired.

My knife stills. "How long is gestation for a trollis?"

"Twenty-three months."

No wonder they're so huge.

"Some try to cross the bridge," she continues, "to . . . I don't know, pick at the old city? Not many anymore. And then sometimes the scout parties intermix." She shrugs. "Regardless, Grodd has fought and kill—fought many humans. And no offense, Lark, but you're hardly terrifying."

I could laugh, but instead I peel.

Unach walks over and stares at me headlong, perhaps trying to see what it was Grodd saw. I vow to myself never to show her. I won't risk losing the few allies I have. I won't risk being sent away. *Please don't send me away.*

"Maybe you should ask Grodd," I try.

"Grodd is likely hiding as much as you are." Azmar retains a low and level tone. He hasn't left the apartment, either. Unach did, but only once, and she fought off curious trollis even as she came home again. "He put on a show and failed in the most dishonorable way possible."

I set down the sweet potato. "Is it so horrible?"

Azmar regards me. There's something deep and interesting in his gaze that I can't define. "Humans rally in their numbers; trollis rally in their strength. No human could best a trollis in hand-to-hand combat. That's why Perg has struggled so. It's biology."

"It's like you losing to a rat," Unach suggests.

I frown, and again Azmar pleads, "Unach."

She glowers at her brother. "It's not an unfair comparison."

Despite the difficult subject, I'm comforted by their conversation. By their fraternity. I almost feel a part of it. For whatever reason, that almost-feeling makes me sad.

Turning to me, Unach asks, "You're friends with Perg?"

I nod.

"Think of him, of how badly he's treated. Grodd is at least that now." She spits on the floor. "I can hardly believe it myself. That self-serving oaf is a thorn in my side, but he's a damn fine soldier. I'd even considered trading bloodstones with him once, just for the fine stock he'd put in me."

I flush. "But he's horrible."

Unach shrugs. "It is what it is. I could always take the stone back with a witness."

I glance at Azmar, surprised to see his gaze more intent than before. My pulse quickens, and I self-consciously tuck some hair behind my ear.

Rubbing my hands together, I say, "I want to see Perg."

"He's fine." Unach scratches her nose.

"*Alive* and *fine* are not interchangeable."

"Lark." The softness in Azmar's voice startles me. "Even if Unach and I went with you, you'll be barraged by trollis. They might not be as understanding that you won't answer their questions as we are."

I clench my hands into fists. "I already answered your questions. I don't know what happened. I just . . . I just had to defend Perg."

Both Azmar and his sister look unsure.

A knock sounds at the door.

Unach wheels around. "I'll break that damn door down on your wretched face!"

A beat passes. "The human has been summoned by the council."

My heart lodges in my throat. Standing, I look between them. Familiar fear dribbles down my legs and freezes in my toes. "Please don't make me go alone."

Azmar moves to stand beside me, and the ensuing relief sweeps through me cold as canyon wind.

Unach answers the door. "She's coming."

The messenger waits.

Before Unach turns away, she adds, "And the human's name is Lark."

The messenger is a short trollis—which still makes him notably taller than I am—with a round gut, the least warrior-looking trollis I've seen since my arrival. He leads the way through Cagmar, down the tunnels, through the market, up a special set of stairs I'd never noticed before. The council chamber rests at the very heart of the city, making it the last place a monster—or a human—would ever reach.

It's rather clever. My father would have agreed.

No one bothers us on our journey. The messenger holds a short red flag in front of him, which somehow signals the importance of our travel. Everyone gives us deference, regardless of caste. But their eyes . . . They stare unabashedly, making me feel naked beneath my trollis-spun dress. Even my hair can't hide the intensity of the glares. Most do not appear malicious, but I've never been gawked at so thoroughly in my life. Even enraged mobs never stared me down with such unrestraint.

I curl in on myself, even when we reach the council doors, my head nearly touching Unach's back. To my surprise, Azmar's hand settles gently on my shoulder. I don't look at him, but I relish the comfort of its weight.

Who would have ever thought I would find comfort at the hands of a trollis?

"You will have to wait in the antechamber," the messenger tells Unach and Azmar.

Unach's brow furrows. "We're her employers." Not quite the truth. "We have every right."

Unfazed, the messenger replies, "Do you care to bring up the complaint with Qequan?"

Her lips press into a thin line.

Azmar answers, "No."

Appeased, the messenger opens the door to a narrow, unadorned antechamber. It doesn't even have chairs, only one window that looks out to the distant marketplace. Unach moves toward it, rippling with displeasure. Azmar begins to follow her, but he glances my way and nods.

He doesn't think I'm in danger, then. Stars let him be right.

On the far side of the antechamber stand two massive trollis, both well armored and armed. Each carries a long axe, not unlike Perg's, which makes my heart hurt for my friend all the more. The image of his beaten face . . . I don't think that will ever leave my memory. It certainly haunted my dreams last night.

The guards stand aside and allow me entrance. The messenger does not follow.

The main chamber is not as large as I remember. Wide swaths of fabric hang from the ceiling and connect to the walls, looking brighter than they had at first. I must have gotten used to the dim colors of Cagmar. As before, I stop at the edge of the enormous fur rug in the center of the room, still unable to identify what monster it hails from. All five council chairs are filled.

Somehow, the Supra seem more menacing than when I first arrived.

If Unach thought Grodd was a great soldier, then these trollis are gods.

Unsure of myself, I bow low. I don't stand until the first trollis speaks.

"Lark."

Qequan leans on one stone armrest, his hand pressed into his massive jowl, which makes him look frog-like. His widow's peak pours over his scalp and ends in a daggerlike point.

I muster everything I ever learned from my father's study, from every politician and landowner who ever graced his floor. I straighten, but not enough to appear haughty, ignoring the heavy thudding of my heart that threatens to echo between the brick and iron walls. "Master Qequan."

The trollis grins. "Ah, I forgot about the title. Yet I still like it. *Master.*"

Agga, the only female on the council, rolls her eyes.

Qequan scrutinizes me up and down, and I lock my knees to keep from fidgeting. "I took my time with this one. Do you know why you're here, little Lark?"

My mouth dries. "I presume you mean to speak with me about Grodd."

"She presumes." Qequan chuckles, and Ichlad, to his right, scowls. "You're a very polite human. Remind me where you hail from?"

The question again discomforts me, but I would do well to be honest and humble before creatures that could tear me limb from limb, either with their own hands or by a simple order. "Lucarpo, sir."

"I do not know it."

"It's far east from here. Too far for a reasonable raid."

Qequan raises an eyebrow. "But not too far for a little bird to walk?"

"I did not come directly from Lucarpo, sir, but traveled many years." A spot on my back itches fiercely, but I dare not scratch it.

"Hmm. And Perg 941. What is he to you?"

"Merely a friend." I squeeze as much softness and respect into my voice as I can. "He is, a little, like me."

Agga snorts in disgust. "Understandable."

Qequan leans back. "Perg cannot keep his victory, but Grodd's behavior was . . ." He waves his hand like we're casually discussing the sale of a goat. "Unseemly. He will remain a Pleb, and your *friend* will retain his Nethens status."

Oh, Perg, after all that work. But at least he will also retain his life.

A spike of fear courses through me. Is it more honorable to die in a tournament, or to lose? Especially with a human protector? Have I done him a disservice?

No, he was fighting to stand. He was ready to surrender.

"As for you." Qequan sits upright and leans forward, sobering. "You will not take any status within Cagmar."

I lower my eyes. "I did not intend to."

I feel his gaze through my hair. I clasp my hands together, grateful that I left Perg's knife in my room. I can't imagine what would happen if I were caught with it.

"I had a feeling you were involved with the leckers' attack." Qequan's words carry practiced precision. *Leckers* were the monsters that attacked Cagmar. "You did prove my judgment to these." He jerks his thumb to the other council members, who take the thin scolding with silence. "I was right about you. And in truth, Grodd could stand to be taken down a few pegs. Mayhap not *all* of them"—he grimaces—"but a few. Give him a couple years and he'll climb his way back up, if he's strong enough." He laughs. It's a rich sound that echoes off the walls of the council room, making it sound as though there are four of him.

Something about that phrasing, *strong enough*, sickens me.

"But, Lark." The stringent use of my name cuts through his joviality. "If you *ever* use your gift against one of my people again, I'll throw you into the canyon myself."

True fear bursts through the soles of my feet and roots me to the spot. It crusts over my joints and constricts my lungs. No humor glimmers in Qequan's eyes. The council looks at me with a familiar disdain, disdain I've seen in countless faces, whenever my secret has come to light, all throughout my life.

"B-But you will let me stay?" Were it not for the amplification of the walls, the council might not have heard my weak voice.

Qequan tips his head, and my legs nearly give beneath me. "For the leckers. But my words are a promise."

I drop to my knees and prostrate myself before them. "Thank you for your mercy. I will obey. It will not happen again."

With my nose pressed to the fur rug, I don't see what Qequan or any of the council members do. But Agga says, "Take your leave," and I scramble to my feet, my heart pounding, my head dizzy, and hurry to the doors. Trollis guards open them. When they shut behind me, I bend over, taking in air like I've been underwater the entire time.

Azmar and Unach appear at my side.

"Lark?" Azmar asks.

Unach says, "What happened?"

Once I catch my breath, I answer, "They're letting me stay."

Unach lets out a long breath. "And? What did you tell him? About the tournament?"

Tension warps my spine. "The same thing I told you."

Unach blanches. "You gave those excuses to the *council?*"

I whirl on her, fear igniting to anger beneath my skin. "The truth doesn't change when a different person asks." But it's a lie. It's all a lie. I know exactly what I did, and so do they.

And I can never, *ever* do it again. I have nowhere else to go.

Azmar steps between us, one hand on his sister's arm, the other on my shoulder. "Leave her be. We must accept that she doesn't know."

"How can she not know?" Unach protests, even as Azmar guides her toward the exit. "Why would she run into a battle like that without knowing she would win?"

Azmar's eyes narrow. "Do you know you'll win, every time you plunge into the canyon to face the creatures below?"

Unach works her jaw. Looks away and kicks open the door, storming out ahead of us.

A stale breath passes my lips. "Thank you, Azmar."

He nods, though I sense his own discontent with my answer. But that answer is all I can give. If I'm to stay in Cagmar, I must forget my fear, slough it off like snakeskin and become a new Lark. The thought is both liberating and terrifying.

I suddenly want Perg's knife, but I should get rid of it. I must do nothing to tarnish my name further. I must become a perfect human.

Azmar lets me walk down the stairs first. The council chamber sits higher than the market, so we have a good view of it as we start down the hill. A small group of trollis loiters near the food handlers, jeering and calling names, occasionally kicking or slapping someone amidst them. It reminds me too much of Perg, but Perg is in the infirmary. Thinking of Ritha and the others, I quicken my step.

One of the trollis shifts, and I see it's not a human they torment, but Grodd. He wears the common clothes of a Pleb, and his disheveled hair speaks of ill treatment. He scowls at one of his assailants and raises a hand as though to strike back.

A trollis behind him batters a fist into Grodd's skull. "Raise your hand to your betters, *Pleb*? I'll have you thrown in the dungeon for that."

The others laugh. Unach watches, too, her face grim. "How easily the iron bar bends," she murmurs. I wonder if that's a trollis idiom.

Before I can wrench my gaze free to follow Azmar, Grodd looks up and meets it. In his vivid green eyes, I see hatred deeper than any I've ever encountered. Hatred sharp enough to steal my breath away.

He knows, more than anyone, that I'm hiding something.

And in that embittered glare, I see the promise of revenge.

Chapter 11

I don't know if the excitement of my brief encounter with Grodd has died down or if the council sent out some missive I don't know about or even if Unach's rage can quell the entire city, but a few days after the caste tournament, the glares and whispers reduce to a simmer, and I'm able to visit Perg. Trollis still examine me when they pass by, but I don't fear being mobbed by them, and very few speak to me outside of small comments, like an awed "a human, of all things" or "would-be Montra." Some even salute to me. I seem to have earned some respect among the more open-minded. While it pleases and astounds me, I wish even the compliments would end. The sooner Cagmar forgets about me, the easier my transition to a defenseless, boring human. The sooner I will be safe.

Perg looks better. Bruised, but better. Blue cuts and abrasions speckle his skin. Heavy bandages encompass his forearm and torso. A thick blanket hides the rest of him.

"But it's worth it," he says as we discuss what happened on the bridge. He doesn't remember my being there, except hovering over him as he lost consciousness. "To see that teat-sucking mole in squalor. Or it will be, when I do see him."

I don't answer. Looking around the infirmary, I see that everything here is trollis-made, all beams and steel, some wood and mortared stones. Lamps hang from the ceiling over each bed, making it the brightest room in Cagmar. There are six beds in total, two of them pushed together against a far wall to make more space. The nurse, a slender trollis with tusks too big for his mouth, stepped out just a minute ago.

I do think Grodd deserves punishment for his cruelty, but I don't believe in fighting malice with malice. It seems everyone in Cagmar hates him now. Just as they hated Perg. And yet Perg has no empathy for him. I don't blame him, but it makes me wonder.

"How long will you be here in the infirmary?" I ask.

Perg tries to shrug, then winces. I wonder how trollis medicine compares to humans'. "At least a few more days. Make sure infection doesn't set in. But then I'll be confined to quarters after that. Don't know which I'd prefer. But as soon as my body catches up with me, I'm training again."

I blanche. "Will you be ready for the next tournament?" It is only three months away.

Perg grimaces. "No. And not the one after that, either." He focuses on a spot on the wall. "He beat me, Lark. Tore and broke so much . . . even when I'm healed, I'll be soft. I don't hold my musculature as well as a full-blooded trollis. I have to work twice as hard for everything . . ."

His voice cuts to a whisper. I place my hand on his bicep, above his bandages. "But you'll do it, Perg. You're already a Deccor at heart. You did it once, and you'll do it again. I have faith in you."

He offers me a half smile at that, but a heaviness pulls at his features.

"I'll visit you every day," I promise. "What's your favorite meal? I'll steal from Unach's stores to make it for you."

He laughs, then winces as it shakes his broken ribs. "You'll think it's ridiculous."

"Why would I think it's ridiculous?"

"Because"—he glances around, checking for nurses, but we're alone—"it's carrot soup."

I blink. "Is that funny?"

He shrugs. "Well, it's not *meat*."

The trollis *do* have a meat-heavy diet, I've noticed, and meat seems the more masculine food group. Azmar's favorite food is boar belly.

I pause, wondering when I learned this. I've never even cooked it for him. I try to think what Unach's favorite meal is, but my mind comes up blank.

"I'll make the best carrot soup you've ever had. And I'll even spoon-feed it to you."

Perg rolls his eyes. "Please no. Any respect I earned from my first battle will be gone the moment someone sees a human babying me." He says *human* like it's a totally foreign concept, not like it's half of who he is. "It's bad enough that—" He stops abruptly.

I pull back. "Bad enough that what?"

He waves a hand. "Don't worry about it."

But in my gut, I know what he was going to say. *It's bad enough that I'm friends with one.*

A sharp shiver runs through my heart. I swallow in an attempt to relieve it.

After Perg heals, he'll train again. He'll find someone to battle. He'll become a Deccor, maybe even reach Intra. Will there be a point where befriending me is no longer in good taste? Is our friendship based not on our shared humanity, but on our shared lowliness in the trollis caste system?

But Azmar is Centra, and Unach Montra. And they're my friends. At least, *I* consider them friends.

Rubbing my hands together to warm them, I say, "I should be going. Errands to run and all." I have to return to my shifts at the south dock tomorrow.

Perg nods. "Good luck."

I offer him a weak smile and find my way out, grateful not to encounter any other trollis in need of deference.

I keep alert as I leave the infirmary. In truth, I haven't hid solely from prying trollis, but from Grodd. That look, so full of loathing, that he gave me. I see it behind my eyelids when I turn in for the night, and I don't want to risk crossing paths with him. Surely he'll convince someone to battle him at the next caste tournament, and all will be well again, but until then, it's best we stay away from one another.

Then again, I could be overthinking things. It's been a habit I've struggled to break since I was a child, analyzing every movement my father made, every sound, every word, determining how he would use me next or what I'd get in trouble for. I'm likely being overly sensitive to Grodd. I had been wrong about Colson, after all. Perhaps I was also wrong about Grodd.

Remembering the way he strutted about on the bridge, and the way he beat Perg . . . I have my doubts.

When I get to the market, I startle to see Colson loading up a small cart with foodstuff, as though my thoughts had summoned him. Near the head of the cart stands Ritha. I hesitate, unsure if I should approach, but Colson dusts off his hands, turns, and sees me.

The exuberance on his face shocks me to my bones.

"Lark!" He waves like he wants me to approach. Ritha notices me, and waves me forward.

I approach hesitantly, clutching the strap of my bag with both hands. When I arrive, young Etewen comes from around the cart, surprised to see me.

"Lark. *Lark.*" Colson reaches forward and grabs my elbows. I turn stiff as brick. "Thank you, Lark. I—we—owe you so much."

Confusion twists its way through me as I pull from his grasp. "What . . . do you mean?" Has he realized what his fate would have been had I and Azmar not interceded on his behalf?

Colson's grin lights up his face in an almost handsome way. He looks like an entirely new person. "Don't you see? A Pleb can't lead the task force."

A sudden buoyancy fills my chest and raises me to my toes. "Grodd?"

He chuckles and scratches the back of his head. "He's been replaced with someone else, of course, but . . ."

"No one hates humans more than Grodd does," Ritha whispers. "Why do you think he beat the half troll so badly? He detests us."

"From what we've heard," Colson adds, "Tartuk isn't cruel. We'll be treated with more leniency."

"That's wonderful." As wonderful as it can be, anyway.

"W-We're sorry," Etewen says, his voice barely audible. He shies behind the cart. "About what happened. Didn't . . . think it through."

Colson dips his head at the remark, a streak of pink climbing up his neck. "I don't know how you did it, but we're grateful, Lark."

"But be careful," Ritha adds. "Don't get uppity about the win. Keep your head down until the amusement passes."

I hug myself. "I only want everyone to forget about it." I'm glad the other humans aren't here, or they'd be asking me questions I can't answer as well.

Ritha considers this, appearing satisfied. A heartbeat later, her countenance slackens. "Step out of the way, Colson."

I turn to see what's alarmed her, only to spy Azmar headed our way. "Don't worry," I assure them. "Azmar is kind."

If only Colson knew how kind.

Etewen glances between me and Azmar, as though uncertain if he should stay or go. When Azmar reaches us, pausing beside me, Etewen stops breathing. And honestly, I can't blame him. Being around trollis so much, I forget how intimidating they are. I forget that Azmar's height, the breadth of his shoulders, and the thickness of his arms easily ignites fear in our smaller species. Compared to the rest of us, he's imposing.

"Have you been to see Perg?" His casual manner contradicts his hulking presence.

I nod. "He's doing as well as can be expected. Do you have any spare carrots?"

He raises his brow in a remarkably human expression. "Carrots?"

"For a meal for him."

He considers this, his lips almost frowning. "I'll see what I can manage."

"Oh no, if there aren't any, you don't—" I start, but Azmar dismisses my objection with a wave of his hand.

Colson, Ritha, and Etewen all stare.

Unsure of the decorum here, I fall back on my human instincts. "Azmar, you remember Ritha. And this is Etewen and Colson." The weight of Azmar's stare grows heavy at the last name, and I wonder if I should have skipped introductions. I also wonder at the weight of the glare, given that we are but humans who had a human struggle, so easily dismissed by most trollis. Oddly, that glare warms me in the strangest way.

He glances at the bags still outside the cart. "Do you need help?"

Colson blanches. I wonder if he sees the inquiry as a threat, which it isn't. "N-No, it's fine." He grabs the last two bags and heaves them into the cart. "Th-Thank you, though."

Azmar nods. I notice a ledger—a new one—beneath his arm. "Off to work?"

"Always." He tips his head to me before heading down the street toward Engineering.

"Never seen comradery between human and troll before," Ritha mutters.

For some reason, I find myself flushing again. "Not all trollis dismiss us."

The expression on her face cautions that she doesn't believe me.

"We should go," Colson interjects, moving to the front of the cart to pull it. Etewen gets behind to push. "Thank you again, Lark. And . . . sorry."

It's an uncomplicated apology, but it gives me hope.

They take off toward the enclave. As I watch them go, I spy a large wagon pulled by a familiar shape, Grodd, and the hope Colson planted immediately shrivels.

As though he senses me, Grodd's hard glare finds me. I feel it like knife points against my skin, pressing just to the point of breaking through. His wagon is loaded with iron ore, and Unach's earlier words ring in my mind. *How easily the iron bar bends.*

Grodd's nose wrinkles, like he's smelled something bad. His wagon veers toward me. Does he need to come this way, or does he mean to confront me?

Unsure of myself, I hurry in the direction of the others and catch them near the middle of the tunnel, near a lift. I didn't think I'd moved very quickly, but I'm out of breath when I arrive.

"Lark?" Colson asks.

Smoothing back my hair, I ask, "Do the trollis believe in witchcraft?"

Ritha's eyes narrow. "No, why?"

I shake my head. There will be no accusations of witchery against me here, at least.

And yet that does little to reassure me.

My shift overlaps with Unach's the next day, and I get to take a rope bridge farther down the canyon to another station. Monsters called cretons have been spotted recently, so the slayers stay on alert. After a couple of hours, we see one a ways off, and I learn exactly where the council got its floor rug. Hanging back, I let Unach load a large crossbow and take a shot at it. She doesn't hit it, but the creature scurries away, out of sight. If we monitor them for a few days, they'll lose interest and move on. Most monsters do, or so I've heard.

When we climb back inside the dock and start sloughing off our harnesses, Kub remarks, "A lecker is one thing. I'd like to see how she fares against a creton."

I drop my harness wordlessly into the chest.

"I'd like to see how you fare against me," Unach says offhandedly, but there's a hardness to her tone. "Leave her be. She has ears, you know."

I bite my lip to hide a smile, because I don't think Unach would react well to my pleasure at her defense of me. I hand her my weapons and a few pitons, and she returns them to the closet.

Afterward, I pick my way back through the city, considering what to do with my few hours of free time. I could visit Perg again, but not a day has passed yet, and he needs his rest. That, and I'd like to have that soup when I see him again.

I wonder if I could barter some writing supplies from someone, just to draw or tell a story, not that I'm talented with either. Thoughts of writing make me think of Azmar, so I turn up toward Engineering. Surely he will have some use for me there, even if it's just teaching me a new concept and letting me sit in the corner while I work it out.

The uphill climb is tiring. Sleet is on duty, the same guard as the first time I visited. He scrutinizes me but says nothing. I scan the tables but don't see Azmar's familiar knot of hair.

"Is Azmar in today?" I ask the guard.

He frowns at me, and I suspect it's at my boldness, asking him a question when I am without rank. Or perhaps he finds me curious, like so many trollis do. "No."

I frown and scan the room one more time. Surely it can't be that hard to entertain myself. Yet I find myself wishing Azmar were here, even if he didn't need my help or have time to teach me mathematics.

I thank the guard and head up toward the market, stepping aside to let a group of trollis through. The last two notice me and put their heads together, whispering. I wonder what they're saying, but think it might be better that I don't find out.

In a little while, they'll forget, I tell myself, though I'm not sure how true it is. I've never stayed anywhere after others "found out." But surely some other spectacle will happen in Cagmar, and I'll be forgotten.

The noise of the market filters down the tunnel. I look at Wiln's clock on the wall. Nearly a quarter past five. I wonder if I could go up to the Empyrean Bridge and watch the sunset, but I imagine I'd need an escort. Might as well head to Unach and Azmar's apartment and cook dinner. If they're both out, I can use their bath.

I keep to the side of the tunnel out of habit. Here the trollis are busy, focused on their own tasks, uncaring about a human, even a novel one, in their midst.

I'm halfway through the market when the hairs on the back of my neck stand on end. I rub them with my hand and lift my head. No one has noticed me, no one stares. Swallowing, I continue on, shoulders tense. It's a strange but familiar feeling that something is wrong. That I've forgotten something, or that I'm late—

Grodd.

I spy him across the way in a narrow alley between the launderer and leather repair. The way the shadows fall, the way the lamplight gleams across him, makes him look like a feral cat, eyes aglow, joints poised and ready to strike.

A tremor of fear pulses through my body. Quickening my pace, I pull my braid over my other shoulder as though it can shield me from that glare, but more than my face can give me away in a place like this. I think I'm almost safe when, from my periphery, I see the shadows move.

Grodd is following me.

Oh stars. I hasten my steps even more. I just need to get back to the apartment . . . but Unach and Azmar might not be there, and I have no trust that a trollis, especially one of Grodd's size, couldn't get past that lock. And if I move aside for every trollis going the other way, he'll catch up to me.

Would anyone stop him? He might be only a Pleb now, but I am without rank. I am the lesser species here. Weren't the trollis ready and willing to kill Colson for his infraction? Didn't Unach say that all trollis have fought humans, so casually that she might as well have been speaking of crushing roaches?

I grab the handle of the first door I reach and slip inside. It's a small wainwright's shop, just enough room for three trollis on one side of a narrow table and two on the other. The trollis manning the table within is older, his hair white, his face wrinkled, his massive back humping. He glances up at me, dismay in his face. "What's your order?" he snaps.

"I—" I wring my hands together. "I don't have—"

"Then get out!" He mumbles something under his breath and returns to his lathe and spoke. When I don't move immediately, he picks up the latter like it's a cudgel. "Didn't you hear me, louse?"

I step outside.

Grodd is twenty feet away.

My thoughts cluster into knots, my heart gallops like a warhorse, my skin sweats as though that giant clock were the sun.

I dart down the next tunnel, vaguely recognizing it as the path to the military training grounds. A guard comes up the other way, and when I don't immediately move aside for him, he shoves me with his forearm, the bony spikes bruising my skin. I teeter and hit the stone wall, then continue onward, trying to look small. If I can find a crowd of trollis, I can hide among them—

I stop short, knowing that going into the training grounds will get me in trouble. But if I'm in the dungeon, Grodd can't get to me. Or can he?

Backtracking, I take the next offshoot going down and east. It's empty, so I rise up on my toes and sprint. I just need to hide. I wrap around military storage, which two trollis guard, and pass the food stores. Next should be Engineering, but this corridor juts to the right and forks off, and when I take the path I think will lead to Engineering, I end up at a drop with a lift and several ladders. The lift is in use, so I take a ladder. When I turn to descend, I see Grodd coming around the curve in the tunnel, his face alight like fire, his hands forming boulder-like fists.

A sob chokes halfway up my throat as I scrabble down. My fear bubbles up like vomit. I could just release a tendril, just enough to slow him down . . .

I'll throw you into the canyon myself.

I grit my teeth and keep going, my lungs beginning to burn. I'm not sure where I am, but it might be Deccor housing, judging by the clothing. I see a woman watching a trollis child and rush to her.

"I'm so sorry, but can you hide me?"

Her expression opens. "You're the one from the tournament."

I glance over my shoulder. "Yes. Can you hide me?"

Her expression closes. "I'll not break the law if you're fleeing the task force."

"I'm not—" But I check again, and Grodd stalks toward me like he has all the time in the world. I couldn't hide here anyway, not anymore.

So I run. Anywhere, as long as it's away. Up, down, left, right, wherever there's a clear path. I run as hard as I can, stone and brick passing under my feet, lights flying overhead. The lamps grow smaller, with more and more space in between. The sound of metal echoes through another atrium as I dart down a long bridge-like platform. I barely register the school in the distance as I slip between two more trollis, one of which curses at me as I fly by. I enter a narrow corridor. Darkness envelops me, and for a terrifying breath I don't know where I am or where I'm going, and I'm forced to slow. My lungs work like bellows and my calves burn like new embers. When I see a glimmer of dull lamplight ahead, I hurry toward it and nearly topple over another drop, barely catching myself with windmilling arms.

I hear approaching footsteps between wheezes, so I turn and take the ladder down. My feet slip more than once, especially when Grodd appears as a hulking shadow at the top.

I jump down the last few rungs and land harder on one side than the other. Sharp pain laces through my ankle. Gasping, I hurry onward, favoring my right side. Just a jam, but it smarts. My lungs heave for more air; it feels as though I cannot inhale deeply enough. But neither can I stop. I'll have to plead with someone, *anyone*, for sanctuary. Surely the council cannot fault me that.

But there are no trollis down here.

I limp toward light, only to realize it lacks the hazy glow of lamp-light. It's dull and a strange shade of purple. As I hurry, pleading with my lungs and leg to follow, the sound of running water strikes my ears. The light expands until I realize it's a window without netting or glass, and the light comes from the setting sun far overhead, choked by the canyon's wall.

I collapse against the thick, stony sill and peer into utter blackness. A sort of aqueduct hangs immediately to my right, gushing with running water.

I'm in the waterworks, somewhere near the bottom of the city.

A cold breeze climbs up from the depths of the gorge and raises gooseflesh on my skin. Simultaneously, Grodd's voice echoes. "Little bird, little bird, why do you run?"

Closing my lips around a whimper, I follow the duct. There's another window ahead, this one with a platform, conceivably for the water bearers to descend into the canyon like the monster slayers do.

Too much light. I pull away and duck under some tubing, then wedge myself behind a column. I crouch, my legs trembling with the effort, desperately in need of air.

"How did it taste, hmm?" Grodd asks in an almost singsong way. "Feast on all my hard work? Devouring my *life*!"

A crash rattles through the waterworks. I think he struck one of the ducts, thinking I was hiding there. I suck air through my raw throat, slow and steady. My pulse beats in my ankle. My calves seize.

Grodd's footsteps near, and I peer through the darkness, trying to find a way back to that ladder. Was it this way, or that way?

If I use my fear on him and he doesn't see me, will Qequan know?

"I only want to talk, little bird," Grodd croons, and I see his silhouette by one of the windows. "I'm not scary, am I? You didn't think so on the bridge."

He turns slowly, scanning. Stops with his face toward my column. He advances, and I scramble to my feet, gasping as pain shoots up my legs. I slide under another duct and run—

Then fall forward with a *splash*.

I cough as I struggle to tread water. I can just barely make out the shape of a pool. It isn't large. Some sort of reservoir. I swim hard, my hips aching, and clamor up the other side, slipping on the hard lip as I do.

"Tell me what you are!" Grodd shouts as I run. The water dripping from my clothes and hair gives him an easy path to follow. I nearly strike my head on another pipe. Some sort of pump heaves to my left. I dart around it, toward another window.

Grodd's pursuit has stopped, or at least, I can't hear his footsteps. He may have fallen into the pool as well. Close to the window, I use the better light to gain my bearings. A narrow path stretches up ahead, heading upward—

A vise closes around my neck, cutting off my air. I jerk forward, my feet leaving the floor. Toward the light. Past the window, until I'm dangling over the darkness below.

Fear, pure and unadulterated, blooms in my chest, filling my head with a strange, twisted sensation of euphoria. My scalp tingles. I look into Grodd's face, his heavy brow pulled so low I can barely see his eyes. His short nose wrinkles in a sneer. Spittle clings to the sides of his thick tusks.

I grab his hand, his wrist, anything to pull up my weight. To keep my neck from snapping. To get air. The dozens of turquoise beads on his sleeve clack with the effort.

Fear.

But if Grodd reacts as he did last time, he might drop me.

His grip loosens a hair, allotting me a trickle of air. Holding on to the edge of the window, he leans out even farther. The canyon opens beneath me like a wintry mouth, cold and dark and ready to consume.

"Tell me what you did," he growls.

My cold hands try to find purchase on his thick wrist. I reach for the spikes on his forearm, but they're too far, and my throat closes completely in the attempt. If I can just *hold on*, I can scare him and he won't drop me. I'll be banished, but I won't be dead.

"Some kind of human *magic*. No other way a weakling like you could best me." He spits the words and squeezes until my eyes bulge, then loosens his grip again. My chin and jaw throb. I've never felt so frail, so helpless. "I'll prove what you are. You'll tell the council yourself and have them reinstate me. They might give you a clean death afterward. Otherwise . . ." He brings me in closer so his breath falls across me, but not close enough for my feet to find purchase. "I'll leave you broken at the bottom of the canyon and let the monsters strip the skin from your bones."

"Grodd."

The unexpected voice hits me like a fist to the gut. It isn't loud, but in the stillness of the space, it carries. Grodd shifts and looks behind him, and though I can't see for myself, I know who's there. When he speaks again, tears trace my cheekbones.

"Put her down." Calmness and precision limn Azmar's every word. Stars, how did he find me? How did he *know*?

Grodd's grip tightens. I struggle for air, claw at him, but no relief comes.

"This is no business of yours, *Centra*."

Lights bloom in the corners of my vision.

"But it is, *Pleb*," he replies, and I can barely hear it over the ringing in my ears. "She is my sister's colleague and my assistant. You'll be punished if you kill her. But if you set her down and walk away, I won't report you."

Grodd shifts closer. I spy Azmar's face over Grodd's shoulder. I try to cough, but can't. My feet go numb.

"I'm a witness," Azmar adds. "Given your new status, I don't think this is what you want."

Cold calculation weighs down his tone. Grodd lowers me, but not enough for me to touch the floor. I focus on that trickle of air. *In, out. In, out.*

"You'll witness, huh?" Grodd's words are husky and raw. "You want to fight for her? You'll lose."

"Perhaps," Azmar concedes, "but then again, I've never had the opportunity to challenge you."

Grodd hesitates. I pull back his thumb just a little as he looks Azmar up and down. Grodd is everything a trollis warrior should be, but Azmar is not weak. Even if he did lose in combat, Grodd would not come out of it unscathed like he did with Perg.

"You *can* fall lower." Azmar folds his arms across his chest. "Neither of you came down here unseen."

A growl sounds low in Grodd's throat. He stiffens, livid, the heat of his anger burning from his fingers into my neck.

And then he hauls me inside and drops me.

My lead feet can't hold me up. I fall hard to my knees and palms, gasping for air, coughing nearly hard enough to empty my stomach. The dark room spins around me. My ears whistle. *In, out. In, out.*

"You are nothing," Grodd spits at Azmar, and he stalks away, making sure to strike Azmar's shoulder with his own as he goes. His footsteps fade, each a hair quieter than the last. My hand moves to my throat, to the bruises forming there. I look through mussed hair, watching Grodd's shadow leave, watching him pass window after window until I can't see him anymore. All the while Azmar stands there, head turned as though he listens as well, unmoving as the canyon wall so near to us.

And then the footsteps cease altogether, and I know Grodd is gone. Only then does Azmar approach me. As if he didn't want Grodd to see.

I swallow against my raw throat and stare at Azmar. He must have seen me in the market, or in Engineering. Maybe another trollis warned him of Grodd's pursuit. I don't know, and I don't care. He came. He saved me.

Never, *never* in all my life has anyone protected me from anything. My father, my siblings, neighbors, servants, friends, strangers. None of them ever stood up for me. None of them ever cared to put themselves in jeopardy for my sake.

The purplish light from the window washes away the earlier coldness from Azmar's features. "Lark." He touches my shoulder and kneels. My name sounds like the wind.

I cry, hot tears streaming over my cold cheeks. The sob that follows hurts. Throwing my arms around his thick waist, I weep into his shirt. Hold on as if the canyon's maw still gapes beneath me. I want to speak, to thank him, praise him, bless him, but I can't. The fear trickles out of me in the form of salty water, and I shake with the realization that I am safe.

Gradually, Azmar's arms encircle me as well, and the maw beneath me closes and recedes. We stay like that for a long time, until my body no longer shakes, my tears stop, and my skin starts to itch beneath my wet dress. And in that moment, right before we pull apart, I realize I might be in more trouble than I thought.

And it has absolutely nothing to do with Grodd.

Chapter 12

No one knows what to make of me when I arrive. I'm sixteen, barely a woman but already taller than the others in the township. Andru's mother takes pity on me, feeds me, puts me to use. I work hard. I want to repay her kindness, to carve a place into their family the way I carved lines into the water-starved earth with prayers that something, this year, would grow there.

Andru is older than me. Midtwenties. But he's kind. Bandages my blisters, listens to me prattle on about stars. His demeanor is so calm, his expressions lively, his smile contagious. It's easy to fall in love with him.

Maybe he thinks the same about me. Or maybe it's the lack of available women. But he asks me to marry him two weeks after meeting me. I say yes. Happiness laces my every step, my every breath. Finally, finally, I have the family I've been searching for. Andru will make a kind and gentle husband. Our babies will have his dark eyes, maybe my blonde hair. Regardless, they will be beautiful, and we will raise them in a little cottage all our own. He starts building it the day after he proposes.

The crops are, indeed, doing a little better this year, thanks to a deep well built the autumn previous. The aerolass must have noticed. They are creatures of the sky, whom I thought had abandoned the human plains. They raid us mercilessly. Run down women and children, take precious oil and herbs by the sackful. Light homes on fire. Break us, so we won't follow.

They come to our half-finished home. But I won't let them have it.

I think Andru will be proud of me, defending our little bit of land and our promise to one another, a promise we'll fulfill at the week's end. I think he'll understand.

I think he loves me.

But his parents mark me as a devil. Other villagers blame my presence for the raids. My heart breaks as Andru joins them. He never openly reviles me, and he does, at least, convince the others not to kill me.

And so I leave that little half-finished house, and all my dreams of our future together, behind.

That was Ungo.

I'd gone seeking refuge, with the faint hope that I might come across the Cosmodian and ask her to teach me, but I didn't know her name, and she didn't call Ungo home. But I found someone else, however brief his companionship may have been. Even now, nearly four years later, I think of Andru. Even now, I sometimes wish I had let the aerolass band destroy everything so that I might have kept *something*.

Unach notices my bruises the next morning, despite my attempt to hide them with my hair.

"What in the black pits is this?" She grabs my chin like I'm a dog and lifts my head, taking in the dark marks left by Grodd's fingers. "You'd think you'd learn, getting mixed up with those humans!"

I pull from her grasp and rub my neck. "They're friendly to me now, Unach."

Her thick brows furrow. She spins toward Azmar, who winds the cords of his hair behind his head. "Do you know about this?"

Azmar hunches over in a chair, reading something, his dark, twilled hair falling over either shoulder, save for the top half that's been spun into a knot at the back of his head, a pen sticking from it like an over-long thorn. The way the light falls, he's half in shadow. The darker half shades him deep viridian, while the lit half colors him more like young buckthorn. His eyes glint like sunlit sandstone, and when he glances toward me, I can't read his smooth expression. His words from last night flash through my mind. *If you set her down and walk away, I won't report you.* And Azmar is a man of his word.

He doesn't lie, he simply doesn't answer, stands, and walks into the narrow kitchen.

But I didn't make such a promise, and I have no desire to protect Grodd or to keep more secrets than necessary. "It was Grodd."

Unach whirls back to me. "*Grodd?* That piss-licking son of a whore! He'll see his head on the chopping block—"

"It isn't illegal to harm a human," Azmar says coolly. The words sting more than they should, deep in the center of my chest, though I know he's merely stating facts. He didn't write trollis law.

"Grodd forgets he is *Pleb*." Unach names the caste like it's tar on her tongue. The muscles in her neck bulge between her tight shoulders. She grabs her sword and hooks its sheath onto her belt with more force than necessary, then takes up her club. "Seems he needs a reminder." She starts for the door.

"Keep it private," Azmar warns. "Lark doesn't need more attention."

Unach hesitates only a second before exiting the apartment and slamming the door behind her.

I roll my lips together. Tie back my hair, since it failed to cover me. "Grodd may be a Pleb, but he was a Montra before. He could hurt her."

Azmar steps out of the kitchen, mixing his morning brew in a large tin cup. "Grodd knows the laws. If he raises his hands against someone of a higher caste, especially *five ranks* higher, he'll risk execution, especially given his current ill favor. If he's smart, he'll take the beating and move on. If he's not, we won't have to worry about him anymore."

We. My chest warms at the word. I think of the night before in the waterworks, crying against Azmar's chest, feeling *safe* for the first time—

I turn back to the fire before he can see me flush. I envy the trollis, the colors of their skin and blood. It lets them hide so much. Then again, perhaps Azmar isn't familiar enough with humans to understand the flushing and blanching of our faces.

He isn't human, I remind myself, crushing embers in the ash.

When the fire peters out, I pick up the iron pot and take it to the back room to soak. When I return, Azmar says, "Do you want to come to the bridge today?"

My heart skips. "Above the city?"

Folding his arms, he leans his weight onto one leg. "A team of engineers is conducting a routine survey today. It will take a while, but you appear to enjoy the sunlight."

I glance to the small window in the hallway and find myself grinning. "Absolutely. If I won't be a bother."

"Not at all." He sets his empty cup on the table. "Find something for your midday meal and we'll go."

Excitement bubbles within me, but I try to stay calm as I scramble to wrap something up for both myself and Azmar. He smiles at my enthusiasm, though his smiles always look like he's trying to suppress them. For the most part, he succeeds. When I'm ready, he leads me out into the tunnels. It's nice having a trollis escort, because I don't have to wait for foot traffic to pass. It's nice because it's Azmar, and even if Grodd were to step onto the lift with us, I wouldn't be afraid.

We go up past farming, Intra housing, and the guard barracks. Azmar points out extra braces, struts, and beams below the original bridge, put in place to hold up the city.

"How old is Cagmar?" I ask as we near the surface.

"Old," he replies, waiting at a ladder as another engineer climbs up. "But not as old as Eterellis. The deeper into the canyon you go, the younger it is."

He lets me climb up next. The air warms with every rung, until it grows hot. The crispness of the morning has already been burned away by the relentless sun. I squint as I climb onto the deck, the air above the bridge's stone rippling with the heat. Shielding my face, I look into the distance, to the near nothingness that surrounds the canyon. A few skeletal trees and bushes break up the expanse. To the west, beyond my sight, rests the fallen city of Eterellis. The townships holding what's left of my people lie far to the east.

Azmar's shadow falls across me. I ask, "Where are the other trollis cities?"

"There is one north, in the canyon." He pulls a grease pencil from his belt. "Many days away."

"Does it have a bridge?"

He shakes his head. "It stems from a cavity in the canyon wall. I've never been there, but it's about an eighth the size of Cagmar. The others, I'm not sure."

I gaze up at him. "Not sure?"

He offers a sad tilt of his lips. "Our people were lost before the drought ever scattered yours, Lark. It would be a waste of soldiers to send scouts to find them in this landscape. When it rains again, the council might see it fit to explore."

I consider this, wondering what it would have been like to live back then, in wealth and luxury, banishing trollis left and right until they were never heard of again. I do not know much of the earth's other peoples—the merdan and gullop of the sea and the fette and aerolass of the sky—but I do not think they hate each other as much as humans and trollis do. At least, I hope that's not the case, for when the drought hit, we were unable to help one another through it.

And now both our people are scattered and lost.

Azmar starts down the bridge, toward the east lip of the canyon. I follow behind and accept a sheaf of papers that he hands to me. A few other engineers dot the bridge. One takes notes and sketches something as we pass. I recognize one of the trollis standing near the bridge's end, his thick gray arms crossed over his chest. He was the first trollis I'd ever met, the one who, I think, threw me over his shoulder upon my arrival and dropped me before the council.

Azmar doesn't look up as we pass, but he greets, "Homper."

Homper studies me, equally suspicious and curious. At the last moment, I decide to smile at him, and he looks shocked, as though a wasp has stung him. I note the single bead on his sleeve, like Perg.

I try not to laugh. It's easy to see how the trollis would be feared, but beneath their size, their bony protrusions, their gray and green skin, they are not so unlike us.

Azmar takes a few measurements, leaving me to my thoughts. After stepping off the bridge, I walk the length of the canyon a ways, then return. Azmar hands me a measuring tape and a sketch and asks me to double-check his numbers. I'm happy to do so, enjoying the sun on my shoulders and in my hair. Other trollis in harnesses slide down the sides of the bridge, inspecting its underside. Azmar closely examines the deck, writes numbers, examines it again. Then he reviews parts that were already reviewed by other engineers. There's no room for error. He explains some of the math to me, but it gets complicated, and I struggle to keep up. I don't think he notices.

Soon the sun burns high and hot, and Azmar hands me a rope and swings down beneath one of the girders, shaded from the sun. He helps me down, and I settle next to him. We open our lunches and let our feet hang.

"We'll have to use cables," he says halfway through his meal. "The canyon wall is strong, and the existing connection to it was overdesigned, but we have added so much that we really need additional connections. If the council wants continued expansion with the same protections Cagmar has now, we'll have to use cables."

"You don't sound happy about that." I pick at a piece of flatbread.

"I would prefer a straight steel connection to the canyon wall." He shrugs. "Cables are better than nothing, but they're also easy to besiege."

I consider this. "Is Cagmar at risk of besiegement?"

He glances at me, his eyes warm. "Humans are not the only threat."

I think of the aerolass raiders, of the monsters below.

Azmar finishes his food first. Before he rises, I ask, "Azmar, why are you kind to me?"

I can tell the question takes him off guard, for genuine curiosity limns his usually carefully guarded features. "I don't think I am, particularly. Unach and Perg are also kind to you."

I shake my head, looking down toward the city. "Not in the same way. Unach is . . . reasonable. She sees use where there is use. And Perg . . . Perg is so desperate for belonging, for understanding, that he would be kind to anyone who was first kind to him. But you, Azmar, you've always been kind. A little blunt at times . . ." I remember our first meeting. "But always kind. You've never scowled at me or ignored me the way the others do, even from the beginning. Why is that?"

I peek through loose strands of hair at him. He regards me in a way that makes him look younger. He looks out across the length of the canyon. Enough time passes that I think he won't answer me, and my question will be left hanging. But then he speaks.

"All trollis must enroll in military training for seven years, from ages twelve to nineteen."

I don't see what that has to do with my question, but I remain quiet and listen to the cadence of his voice.

"When I was sixteen, I was in a raiding party that attacked a human township," he continues, his voice low, like he doesn't want to be overheard. I lean closer to hear him. "We were a small band, overconfident, and most of our numbers were youth. I suspect a scout from the township saw us coming, because the humans were prepared for us when we arrived. The battle was brief but intense. One of the men picked up my fallen comrade's sword and ran me through with it."

"The scars," I say before I can think. I pinch my lips closed.

Azmar regards me and nods. "I fell, and the others retreated. I was headed for the eternal black."

I presume that's their name for the afterlife, but I don't ask. Later.

"But I didn't die. I woke up in a house, on a pallet on the floor. Someone, a widow, I believe, had taken me in. I didn't understand it. She took no risks. My arms and legs were securely tethered to the floor, not that I could have moved anyway. My injury was deep, but her husband had been a surgeon and taught her most of what he knew."

Quietly I ask, "She told you this?"

"Yes. She knew I was young. Felt bad for me, being left behind. I couldn't fight her. I could barely move, and half the time I was unconscious from whatever she gave me for the pain. I spent a week and a half there, slowly healing, and I learned that not all humans are savage 'troll' haters. We're taught that your kind ravage the world like roaches and breed like feral rabbits."

My skin warms. "Only partially accurate."

His lip quirks, but somberness quickly overtakes it. "My band returned with reinforcements and completely brutalized that village. They killed her, the woman who took care of me. Aleah, her name was. They didn't ask questions, just came in and killed her and took her supplies. Dragged me out, burned the house."

My hand flies to my mouth. "Oh no."

"In our culture, women and men both train as soldiers. It is not so with yours." He looks to me as if to confirm. Mortified, I nod. "I protested. I tried to fight—she'd taken off my restraints by then. But I was still too weak. And, admittedly, I feared them seeing my weakness. I feared losing my caste." He pauses, looking down into the canyon. "I was happy to take the demotion when I became an engineer. I'd lost my taste for battle."

It takes several heartbeats for me to digest all of this. "You were Montra."

"Both my parents were, so it passed down to me. But, Lark—" He shifts toward me, and in that moment he is more human to me than ever before. "I learned much of your kind during my stay in that house. I took many truths for myself, which I've kept close to my heart. Even Unach doesn't know that story. She just thinks I am hard to kill."

I search his face, feeling both comforted and anxious at the same time. "Then why trust it to me?"

That soft, barely there smile resurfaces. "Because you asked. Come." He stands and holds out a hand. I take it, and it's barely any effort on his part to lift me to my feet. "We've work to do, and Unach will find it funny if you return red."

I touch my shoulders, which indeed have begun to pink with the heat of the sun. My time in Cagmar has stripped the protective tan that had built up day after day, year after year in the sun. Azmar lifts me back to the bridge, and I unbind my hair for some protection.

We get back to work, taking measurements, surveying rust, sketching damage, but all of it feels different now. Azmar moves, and in my mind's eye I see the silvery scars beneath his shirt, a permanent reminder of a kind soul lost. I wonder if I somehow also serve as a reminder of the human who'd taken him in, and whether or not he wants to be reminded.

For now, it appears Azmar does not mind my company, and I certainly want to stay in his.

Chapter 13

My usefulness soon runs dry, but I'm loath to return to the city if I don't have to. I don't know when I'll get another chance to be outside. It's odd; when I ran between townships, all I wanted was a roof over my head. Now that I'm settling into Cagmar, all I want is the open sky.

In time, I'll be trusted enough to come up here on my own. Perhaps after this whole thing with Grodd passes, though I'm not sure how long that will be. I certainly won't be attending any caste tournaments in the meantime.

I consider introducing myself to Tartuk, the new trollis head of the human task force, and seeing if she'll befriend me.

As the sun makes its slow way to the western horizon, Azmar compares charts with others. I watch them, trying to understand their conversation, but I soon find my attention drawn to the canyon, wondering if any strange beast or monster will climb out of it, trying to see beyond its shadows to the river deep below. I can't, even shielding the sunlight from my face. I search the other direction and think I see a glint of something where the canyon widens before it turns, but it could be a climbing bud or embedded stone. But I imagine it's the river, that the canyon is clear and monster-free, and that I am in some long canoe, rafting down it, beyond the other trollis city and far from this land, to where the drought doesn't reach. Where a city greater than Eterellis awaits on the other side of the world, and perhaps there, humans and trollis get along splendidly.

I snap from the daydream and catch movement not far down the canyon, on the east side, a shifting of shadows. Thinking it rare game, I stand on the parapet and peer outward, the sun glowing at my back. The shadows scatter and head away from the bridge, and in their scramble I see defined human arms, legs, and heads.

Azmar must have noticed, for he says, "Lark?"

I bite the inside of my lip, wondering what I should say. These trollis are engineers, though military trained . . . Would they harm these folk?

Did these shadows mean to harm the trollis, before I spotted them? What other reason would they have to hide?

"Humans," I murmur, pointing. "There's a band of them, there. They ran when I stood."

Alarm crosses the faces of the engineers, and nearby, Homper springs to attention, pulling a club the length of my leg from his back. Several of the engineers drop their tools and notes. Even Azmar looks worried.

One engineer, named Dart, says, "Southwind formation, split three." Then, to Homper, "Alert a rear guard."

Dart is not one of Homper's colleagues, but his caste is higher, so Homper immediately turns for the city and starts yelling to the guard barracks.

I jump from the parapet, heart thumping, worried I've just sent my own kind to their deaths. "Azmar?"

"They'll be captured and questioned, if we can catch up," Azmar says, low and quick, as half the engineers, armed with Homper's weapons, rush in the direction the shadows went. "Hopefully they surrender and no blood will be shed."

I clutch my hands to my chest. "But they haven't done anything."

Azmar looks at me with a sadness that presses like a yoke. "You and the refugees are anomalies. Humans don't come to Cagmar. If they sought refuge, they would approach openly."

I press my lips together. Most likely this troop was a band of spies. Possibly raiders too eager to wait for nightfall to approach. Part of me wishes I had not seen them.

Homper returns to the top of the bridge. Softly, Azmar asks, "Lark, do you stay or come?"

Cold energy pulses through my body. Stay in the safety of Cagmar, or run with the trollis? It might help to have a human with the party. An ambassador, of sorts.

"I'm coming."

Azmar turns to Homper and nods, and the three of us take off after the first party. The bridge guards will follow our trail. The humans have the advantage—they were terribly close when they fled—but there is little cover to be had in this dry expanse, and dust clouds from their feet mark their path.

My legs crave the race and keep up decently well, though Azmar and Homper sprint faster. Skeletal brush scrapes at my legs as we push forward, Azmar in the lead, then Homper, then myself. I follow Homper's path, and his thick, armored shins break the brush for me. My lungs have begun to burn when Azmar slows, then juts suddenly to the south.

"They split!" he calls over his shoulder, concern edging his voice.

I pull up to Homper's side. "What's wrong?"

Homper growls. "They know evasive tactics," he says. Which confirms that these men are no refugees, but trained to lose pursuers.

A shiver slips up my arms. They are not my father's men, are they? Surely he wouldn't come to Cagmar to find me. Surely he would never believe he could break me out of the city.

Breathe, I tell myself. *Azmar is here.* I'll be safe.

The land drops and rolls. We cross a broken bridge, a dried stream bed, a cemetery of dead trees that might have once been part of a forest. Their roots and branches make the chase more difficult, and I suck in great mouthfuls of air to keep my sides from stitching. I spot movement ahead; we've caught up, but the human band—or half of it—still has a good lead.

Azmar lets Homper take the advance and falls back to me. Between huffs, he says, "Can you do anything to help? Slow them down?"

The request rankles down my skin like sunburn. I look away. "I can only make them run faster."

It's the closest I've ever come to confirming anything special about me, but Azmar accepts what I say and continues running, pulling me to one side when the ground takes a sudden dip. I'd been so focused on him I don't think I would have noticed it, and my ankle would have snapped had I fallen.

But there's no time for gratitude. These humans are practiced runners with impressive endurance. Homper pulls a sling from his belt and swoops down to grab a stone as we pursue. He sends it flying overhead and misses, but his second attempt hits true. One of the humans drops. It takes a beat for the others to notice. One turns back, then another. The group splits, and we gain.

One of the runners pulls the fallen human to his feet. He wavers, then stumbles. Two of his companions rush to help. I count six humans in total.

We approach them, and when two of the six see us, they bolt after the group.

"Halt!" Homper bellows. "You will be taken for trespassing!"

The humans don't respond with words. One pulls out an axe, another a dagger. Their glares flash to me.

I slow as I near them and put up my hands. "Please!" I wheeze. "We just have questions! Don't fight or—"

The axe man shouts and runs at Azmar.

"Stop!" I scream. Azmar is unarmed save for a knife at his belt, which he doesn't draw. He feints and grabs the axe man's forearm, stopping the deadly blade. Behind him, one of the unarmed men puts the injured man's arm over his neck and starts pulling him away from the fight.

Homper engages the man with the dagger. I cry, "Don't hurt him!" just before an arm comes around my neck and hauls me back. Stars flash in my vision as the bruises I received from Grodd dance with pain. My frantic pulse beats between my thoughts. The two humans who just ran? Did the party split into three? Did they manage to hide among the dead trees?

Three humans, all men, rush out from behind me and charge, two for Azmar and one for Homper. Knives glimmer in their hands. I distantly think about what Unach said, that humans' strength comes in their numbers.

I fight against the restraint. The man behind me says, "Let us free you!"

I throw my head back and feel it connect with his nose. He releases me, and I bolt forward, only to have his foot catch mine. My knees scrape on the hard, dry earth.

Azmar throws off the axe man and barely misses a jab from one of the knives.

"Let me go!" I grapple with the man, roll over, and kick him in the chest. He's about forty, with dust clinging to every line in his face and seam in his clothing.

He growls at me. "Traitor!" he shouts.

I twist from his grip and scramble to my feet, then feel a hot pain stab down my thigh.

A knife. He had a knife.

The blood seeping through my ruined skirt rims my vision with fire. I am human. I am trying to stop the fighting. I am trying to *help*.

I whirl around and punch him with the side of my fist. When he stumbles back, I strike with fear. He drops his knife as though I punched him in the gut, but doesn't otherwise move.

I do. Fueled with the backlash of the terror I just dealt, I run, limping, toward Azmar. I focus on the two men fighting him—one lies on the ground—and push out my fear.

Qequan only said I couldn't use it against the trollis.

I've never done it this way before. I've always been able to see their faces. See their eyes sparkle and skin pale when the terror touches them. But the fear still takes. One backs away, shuddering as though Azmar has grown twice in size. The other attacks with renewed vigor, fighting over fleeing.

His knife tip nicks Azmar's arm. Azmar snatches him by the elbow, and a sickening *crunch* nearly makes my stomach empty itself as the arm breaks. The man shouts and runs. Azmar lets him.

The man who held me dashes away, back through the trees. Homper races north, after the other two humans, a shrinking gray dot on the amber landscape as the sun sets against him.

I limp to the fallen man first, not the one quaking in terror. He still has a pulse. The cowering man, who covers his head as though fire were raining from the sky, is barely a man at all. I think he must be fifteen, sixteen at most.

Azmar and I exchange a look. He tips his head toward the adolescent.

I approach the boy, hiding a grimace as the skin on my thigh pulls when I kneel beside him. "It's okay, we won't hurt you." If only I could pull the fear back in the same way I dole it out. But I can't. I've tried before.

He lifts his head, his face dirty and streaked with sweat. "Then why did you attack?"

I frown. "You attacked us."

"Y-You chased."

"You trespassed."

His eyes, a bright blue, shift from me to Azmar. He swallows. "Why do you help them?" he whispers. "We could free you."

"I'm not a slave." I say it as compassionately as I can. My thigh stings, my hair sticks to my neck, my legs ache from the run. "We just want to know who you are. Why you were spying on us."

"We weren't . . ." But he doesn't finish the sentence. Glances uneasily to Azmar.

I cut the air with my hand. "Oh, he's hardly terrifying."

Azmar lifts an eyebrow, curious, if not surprised, at the statement. The boy looks unsure.

"My name is Lark," I try. "What's your name? And his?" I gesture to the unconscious man. He's starting to stir. Azmar notices and moves to stand guard.

The boy watches Azmar's every move. "T-Tayler," he says, low, so only I'll hear him. "That's my cousin."

"I think your cousin will be okay." I look up in the direction Homper went. I don't see him, and I don't see the injured human and his companion. I hope they're safe. "Just tell me, please. We'll let you go if you tell us."

I give Azmar a look. If he's uncomfortable, he doesn't speak against the idea.

Tayler hesitates. "We're just . . . We're just low on supplies. Mountain runoff dried up. Knew about the troll city. Were only watching to see where they got their food from. Nothing says only trolls can harvest the land around the bridge."

"You wanted their resources."

"Weren't going to take it from *them*." He shoots a scathing look to Azmar. "Just . . . Just see where it came from. How their lures work, or if there was a river . . . I don't know. My pa had me come. We're not thieves."

I rest a hand on his shoulder. "I didn't say you were."

He relaxes a fraction. "You'll let me go?"

Azmar says, "That's all you wanted?" He sounds skeptical.

The tension surges up in Tayler's frame. "I'm not a thief. I'm not a liar." He turns to me and, almost pleading, says, "I mean it. We've come a really long way. We weren't going to hurt no one. This was just self-defense!" He looks around, either for injured friends or for a way out, I'm not sure. I silently urge him not to run, for Azmar might not be gentle if he tries. "Should have brought Baten. You'd listen to him."

He says the last bit to Azmar. "But they said it wasn't a good idea, even though he's faster than all of us."

Tayler's companion groans and rolls over.

"Baten?" I ask.

Tayler chews on the inside of his cheek. "He's one of them." He tips his head toward Azmar. "Half, anyway."

Just like Perg. I lean back, then wince when it pulls at my injury. "You have a half trollis in your camp?"

Tayler glowers, skeptical. "Why not? Their kind won't take care of them."

Azmar looks equally stunned, though I try to keep my focus on Tayler. "We . . . There's a half trollis in Cagmar as well. He's a friend of mine. His name is Perg."

Tayler eyes me, but I think he believes me. And then I'm aware of Azmar standing near me, the sun casting his shadow long across the ground. His kindness to me. His arms around me in the waterworks.

I swallow, hard. "Your township accepts him?"

Tayler shrugs. "He's been there since he was a baby. He's older than I am."

"Where is your township?"

Tayler's face closes off instantly at my thoughtless question. Of course he won't tell me where he lives, not with Azmar right there. Wherever it is, it's far enough away not to be on my father's maps.

I look around, licking my dry lips. The monotonous land has little in the way of notable formations or vegetation, save for the copse of spindly trees. Then I realize something.

There's a township I haven't been to. Another place of refuge.

The Cosmodian, the only person to instill hope in my fearful heart, might live there.

I want to know. I want to know so desperately that a chirp escapes my lips. At the very least, to be able to *thank* her . . . and if given the chance, I want so badly to learn from her. To learn more about myself and the workings of the gods and their messages in the stars. To understand my place in the universe and, one day, to brighten the future of someone else, the way the Cosmodian did for me.

It feels too forward to ask outright. I think for a few beats, then pull close to Tayler. His eyes widen, but I seek only to reach his ear. "The flowers that grow in the canyon's shade are edible. They can be replanted." I think of my schedule. "The day after tomorrow, if you can, would you meet me here? If your camp isn't moving too far. I want to know more. I know you can't trust me now, but I want to know."

I pull back. Tayler studies me. I can feel the weight of Azmar's stare as well, but I don't meet it. Tayler mumbles, "Give me four days. Evening."

Relief puffs up like the smoke of a newly lit pipe.

I stand, faulty on my injured leg, and say, "Let them go, before Homper gets back." I turn to Azmar. "Please."

His mouth sets into a line—I imagine this goes against his training—but he nods.

Tayler moves like a snake, bolting toward his cousin, who blinks, confused. Tayler hauls him to his feet. The cousin sees Azmar and reaches for his belt, but his weapon is gone. Tayler mutters something to him and drags him north. I watch them go. After about thirty feet, they both take off at a run.

Azmar steps closer to me, watching them like a hawk. "You believe him?"

"I do. I don't think he'd have a reason to lie to me."

Azmar's gaze penetrates, as though he's trying to unravel me, seeking my sincerity. Or perhaps he senses I performed as I did with Grodd at the caste tournament, and the humans were not simply afraid of him—though not long ago, I would have feared Azmar myself. I meet the gaze head on. Azmar looks away first.

A sizable stone protrudes from the ground nearby. He gestures to it. "Sit."

"Why—"

"Your leg."

I glance down. Blood shows starkly against the light beige of my skirt. It's not a bad wound—the knife didn't reach the muscle—and it's on my outer thigh, away from the spot where a blade could have ended my life. Azmar takes me by the arm and helps me sit. Then he grabs my skirt and tears a long piece off the bottom.

"Hey!" I protest.

He doesn't look up from his work. "We'll mend it."

I bite my lip as he tears another piece. "Thank you," I murmur. He puts a warm hand behind my knee and lifts it to bend my leg at an angle. His hands are very human, save for their color. He hesitates for a second before pushing the skirt up to see my wound, which starts about six inches below my hip.

My face heats, and I dare not speak. Azmar takes a canteen from his belt and cleans the cut, and I'm grateful he can't see my face scrunch when he does. I know how trollis feel about strength and weakness, though Azmar is not like most trollis. I'm silent as he works, but I can't help but notice . . . his usually fluid hands move artlessly. His cloddish touch sends prickles of heat through my skin, and yet it's as though he's trying not to touch me. Certainly not the way a soldier trained in field wounds would touch a patient.

I've never seen Azmar so . . . awkward. And my silly, spinning mind can't help but speculate as to why. I wonder what his hands would feel like running down my leg, touching the skin just to touch it, and I look away, berating myself. *He is trollis.*

But there is Perg. And there is Baten. And there is apparently no limit to how foolish a woman like me can be.

Azmar finishes his work and pulls my skirt back down. I meet his gaze again, and yet this time it's different. I feel clumsy without moving and hot despite the half-set sun. And Azmar . . . Damn him, I can't read him, but there's something so stiff in his expression, like he doesn't *want* me to read him.

And maybe it's better that I don't.

He stands and offers me a hand. I take it, the bandage on my leg pulling tight. I waver, and Azmar doesn't release me until I'm steady. In the distance, I think I see Homper returning, thankfully empty-handed.

Clearing my throat, I search for something to say. "You're always so serious, Azmar."

Stepping back, he folds his arms. Considers. "Cagmar offers little opportunity for merriment."

That much is true.

The air cools, and I rub my arms when the skin starts to pebble, though I'm eager to see the stars again. "Do you think the others got away?"

"I don't know."

Homper gets closer and closer. He looks mad. Good. As for the rest of the human band . . . I'll have to find out after we return.

"I hope they did," Azmar says. "Get away."

I offer a small smile.

Azmar turns back for Cagmar. "Let's go." He puts a hand against the top of my back to guide me toward the Empyrean Bridge. "We don't have to wait for him." He drops his hand.

I can still walk, though my thigh smarts with every other step.

Azmar notices. "Do you need me to carry you?"

"No, thank you. Though I admit I'm growing tired of being injured all the time."

"You're a fragile human in a trollis city."

"I'm not fragile."

We walk for several steps. "No, you're not," he says.

The comment pleases me. We walk slowly, for my sake. Homper catches up with us and looks to Azmar, who shrugs, the easiest way to say that the humans got away without explaining how. And he doesn't have to explain, thanks to his caste. Homper grumbles something foul and stomps past us.

"The stars will be out soon," I say.

Azmar glances up. "I haven't seen them in a while."

"At this pace, we both will. Would you . . . Could I have a piece of paper? To map them?"

He eyes me for a beat. "Yes."

I'm so pleased that I fail to watch where I'm going and trip on a root. Azmar grasps my upper arm to keep me upright. I want to lean into him, and not just to help me walk, but I don't, and he releases me.

We're just past the dead trees when he says, "Why doesn't the sun shine in Cagmar?"

I glance at him, confused at the question. "I don't know. Why?"

His lip twinges ever so slightly. "Because it's already full of beams."

It's a terrible joke that makes me gawk. It's out of character and it's awkward, but I love it anyway.

Or maybe I just love that Azmar wanted to show me that he isn't always so serious.

Chapter 14

Night falls sleepily as we approach the Empyrean Bridge. I stare up at the wide expanse of sky. It feels like looking at a childhood portrait—nostalgic and *mine*. I trace the hundreds of budding stars, seeking out the South Star first and offering it a silent thanks. I search for the queen and the oak, but neither has risen above the horizon yet. After pulling my gaze away, I spy Homper's shadow far ahead. I would not have seen it if it hadn't been against the whiteness of the bridge itself, which leads me to wonder how well trollis see in the dark.

Azmar walks about five feet to my right, ensuring I don't get lost while in a world of my own. I smile at him, but it might be too dark for him to see.

When dust gives way to wood under my feet, I hesitate, again peering up at the night sky. Moments later something brushes my arm. I think it must be moth wings at first, but it's a curled half sheet of paper.

"Thank you, Azmar," I whisper, accepting it and a charcoal pencil. I draw a circle on the paper and section it into four equal parts, marking the axis with the South Star. I utilize a lot of guesswork as I try to make my chart look like the almanac. All the while, Azmar waits patiently, a presence as still and calm as the barren trees. He is marked by Ura, through and through.

"Why do you copy them down?" Azmar asks as I work.

I place a careful dot on the paper. "To learn."

He hesitates. "Their movements?"

"That's part of it." Another delicate dot marks the tip of the constellation Ceris, the mother. The rest of her hides behind the horizon. "We're all part of the cosmos, and understanding the cosmos can help us understand ourselves. Or, I like to think so."

Finished, I hand back the pencil and stare upward. Take a deep breath, hold it, release. "When I look at the stars, at the universe, I realize how very small I am. And how very small others are. Small people, small problems, and none of it really matters in the great vastness of it all. Somehow, that makes me feel better. Somehow it encourages me to be . . . bigger."

Azmar considers me silently. I only ever shared that idea once before, with Andru. Thought of him pings sharp in my chest. He had the opposite view. The universe made him feel small, too, but instead of being encouraging, it instilled in him a sense of worthlessness.

I'm hesitant to turn in, though Homper has already vanished into the city. Today has been a good day. Yes, I have a new wound to nurse, and yes, we were attacked . . . but the rest of it was good. The stars make for a happy end to it all.

I point to a cluster of them peeking just over the horizon. "Territopus." Azmar follows the line of my arm. When he doesn't respond, I add, "It starts with those two stars close together, then goes up to that bluish one, and down. It's a scorpion. Its tail points to Mirras." The fourth planet, the snake. One of the few that I've been able to find with unaided eyes. It looks like a tiny star with a faint red halo.

A soft hum radiates from Azmar's lips. "Ours adds on a cone." He indicates several stars above. "The warrior. He's holding a club."

It takes me a second. "Oh! It does look like that. More than a scorpion." I scan the sky. "I never realized there might be different interpretations of the stars." The very idea sends an excited chill through my skeleton. I point again. "That one is Swoop, the spoon."

He finds the six-star constellation. "Here, it's Makog, the spider."

"It looks nothing like a spider."

He shrugs. "I did not name it. But above is the web."

The dozens of stars above the constellation cluster so closely it's nearly impossible to draw lines between them. I can see it as a web, a great, tunneling web full of prey. A spider, just like me. Just like Unach. "A spider that eats stars."

We point out a few more, some completely different, others similar, and I repeat each trollis interpretation in my mind so as not to forget. We have one constellation with the same name, a set of twelve stars simply named "the arrow." It points north.

"I use that one the most." I lean against the bridge, the wood still warm from the sun. "That, and the South Star. I never got lost if I could see the stars." I always made sure I knew how far and in what direction the next township was, just in case. And I always ended up needing the information, until I ran out of townships and the old bard's song was the only hope I had left.

"Lark," Azmar's voice rumbles, nearly as quiet as the night itself, "why did you come here?"

I keep my gaze on the arrow, the bright star at its tip. "Because I'm different. And my people fear difference."

I feel his gaze on me like the fur blanket he draped over my sleeping form so many times. "Are you so terrifying?"

A few heartbeats pass. "I can be."

I feel I should be more forthcoming, as he was with me earlier, but I can't bring myself to confess my secrets. In truth, I worry Azmar will look at me the way Andru did after the attack from the aerolass, and I don't think I could bear it.

"Are you afraid here?" His voice sounds closer. Close enough to touch him, if I reached out. The tips of my fingers would graze his chest. Caress the silvery scar beneath his clothes.

I don't try, of course, even in the safety of the dark, and the privacy of the night. I'm too afraid, though that isn't the fear Azmar meant.

"Fear is an interesting thing." I match his hushed pitch, search for his shadowed eyes. "It isn't instinctual; it's learned. Learned for self-preservation. It can cripple the strongest of men, and yet it can strengthen the weakest of them, too. It's both debilitating and invigorating. It's a curse we all have in common—human, trollis, aerolass—and when handled in the right way, it can be almost . . . comforting. So yes, I'm afraid. I'm always afraid. But I don't think I would have made it this far if I weren't."

He's quiet for several breaths. "You are an anomaly, Lark."

I warm. "So you said."

"No, not like the rest." His voice is sober, direct, yet soft. "You're very different than anything else in Cagmar."

His words burn in my chest. I want them to be complimentary and fear they're not, but I don't ask for an explanation. I don't ask or say anything, and neither does he. Our silence is comfortable, comforting, alone with the stars and the endless sky, like we're the only two beings beneath it.

It's late when we finally climb back into the city. So late that Unach has already retired to bed. I check on her before making my way down to my own room. Quiet, so she doesn't know. Unach isn't someone who likes to have tabs kept on her.

But Azmar is my only witness, and he won't tell a soul.

The good news is that the other humans got away. Dart's team returned empty-handed. Whether they were outpaced or the human band knew of tunnels or such to get away, I don't know. I wasn't told.

The unfortunate news is that the next morning, while I'm collecting water and prepping a meal, I am utterly clumsy in Unach and Azmar's apartment, and not because of the injury to my thigh.

For whatever reason, I am aware of Azmar's every movement, his every breath, his every gaze. And not simply because I served him breakfast. And not simply because he thanked me.

It's because I am a fool woman who can't keep her head straight to save her own life.

What's worse, I feel that Unach senses my awkwardness, my looking but not looking, and yet at the same time, I'm sure it's all in my head. My senseless thoughts tumble over each other again and again, and all I want to do is haul the water down to my own apartment and run to my shift at the south dock. Monsters would be easier to face right now.

Unach picks at her nails, frowns, and says, "Would you get the rest of that hot water in the basin?"

For a bath, she means. I oblige, eager to be out of the main room where they're eating. I feel like I'm being watched, but I don't dare turn around to see if I am. I carry the iron pot from the fire to the little back room and fill the basin there, then carry in cold water from the pump until it's half-full. When I return, Azmar glances up from his reading, and I think of the bath, of him half-dressed, and how human and trollis physiques really aren't very different, and how his is rather spectacular.

I grab my pitcher and leave without excusing myself, closing the door behind me, harder than I should.

Perg can sit up now. The swelling in his face has gone down, though he's still in the infirmary until he has the strength to walk unaided. He cups a bowl of carrot soup in his hand and happily brings an oversized spoon to his lips.

"I'm going mad," he admits. "I'm so bored, Lark. I'd rather be a slave than an invalid. At least I'd be doing something. At least I wouldn't be . . . *weak*."

I look up from studying the book Wiln gave me. "You're not weak."

He sighs.

I turn a page. I don't want to be seen with the book, in case someone recognizes it as something I'm not meant to have, but I thought it might be handy with Perg. "Do the trollis keep slaves?"

"Not anymore. Used to." Perg taps his leg, thinking. "There's a few books, but I can't read any of them."

That startles me. "You can't read? But the school—"

"Education is based on caste. And I am what I am." He takes another sip of soup.

I slouch. "Then to use education to advance in your caste—"

"You have to have access to it already." He shrugs.

Chewing on my lip, I look over the open page of the astronomy book, then hold it up for Perg to see. "Merces—your planet—is moving into the northern sky."

Perg glances at it. "That map looks a century old."

"I thought you couldn't read."

"I can read numbers." He gestures to the date in the corner.

Withdrawing, I say, "North is good. Think of it as being . . . on top of things." That is, at least, my understanding of it. If only I had a teacher to help me unlock the skies! "I think it means you'll have success soon."

Perg snorts. "Does any of this look successful to you?" He gestures at his bandaged body. Winces.

Distantly, a horn bellows.

My spine stiffens, and I sit upright on the stool beside Perg's bed. I finished my shift at the south dock two hours ago. It was uneventful.

Perg lowers the bowl. "Don't worry. Last time was a fluke. They usually don't attack the city directly, and they never breach it. Could be just a sighting, even."

I frown at him. I know how the horn works. "If the horn blows, they're close." The others will attempt to scare the monsters off, but still, I listen for the horn to blow again. If it does, I'll have to leave for the dock.

Perg shrugs. "Usually it's the new hatchlings you have to worry about. They haven't learned."

I think about Unach, who's on shift now, and say a small prayer of protection on her behalf. What would happen, were she to die in the line of duty? Certainly she'd be honored in her passing. As for me . . . I suppose I would keep trekking on as I was. Unach was only required to see me fitted to the position. She doesn't *need* me. Neither does Azmar.

"Perg," I speak carefully, "do you know . . . did your parents love each other, at all?"

A dribble of soup spills from Perg's lips. He wipes it with the heel of his hand. "Are you serious?"

I swallow and move my hair over one shoulder to keep my neck cool. "Did they?"

His thick brows draw together, like he's trying to discern what sick joke I'm playing on him, but the expression gradually relaxes. "I don't think so. I mean . . . ugh, maybe they found each other attractive? Ugh, Lark, I don't think about this stuff. I don't know."

"They're not around anymore?"

"No. My father escaped to the settlements, and my mother jumped into the canyon when I was little."

My mouth dries. "I-I'm so sorry—"

He stirs the spoon around. "It's fine, Lark. I don't remember them. It's just what I'm told. Might not even be true."

My stomach twists. Still, I push a little more. "Have you . . . ever met another like you?"

He swallows a spoonful of soup. "No."

"What if you could?"

He glances sidelong at me. "What are you getting at?"

I rub my hands together above my lap. Lower my voice. "Did you hear about the band of humans caught trespassing near Cagmar yesterday?"

His features slacken. He shakes his head.

"I talked to one. Just a little, before he escaped." I trust Perg to keep my secrets, but I also want to tread carefully. "He mentioned someone named Baten from his township. A half trollis."

Perg snorts. "Yeah, right."

I touch his wrist, stopping the spoon over the nearly empty bowl. "I mean it, Perg. I believe him."

Perg looks down to the soup. He sets the bowl and spoon on the small table beside him, wipes a hand down his face, and winces. "I don't know, Lark. I don't know why humans would keep any trollis around, even a half one."

"I would. And I'm not special, Perg. I'm not the only decent human being in the world. A lot of us are sane, caring people." The cruel ones merely scream the loudest.

He frowns. "So what, some trollis soldier got weird on an excursion and raped one of you, and the rest felt bad, so they kept the infant?"

I blanch. I had never considered a malignant conception. I had hoped . . .

It doesn't really matter what I hope. What I feel, or was starting to feel. And yet I ache to meet with Tayler, to ask him about the Cosmodian . . . and Baten, his origin, how he was treated by the others. I have a deep, sick desire to know. I'd thought the humans in Cagmar my last chance at a family, but if there are others . . .

And perhaps, Tayler might justify the strange tilting of my heart.

I think of Azmar, the hooded way he looked at me, his hands on my leg. Were he human . . . the expression and behavior was not so different from that of Andru, my former fiancé. But Azmar isn't human, and I have not lived in Cagmar long enough to understand the countenances, emotions, and behaviors of trollis. At least, that's what I keep telling myself.

"I don't know Baten's story," I admit to Perg.

He leans back into his pillows. Standing, I help adjust them. "Who knows, Lark. Probably just a distraction anyway." He sighs. "I'm going to sleep."

I lean over him and take the bowl, then rinse it in the small sink on the other side of the room. When I'm done, I murmur, "I don't mind teaching you."

He snorts. "Monster slaughter?"

I click my tongue. "Reading."

He shrugs. "Maybe. With luck, I won't need it."

With that dismissal, I slip out into the stony corridor. The monster horn doesn't sound again. Perg must have been right about the sighting. I hug the right wall so two Nethens can pass by me, and as they do, I hear a sharp word pass from the lips of the closest.

"*Witch.*"

I stop. Turn around, cold from the stonework seeping into my joints. The trollis looks back at me, briefly, eyes hard as iron.

Witch.

My heart pounds against my ribs. Did I hear wrong? That name has been flung at me so many times over the years I'm sure I didn't. Ritha had said the trollis don't believe in witchcraft. So why . . . ?

Hugging myself against the chill, I walk briskly back to the market. I step aside for several more trollis, who pass me silently. I'm too stuck in my own head. I should find something to do. Unach always has something that needs doing.

I've just barely stepped into the market when I hear my name, almost as hushed and sharp as the Nethens's voice had been. Turning, I spy Ritha, over where the massive walls of the cavern meet their joists in the shadows. I hurry to her.

Then I see the bruise. It's large and purple and covers a quarter of her face, starting from the jaw and crawling toward her eye.

"Ritha!" I reach forward, but she pulls away. "What happened?"

Ritha shakes her head. "I was hoping to talk to you, but not here. Do you have private quarters now?"

I nod. "But tell me what happened."

She presses her mouth into a hard line, then sighs through her nose. "I had a run-in with Grodd."

His name shoots ice through my center. Azmar said, *It isn't illegal to harm a human.*

Because even a Pleb is greater than we are.

Ritha gives me a long, piercing look. "I learned a long time ago not to interfere with troll politics. Something you should remember, too. But I do want to speak with you."

"Now?" I try.

She shakes her head. "After sundown."

I tell her how to get to my tiny chamber.

She turns, but hesitates. "Be careful, Lark. Grodd may have fallen in the tournament, and in his caste, but he still has allies. I've heard rumors."

I swallow. "That I'm a witch?"

She frowns, but nods. My sense of safety shatters.

"You're a human," she warns. "Remember your place here, beneath the feet of even the lowliest troll. Do not forget it."

She glances around, heaves her sack onto her other shoulder, and hurries away, leaving me shivering in the shadows, alone.

After dinner I sew a patch over a pair of beige slacks that I tore while climbing the city. I'm in Unach's apartment, using her thread and my needle. And I'm distracted. Did Grodd strike Ritha out of anger, or did she provoke him? Ritha is so demure . . . I couldn't imagine her so much as crossing a trollis's path. And what does she want to talk to me about that she feared speaking of it in the marketplace?

The fire diminishes, and the sunlight has already gone from the window. I poke myself with the needle.

"You're distracted." Azmar's voice resonates cool and calm. He approaches me—from where I sit on the floor, he seems enormous—and lowers himself into the oversized cushion beside the dying embers. Unach busies herself in the kitchen, violently shucking the scales off a fish.

I pull the thread through my stitch and sigh. "Something one of the other humans said to me today."

Azmar leans forward, resting his elbows on his knees. "Ritha?"

"How did you know?"

He offers a one-sided shrug. "I do remember their names. You interact with her the most."

I know Azmar is different, but I'm again surprised at his impartiality toward my kind. I chew the inside of my lip and push the needle through the fabric again.

"You can trust me, Lark."

"I do." I look up at him. Surprise widens his eyes, just a bit. I smirk at him. "Why would I not?"

He leans back, and the air grows decidedly cooler. "There are many reasons."

Lowering my work, I dare to put a hand on his bare foot. "I do trust you, Azmar."

His gaze shoots to my hand, and remembering myself, I draw my fingers away, curling them into my hand one at a time.

"Ritha didn't *say* much at all. But she had a bruise on her face from where Grodd struck her. In passing, I assume."

Azmar's brows pull together. "I'm sorry."

I shake my head, pinching the needle. "Nothing can be done?"

"No." Regret colors his words. "Not unless he kills her."

And then what is the point of justice? I don't need to say it. It hangs in the air.

I hesitate, but if I cannot tell Azmar, whom would I tell? "A few of the trollis have said unkind things to me. Ritha says Grodd has allies."

Azmar looks away. He's thinking. I take the opportunity to look at him, the line of his jaw, the way his hair coils and falls into thick ropes, currently unbound. The divots of his neck, shaped just like a human's.

"Perhaps you should spend more time here," he suggests.

My needle stills. I look at the small fire, the glimmering coals. For a moment the apartment isn't a hole in the great rock of Cagmar, but a little cabin tucked away on a plain of dust and sagebrush. A safe place to be . . . with family.

"Her hide's thicker than that," Unach chimes in, snapping me from the reverie. "A few foul words never hurt anyone."

It's true—but *that* foul word, *witch*, has always led to suffering. I hear it in all their voices: my father's men, Danner, Andru, even Finnie.

"If you walk with her to her shifts"—Azmar raises his voice—"it might remind people who her allies are."

"I'm no Alpine." Unach comes out of the kitchen, wiping her emerald hands on a dishcloth that's a few threads from falling to pieces. In Cagmar, supplies are sparse, so they're used and worn until nothing remains of them. "But I suppose I could." She frowns. "You require a startling amount of maintenance, Lark."

I tie off the patch. "I'll make up for it." I glance to the window. "What time is it?"

Azmar pulls a clockwork device from his pocket, and I wonder if Wiln made it. "Five to nine."

Standing, I fold the trousers and stick them under my arm. "I've decided to turn in early tonight." I glance tentatively at Unach. "My shift's at eight . . ."

She rolls her eyes. "Remind me in the morning."

I pull my braid over my shoulder and turn back toward Azmar. I meet his gaze a second too long before I say, "Good night," with the voice of a cricket.

"Lark."

I hesitate.

He reaches behind him, pulls a small booklet from a trouser pocket, and hands it to me. The cover is made of the same paper as the rest of it, and it's warm. I wonder if it's extra paper for my star charting, but when I open it, hundreds of circles drawn in colored ink already occupy the pages, with connecting lines and dots representing stars.

I gape. The writing isn't Azmar's, and age has stiffened the pages. He must have retrieved it from a trollis library, another place humans aren't permitted to go. The star charts blur, and I blink away a tear.

"Thank you," I whisper, and clutch the precious gift to my heart, all the way home.

My nerves make time drag, and I soon find myself pacing the narrow strip of floor between the wall and the edge of my cot. I try to time my steps to what I think would be the fast hand of a clock. Judging by the candle, it's about the twenty-second hour when a soft, barely perceptible knock sounds at the door.

I rush to let Ritha in. She's bathed recently and has pulled her hair into a tight, wet bun at the base of her skull. The candlelight glimmers off several gray hairs hiding in the auburn. Her bruise is stark against her cheek.

"Away from the door." She checks it for a lock, but doesn't find one. She shifts toward the candle, the moving shadows making her look ten years older. She glances at the dark, slatted window. Turns to me. "Are you a Thellele?"

My chest seizes at the sound of my surname. My true name. I can't recall the last time I heard it, but the syllables hit me like gut punches. I bump into my little table, and the candlelight flickers.

Ritha says, "I'm guessing I'm right."

I struggle to swallow. "How did you know?"

Letting out a long breath, Ritha sits at the edge of the cot. "Because you look like your mother. Though in truth, you've more of your father in you."

My fingers turn cold, my heart races, but I approach her and kneel at her feet. "Ritha," my voice scratches the name, "did you know my parents?"

"I didn't know your father. Not personally. But your mother, yes."

The stone might as well crumble beneath my feet. My hands twist a fistful of my skirt. "I don't look anything like my mother—"

177

"Your real mother, child."

She looks at me pointedly, maybe expecting another reaction, but she's only confirmed what I already believed. That the mother in my household—she didn't raise me, the nursemaid did—is not my mother. She's too young. I don't look like my siblings. And that mother never liked me. Like she knew there was something wrong with me even before I did.

I lick my lips. "What was her name?"

"Artlina." Ritha's tone is reverent. "I knew her through her sister."

"I have an aunt." My eyes sting.

But Ritha shakes her head. "She died of fever before I ever came here. But your mother. I was supposed to help her escape."

"Escape?" Gooseflesh sprouts on my arms.

"From your father. She was a servant in his household. Not as pretty as you, my dear, but a woman's body has always been a temptation for villains like Ottius Thellele."

My ears ring at the sound of my father's name.

"She was with child and hid it a long time, not sure what he would do when he found out," Ritha says.

My thoughts verge on the horrors of how my father would react to such a situation. To having control taken from him, or leverage used against him. It's a dark, bubbling pit, and I stand at the brink of it, but Ritha's story pulls me back.

"I knew my cousin would take her in," she continues. "She was a widow of ten years and lonely. We had the story all worked out, how Artlina was a distant niece, and the drought ate up her farm and took her husband. All we had to do was get her away before Ottius learned the truth."

I'm trembling, and I grip the cot with one hand to steady myself. "He did," I guess. My father is not one to be duped.

Ritha nods.

"Tell me," I press.

She rubs the cuticle on her thumb. "Guessing from how I found her—"

I wince.

"—she took the path we had planned for her, off the main road. She was dead and bloody, but I didn't see any stab wounds. And her womb was empty."

The fire eating up the candlewick feels like winter.

"I don't know if he killed her or if she fell by the way in the pains of labor and passed giving life to you. But she was there and you were not. And you're the right age, the right look. I knew it from the moment I first saw you."

I blink back tears. My body shivers, but my face boils, and I press chilled fingers against my cheeks. I can't help but see it, a woman round with pregnancy, fleeing through the hills, ravaged by pains she can't control. Falling by the way . . . or did my father push her?

How is it that in a single instance, I've both found and lost my mother?

"I told you trolls don't believe in witchcraft." Ritha leans close to me. "But I do. And while I don't think you're a witch, I do think you're shifted."

I search her face for meaning. "Shifted?"

She knits and reknits her hands. "It's so rare, especially with our people scattered as they are. I've only seen it one other time, years ago, before you were born. And only heard about it once besides that."

I want to both tear the words from her mouth and clamp my hands over my ears.

"There is something different about you, isn't there, Lark?"

I don't answer.

"Colson babbled about it after that night." She's barely audible. "And for the council to assign you to such a task . . . and the caste tournament. Others may dismiss it, but I know better. I understand fear, Lark."

I stop breathing.

"I think . . . ," Ritha says carefully, "that Artlina was terrified in her last moments. As scared as a person can be. And you were born in that fear. You drunk it in and came to life through it. And it lives with you now."

Abruptly I'm on my feet, a swirl of dizziness beneath my skull. My erratic heartbeat consumes me.

"I was there," Ritha says. "At the tournament."

I shake my head. I hadn't seen any other humans. But neither can I discount her story.

"I saw the look on Grodd's face. And Etewen . . . he told me *his* account of that night in the schoolyard, before Perg ever came your way." Her gaze drops to her hands. "I knew it then. That you were the lost child. That you were Artlina's. I don't know how you ended up in Cagmar, but given the choice between the trolls and Ottius Thellele, I would choose the trolls."

I press a hand to the wall, forcing air into my lungs. It's alarming and yet relieving to hear my secret spoken aloud. To see it in the hands of another . . . and not be cast out. Ritha has used discretion so far. I have no reason to believe her story false. She knew my mother. My *real* mother. Tried to help her. And she has helped me. She's trustworthy.

And yet that does nothing to calm the blood racing through my body, the ache blooming behind my forehead.

"Wh-Who was the other?" I ask. "The other you called . . ."

"Shifted? An old man in Ungo."

I perk up at the name of the township.

"He passed away some time ago."

Which means I never could have met him.

"He was very open about it," Ritha continues. "Anyone who came into his home left feeling light on their feet, good in their heart." She chuckles to herself. "When I asked, he told me he'd been an only child, born to parents *fifty* years of age, who had been barren. The joy of his coming passed on to him."

I stare at her a long time. "Joy?" I repeat, raspy. "He gets blessed with joy, and I'm cursed with fear?"

"You seem to have used it well."

I turn away. "It's the reason I had to come here. People don't cast joy from their homes, their townships." *Their families.*

Several heartbeats pass before Ritha says, "I'm sorry."

"Who was the other?" I meet her gaze. "You said you knew of one other?"

"The other was just a story. A story of a child who could cast fear into the heart of any man, just by looking at him. But"—she pauses—"that child would be a woman now."

My lips part.

She holds up a hand. "I know nothing more than that."

I hug myself, trying to process Ritha's words, trying to piece together the dark history of the mother I never knew and the person I've become. So often, I've wanted my fear gone from me. I wanted to be normal. Had I been normal, perhaps my father would have seen me as a human instead of a tool. And yet in some sick, disturbing way, this *shifting* is all I have of my mother.

I think of how frightened I'd been when Grodd had his thick fingers around my neck, dangling my body over the chasm. Was that what Artlina had felt like, running through the dusty dark, while in labor, with my father at her heels? Or had it been worse?

What a terrible, *horrible* way to die.

"I shouldn't tarry." Ritha stands and places a hand on my shoulder.

"O-Of course." I wipe my eyes and pick up the candle, taking it to the door. I open it and move aside, allowing her to pass through. She bids me no farewell. Doesn't even look back, but heads west, down one of the narrower tunnels with no lifts. I know there are more servants' quarters down that way, but I didn't know it connected with anything. I wonder where it leads.

I turn back too quickly, and the small flame of my candle extinguishes. Lamps dimly light the corridor. I glance down the other way just as a familiar form in the lift drops out of sight.

My hands go limp. The candle holder clanks against the stone floor. Ritha had been followed.

And as Grodd vanishes, I choke on the realization that he now knows where I sleep.

Chapter 15

My fear doesn't linger.

It's one of the disadvantages of wielding it: even if Qequan hadn't threatened me with my life should I use it against one of his kind, Grodd's fear would dissipate after he left. I had to actively project it into him, to keep him afraid. In truth, I will always be afraid of Grodd, but he will not always be afraid of me.

I can't leave Cagmar. I have nowhere else to turn. And even if I did, I wouldn't want to leave. I have a place here, though it feels as precarious as a harness without a rope.

I think of Tayler and wonder if he'll keep his promise to meet with me. If the worst happened and I had to flee . . . perhaps he'd trust me enough to take me with him.

And then I think of Azmar, and misery darkens my thoughts.

I don't sleep. Every creak, every imagined footstep, keeps me alert long after my candle drowns itself, until the early rays of dawn brush my little window. Grodd does not come. I need to bathe, so I drag myself upstairs. Neither Azmar nor Unach has woken. I pump water to get the job done, only what I need, not even bothering to heat it first, and work quickly, scrubbing dirt from my hair, my skin, my nails. I clean everything up when I'm done, and I've a little time left until my shift. Dragging myself to the kitchen, I start breakfast, yet I'm unable to compensate for my sluggish movements and sloppy knife cuts. Gripping the end of the short counter, I close my eyes and breathe deeply, trying to find some semblance of peace.

I hear his footsteps as though they come from very far away. It's an effort to open my eyes. Azmar moves beside me, folds from his pillow creasing one side of his cheek. He puts a hand under my chin and guides my face up.

His brow creases. "What happened to you?"

Unach's bedroom door opens and Azmar's hand immediately drops.

Unach comes around the corner, surprised to see me so early. Her mussed hair bounces as she wipes a forearm across her mouth. Her gaze moves between me and Azmar.

"I didn't sleep," I admit.

Unach massages the bridge of her nose. "I wish I still was. *My* shift isn't until noon."

"Why?" Azmar asks me.

I blink, trying to wake myself. It helps a little. I pull my hands from the counter. "Grodd knows where I live."

Azmar tenses.

"I saw him last night in the corridor."

Unach frowns. "What reason does he have to visit there? His Pleb housing is on the east side." She curses. "That bastard's pride. I didn't beat him thoroughly enough."

"You're sure?" Azmar murmurs.

I hug myself. "Ritha came to visit me. I think he followed her."

Unach grabs a cup from the kitchen and crosses to the water I have boiling over the fire. "He won't kill you. He wouldn't dare." She dips the cup. "Not with the law and his caste."

The assurance doesn't ease the anxiety rooted in my chest like a thorn tree. "He can do worse than kill me."

Unach frowns.

I glance to Azmar, noting his tight jaw. He's thinking again, but he must feel me watching him, for he meets my eyes.

Unach stirs her morning brew and takes a sip. "I'll file with the council to make you an official servant. You'd be more or less my property. It would give you some protection. After that, he wouldn't dare. I'll kill him if he does. It would be my right." She must see my discomfort, for she frowns. "He won't, Lark. I'll file today."

The idea of being *property* whisks me back to my father's house in Lucarpo. But Cagmar's laws are different; this is the best we can do, and I'm grateful. I don't love the idea of being an official servant, but I have the feeling Unach won't abuse the new relationship. If it protects me from Grodd and keeps me close to her and Azmar, I'll consent to just about anything.

At least the anxiety drives back the fatigue. Keeping my head down, I finish breakfast quickly so I won't be late for my shift. Unach doesn't complain about escorting me to the south dock. I search the shadows the entire way. She does, too. We run into no trouble, and Unach leaves me to my harnessing, not even bothering to greet Troff and Kesta.

The only monsters I see are small ones, about the size of a large dog, rooting around nearby for nesting materials. They're called trudeis, fat-bodied bird things with wicked-looking talons on long, spindly legs. Not a threat to the city, but I scare them off anyway. I'm actually getting used to the sling. I can't hit any of them, but I get close enough to dissuade them from exploring any closer.

Neither Unach nor Azmar can escort me back when my shift ends; they both have work of their own. But it's a busy time of day, so if nothing else, I feel protected by the crowds. Still, at every corner, I search for Grodd's broad, scrunched face and his inky shadow.

I let myself into the apartment and start cooking dinner. I suppose this will be an official task for me now, instead of a trade of services. Azmar gets home first, looking tired, but he greets me before sloughing off his heavy belt and slipping into his bedroom. Unach arrives only half an hour later. There's a bandage wrapped around her calf. She's in a foul mood, so I don't ask. When Azmar returns, I serve them dinner, eating my own near the fireplace. I couldn't eat with them even if they invited me—the high table seats only two.

As the sun pulls away from the canyon, I don the role of servant and take on every possible chore I can fathom: washing dishes, sweeping the floor, organizing the rations, anything to keep me from going down a level to my own room.

I put out the fire. I scrub out the cookpot. Dust. Tighten the nuts on the water pump. Set out grains to soak for breakfast. Rearrange the cold box.

Unach stands over me as I scrub an old stain in the floor grout, her hands on her hips. "Go to bed, Lark."

"I don't mind working," I say, not meeting her eyes. "I can even oil your weapons."

She snorts. "The council will approve my request, and I made a point of sharing it with the local gossips. He'll kiss the canyon floor before he lays a finger on you."

My scrubbing slows. My knuckles ache, and lack of sleep makes my muscles sore. "Do you have anything that needs mending?"

Azmar stands in the doorway to his room. He says, gently yet firmly, "Go to sleep, Lark. You'll be safe."

I should be. Unach isn't a liar. And yet the promise flits away on the air. There might be space to sleep beneath my cot. Then, if Grodd comes in the middle of the night, he'll think I'm gone. The idea lends me a little courage.

I return the scrub brush to its bucket and wipe my hands on my skirt. "Of course."

Feeling small, I keep my head down and slip into the corridor, closing the door softly behind me. I scan both ways, checking the shadows. Something moves to my right, but it's only the trollis in the neighboring apartment.

My clammy hands barely grip the ladder rungs as I drop down to my level. Again I scan the darkness. Hold my breath and listen. Someone converses down the way, too distant for me to make out individual words. I sprint to my door. Open and close it.

I won't light a candle. I won't make a sound. I won't do anything to reveal I'm here.

If I have to use my ability for self-defense, will Qequan still punish me?

Lowest of the low, I remind myself. Even lower than a Pleb.

In the dark, I get down on my knees and feel under the cot. There isn't enough room to crawl under, but there might be if I lift the cot, roll under, and then lower it over me.

I've little space to work with, and I'm clumsy in the dark. I scoot my little table closer to the door, as out of the way as I can get it. Then I roll up my two blankets, including the fur Azmar gave me, and put them on the table, wishing I had moonlight to see by. Tugging the cot out from the wall, I wince when it scrapes across the stone loudly. Then I lift it and push it against the far wall. I stub my toe on the table when I go to retrieve the blankets. The thicker one can go on the floor, to nullify the stone's chill. And the thinner one—

Lamplight peeks through a hair-fine crack in my door. My throat constricts.

A soft knock sounds.

Grodd wouldn't knock.

I steel myself before croaking, "Ritha?"

"Lark." It's Azmar's voice.

All my breath rushes from me. I dart to the door, stumbling once, and open it.

Azmar lifts his lamp and looks into my room. "What are you doing?"

I glance back at the mess. "I . . . was rearranging."

He eyes me.

Picking at a hangnail, I say, "I was going to sleep under the cot. So the room would look empty."

"I see."

We stand there, quiet and stiff, for several seconds, until my wits come to me. "Do you want to come in?"

He nods, and I step aside. He closes the door, then runs his hand along it. "You don't have a lock."

"I don't think any of the servants' quarters do."

"Hmm." He sets the lamp on the table, illuminating my mess. As he inspects my thin door, I set down my cot, oddly embarrassed. "I'll need a steel-bit drill, but I can install a lock here." He prods the mortar between stones in the door frame.

My chest balloons. "Really?"

"I'll purchase the materials tomorrow."

I'd offer to purchase them myself, but I don't make any money. "Thank you, Azmar. So much." *If only I could have the lock tonight.* Surely Grodd wouldn't dare break down a door to get to me. It would make too much noise.

Azmar pulls away from the door. "I'll stay, if it doesn't bother you."

Heat rushes into my cheeks. "S-Stay? Here?" *Oh please yes.*

"If you're afraid."

I swallow. "I . . . I am. I know what Unach said, and I understand the basics of trollis law, but—"

"I can wait outside the door," Azmar gently interrupts, "but if Grodd does mean you harm, it would be better to let him in."

I choke. "Pardon?"

"A guard will scare him off. But if he's caught in the act, he'll be dealt with officially. With so many marks against him, it will not go well."

I consider this.

Misreading my silence, Azmar says, "He will not get past me."

"I have no doubt of that." Grodd is a large trollis, but so is Azmar. His family line is Montra, after all. I meet his eyes. They look gold in the lamplight. "Azmar, thank you."

He pointedly raises an eyebrow. "Don't tell Unach."

The way that sounds, my ears warm as well. I grab the blankets from the table and arrange them on the cot. "Here," I offer.

"I'll take the floor."

"You won't fit on the floor." There's barely enough space for the two of us standing.

His lip twitches. "I don't plan to lie down." He settles against the wall, knees up, elbows atop them. Tilted just slightly toward the door. "You should sleep, Lark."

If he thinks I'll just fall asleep with him sitting there, he's mistaken. But then I realize the anxiety has fled me entirely. I am utterly calm, save for *other* nerves. And I am dreadfully tired.

Taking the thicker of my blankets, I unfurl it over him.

"Lark," he says.

But I let the fur settle over him, as he'd done for me when I was shivering in the hallway. I even tuck it behind his shoulders. In doing so, my face gets very close to his. I meet his eyes. A sort of smoky warmth flickers in them. And I can smell him—white cedarwood and ginger.

I pull away. "Thank you."

He nods, still watching me.

I turn down the lamp, not wanting to waste fuel, though truly I want the darkness to hide my flush, my expression, for I fear it reveals more than I want it to. I lay on my cot, guilty knowing that Azmar will lose sleep over me, and curl into the other blanket. Despite my weariness, sleep feels a long way off.

After a while, Azmar murmurs, "Lark."

I roll over to face him, though in the impenetrable darkness, I can't even make out his silhouette. "Hmm?"

He waits so long that I think he won't speak after all, but finally he asks, "Why did you come here?"

He asked me before, on the bridge. He hasn't forgotten. But now he wants to know more. And how can I deny him, after all he's done for me?

189

Biting my lip, I mull over my life, my reasons, my secrets. I try to line them up in a row, inspect them one by one.

Azmar shifts against the stone.

"I'm the oldest of four," I begin, "though my brothers and sisters are half siblings. My mother—my father's wife—never wanted me. In truth, I don't know why my father did, at first. He's a terrible person. The worst I've ever known. Even when he doesn't notice you, he is terrible. But it's worse when he does. He . . . knew there was something special about me. Figured out what it was and decided I'd be useful to him.

"Grodd fights with his fists, with his strength. My father fights with his mind. That is, he used his fists as well." I shift to stare at the faint indigo glow at the window. "But he was clever. He liked power. He knew how to manipulate people around him, whether to bargain an unfair trade or to intimidate someone into giving him what he wanted. He made me help him.

"I'm from a township called Lucarpo, near the last river. My father was mayor of the place when I left. Mayor in name, lord in action." Though human lords had died out with Eterellis. "He got it through fear. Through owning more land than anyone else. Through intimidation. He was creating a nation unto himself, and I was meant to be part of it, whether I wanted it or not. And I didn't. I met a woman . . . a woman who didn't know me, but she believed in me when no one else did. She gave me the courage to seek a better life. So I left. I did what my mother couldn't. I was twelve years old. I went as far as I could on what I'd stolen from the house. Then I found a township and a family who would take me in. But . . ."

Secrets dance around my teeth and tickle my tongue.

Very quietly, I repeat, "But . . ."

But I am more like my father than I want to believe. I wield fear, just as he does.

"But they inevitably learned that I was different, just like Grodd did. And I had to leave. There aren't many human townships to take shelter in. So I took my chances with Cagmar."

Silence weighs down the room. I wonder if my tale put Azmar to sleep. But I hear him shift, his heels sliding against the floor as he stretches out.

"You could have spun that into a much different answer," he says quietly.

"I could have. But I meant what I said, Azmar. I trust you." Though I still hold back my deepest secret, I have told him more than I've told anyone.

"Why?"

"Why do I trust you?" I whisper. "Because you are sincere and noble. Why did I tell you my story?" I think of his words on the bridge. "Because you asked."

He doesn't respond, but I think I feel his small smile cut through the darkness.

I tuck my head down and focus on my breathing, feeling safe with Azmar between me and the door. My thoughts feel lighter, my chest warm, and sleep soon encompasses me.

When I wake the next morning, both blankets cover me, and Azmar is gone.

Chapter 16

Azmar is angry when I get to his apartment.

One who did not know him well would not see it, but to me, and certainly to Unach, it's obvious. The sharp way he moves. His curt responses to questions. The heaviness to his silence and the way his gaze unfocuses, like he's lost in thought. I gape at him when I arrive, and find it difficult to look anywhere else. He laces his boots so tightly he nearly breaks the string.

Unach is oddly quiet, but not angry. At least, I don't think she is. Unach is loud when she's angry. She doesn't feel the need to temper herself like others do. She merely sips her brew and watches her brother in a curious fashion. It's not until Azmar retreats to his bedroom and comes out with a leather belt, laden with three menacing daggers, that Unach speaks.

"Are you going to tell me or not?"

Halfheartedly measuring millet, I ogle the daggers. Why is Azmar arming himself? I try to meet his eyes, but he doesn't look at me.

"Tell you what." It's more a statement than a question.

Unach snorts. "Why you're acting like a bitch in heat?"

Azmar glowers at her. "There's a lot to be done in Engineering today."

"So you need your knives."

"Right now, I prefer them."

Rolling her eyes, Unach grabs a slate and a piece of chalk and scrawls across it. Her handwriting is much more legible than Azmar's.

Azmar writes as though his hand can't keep up with his thoughts, and he cuts every possible corner to speed it up. "Once the workforce heads approve your paperwork, Lark, which should be today, your shifts at the south dock will likely be cut—"

"I would like Lark's help in Engineering," Azmar interrupts.

I bite the inside of my cheek, glancing from sister to brother. My pulse quickens. Azmar isn't upset with *me*, is he? Did my confession last night rankle him? Did I say something wrong?

My spirit sinks. *Nowhere else to go.*

Unach turns toward him. "For how long? She has a shift today."

I do, but it's not until this afternoon.

Azmar shrugs. "Until the work is done. We need extra hands, and she can do the numbers."

Unach frowns. "She's *my* servant, Azmar. Not yours."

"I'm requesting her."

Unach holds her brother's gaze for a second too long to be comfortable.

"I'm not anyone's servant yet," I murmur.

Unach huffs and drops the slate. "Fine. Go." She pushes off the chair and strides for the door, closing it a little too hard.

Azmar waits a minute before grabbing his pack. "Come."

Drying my hands, I hurry after him. Fortunately, I don't have to prod for the information I want; Azmar offers it freely. "Someone came to your door last night."

I trip. "Wh-What?"

"I heard him approach and turn the knob." Azmar's set jaw emphasizes its bony nubs. "I stood to intercept him, but I hit your table. Scared him off. I didn't move swiftly enough to identify him. Or her. It may not have been Grodd."

My heart flitters. Who else would it have been? I didn't hear a noise . . . or if I did, my mind must have encompassed it into a dream that I've already forgotten.

The table was my fault; I never moved it back. Were it not for that blunder, Azmar might have caught him.

"I didn't hear anything," I whisper.

We reach the lift. Azmar grabs the rope and begins hauling it upward. "It happened less than three hours after I arrived." He slows, holding the rope with one arm, and turns to me. "Could you do it again? What you did in the caste tournament?"

Lightning pops up my spine. "I . . . I don't . . ."

"Could you do it again?" His question is firm, unrelenting.

I swallow. Tense. Nod.

To my astonishment, relief relaxes his features. He's not wary of me, not afraid. Does he comprehend, even distantly, what I can do? He's a smart trollis; of course he must. And yet if he does, he would surely hate it, as others have.

I break his relief with three words. "But I can't. I promised Qequan that I wouldn't, and his punishments will be swifter than anything Grodd can do if I don't keep that promise."

Azmar's eyes widen. I don't know what shocks him more, the fact that Qequan knows, the law restraining me from protecting myself, or the punishment that awaits me if I do. We stand there, staring at each other, neither of us able to speak, until the rope starts to jerk. Someone on another level is trying to use the lift.

Azmar turns his attention to the ropes and continues to lower us.

So he has the daggers for my safety. He must have been confused, knowing I'd made Grodd wet himself on the bridge, and yet I nearly lost my life to him in the waterworks. But Azmar was there when the council summoned me. And now he knows why.

I think of Grodd, holding me out that window, the dark canyon gaping beneath me, and touch my neck, remembering the prints of his thick fingers.

We're nearly to the market floor when Azmar pulls the ropes tight a second time. "I want to know, Lark. But I will not pry it from you."

The utter respect with which he makes the request nearly makes me weep. A sore lump builds in my throat, and I nod my thanks.

Azmar escorts me to Engineering, which isn't busy in the slightest, now that the damage caused by the recent monster attack has been passed to the construction team. He lied to Unach to keep me close.

Surely she would be furious if she knew just how close I wanted to be.

In the afternoon, Azmar walks me to my shift at the south dock. I climb and stand guard on outposts until the low sun starts coloring the sky. I take some time after my shift ends to watch the sky and read the stars. When I climb back down, my arms feeling like noodles, Azmar waits for me in the corridor. I know his shift ended hours ago, and I could kiss him for his kindness. But that thought skirts too close to the edge. I banish it, and instead whisper my thanks as we head back toward Montra housing. We stop at the market for polishing oil for Unach and the materials to construct a lock. Azmar gets them easily; higher-caste trollis have priority everywhere in Cagmar.

Using tools borrowed from Engineering, Azmar leans in my doorway and drills a hole into the hard mortar between stones, then carefully twists screws into the wooden door to secure a latch. A long iron bolt slides into the new hole. An elementary but expertly crafted lock.

He closes the door so I can test it. He shakes the handle, trying to get in. He makes a few adjustments before he's satisfied.

I run my fingers over the device. "Thank you, Azmar. For everything. I'm in your debt."

His lip quirks. Our eyes meet. Lifting a hand, he brushes a few strands of my hair behind my ear. My skin heats beneath his touch.

One of the other servants down the hall exits her room, and Azmar's arm jerks away. Stepping back, he says, "We should go, before Unach wonders."

When he starts toward the lift, I touch my cheek where his fingers grazed it and hope the corridor's darkness hides the secrets that my skin would shout to all who might witness.

The lift isn't empty this time. Because Azmar walks with me, no one complains when I step onto it out of turn. I push myself into the corner, trying to be small. Azmar leans against the wall beside me, his arms folded across his chest, his head dipped in thought. I wonder what he's thinking, but I don't want to ask with others around. I don't know if it would hurt his reputation, acting friendly with me.

The lift rises to his floor, and we exit with two other trollis, who disappear into apartments closer to the lift. As we near his own, Azmar's steps slow.

I stop. "What's wrong?"

He lets out a long breath through his nose. Glances up toward the decking and joists overhead. "Lark." He says my name like it's a secret. Then he pauses again, unsure of his words.

I step closer to him. I want to take his hand, assure him, but I'm afraid to.

Finally he says, "I'm not human."

My heart thuds in my chest. I could think of a few reasons why he'd feel the need to point this out to me, but only one prevails.

I lick my lips. Try to calm the whirling of my mind and the speed of my blood. Once I orient my thoughts, I tip my head into his line of sight so he'll look at me. When he does, I say, "Sometimes I think I'm not, either."

His left brow twitches. He rubs his eyes with his thumb and forefinger, then drops the hand and presses it between my shoulder blades, guiding me toward the apartment. The tips of his fingers might as well be hot pokers, the way they burn through my shirt.

When he opens the door, Unach, who appears to have been pacing, whips toward him. Where Azmar's anger is bottled and hard, Unach's is as ferocious as the monsters she hunts. Where Azmar suppresses his anger until it's hard as granite, Unach feeds hers until it's as jeopardous as the monsters she slays.

"What the actual hell, Azmar?"

My lungs seize. For a terrifying moment, I'm certain she's discovered that Azmar stayed in my room last night. My terror-filled mind scrambles to find an excuse—

"I know about Kesta," she spits.

Confusion bubbles up in my chest, extinguishing the fear.

Azmar says nothing. Unach marches right up to him, her hands in fists. She looks at me and says, "Out, Lark. *Now.*"

I obey immediately and skitter into the hallway. The door slams behind me.

I take only two steps before turning back and pressing my ear to the door. They've moved away from it, but I can still make out Unach's iron words.

"She basically dropped her bloodstone at your feet, and you said *no?*"

I press a knuckle into my mouth and bite down. Bloodstone? Perg said trading them was the closest thing the trollis had to human marriage. And *Kesta* offered hers to Azmar?

My stomach twists so hard I slouch to compensate for it.

"I am not required to accept," Azmar replies, so quietly I can barely make it out.

"She's *Montra*, you fool! Why wouldn't you? To say she's offended is—" Unach's words dwindle. She's pacing again, away from the door. When she returns, I catch, "—chance again!"

Azmar says something I can't discern.

The wall shakes, and I jump back from the door. Unach must have hit it. "You realize that if every trollis in Cagmar waited for fuzzy feelings to trade, we'd be extinct." The words scathe.

After retreating from the door, I hurry to the ladder and start climbing down, pausing halfway to my floor. My hands tremble, palms slick on the metal rungs. I don't want to make assumptions. I don't want to jump to conclusions. History has proven time and time again that someone with my abilities is not meant to be loved. And yet my cheek burns where Azmar touched it. My mind flies to Tayler and his secretive township. To the half trollis Baten. To Perg.

You are human, he is trollis, I remind myself. *He* reminded me of that himself.

And yet I cannot believe we're entirely impossible.

Shaking my head, I scurry down the ladder and wring my hands together. Desperate for a distraction, I climb down again, and again. I'll visit Perg, take my mind off things.

For as long as I can.

It's late, close to the twenty-third hour, when I return to the apartment. I stayed late with Perg, who now rests in his own chambers, which measure roughly the same size as mine, so that he also has to use public waterworks and baths, which will be hard with his injuries. Boredom and depression overwhelm him, so I stayed to play a board game that his nurse lent him. Unsurprisingly, it's a war game, with so many pieces and strategies that it took me nearly an hour to get the hang of it. Perg won every match, but he deserves to win *something.*

I worry I gave him false hope, stretching myself to interpret the stars, the gods' will for his future. Especially when I can't even read my own.

Hoping Unach's anger has fizzled out, I carefully knock on her apartment door.

"What?" she responds sharply.

I pull the handle and step inside. Unach sits at the tall table near her bedroom door. She rubs her temples and glances up at me.

"Oh, I forgot about you. The request got approved. You're welcome."

I let out a long breath. I now have a lock on my door and legal protection. "Would you like me to tidy up?" I ask not only to fill my new role, but in hopes of cheering her up as well.

Unach waves a hand. "Go to sleep. I'll have plenty for you to do in the morning."

I think of my dark chamber, of Grodd's slinking shadow. But I'm safe. I'll even run through the market screaming that I'm protected by a Montra, to make sure Grodd knows it, too. And if he comes anyway, I think I could scream loud enough for it to carry through the walls to this apartment. At least my neighbors would hear . . .

As I turn for the door, I notice Azmar's bedroom door ajar. It's dark within. He always sleeps with his door shut. "Where is Azmar?"

"Hell if I know," Unach grumbles. "Probably knocking down a pillar somewhere."

I hesitate, peering into Azmar's room. I think of Kesta and frown.

Unach's chair pushes back, and her tired countenance suddenly morphs into suspicion. "What were you and Azmar doing? You came here together."

I flush. "I assisted him in Engineering." Unach knows this.

"And got back later than usual." She looks me up and down, and I try not to cow beneath her gaze.

"He helped me with some purchases. I've been . . . concerned about Grodd."

She doesn't hear my words, and her voice takes on a chill. "Are you in love with my brother?"

My heart slams into my ankles, and I step back. "I . . . What? Of course not!"

Unach closes in on me. "I've seen you moon-eyed with him. Flushed and eager to please—"

"U-Unach." I hold up both hands and scramble for an excuse, landing on the first one she'll believe. I try to smile, like it's all a joke. "Y-You're mistaken. Humans don't show affection the way trollis do. I've been here long enough to know. I'm just trying to be a good . . . servant."

Unach cocks her head to one side, considering this. If I have any upper hand with her, it's that I understand trollis far better than she understands humans. She's never lived among my kind.

199

To hammer in the nail, I add, "No offense, Unach, but he's . . . trollis."

The suspicion leaks out of her immediately. Of *course* humans are bizarre. Of *course* one would never be interested in a trollis! This is something she understands completely. And while that fact settles my fear, it also cracks my hope.

I'm not human, Azmar said. It was likely less a declaration than a response to my "moon eyes," putting me in my place.

And yet.

Unach is not one for apologies, so she merely waves her hand in my direction, as though swatting at a fly. "You can go."

I exit before she can question me further.

Somehow the shadows have intensified in the long corridor outside. I wonder at Grodd, at Azmar's claim that someone came to my door last night. I have not seen Grodd today, thankfully. Perhaps he's lying low. Perhaps his labors as a Pleb have kept him busy.

But I worry about Azmar. I didn't hear his entire conversation with Unach, but I know he took the full brunt of her anger. *Knocking down a pillar somewhere.* I've never witnessed Cagmar's engineers demolish anything, only make plans for it.

Then I remember the pillars in the military training rooms, and before I realize what I'm doing, I'm in the lift and heading that way.

I scan the shadows as I enter the market, the faces of the night workers now familiar to me. For a terrifying instant, I think I see Grodd, but the trollis turns toward a lamp, and it's the blacksmith. Sucking in air to calm my heart, I hurry down the corridors toward military training, where no humans are supposed to be.

As before, with Perg, I meet little resistance. At the first chamber, I crack the door open to peek inside. Two very tired, very sweaty trollis linger in the far corner with wooden staffs, comparing stances. A female trollis walks on the bridge overhead. In the opposite corner, I spy Azmar at a great punching bag, his knuckles blue with abuse. Sweat dampens his shirt, trailing from his chest to his waist. Though he's a modest one—the other trollis are shirtless—the sight of him lights something deep in my core, and the desire to touch him inundates me.

Feeling daring, I slip inside and hug the wall, moving toward him. He throws another fist into the column, then wipes his forehead with his forearm. He spies me as I near him. His guard is down, leaving the surprise clear on his face.

"Lark," he says between breaths.

One of the other trollis turns our way. "No humans in training!"

"Crave off!" Azmar barks, and the trollis frowns and turns away. I don't understand the idiom, but I can imagine what it means. Those trollis must be lower caste, for Azmar to speak to them so. And he must be angry; I've never heard him yell.

Taking the defense as permission, I draw closer and lean against the padded pillar. "Are you all right?"

He lifts the hem of his shirt and wipes his face, and I chide myself for admiring his torso as he does so. Not enough shows to reveal his scar, but I note the dark hair flowing down from his navel, and that space deep within me ignites anew.

I avert my eyes as he says, "I'm well."

"Unach can be fierce."

He chuckles and drops his shirt. "You say it like it's something she ever stops doing."

I hug myself against the chill. "I didn't know you knew Kesta."

He must be too tired to school himself, for his features open in what looks like . . . guilt? "She is close to Unach." He runs the pad of his thumb over the bony nubs of his jaw. I want to ask about the bloodstone, but I don't want to reveal just how long I'd been eavesdropping. Watching the other trollis, who seem to have forgotten about us, I push off the pillar and step closer to him. He looks down at me, so close yet so distant, his eyes warm as honey.

"I need to go to the surface tomorrow," I whisper.

His brow lowers. "Why?"

"To rendezvous with the human boy we caught. From the spying band." His expression hardens, and I rush to add, "Just for information. He's very secretive about his township. Azmar, there's a half trollis like Perg there."

His brow releases, and he looks away in thought.

"I can't go alone." My pulse races as I gather courage, and I reach for Azmar's hand, clasping it in mine. His gaze immediately falls to our entwined fingers.

"If you take me . . ." I'm so quiet I can barely hear myself. "I'll tell you what you want to know."

His eyes widen. He studies me, and I try not to flush under the scrutiny. One breath, two, and his hand tightens around mine.

"I'll take you."

Chapter 17

We set our rendezvous for evening, when it's harder to be seen, so between the south dock and my shift with Unach, I work relentlessly, dispelling any possibility of her suspicion. After dinner, I make my way up toward the farming walls, where Azmar said he would meet me. I find him easily, and he takes me up to the bridge, tipping his head once to Homper as we go.

No one questions him. They are Deccor, and he is Centra.

I breathe deeply as we step out into the fresh air, the sun nearly set. It paints the sky with swaths of orange and pink, casting long blue shadows across the dry ground, coloring the bridge pastel and deepening the blackness of the canyon.

I walk behind Azmar, the picture of the obedient servant. He even has his toolbelt and pack with him, making him look every bit the engineer on duty. When we reach the skeletal forest, I walk beside him for a few minutes, then I step in front, blocking his path.

"You need to wait here," I say.

He doesn't even hesitate. "No."

"I promised I would go alone." I look up at him, pleading. "They might have a half trollis in their township, but they're afraid of you, and I have to keep my word. I don't think he'll hurt me."

He frowns. "They have before, Lark."

He means Colson and the other humans in Cagmar. Shaking my head, I put my hand on his wrist and repeat, "He won't hurt me. He's supposed to be alone, too."

"And if he's not?"

I smile at his protectiveness. I'm still unused to having someone worry over me. Defend me. "Azmar, I've been honest with you. Just trust me."

His jaw works, but he nods. "Quarter hour."

I roll my eyes. "You are not my nursemaid." I turn and head through the trees, but then I stop. "Only come for me if I scream."

Azmar's expression darkens, but he acquiesces, and I am undone by his trust. So I put my arms around myself, holding my pieces together, and hurry through the wood. I don't want to miss Tayler.

He isn't there when I arrive at the boulder that marked the spot where we'd caught up to him and his friends. Nervous, I search the forest behind me. No sign of Azmar, and no sign of any predators—it's too difficult for them to survive here.

I wait another ten minutes or so, standing on the boulder so Tayler will see me. If he doesn't come . . . I could leave a note, but what if someone else finds it? I've no idea how far off Tayler's township is. It might not be easy travel, if he even planned to return. And I hope he returns. Tayler *is* hope, hope that there are more of my kind out there who might accept me for what I am, like Ritha does. If this township welcomes Baten, if he belongs and has a family . . . maybe they could spare some acceptance for me, too.

I murmur a silent prayer to the stars. As if in answer, they begin dotting the sky. Minutes later, a narrow shadow moves toward me from the east—too small to be a trollis. Stepping off the rock, I call out, "Tayler?"

The shadow takes a few more steps before snapping, "Keep it down."

Relief cools me as I recognize his voice. *He came.*

He stops about four paces from me, hands shoved into his pockets. His attire differs this time—it's darker and closer to the skin. He's about two inches shorter than I am.

"I'm glad you came," I say.

He shrugs, not meeting my eyes. "You spared me. I'm honor bound."

I've never heard a human say such a thing. Many in the past didn't care if I used my abilities to save their lives. "The trollis wouldn't have killed you." Though I cannot speak for Homper.

Tayler scoffs.

"I heard the rest of your band escaped?"

"Barely."

"How?"

He glares at me.

I hold up both hands in surrender. "You don't need to tell me."

"Are you a spy?"

Lowering my hands, I say, "No. I came to Cagmar as a refugee. There are dozens of us."

He glances behind me. "Liar."

"I'm a refugee," I insist, also glancing behind me. The darkening forest appears empty. "My friend, who was with me before, is back there, but he promised to stay put."

Tayler hisses through his teeth and steps back. "You said you'd come alone."

"I did. He's at least a quarter mile off. I can't leave Cagmar without an escort."

Tayler shakes his head. "I don't believe you."

Rubbing my hands together, I try to think of a way to persuade him. Remembering my satchel, I pull from it a floral disk and press it into his hand. "This is all I have right now. If you look carefully, there are small seeds inside. They come from one of the vines the trollis harvest for food."

Tayler's brows knit together as he examines the pink disk.

"I . . . am different from most of our people," I try. "I've struggled for acceptance in many of the townships. So I sought out Cagmar for my shelter. The trollis are a hardened people, yes, but they're not terrible."

The floral disk vanishes beneath Tayler's cloak. "They kidnap humans and make them slaves."

I consider this. "I . . . heard that they used to, yes. But not anymore. We're . . . not respected there as a general rule. But I have friends who are trollis. Just like you do."

Something about that strikes him, for he instantly sobers. "I suppose."

Taking a deep breath and treading carefully, I say, "You said you have a trollis in your township."

"*Half* trollis."

I nod. "Baten."

He studies me in the dark. "What about him?"

"He's accepted? Among the humans? And he's the only one?"

Adjusting his cloak, Tayler asks, "Why do you care?"

"I told you about Perg. He's also half-human, and a friend of mine. But he isn't treated well in Cagmar. Not by most. They have a strict caste system there, and it's . . . difficult to raise his status."

"Not surprised."

I push onward. "But your people accept Baten?"

Tayler shrugs. "We're not cruel to him. So . . . yeah. His mother is from—" He stops abruptly. "His mother is from our township."

He must have almost slipped and said the township's name, not that a name would tell me where it was. My father had extensive maps of this area, but Tayler's township was not included on them. If it had been, I would have sought out its shelter before turning to Cagmar.

"If you would . . . sate my curiosity," I try carefully, "how was it that Baten came to be?"

Tayler hunches and shrugs again. "Don't know. His mother never talks about it. Or talked about it, so everyone says. She ran off, once upon a time, before I was born. Came back a couple years later bursting at the seams." He clears his throat. "Pregnant, I mean. We all just assumed she got caught up in a raid and taken advantage of."

I wince at the bleak theory, so much like Perg's. "Is she happy?" I whisper.

His head snaps up. "What?"

"Is she happy? With her son?"

Tayler looks confused. "I mean . . . yeah. They live in the same place and all."

A long, slow breath passes my lips. "Good."

"Why do you care?"

A tickle like floating dandelion seeds erupts beneath my breastbone. "Because you seem so accepting of him. Of Baten." *Accepting of someone like me, maybe.* "And Perg . . . once he heals, maybe he could be accepted, too."

Tayler goes wide eyed. "Heals from what?"

I think he fears disease, so I clarify. "Perg was in a caste tournament to better his status and was badly beaten by another trollis."

Tayler frowns. "I see."

"Tayler, where is—"

"Don't ask," he interrupts. "I won't tell you where we live. Don't try to follow me back."

His harshness hurts, but I accept it. "Of course. You don't know me. Not yet."

He regards me again. "Not yet?"

I offer a smile, though I don't know if he can see it. "Meet me again. In a week? I'll bring you food, whatever I can carry out."

He stiffens. Considers. "I need nine days. And . . . we need seeds."

Surely I can find some on the farming level, even if I have to harvest them myself. "I'll bring you seeds. But what we have—they're cooler-climate shade flowers. They have to grow in the canyon."

Tayler frowns. For a moment I think he'll tell me the canyon is too far from his home, but instead he mumbles, "We'll have to clear out the crag snakes."

I lean forward. "Just meet with me again, here. Same time. Please?"

He hesitates but eventually relents. "Alone. No trolls."

"I can't leave without—"

"*No* trolls, if you want me to trust you," he insists.

I swallow. Nod. I could likely hide Azmar again, assuming he'd return with me, but if Tayler is watching . . . I could ruin everything. I know the city inside and out. I can probably manage coming alone.

Tayler extends his hand, and I shake it, surprised at the hardness of his calluses. He is not yet a man, but he knows hard work.

I grip his fingers tighter. "Tayler, is there a Cosmodian, where you come from? A reader of the stars?"

His grip tightens. I release mine, and he pulls back slowly. Eyes me in a way that makes me think of Unach.

"Why?" he asks.

I hold his gaze. "I met one when I was young. A woman. I've been praying to meet her again someday. I've been to all the townships on my map"—on my father's map, that is—"and I've never crossed paths with her. I don't know her name."

He chews on his lip, contemplating. There must be *something*, for a simple no would be an easier response.

"I'll tell you," he says hesitantly, "when we meet again."

He whips his hand back and dashes away, again to the east, leaving me with blossoming anticipation. I've found her. I'm *sure* I've found her!

I wonder if the hidden settlement lies east of here, or if Tayler travels around so I won't be able to guess where he's headed. I suppose it doesn't matter now. I'll meet him again. I'll earn his trust. I'll learn about Baten and the Cosmodian and a safe place to go, should my time in Cagmar end . . . poorly.

Touching my neck, I wince, though the bruises Grodd left there have healed. I force my hand back. This is good news. A *good* day. I will not let fear ruin it.

I turn back for the scraggly trees, careful in the darkness. Out of habit, I lift my head and find the South Star. The sun has slumbered long enough that the sky brims with stars, glittering and beautiful, orderly and chaotic. Still, the South Star blazes where it always does, pointing me back to my new home, promising me I'll never be lost . . .

My steps slow as I peer into a pattern of stars I don't recognize. And they're . . . blurry. I blink to clear my vision, but it's fine—everything else in the night sky is crisp. I squint again, almost able to make out Ufreya, the queen.

My footsteps stop altogether. The constellation isn't blurring, it's just overlapping with another. With Sankan, the oak tree. Just as Wiln's almanac said it would.

A shiver courses up each arm, colliding at my neck, as though the gods themselves whisper in my ears. I've read that almanac so many times. I know its astronomy passages by heart. Every twelve years those constellations meet, either to bless us with fertility, or to curse us with war.

I look back the way I came. Even if Tayler lingered, I'd never pick him out among the shadows. Steadying myself with measured breaths, I continue into the trees. Azmar has lit a lamp, so after picking my way through a maze of elevated roots, I'm able to spot the light in the distance and work my way toward him.

Hearing twigs snap underfoot, Azmar stands and draws a knife from his belt, but he sheathes it immediately when the light falls over me.

"Thank you," I say.

He looks over my head. "He came?"

"He did." I relate the brief exchange with him. "I hope to earn his trust."

"You're meeting him again?" Concern lines Azmar's brow.

No trolls, Tayler said. Do I risk that trust? I give the safest, truest answer I can. "I hope so."

Azmar picks up the lamp, and we start back for Cagmar. We're nearly to the edge of the forest when he says, "Do you wish to leave?"

I glance up at him, but he faces straight ahead. "Leave Cagmar?"

He gives a nearly imperceptible nod.

Would I leave, if Tayler invited me to his township? I'm not sure. But the choice, for now, is easy. "No. Other than Grodd . . . I'm content there."

"Only content?"

I step over a raised root, drawing closer to him as I do so. "Yes. With you, and with Unach and Perg." Encouraged, I ask, "Why, worried I'll run off with a fifteen-year-old boy?"

He doesn't respond. His guard is up, and in the poor light, I can't read his expression. I may have overstepped my bounds. It's easy to forget myself when we're alone. I wonder if I should apologize, but that would be to acknowledge the overstepping, to highlight it, and the thought makes me curl in on myself.

Another thought presses into my mind. *I promised.* To tell Azmar, that is. That was the bargain. And yet when I open my mouth to explain, no sound emerges. My own fear clogs it. Azmar is different, yes, but I've met plenty of kind souls who couldn't endure my truth. Outside of the council, which forced my hand, I've never willingly offered up my secret. First, because my father threatened all manner of suffering if I did—he couldn't let others know the secret of his influence. And second, because it has always been the reason, one way or another, that my chances of a new home and a new family have broken apart.

If Azmar rejects me now, if I become just another casteless human wandering Cagmar in between work shifts, with no enclave to take me in and no trollis to speak to, I'll wither away to nothing. I know I will. I've allowed too much hope to take root.

The stars warned me that my path would be a hard one, but if this turn proves too sharp, I might not have the strength to keep going.

The lamp swings between us. We walk in silence for about twenty paces, thirty. The sun has set, but the quiet burns hot and sticky. My tongue seems to swell in my mouth, forbidding me speech.

I draw in a long, slow breath. I trust Azmar. Truly, I do. And he trusts me. He's shown me as much tonight. I rub the clammy skin of my palms together. My breath shakes. My pulse sputters. Strange how my own true fear discomforts me so much more than the fear I project. I can't control or temper it, can't turn it off. I must simply push through.

So I suck in another breath and push it out all at once, forcing my voice. "I have an ability to project fear into others."

His gait slows. "What?"

"What I did with Grodd, and what I do with the monsters." I look up ahead, though in the darkness, I can't see anything beyond the light of the lamp. "I've had it since I was a child. Since I was born. Ritha thinks it transferred from my mother. That's why my father found me valuable. I helped him intimidate those who had what he wanted, or who complained about his power. It's why I haven't been accepted in other townships. Somehow I always end up using it, in self-defense or otherwise, and everyone thinks I'm a witch. We're very superstitious, we humans."

I try to make the confession light, but inside my organs coalesce into a tight iron ball. I can scarcely breathe as I wait for Azmar's response. Will he take this in stride, as the council did? Will he say *I knew it!* and strike me down? Will he distance himself from me once we return, leaving me to my servitude and nothing more?

"The monster that broke through the wall," he says.

I swallow. "Yes. I'm still a poor shot with the sling."

He considers, and I allow him time to think, but each passing second kills me, making that iron ball a little bigger, a little harder. My feet drag in the dust.

"I've never told anyone," I whisper. "Except . . . the council. I had to, to stay."

Azmar shifts the lamp to his other hand so that it no longer sways between us. "I've heard of a similar thing, with a trollis who lived seventy years ago," he murmurs. "He was renowned for leading troops because he could effortlessly inspire bloodlust in them."

"Bloodlust," I repeat, croaking. "Fear. But there are more pleasant things one could be cursed with."

"It's not a curse," Azmar says, and the iron ball stops rolling. "You saved us that day. And you saved Perg when no one else would take a stance, myself included."

Tears blur my vision, and I blink them away. "Thank you for saying that."

He nods.

"Please don't tell Unach. Or anyone else. I don't know how the council will react. They've been very clear that I'm not supposed to use it, outside of the dock. Grodd already suspects—"

"You have my word."

I stop, and after a pace, he notices and stops as well. Turns toward me.

"Just like that?" I ask, my voice shaking. "I tell you I'm a creature who terrifies even monsters, and you accept it, just like that?"

He regards me, lamplight glinting his eyes the shade of honey. "It is not a curse, Lark. It's a gift."

"But do you mean it?" I whisper. "Or will you despise me once we crawl back under that bridge?"

His shoulders loosen. The lamp swings as he closes the gap between us. He smooths back hair that has escaped from my braid, and cups the side of my head in his hand. "I would never despise you."

I want to kiss him. I want to grab him by his corded hair and pull him toward me. Taste his lips. Touch him. Be close to him. But instead I just cover his hand with my own. "Thank you, Azmar."

He runs his thumb over my cheekbone. "Thank you, Lark. For telling me. And for staying."

Butterflies spring to life in my stomach. He lowers his hand to my back and guides me toward the bridge. I practically lean on him as we walk, but when the great bridge's struts come into sight, I pull away. Homper is still on duty. We descend into Cagmar, and Azmar puts out his light.

We reach the lift. Azmar pulls the ropes. I wait a few heartbeats before saying, "Thank you for the lock."

"You already thanked me."

"But will you stay with me again tonight?"

The rope stops. Azmar looks over his shoulder at me. "Yes, after I put my things away."

Pressure builds in my chest. It's both unpleasant and . . . not.

He stops the lift at my level, and I hurry to my room, searching the shadows. No one lurking, not yet. I close my door behind me and slide the new latch into place, letting out a long breath. Fumbling with my flint, I light a candle. I'm not allotted many, so I light only one. Then I pull off my dress and change into a lighter one for sleeping. Sit on the edge of my cot.

I can still feel the weight of Azmar's hand on the side of my face. *I would never despise you.*

My heart races, making me feel too warm. Hugging myself, I hunch until my forehead touches my knees. I had hoped Azmar would react well. He's so calm, so open-minded. But to have it go so smoothly . .

I lift my head and stare into the dark. *Wholly unexpected,* the Cosmodian said.

Couldn't I . . . Couldn't I still find a family in Cagmar?

The humans here haven't rejected me. Wiln and Ritha are kind. But . . . could I not have Perg as my brother, and Unach as my sister? And Azmar . . .

Unach's voice echoes in my head. *Are you in love with my brother?*

I close my eyes. *Yes, I am.*

My heart still thuds when I hear a soft knock at my door. It's Azmar's knock. Leaving the candle on my table, I hurry over, pull the latch, and let him in. He has a spare blanket with him. I lock the door behind him, relishing the security of the bolt. The security of him.

Azmar drops the blanket on the floor. "I don't think he'll try again so soon," he says, looking at the lock. "But I don't know Grodd well."

"You are amazing, Azmar." I don't think I meant to speak it out loud. It was just a whisper, but in the silence of the room, it carries. Azmar turns toward me, solid and mesmerizing in the candlelight. Embarrassment heats my neck. "You are. Everything about you is amazing."

He regards me a long time, making me self-conscious. "You're different, Lark." He matches my tone. "Not because you're human. The way you speak, act, move—it's everything Cagmar isn't."

I smile. "Hard and purposeful and full of joists?"

His lip quirks. "Purposeful, yes. But graceful, compassionate." His gaze shifts to the candle. "Like that flame."

"Easily extinguished." I touch my neck, remembering the press of Grodd's fingertips.

Azmar moves toward me. Touching the other side of my neck, he grazes my jaw with a knuckle. "No one will extinguish you, Lark. Not so long as I draw breath."

I want to cry and laugh at once, but I do neither. I just stare up at him. The candlelight makes his eyes look like jewels and his skin look like agave leaves. There is nothing human about him, and yet he's so human to *me*, so much more like myself than any creature I've met before. He is beautiful, and his beauty warms my skin, even in the cool air of my narrow room.

His hand has not left my face. He studies me, and I'm desperate to know what he's thinking. What he sees in my face, what he hears in my breaths. What questions and theories turn inside that mind of his.

I step closer without thinking. The fine hairs on my arm stand on end when he bends, his face close to mine, closer still. The warmth of his breath grazes my cheekbones.

I'm the one who closes the gap. Who rises to my toes to brush my lips against his. The contact sends a thrill through my bones that makes my ears ring.

And yet as soon as we touch, he jerks away. Steps back and runs a hand down his face.

My very spirit sucks toward the floor.

"Azmar—" I blurt.

At the same time he says, "We shouldn't do this."

Despair trickles down me like freshly pumped water. My lungs shrink, as if I'm wielding my fear. "Azmar, I'm so sorry. I shouldn't have—"

"I shouldn't be here." He steps toward the door, hesitates, and glances at me. His stony face reveals nothing, but the light in his eyes bounces between regret and frustration. When his irises shift toward the shadows, my very bones start to crumble. "You'll be safe tonight, Lark. I'll make sure of it. But I can't stay here."

And just like that, he leaves, unbolting the door and slipping into the dimly lit hallway, forgetting his blanket. Perhaps he's discarding that, too.

I am frozen, swaying on my decrepit skeleton, staring at that door and wishing, praying, pleading with the stars to reverse time. But forward the seconds tick. Several minutes drag by before I remember how to move, and I sit numbly on my cot, hollow, confused, and humiliated. Biting my lip, which tingles from the touch of his, I drop my face into my hands and curse myself, squeezing my eyes against oncoming tears. *Stupid, stupid, stupid.* There was such a delicate boundary between us, tight as a stuck thread. Yet instead of easing the knot, I've broken the filament. Practically thrown myself at him. And *I'm a human*, as everyone here reminds me daily. As *he* reminded me. I let hope blaze too bright and destroyed everything.

Shaking, I bite down hard enough to draw blood. Numbly cross the room to bolt my door before dropping back to the cot.

The fledging hope of *family* wilts before it could truly bloom, and I wilt with it, growing small and dry and insubstantial.

At least Azmar is trustworthy, I remind myself. He is a good man, a good *trollis*. He won't share my disgrace. It isn't in his character. And why would he, anyway? How embarrassing it would be for him, to admit to letting a *human* get that close.

Stupid, I chide myself, slapping a tear off my face. The flame of my candle flickers, as though laughing at me. I pinch the wick to extinguish it, not even flinching when it burns.

Chapter 18

"You're quiet today, Lark," Perg says.

I push a pair of large pliers—made for trollis hands—down on a stud in a leather vest refitted to my frame, curling the prongs. I've ripped through so much clothing that the tailor finally complained and got me approved for armor of my own, but much of the labor was left to me. I've gotten only two rows of the brassy studs intact. I flex my hands after setting down the pliers, then pick up the awl again.

"I suppose I have a lot to think about," I offer. We're in Perg's quarters. His cot is a mess, and he sits up on it, dishes littering the floor beside him. I should offer to take care of them.

I jab the awl into the leather.

"You'll hit your leg, holding it like that," Perg says.

"I haven't yet." But I think of the scar on my thigh from Tayler's comrade, which makes me think of Azmar's hands as he bandaged it, which makes me feel small and idiotic all over again.

Perg watches as I press the next stud into place and pinch it with the too-large pliers. At this rate my hands will be useless tomorrow.

"Are you angry with me?"

I set the pliers down and lift my head. "Why would I be angry with you?"

He shrugs. Doesn't wince. That's a good sign.

I pick up the awl.

"I'm back to work tomorrow." Perg runs a finger along the edge of a scab.

That gives me pause. I take in his splints, his bandages. "Already? Perg, you need to rest longer."

"I'd love to, even though I never want to sleep again." He sighs. "But I can't earn my rations without working."

I set the awl and vest on my lap. "You can't work with your injuries!" Not in construction, with all that heavy lifting. "Does the council not allot recovery time to injured trollis?"

"They do. I've just used it up."

I'm incredulous. "But you'll hurt yourself and then need it all over again. You're not ready."

He flexes his hands. "I can manage lighter loads. It will just take me longer."

I shake my head and wield the awl like a weapon. "If they can't give you the proper time to recover, then they shouldn't have allowed Grodd to have his way with you."

I sense, more than see, Perg deflate.

Frustration curls in my chest. "I'm sorry, Perg. I didn't mean it that way."

"Mean what?" He reaches into my bag and hands me a stud. "The truth?"

I shake my head. I can tell Perg wants to ask me more about that day, but I keep my focus on the vest.

I've told only one other person my secret, and now I can't speak to him at all.

I close the pliers, harder than I need to. I saw Azmar only briefly this morning, while Unach demonstrated how to stud the leather. He didn't speak to me. He didn't look at me. He just got his things together and left for work, leaving me smothered in my own shame. Something about my apartment's walls felt claustrophobic, so I came to see how Perg was. Not that I'm good company.

Is this how it is to be, then? My fears realized, and not because I am a human endowed with fear, but because I dared to kiss a trollis? Is that what I am now, not a monster or monster slayer, not a servant, but a mistake?

I think about the men of my past, their propositions, their eager hands, their judgmental stares. Then I think about Azmar, and that brief moment of contact, and the tip of the awl bites my thigh. I hiss and pull it away.

"Told you," Perg says.

Moving the vest, I inspect the damage, but it's minimal. I put my elbows on my knees and my face in my hands, allowing myself a few deep breaths.

"Lark?" Perg sits up straighter. "What's wrong?"

"Nothing."

"Is she beating you?"

I laugh, though it's dry and hard. "Unach? No. She's prideful and hard skinned, but she wouldn't lift a hand to me."

Perg nods. "I'm glad."

A bit of frustration ebbs out of me. Setting the vest aside, I gather up Perg's dishes.

"I can do those," he insists.

But I carry them to the tiny tin tub that serves as his sink. "I need something else to do."

Perg frowns. "If you insist."

I pour the last of his water over the dishes—I'll need to fetch more for him so he can rest before returning to his labor. "Can I stay here for a while, Perg? Until Unach comes home." I don't have a shift today.

He regards me skeptically. "Are you lying about the beatings?" He touches his chin. "But I suppose if Grodd is nothing to you, Unach wouldn't be, either."

I deflate. "Let's not talk about that, please." *Let me just be normal for a little while.* Despite there being absolutely nothing normal about me.

"Yeah, if you want."

Relieved, I turn my full attention to scrubbing.

Unach's schedule has her returning at the eighteenth hour, so I plan to arrive a few minutes after that to start dinner. I prefer her rage to Azmar's awkward indifference. When I arrive, though, Azmar sits at the tall kitchen table, a workbook in front of him. Unach is nowhere to be seen.

I almost retreat, but instead I take a deep breath and head to the kitchen. Being at the end of their rations limits our dinner options. I might as well pick up all our rations tomorrow.

I prepare the food in silence, skewer a hunk of liver over the low-burning fire, and occasionally glance at Azmar from the corner of my eye. He rests his chin in his hand, staring at the same page, tapping a pencil lightly.

Desperate to get over myself, I ask, "What are you looking at?"

He shifts, lifting his head. "The addition off the master armory. We've determined we should add a cliff anchor there, and I'm trying to decide how to do so with our budgeted resources while maintaining the city's integrity."

I glance over his thick arm to the book. Numbers and equations consume the left page, while sketches dominate the right, one of them unfinished. It's all very symmetrical and familiar.

"Have you ever considered making it . . . pretty?" I suggest.

He glances at me, a short line forming between his brows. "Pretty?"

I shrug and continue into the kitchen. "Everything in Cagmar is so utilitarian. Even the council room limits its aesthetic."

"It's utilitarian because we must make do with what we're given."

"But even basic things can be beautiful." Our gazes meet, and I look away, busying myself with dishes. "Where is Unach?"

"Charming another Montra at the south dock. She'll be home late."

I wonder. Not Troff, is it? Or maybe the south dock purely provides the meeting place. I reach for a plate and nearly drop it, the muscle at the base of my thumb cramping from overuse with the pliers. I move the plate to my elbow and rub the spot until it's a dull burn.

The workbook shuts too loudly, or maybe we're just too quiet. I peek over at Azmar, who sits with his hands together under his chin, looking toward the door, but nowhere at all. I cross closer to him and set the plates down.

"Lark."

My pulse quickens when he says my name.

He waits for a breath. "Will you use it on me? Your fear?"

I blanch. "I would never—"

"That's not what I mean. I want you to. I want to . . , understand what it feels like."

My stomach clenches into a sick knot. "You don't want to know what it feels like." I know what it feels like, and it took me *years* of using it almost daily to learn how to compensate for the backlash, to understand the fear coursing through my veins, mirroring what I dealt to others. Even then, I'd only just learned how to fall asleep with dry eyes and keep nightmares away before I fled Lucarpo.

"I do." Such an easy response.

I stare at him, the breadth of his face, the lines of his jaw interrupted by studs of bone, not unlike what I've been punching into that vest. My belly grows hot.

"Why, Azmar?" I'm angry, but my voice leaks out like I'm about to cry, and I hate it. "Why? So you can detest me, too? So you won't have to feel this way about me anymore?" Maybe that's an assumption, but Azmar came to *my* room. He told me those kind, heartrending things of his own volition. He *let* me get close enough to kiss him.

He also rejected me the moment I did.

His expression darkens. "That's not why I ask. I simply want to understand."

I shake my head and cross into the kitchen, though I've nothing to do here. I start reorganizing utensils to keep my hands busy.

Azmar follows me as far as the doorway. "I know it's a trick of the mind. It will not change how I view you."

"Please, Azmar." It's almost a whisper. "It will. And I cannot bear that."

Several heartbeats pass. "It's a blessing, not a curse."

I drop the utensils and whirl toward him. "Then why has it brought me nothing but sorrow? Can all your fancy Engineering education and structural drawings tell me that?"

He's unaffected by my outburst. Cool, calm, collected, as always. "Is Perg's life sorrow? Is mine?"

I shake my head. "That's not fair."

"Perhaps not," he agrees. "I will not ask again, if that's what you wish."

I glance at the door, wondering how late Unach will be. Wondering how I'll be able to mask myself if she walks in right now. Becoming a legal servant was a bad idea. I wonder if such a thing can be revoked.

I feel closed in again, so I push past Azmar toward the fireplace, sinking onto one of the giant cushions. I rub an ache from my temples. "I won't, Azmar. Not for curiosity, not for science, not for anything."

He follows me, surprisingly silent on his feet, until he towers over me, like some ancient sentinel, and I . . . I am a mere human. "Even if I hurt you?"

The question startles me. "You would never hurt me, Azmar. Your promise aside, I know you. I'm not afraid of you."

He considers this for a minute. The fire cracks behind me. I reach over and turn the meat.

Azmar sits beside me, making the cushion dip with his weight. "I've petitioned for my own quarters," he says. "Unach won't like it, because it will require her to downsize as well, or share with someone else."

I stiffen. My heart beats too hard, catching on barbs in my ribs. "I see." With Azmar out of Unach's space, I'll never see him. On occasion

I'll pass him in the corridors, or on the lift, or when Unach needs something delivered to him. It will be easier for him to forget me. Easier for me to forget him, too, I suppose, but the hurt blossoms like a poisonous flower, regardless.

"I would appreciate if you didn't mention it to her until after Housing approves the request," he adds. "Best to minimize her reaction, as much as possible."

I rise. I should work on the vest. I need something else to think about.

Azmar grasps my wrist. His grip is like a stone left by the fire, pleasantly warm at first, but more and more scorching the longer he holds on.

"Lark," he murmurs.

I twist from his fingers. "My name is Calia."

He doesn't respond. I dare to meet his eyes. They're unsure.

So I repeat, "My real name is Calia Thellele. My nursemaid called me Lark. I didn't want to be found after I left my father's house, so I changed my name."

I've had more names than those two, but they don't bear repeating.

Azmar's gaze is an iron manacle holding me in place. "Which do you prefer?"

I swallow. I want nothing to do with that sad, scared little girl, and the sad, scary life she left behind. "Lark."

He doesn't move. Doesn't confirm the name in any way. He's about my height, sitting on the overstuffed cushion, with me standing. A little shorter. Staring at him, being close to him, is awful and agonizing. His presence is hotter and brighter than the fire at my back. I want to fall into him and be burned.

But I am nothing if not a survivor.

I turn away. Take half a step. Fight with my warring mind. But I've already thrown myself at him once. What more damage could I do? If he's leaving Montra housing, I might not get another chance.

"I know what I am, and what you are." My voice is quiet, my throat too tight, so I force myself to turn back. The fire feels too hot now. "I haven't told a soul about you, and I won't speak of it again after this. But I need to hear it from *your* mouth, Azmar. I need you to remind me that I'm human, that I'm repulsive and below you, that the only thing you feel for me is pity." His stare is too intense, so I lift my focus to his brow. "Just tell me that I'm a fool. That I'm in the way. Just tell me, and I'll leave you be. I'll change my shifts so our paths never cross. I'll even leave Cagmar, if that's what you—"

His calloused hand finds mine again, but this time he tugs me toward him. My words jumble on my tongue as his other hand touches my hair. I barely process that I'm falling before he kisses me. Not a meager brush of the lips, but a true kiss, and something inside me shatters and is rebuilt again.

His lips are warm and soft, thicker than mine. One of his short tusks glides across my cheek. My pulse roars in my ears. *Wrong, wrong, wrong.*

But Azmar's hand clutches my hair, his other encircling my waist to pull me closer, and it sings, *Right, right, right.* The flames seem to leap from the fireplace and ignite every inch of me, and the complicated plait of my thoughts loosens and disintegrates, until there is nothing in my head but the ashes of him.

Our mouths learn one another slowly, measurably. It's tantalizing, invigorating. I cup his strong jaw in my hands. He turns his head and coaxes my lips to part. I give in eagerly, and the heat of him flows through me, over my tongue and down my throat, feeding that secret space deep within. And then I am on his lap, tracing his mouth with my tongue, crazed on the scents of white cedarwood and ginger. His fingers map the length of my spine, each pad a smoldering ember against my skin. It makes me feel so fragile, and yet so strong at the same time. Our breaths mix together, dancing. I lean into him, desperate to be closer to him, relishing the feeling of his hard body against mine. Our tongues intertwine, and he makes a low sound in his throat that is as delicious as it is addicting.

The kiss slows, gradual and reluctant, until our lips break apart and I can feel blood swelling in mine. I search Azmar's eyes, his pupils so large and dark there's barely any topaz left in them. I'm sitting on him, the cushion bulging against either side of my thighs. There would be no easy explanation for this, should Unach walk in.

My heartbeats thrum too swiftly to count. I search Azmar's face. "Your fault this time," I whisper.

He runs a hand behind my ear and over my braid. "Perhaps do not tell Unach about this, either."

A sudden shyness overtakes me. Leaning back, I pull my legs to myself so I'm no longer straddling but sitting modestly beside him. Trying not to think of the telltale sign of desire I'd felt, which is definitely the same with trollis as it is with humans. I murmur, "What would she do?"

"She would not take it well." He wipes a hand down his face. "None of them would."

I'm glad he doesn't sugarcoat it for me. And yet it stabs me in the chest like a rusted nail. I think of Perg's mother, casting herself into the canyon . . .

Unach would never support us. Even Perg would never support us. And if they won't, no one will.

We're doomed before we begin.

"Which is why I've requested my own quarters," he continues. "They would be much smaller, but more . . . private."

My face warms. "Oh," I say stupidly. "But this . . . The law . . ."

"There is no law against it . . . officially." He leans his elbows on his knees.

I study him, the concern knotted at the corners of his eyes. "Because it should be obvious without the council declaring it."

He nods. "Because aside from Perg, it's unheard of."

That wilted hope from last night grows new roots.

A moment passes in silence before I ask, "Why did you change your mind, Azmar? Last night . . ." I can't find a way to finish the sentence without feeling foolish. I can still taste him on my lips. My pulse is erratic in the aura of his calmness.

"I did not change it," he said, allowing an iota of panic to surge into me. "I merely accepted it."

I study his profile, and then his eyes when he turns toward me, so resolute. I reach forward and splay my hand on his chest, over his shirt, where his heart is. Despite the firmness of his voice and the stoniness of his features, his heart beats swiftly, one hard pulse for every two of mine.

A strange jubilation burns in my core, and despite everything—Cagmar, Unach, the council, the laws—I find myself smiling.

His lip quirks at my countenance. "Did you think me heartless, Lark?"

I don't pull away. "Only worried."

His hand touches my thigh, and he leans in, but before I can kiss him again, loud footsteps sound outside the door.

I'm up so fast—smoothing my skirt, skittering away from the fire—that the room spins.

Unach barges in with such intensity that the door crashes against the wall behind it. Azmar stands, his expression utterly stoic, his body poised as though ready to fight.

My gut hits the floor. There is no way Unach could already know—

"Seven trollis," she says, and confusion replaces my trepidation. "*Seven* trollis adolescents murdered, their heads left on pikes for us to find!"

My jaw drops in shock. And given the scathing look Unach throws my way, I know exactly who the perpetrators are.

Humans.

Chapter 19

Ufreya the queen and Sankan the oak tree.

Did the stars predict this?

Azmar answers Unach first. "Where? When?"

Unach whirls around and kicks the door shut. It seems all of Cagmar shakes with the frame. She stares it down, as though it might attempt to war with her, before turning to face us. Her green skin is especially bright, her glare hotter than the fire behind me.

"East fan," she says. It's a trollis district, not anything labeled on human-made maps. "Right on the border of the East Arrow."

From what I can remember of trollis geography, she means somewhere south of Dorys, the township I'd run from after my father's men attacked me in the stable I was sleeping in, in the earliest hours of the morning.

I shudder and hug myself. "Were they scouts, or—"

Unach reels on me. "Or *what*?"

"Unach." Sadness brims Azmar's calm cadence.

"Or raiders," I finish, trying to match Azmar's tone. "I assume it was my kind who did this."

"You're damn right it was your kind." Unach marches closer, jutting a thick finger in my direction. "And what does it matter?"

I frown. "It matters." Though even in self-defense, to put the trollis' heads on pikes . . .

My stomach twists into a hard knot.

Unach growls, but she's too sensible to take her anger out on me. Instead she grabs the side of her head, as though her skull struggles to contain her rage. "They were trainees. Innocent! They were running drills when they were attacked."

I glance toward Azmar. Hadn't he been in a similar situation when he got that scar?

I swallow, tasting the danger of the line I'm about to walk. "Perhaps the people of Dorys felt threatened—"

"Dorys?" The township name cracks whip sharp on her tongue. "What the hell is Dorys?"

I forget that the trollis have an entirely different way of mapping the world than we do. I know this land by its subtle roads and townships; they know it by great geometrical tracts and ranges. "A township—"

"They weren't *near* any human townships!" Unach's roar echoes between the stony walls. "From what our scouts saw, they were swarmed! An army took them out and left their heads for us to find. Regret knows where their bodies are."

I step back as though she'd pushed me. "Swarmed?" Dorys is a small township; they don't have a large number of fighting-ready men. I would guess they'd avoid a fight, not seek one out.

Azmar studies me closely. "Did the report estimate how many humans?"

"We can guess, can't we? Two humans to every trollis, maybe three. No human remains found nearby. It looks like an ambush." She grits her teeth. "That's all I know. Damn it, that's all I know." Unach slumps down on the cushion that Azmar and I just occupied, her head in her hands.

I'm not sure what to do, what to say, but I can't do *nothing*. Inching closer, I offer, "I'm so sorry, Unach. Did you know any of them?"

She barks a sour laugh. "Hardly. Kesta told me. The whole city will be alive with it soon enough." She drops her hands, fingers curling into fists.

A coil of fear wraps itself within my belly, a snake made of iron and thorns. Surely Dorys doesn't have so many armed men. Surely the township hasn't changed so much in the few years since I left it. Terysos is the next closest, but still . . . something feels off about the tale, like the first stench of rot on a cut of meat. After the drought, my people were left so scattered, with so few resources. I can think of only one place where such an army might be tacked together. Or rather, one person who'd be able to form and lead it.

Ottius Thellele, my father.

In a world of drought and desperation, he had more power than any I had met, and I'd met them all, as far as the east side of the canyon stretched. My father had a way with people. He didn't need me to intimidate them, to coerce them, to control them. I just made the job swifter.

And if it wasn't my father . . . could it be Tayler and his band? Could they have set a trap for the trollis, or sought revenge for being chased off? But Tayler sounded so genuine, even if he was scared. Surely it wasn't him.

I dread either answer.

I come back to myself and glance at Unach, then Azmar, who meets my gaze. Apology limns his countenance, and he tips his head toward the door. I should leave, though I've not finished dinner yet.

I look at the pot in the tiny fireplace, and Azmar subtly waves for me to forget it. His jaw tenses, like he's about to set a bone.

Oh stars, he's not going to tell Unach about his new apartment *now*, is he?

Suddenly motivated, I step quietly to the door and slip into the cool hallway, pulling it shut behind me. I wait a minute, then another, before Unach's voice booms, "You did *what*?"

Azmar knows his sister well. Perhaps it's better to get all her rage out in one burst than to drag it out over days. Because if this attack wasn't a single skirmish, if it's something larger, it will be days, weeks, even months. And every trollis in Cagmar will be involved. All are trained soldiers.

Vile words erupt from Unach's mouth, each a nail to my chest, knowing Azmar bears them alone. Rubbing my sternum, I make my way to my quarters, wondering at the revelations of the last quarter hour. They're too big to fit in so small a space. I don't know what either will bring—the death of the trollis adolescents, nor the kiss Azmar and I shared.

The strain between Azmar and Unach hangs in the air like steam, and no attempts at conversation or bad jokes can lift it. Unach has always been the bold one, Azmar the quiet one, but in his presence, Unach simmers like hot oil, waiting for the first taste of raw meat to explode and burn.

She's concerned she won't be able to keep her apartment to herself, even though she claims to prefer living alone. Space is as valuable in Cagmar as water is in the townships, and none can go to waste. Meaning that either Unach also has to get a smaller apartment, or she has to find a new roommate. She asked Kesta during our shared shift. Given that Kesta's attempt to room with Azmar was turned down, I think she'll take Unach's offer.

"Otherwise, I might as well pick a mate," Unach snaps a few days later, as we man the highest of the slayers' scouting points. She scoffs. "Maybe I'll participate in the next caste tournament and win the stone of an Alpine."

It reminds me that Unach had once been interested in Grodd—at least genetically. Thankfully, he has not crossed my path again. For how much he hates humans, I can't imagine how he'd react if he learned about me and Azmar. Though in truth, I'm more worried about what Unach would think. Or say. Or do. But she's so wrapped up in Azmar's leaving she hasn't thought hard on *why* her brother wants his own space. At least, not out loud, and not in my presence.

Everyone in Cagmar is talking about the attacks. The trollis adolescents were savagely murdered in the middle of unclaimed, barren land. It had to be an act of war, with such a gruesome message left. The trollis mobilize, their movements a little quicker, their conversations a little lower as I pass them on the streets. More and more occupy the training grounds, including Perg. His injuries haven't fully healed, but he's so bent on regaining his strength, on proving himself to those around him, that he pushes himself beyond what I think wise. But he won't hear otherwise from me. In fact, it's hard to find him now that he's left his bedrest. Were I not so occupied in my own matters, I might be hurt by the neglect.

Between my shifts with the slayers and Azmar's putting in more time in Engineering to avoid his sister's anger, I don't see *him* as much, either, save for when he guards my door. But he spends the nights out in the hallway instead of on my floor. Our conversation is still easy, but I worry he regrets returning my affection so readily. I don't visit him in Engineering, either, not wanting to attract Unach's attention. I have to be absolutely careful with Azmar; no one can know our secret, no matter *what*. Not only for my own well-being, but for his as well. I will not do or say anything to jeopardize his standing, his caste, nor his relationships, even at the expense of my own heart.

Six days after our kiss, Azmar stays late in Engineering again, and Unach has an evening shift at the south dock. I let myself into their apartment anyway, to cook dinner. Unach, at least, should be home within the hour. I set two bowls of lecker stew on the table for them.

Then I notice, through Azmar's door, that his belongings are gone. A quick pang stabs my chest, and I stand in the doorway, looking at the empty space. The bed where I recovered from the attack outside the school, the small table where a mountain of his sheaves usually sit, and the cushion in the corner are gone. Azmar isn't a materialistic person—few in Cagmar can be—but the room looks stark without his effects.

The walls still smell like him, white cedarwood and ginger.

I lick my lips, missing him, hating the uncertainty wiggling in my stomach. If he does regret me . . . will this be it? Will he still guard my door? Could I petition to take this room, even though I'm human? At least then I'd have Unach close.

I'll have to ask him. Taking my dinner and newly filled pitcher of water, I make my way to my narrow chamber, checking the shadows, searching for Grodd or other lurking threats. I see only a Nethens, who regards me indifferently before slipping into her own room at the end of the corridor.

Azmar doesn't come at his usual time. I wait for him, burning a precious candle, pacing the length of the cramped room, checking, double-checking, and triple-checking my lock. Azmar is not one to turn a cold shoulder to his problems. But perhaps he would, where a human is concerned.

The room feels a little darker, a little colder, despite the exercise of my pacing. Sitting on my bed, I pull the fur he gave me around my shoulders and am about to blow out the candle when a soft, blessedly familiar knock sounds at my door. I'm both relieved and terrified, though this kind of fear isn't the same as my usual companion. It threatens a different kind of hurt.

I pull the bolt and open the door. The faint light spills over Azmar, though his shoulders, neck, and head remain in shadow.

"I thought you weren't coming," I whisper.

He tilts his head, his expression soft. "I would not leave you, Lark."

And as though a magician snapped his fingers, all my fears and worries dissipate, like water spilled on hot stone in the heat of the afternoon sun. The relief escapes me in a swift breath, and Azmar's lip ticks up at it.

"I have a safer place for you to sleep, if you're not too tired," he offers, his voice quiet as the canyon itself.

I perk up. *He got his apartment.* I'm not sure where Centra housing is. But it makes sense, suddenly, why he is so late. He wasn't standing guard for his sister's hired help. He was coming to escort her away. The fewer witnesses, the better.

I slip inside to blow out the candle and grab my bag. The pitcher, the dishes, and the rest can stay, for now. I follow Azmar into the dimness, walking beside him at first, but when we pass the lift, I fall a few steps behind to show deference to any others who pass by. Azmar glances back at me, a whisper of a frown on his lips, but he knows as well as I that this is safer. I will protect him.

But I want him desperately.

We take a steep road above the trade works to the east side of Cagmar, skimming by the guard barracks on the way. We pass one other trollis, who pays little attention to either of us. We take a lift up. It opens onto a floor identical to all the others, though the doors are spaced more widely apart than in my wing.

Azmar left the door unlocked and goes straight for the handle, pushing it open. It's dark within. I slip inside first; he follows and pulls the door shut behind him. His heat whispers past me, and a moment later, the flame of a candle sparks into existence. The glow is faint, but it's just as bright as the stony corridors outside this time of night.

The apartment is nice. It's smaller than Unach's by half, but it's only meant for one Centra to occupy. No interior walls separate anything. The bed is pressed into the far corner, near a chimney that lets out the faint smell of lignite smoke, despite a fire not being lit. I imagine the chimney connects to other rooms below and above this one. The kitchen space is immediately inside the door. There's a washbasin and some shelves, and a familiar rug lies in the center, taken from Azmar's other apartment. Overlapping it is the cushion from his room.

"That was quick." I pinch the strap of my bag with one hand, then run my palm across the kitchen counter, which is only a foot wide. "It's nice."

Azmar smirks. "It looks like every other room on the Centra floors, but I suppose it is."

I meet his eyes, tasting a grin on my lips. "Did you design them?"

"Hardly." He throws a bolt on the door and strides into the room, stretching one arm overhead. Two pencils poke out from his hair—I wonder if he forgot about them. "These were constructed long before I was born."

I press my hand into the smooth stone wall, a new heaviness dragging on me. "Is Unach still angry with you?"

"Unach is always angry." He sits on the edge of the cushion, elbows on his knees. "She'll forgive me eventually."

"Kesta may take your spot."

He appears completely disinterested by the information. "Grodd won't find you here."

My cheeks warm. "He may have given up the chase. I haven't seen him, even in the market."

Azmar shakes his head. "I don't know him well, but I don't trust him."

Unease bubbles in me, less about Grodd than about the fact that there is one bed in this room. I've never shared a bed with a man, not even Andru. As I cross over to Azmar, thoughts of that bed—of what we could do in that bed—flit through my mind, bringing heat to my skin. But I remind myself that trollis only mate with bloodstones. Between Unach's and Perg's talk of it, that rule appears strict.

Azmar stands when I near and clasps my shoulders in his emerald hands. I look up at him and place my open hands on his chest.

"I was worried you regretted me." It comes to mind, after I've spoken, that the name of the trollis god was embedded in my words.

"Not you, Lark."

I love the way he says my name. I'm so used to the trollis accent now; even some of the humans in the enclave have assimilated it. But I always notice it when Azmar says my name. The roundness of the vowel, the distinction of the *K*.

I lean into him, my bones humming with the beat of his heart. "Does that mean I don't have to sleep on the floor?"

He responds by closing the space between our mouths. I clasp his jaw and invite him deeper, rolling his bottom lip between mine. A soft growl reverberates in his neck. I laugh softly, unrestrained glee building in my muscles, my blood. I shift one hand and run the pad of my thumb up one of his tusks. I've always wanted to touch them. Strange that I'd once thought them so inhuman. Now they are simply Azmar.

He pulls back. "Am I so humorous?"

I grin. "You can be." I reach forward to pluck one of the pencils from his bound hair before waving it between our faces.

"Hmm." He takes the pencil, throws it on the floor, and scoops me into his arms. I muffle a shriek of surprise and grasp his shoulders, unable to get a good hold before he plops me onto the bed. It's a standard size for a trollis, but I won't take up much space comparatively.

He hovers over me, a mischievousness in his eyes that I've seen only in rare glimpses before. But we're alone, with no passersby or sisters to walk in on us. Here, now, neither of us needs to be guarded.

My chest fills to bursting.

Azmar smooths hair from my forehead. "You do not need to sleep on the floor." He grabs my bag, pulls its strap over my head, and drops it beside the chimney. Then he settles onto his side, facing me, his head propped up on the heel of his hand.

"Oh good." I curl into him. "Because it is very cold, and you are very warm."

His free hand glides up my back, over my shoulder, and down my arm, the touch modest and unexpecting. "You're so small," he murmurs.

I roll my eyes. "I am very tall for a human, you know. Taller even than most men."

"Hmm." He tucks my head under his. I press my forehead into the base of his neck, placing a kiss on the spot where his collar dips. He breathes into my hair and wraps a thick arm around me. Its weight is assuring and delightful. I'm sure sleep will never come, but it does, and remarkably quickly.

Because for the first time in my life, the fear dissipates entirely. I am completely and utterly safe.

Chapter 20

I'm slow to wake in the morning, my head flitting between half dreams, my limbs clinging to drowsiness. Fur tickles my skin, and I blink awake to an unfamiliar ceiling lit with a ray of sunlight from a narrow window. But Azmar is not beside me, I drown alone in a bed made for a trollis.

Sitting up, I stifle a yawn and smooth back my hair. Azmar is leaning over that little square of kitchen counter, reading a sheaf of papers, a half-eaten floral disk in one hand, a pencil in the other. His shirt stretches nicely over his shoulders, the seam parting for the bony nubs to protrude.

I get to admire him only for a second. Despite his position as an engineer, Azmar trained as a soldier, and I was hardly stealthy in rising. He sets down breakfast and pencil and turns my way, his topaz eyes warm, his belt already strapped to his hips, his feet shod.

Panic floods me. "What time is it?" If I'm not at Unach's to prepare breakfast, she'll ask where I am—

He reads my mind. "Don't worry about Unach. With an evening shift, she's likely still sleeping." He crosses the room, glancing out the window. "Do you report today?"

I nod, sweeping the mess of my hair into a tail over my shoulder. "Not until this afternoon."

He leans against the side of the bed, arms folded. "Maybe you can gauge the risk of my showing my face again."

I run my thumb over his knuckles. "You know she fights it because she loves you, not because she doesn't want to search for a new roommate."

"Don't say that where she can hear." He reaches over and plucks my hair from my hand and throws it back over my shoulder, undoing my efforts to make it neat. "The wildness suits you."

I blow a pale strand from my face. "I'll have you know I was practically an Alpine, where I come from." I mean it as a joke, but thoughts of my father's household, of his power wars and my part in them, have never sat well with me, even seven years after my escape.

Azmar's countenance softens. "Then I have chosen wisely." He leans forward and touches his lips to mine. All my uneasy thoughts flee. The kiss almost distracts me from his fingers splaying mine and pressing something into my palm. I hesitate to see what it is. He tastes like honey and smells like jasmine. The only thing that keeps me from fully exploring him is the time . . . and the fact that I might not taste so sweet first thing in the morning.

When I pull back, I open my hand to see a piece of jewelry, a green stone with flecks of red entwined in looping copper wire, with a simple chain strung through it. It's beautiful.

"You don't have to keep it." His voice is low.

I might not have realized what it was, had he not said that. Had his words not carried a note of uncertainty.

My heart squeezes, missing a beat. I trace my fingers over the glossy surface of the pendant. "This is a bloodstone."

He nods.

"This is *your* bloodstone." My pulse quickens with each breath.

"Our customs are different than yours," he explains, watching the stone and not my face. "Unach has spoken of this to you before—"

"Why wouldn't I keep it?"

His gaze meets mine. I can only guess what my face looks like. I'm surprised. It's unexpected. So soon. And yet the validation, the *significance*, of such a gesture floors me. I'm falling through the canyon and floating into the clouds all at once.

Azmar . . . Azmar loves me.

No one has ever truly loved me.

My vision blurs. Blinking it clear, I clutch the stone to my chest. It's utterly perfect . . . the green surface has blue hues, just like trollis blood. Hence the name: *blood*stone. But it has red flecks as well, like human blood. Like the very gem itself condones a union that every creature in this city would surely spit upon.

The wire bites into my skin, yet I'm unable to release my grip. I search Azmar's face; there are so many things there. Patience, hope, determination, dedication. A trace of fear.

I swallow. "I-I don't have one. One to give you."

I didn't think his eyes could soften any more, yet they do. He brings a calloused hand to the side of my face, sweeping away a lock of hair and cradling my jaw. "That doesn't matter."

I lean into his touch. "But I would give it to you, if I had one."

Letting out a long breath, he touches his forehead to mine. We stay like that for several seconds, sharing air, sharing thoughts. "I want you to stay here, Lark."

"I'm not leaving."

"Here, in this room." He pulls back and meets my gaze. "In my bed."

I swallow. "The council—"

"It isn't illegal." He frowns. "Technically."

I press my lips together. "Perg told me what happened to his parents. I don't want to hurt you, Azmar."

He slowly drops his hand. "You cannot hurt me."

"Oh, but I can, and you're a fool if you think otherwise." I grasp his hand in my free one. "I love you, Azmar, but you will sacrifice nothing for this. Though I am honored you would consider it."

His other hand slides beneath my knee and pulls me forward so he can kiss me again. This time it's less sweet and more distressed, harder, demanding. He may think me small, but I don't cow to him. The blood-stone bites into my palm, and I battle with him, warmth building deep in my core. My soul sings to him in a way that is both enthralling and terrifying.

I don't know how to read this, Calia, the Cosmodian once said.

But I can. All the stars and planets have aligned, my broken road mends, and the way is clear and straight before me. *Wholly unexpected,* the reading said.

The Cosmodian wasn't wrong.

Azmar breaks away, and we both gasp for breath. Slowly, finger by finger, he releases my leg. Finger by finger, I ease my grip on his bloodstone. I will cherish it like I've never cherished anything else.

"I'm late," he growls, but his frustration isn't with me. Standing, he jerks on the ropes of his hair. Walks halfway across the room, pauses, and turns back to me. He looks angry and sad at the same time, and it's like a needle piercing my heart. "Be careful, Lark."

We watch each other for a moment more, reading and studying and questioning, before he grabs the sheaf of papers off the counter and leaves, shutting the door behind him with a force that reminds me of his sister.

Opening my hand, now covered in red marks, I cradle the bloodstone, memorizing its every facet. It's beautiful, and I wonder if Azmar crafted the setting himself. But I cannot wear it. How would I explain, if *anyone,* even Ritha or Perg, were to find this on me? What believable story could I offer?

Because I *can* hurt Azmar. He's essentially handed me the weapon with which to do it. And so while I wish I could pin this emblem to my breast and wear it with pride, I slip it inside my shirt, under my breast bindings and over my heart, and quickly ready myself for the day. I cannot let these adventures, wonderful as they are, disrupt my normal schedule. I need to be at Unach's apartment and then the south docks, fulfilling my responsibilities. But first, I will hide this, somewhere safe, where no one else can find it. It will be difficult—I have so little space to claim as my own. But I will protect it with all I have.

More difficult will be hiding the elation that I'm sure radiates from every inch of my skin, because despite all the fear tied to this promise, I have never been happier.

"They won't mobilize all of you?" I ask Unach as we take the sloping road down between military storage and food storage. It's the third hour, time for the shift change, and bodies crowd the way.

"Not until further threat." She shifts her jaw to one side and pops it. She has a gruff edge to her voice, like she's still angry, but getting tired of being angry. At this rate, she'll be on speaking terms with Azmar again by next week. "Until then, we go by ticket, and mine's up soon. I'm looking forward to fighting something on level ground for once."

"But you haven't *found* the attackers." I think of Tayler. If he comes scouting again, his band might be put to blame. I fear for him. Our meeting time nears, and I have no way to warn him of the extra trollis scouts. If it's only him, hopefully he can pass under their watch, just as I'll have to. I promised him I would come alone, without even Azmar, and I am still working out how to accomplish that.

Unach sticks out her broad chest. "And what if I do?"

I shrug. "Of course I don't want war, Unach. But if you have to defend yourself, it doesn't matter if they're humans, aerolass, or merdans, in the end."

My answer pleases her.

A passing trollis shoves into my side, sending me sprawling into Unach. She rights me with one strong arm. Then swings around so quickly I question if I ever fell.

She grabs the trollis by the collar and shoves him against the stone wall. "You'd better watch where you're going, Intra."

The Intra gapes, confused, his charcoal eyes flicking between Unach and myself. "She's human!"

"She's *my* human." Unach jerks the trollis forward and releases his collar. Frowning, he adjusts his clothes and merges back into the crowd.

I can't help but smile as Unach continues down to the dock as though she didn't just blatantly defend my honor. I don't say anything, of course. If Unach hates anything, it's feelings.

We're coming upon the tribunal when the horn sounds, loud and sharp, two times over. All the trollis slow at its call.

Two times over. Monster attack.

Unach and I bolt down the lane, hurrying to the dock. Others quicken their steps, rushing to their designated stations to wait out the attack. I think of the leckers' prior breach and push my legs faster.

Two slayers, Kub and Troff, have already set up at the dock when we arrive, Troff holding a rope that must lead to Kesta, already on the city's exterior.

"Hurry!" Kub says.

Troff blurts at me, "I can hold two!"

We rush for the trunk of harnesses. Unach grabs one and shoves her legs into it. I help her buckle and adjust.

Troff says, "It's a spreener. A *big* one. Came up to check out the waterworks—" He grunts and pulls back on the rope as it changes directions.

Unach fastens a rope to her harness before throwing the other end to Kub. I untangle my own small harness, which I usually shove in the bottom right corner of the trunk for easy finding. Once Unach's rope coils up through the pulleys, she climbs out.

I hear her curse at the same time the horn blows again, loud and teeth shaking.

Seconds later I understand why, after a *stip! stip! stip!* of sharp legs shakes the rock and an immense shadow falls over the dock, punctuated by half a dozen acidic eyes.

My breath dissolves. The spreener spider is massive, its exoskeleton hard and faceted as a carved gem, its beak gleaming, sufficiently large to take a trollis—or a human—in a single bite. Kub and Troff both jerk back, retreating, ropes under their arms. In unison they reach for the heavy swords on their belts. My heart pulses hard and heavy. Chills spiral down my arm.

I've never been this close to a monster, even the leckers.

The spreener hisses, revealing two sets of slimy fangs.

Peering into its gaping mouth, I shove my fear down its gullet.

But the spreener doesn't react as the leckers did. It starts, it rears, and it *fights*. The entire dock quakes as it lunges, legs grappling with the stone, beak snapping for *me*. I rush for the chest of swords, hardly able to keep my balance on the shaking floor. Each chomp clacks louder than thunder and echoes against the wall as if an invisible army surrounds us.

Troff slashes at its armor with his sword, striking a joint. The spreener's many eyes shift as it wheels around to face him. In doing so, its curling legs sweep out and strike me in the side, whipping me across the dock floor and out—

I'm falling.

Wild fear bursts through my body, cold and slick and sharp. Everything slows as terror spurs my brain to work faster.

My harness isn't buckled.

I don't have a rope.

The dock looms above me. The canyon below.

I scramble, limbs flying. My nails scrape across the stony side of the city as I plummet, searching for a handle, but there aren't any. The rock skims my knee, rips up my hands—

I catch a sliver of a ledge and cling to it with all the strength in my right hand, crying out when my weight jerks on my shoulder. A shout echoes above me. I barely register it as Unach as I try to find another handhold, but there's no space for another grip. My feet dangle. I flail, my left hand glazing over too-smooth rock. I'm holding myself up by just four fingers now.

And I'm slipping.

"Help!" My pulse thumps like a war drum. I can barely hear the commotion over it. Unach hangs thirty feet above me, sword drawn, torn between the spreener and me. Kesta hangs on the other side of the dock, wide eyed.

Fight or flee.

The spreener fights.

Gritting my teeth, digging in my nails, I glare at the spreener's backside and push the mounting fear out of me, striking it again. As before, it spins and seeks me out, hissing, saliva raining from its beak, bits of broken stone tumbling down.

But it has neglected Kub and Troff. I hear two loud *crack*s, and the spreener screams, a horrible, grating sound that rattles my eardrums and pierces my brain. The spreener falls off the dock, green ooze spraying from two severed hind legs. It falls into the canyon, but its slime dribbles down the side of the city and toward me. I grit my teeth as the hot ooze splatters my cramping hand. I lose a few millimeters.

"I'm slipping!" I scream. There is no way in the gods' dry world that I will survive this fall.

"Hang on!" Kesta shouts, working her way down, handhold by handhold.

Again I try to lift my free hand, higher, higher, but there are no dips or crags to fit even a single finger into.

"I'm falling!" I cry. Of all the ways I have pictured myself dying, it was never this.

Azmar.

The canyon looms below me.

"Troff, I'm going to jump!" Unach bellows.

A rope whizzes overhead. I look up to see Unach falling toward me.

My fingers go numb and release the rock. I scream, but Unach's arm hooks around my waist. Her rope jerks so suddenly my neck pops, and she groans.

I don't breathe. Then all my air rushes out.

Unach laughs. "I've got her!"

I grab her shoulder with my left hand. My right-hand fingers remain curled into claws, unable to release their desperate hold. "Oh stars, Unach. Thank you." A hard ball forms in my throat. My eyes and nose run while my entire body shivers. I clutch Unach's tricep with my good hand. "Thank you, thank you. Gods bless you."

We jerk up a few feet at a time until Kesta grabs my upper arm and hauls us up. All three of us drop onto the dock, safe and secure once more.

I press my head to the cold floor and offer up a million prayers in the space of a breath, pressing myself into it to prove that it's really there. A small part of my mind is still convinced I'm falling.

"Get a tub!" Kesta shouts, shaking slime from her hand.

Spreener blood is poisonous. I haven't swallowed any, thank goodness, but I don't want to contaminate anything, either.

"Ugh." Unach stands, examining the wet goo I left across her shirt and harness. She looks at me and says, "Don't open your mouth."

Kub runs off the dock to do as bidden. Unach barks at Troff to follow, since we'll have to strip out of the tainted clothing. Goo clings to everything, scratches from the carnage of the giant spider mar the walls, and Unach's hair is a mess.

I meet her gaze. And despite everything, I laugh. It's an awkward laugh. I struggle to keep my mouth shut so I don't poison myself. But it's all so ridiculous I can't help it. Unach stares at me a beat, then guffaws loud enough to echo across the dock. She slaps her thigh and cringes at the mess and laughs. Kub and Troff return with a tub, their features twisted in confusion, unease on their faces.

I feel . . . better. Amazing. And I laugh at myself and at Unach and realize how much I love her. She is the sister I never had. She is *family*.

And I realize, with that sobering thought, that my people are wrong. I was *wrong*. It's not all about war and strength and size. All of that is just a veneer, easily chipped and discarded.

Unach doesn't value strength more than anything else. She values family and friendship. Azmar values justice, truth, and love. Perg values relationships and sees to the hearts of others. Kesta is merciful. Troff and Kub are accepting and jovial. They'd rather sit telling jokes, their legs dangling from the dock, than lift a hammer or sword in a caste tournament.

They set the tub in front of me. Warmth blooms in my chest. *I belong here,* I think, fighting against another smile. *This is my home.*

Grateful and exhausted, I shift to get my legs under me, then wince as something bites my scraped palm.

It's a bit of stone, no larger than a coin, from the rock the spreener broke. It has a blue sheen to it, purple where my blood touches it. I pick it up and study it. It reminds me of a bloodstone, though its surface is much rougher, its colors darker, than Azmar's. Yet my pulse spins. Not a bloodstone, but a blood stone. Perhaps for us, it could be enough.

"Take them off." Unach jerks her thumb, indicating my clothes. Then, to Troff and Kub, "Out."

I stand, careful where I drip, and set the stone aside. "Thank you, Unach."

She shrugs, but I detect relief in her stance. And despite the scare, the slime, the cuts, and the absolute chill of the bathwater, I laugh again.

After I'm dressed in the new leather vest I finished studding and the smallest trollis slacks Troff could find, I have to roll up their waist and secure a leather weapons belt around it. But it works, and I'm grateful for clean clothes. The rest get thrown into the canyon.

I'm used to fear, but it takes a while for it to leave my system fully. For my joints to move smoothly, my heart to beat evenly, my muscles to settle. True fear always leaves a deeper mark than the recoil of my strange ability. Unach remains, and Kesta stays around for another hour to chat, then leaves us to man the dock while other slayers go to the lookouts. The rest of the shift flows uneventfully. I imagine that spreener scared off anything else that might bother Cagmar.

New trollis relieve me and Unach at the twenty-first hour, when the sun starts to set. "Just get some rest," she says when the lift stops at my floor, excusing me from any other duties. "We both need it."

I thank her and head toward my room, only to pass it and take the ladder down a level, following a new road east. The stone sits in the empty sword holster on my belt; thinking of it renews my energy. I step out of the way for a few trollis and wait several minutes to use the lift that will take me to Centra housing. When I reach it, another trollis busies himself putting out lights, so I take the lift up to Intra housing instead. Fortunately, at the end of the row of tight-knit apartments is a ladder, and when I take that back down to Azmar's floor, the way is empty. I hurry to his door and knock softly. Wait, listen. But he doesn't come to the door.

The lift starts moving at the far end of the corridor. Not wanting to be seen, I try the handle—unlocked—and slip inside.

A small candle twinkles, but the wick is almost drowning in its own wax. Candles are costly, even to high castes, and it's unlike Azmar to leave one unattended. I quickly open drawers and cupboards until I find another and light it. Azmar's shift should have ended an hour ago. He would be home, unless he had errands, or went to make amends with his sister. But without a note of some sort, I'm not sure when he'll want to meet me. It wouldn't be safe for him to be seen escorting me across the city *again*—

The door bursts open, and I choke on a shriek, my instinct to be quiet, not to let any trollis know I'm here, kicking in at the last second.

After whirring around, I'm relieved to see Azmar, yet taken aback by the panic written over his features.

Have we been discovered?

But no—Azmar slams the door shut behind him and crosses to me in two strides. His arms swoop around me with nearly unbearable pressure. His breath puffs hot in my hair.

"Gods help me, Lark." He holds me a beat longer before releasing me and searching my face. "Kesta told me."

"Spreener. But I'm fine."

His body brims with tension, brows drawn tight. He runs his hands down my arms, eyes raking my body, pausing on a bandage around my hand. He grasps it, his delicate touch a stark contrast to his crushing embrace.

I pull the hand free and flex it. "Only scrapes," I assure him, warmed by his concern. I trace one of the nubs on his jaw. "Only scrapes," I repeat, a whisper. "And you wasted a candle."

A great breath flows out of him. "Only scrapes," he manages, and his brows relax.

I frown. "Please don't tell me you ran around the city in a panic."

He glowers. "I masked it well."

"Did you?"

He shakes his head, not enthralled with the direction of the conversation. Instead of lecturing me on the importance of harnesses or pressing further about my welfare, he asks, "Have you eaten?"

I shake my head.

He composes himself, and his gaze drops to my clothing. His lip quirks, and I know the fear has abated. "You look like a trollis in that."

I glance down at my vest and weapons belt. "As close as I'll get, I suppose."

He takes up the end of my braid and curls it around his hand. His gaze travels to my bandaged palm. I turn my hand to clasp his fingers, slipping by him to bolt the door. I know how easy it can be to eavesdrop through those things. I take him to the opposite wall, before releasing him and rummaging through my belt.

"I know it's not the same." I feel a little silly now, but I've already started, and it's really the gesture that counts. I pull the stone from my belt. Its bluish hue glimmers in the firelight, not nearly as smooth or multifaceted as Azmar's, but it's the best I can do. "This broke off during the attack, and, well, it's what I have to give." Taking his hand, I press it into his palm. "So we'll pretend it's something lovely."

I don't need to explain what I mean. The way Azmar turns the stone over, so reverently, I know he knows.

I should ask how *his* day went, if *he's* eaten, what *he's* thinking, but I don't, because after hanging over death by the strength of a few fingers today, I understand so much more the life I want. The person I want.

I slide my hands around his waist, letting my thumbs dip beneath the hem of his shirt. The touch of his firm skin sends feathers of heat up my arms. Looking into his eyes, I whisper, "I'm not hungry."

His free hand wraps behind my head, fingers burrowing into my hair. I rise onto my toes to kiss him, hearing a soft tap as he gently sets my stone on the mantel. I relearn his mouth, tasting it inside and out, pressing onto the tips of my shoes to get closer to him. He's so damnably tall—

He has the same frustration, for he jerks away, only to bend down and grab my thighs, picking me off the floor, bringing me to his level. A slip of a laugh escapes me as my shoes topple to the floor. I wrap my legs around his waist and snake my arms around his neck. He traces my tongue, and a restrained groan from deep inside his throat lights me on fire. Every part of me feels too warm and too tight, especially where his fingertips press into my legs.

We turn until my back meets the blissfully cool stone wall. Azmar etches his lips down my neck, my collar, and I am undone, grasping fistfuls of his hair to keep me present. My legs squeeze him of their own volition. He presses into me with a ready response. My breath quickens, and that deep, sacred place inside me burns brighter than the noonday sun. It makes me selfish, and I bite and pull, demanding more. He gives eagerly. With the support of the wall, he frees one hand and presses it into my waist. His fingers climb the grommets of my vest, one by one, until they settle on the ties between my breasts. No farther. An unspoken question.

In answer, my toe slips beneath his waistband, and I pull the ties free myself.

We make it to the bed, but we cannot simply give in to our passions. Humans and trollis are compatible, yes, but Azmar is a large man, and I've never opened that part of myself to anyone. But I want all of him, however slow, however painful. And Azmar is everything I know him to be—tender, patient, fervent. I know from the moment we come together that I am changed forever. That I will never again be the woman I was.

Yet neither do I want to be.

Chapter 21

The room is bathed in predawn light when I open my eyes. I lie on my side, facing Azmar, who lies on his, facing me. His arm is tucked under my head, my ear pressed to his bicep. A fur haphazardly covers our hips and legs. My breasts are fully exposed, but I can't find it in me to be embarrassed, even by the fading pink marks left over from the night's ardor. I study Azmar's sleeping form. His face looks younger, relaxed like it is. There's a slight bump to his nose, right below where it connects to his brow. His eyelashes splay darkly with the slightest viridian tint. He has high cheekbones and a strong jaw, emphasized by the slight bony protrusions running along it. A few cords of hair waterfall over his neck and across his chest.

A hand's breadth below them stretches that silvery scar, the one I first saw when I witnessed him coming out of the bath. I trace the length of it, from just below his ribs to about four inches to the left of his navel. The muscle beneath it feels leaner than the rest of him, likely from the way it healed.

The story behind that scar reminds me what day it is. I'm supposed to meet Tayler this evening. I've worked out my shifts for the last week and a half to make sure I'd be free, but with the extra scouts, keeping my promise will be difficult, though not impossible. I wonder if Tayler will bring Baten.

At the thought, my fingers skim over my abdomen. I know the trollis struggle to conceive—it's one of the main reasons my ancestors were able to dominate theirs before the drought. I wonder if that struggle is the same with trollis-human pairings. Would a half-human babe gestate for nine months, or twenty-three?

I wonder what Unach and the council would do if I gave birth to a child like Baten. Like Perg. Nerves flutter beneath my skin. They make me want to talk to Tayler and Baten that much more. I need to know what my—our—options are, just in case.

I want to tell Azmar about the rendezvous, but I'm sure he'll insist I not go, though with some persuasion, he may agree to come with me. Yet I promised Tayler I would come alone. I want so badly to know about him and his mysterious township. If he or one of his friends spy a trollis with me, he may run, and I'll never have another opportunity to talk with him. That, and I fear being seen together with Azmar more than ever. I am his sister's servant now, but Azmar is no longer tied to their apartment. I will not implicate him in any way. I have to keep that promise as well. But I will not lie to him, and the only way to do that is to keep Tayler to myself and confess later tonight, after I return.

I only hope I find Tayler before any Cagmar scouts do.

My knuckle runs back up Azmar's scar. His breathing changes, and a second later his hand moves to encapsulate mine. He shifts; I imagine the weight of my head has cut off the blood flow in his arm. He leans onto his back and pulls me close, lining me up with his side.

I nuzzle into his pectoral muscle and resume tracing his scar. "When is your ticket up? For the scouting parties. Unach said hers will be soon."

His fingers caress the small of my back, raising gooseflesh in their wake. "Not for a while." His voice sounds lower at this early hour. "It isn't based strictly on caste. More on utility. Engineers, school teachers, those on the . . . task force"—a slip of chagrin emphasizes that last one—"will be the last ones assigned. But if there aren't any human parties or attacks reported, the city will calm down within a few weeks. Are you worried?"

My fingers glide down the scar. "Not too worried."

I know I need to leave soon, to change and take care of Unach and her apartment, but everything here is too perfect. Every minute is a gift. I let my hands roam over Azmar's chest, his stomach, his hips, laughing at how quickly his body responds. The hour is early enough for us to engage in our affections one more time, and it's easier the second time, even more tantalizing, and in truth I could lose myself to him all the day long. But we both have responsibilities that tether us: Azmar to the city, and me to Tayler.

When I finally pull myself away, I wish so badly that I could wear his bloodstone proudly. It's a fanciful dream, and I tuck it away quietly. Once I'm home—as much as I can call my dark quarters home—I press a kiss to the stone before tucking it away again, change my clothes, and hurry upstairs to set water boiling on Unach's fire. I notice a new rug and cushion in the main room; Kesta must have moved in.

I have breakfast ready for the both of them by the time they wake.

That afternoon, around the fifteenth hour, I make my way to the human enclave. It's not as blustering as it was before; most of its tenants must be working elsewhere in the city. I spy Wiln at his clock shop and give him a wave, but the person I want to visit sits in the back of the short hall on a blanket, working dried herbs with a mortar and pestle.

"Ritha." I kneel down across from her.

Her face lights up. "Oh, Lark! I haven't seen you around. Were you involved with the spreener yesterday?"

Just thinking of that enormous spider, of my body dangling above the canyon, sends a shiver up my backbone. "I was, but I'm fine." I tuck my bandaged hand under my leg.

"Good." She grinds away at a paste in her bowl. "I don't suppose you came just to chat."

I smile. "I will come just to chat again soon. But I do have a . . . favor to ask you."

Her grinding slows. "I don't like how your voice quieted." She glances around, surveying for eavesdroppers.

"You leave the city to collect these, right?" I gesture to the bundles. So many herbs and plants have long been lost to drought, but the most robust ones manage to survive the dryness, just as we do. "Could you go tonight? And take me with you?" Ritha would have a trollis escort, of course, but it would get me out of the city, and if I happened to venture off toward my rendezvous with Tayler . . . so long as I came back having collected *something*, I think I'd be all right.

But Ritha frowns. "Not today. Not until all this scouting nonsense ends." Her voice drops as she adds, "I bet it was trolls killing trolls, and they just blame it on us."

The assumption makes my gut twist. I leave it be. "I see. Then . . . if anyone were to ask. Say Unach, or . . . Tartuk"—Ritha stiffens at the name of the human task force leader—"would you tell them I spent my evening here with you, preparing these?" I touch a bundle of creeping rosemary. "And I can help you, later tonight. The work will be done."

Ritha chews on her lip.

"Please, Ritha."

Setting down the mortar and pestle, she whispers, "And what are you doing that needs me to cover for you?"

I consider, but I might as well tell someone. "I'm meeting a human outside the city." I keep my voice so low I can barely hear myself. "His name is Tayler. His people need seeds." She doesn't need to know the rest.

Her frown deepens.

"He might have information I need. If I come with a trollis, he'll run. He was very specific about that."

A thin sigh pushes past Ritha's lips. "There's Perg."

There *is* Perg. Tayler has one half-trollis friend, so perhaps Perg wouldn't upset him as much as Azmar would. But then again, he was very specific that I come alone.

Perg could be a backup plan, if I could even convince him to come. He likely wouldn't do anything to jeopardize his caste.

Reaching forward, I grasp her hand in mine. "Please, Ritha."

She looks away. "Fine, Lark. But if anyone *does* come looking and gets suspicious, I have to save my skin."

"Thank you. Wiln just saw me, too."

"Well, that's something." She turns away, riffles through a burlap sack, and begins pulling out tiny packages. "I have some seeds you can take to them. Most will only grow in the canyon, though."

Hope floods my limbs. "Thank you, Ritha. I won't forget it."

I use a window in Deccor housing to slip outside the city.

I saw it before, on my way to the south dock. A window to a small room whose walls had been damaged during the lecker attack five weeks ago. All the windows in Cagmar fit a uniform mold, but when cut in stone, they aren't all precise. This one is just large enough for me to slide through. I don't want to exit via the south dock. First, it's on the bottom of the city, and the climb would be exhausting. Second, slayers always man the south dock, and I'm trying not to be seen. It's a risk, I know, but the slayers' handholds are all over the city and will help give me purchase, even without the security of a rope.

The sun burns a vivid orange, meaning there must be a dust storm a ways off. The breeze picks up the higher I climb. I stay close to the east cliff wall and the shadows, avoiding the slayers' scouting points. Their eyes always point down, not up.

But when I reach the lip of the canyon, my limbs shaking from the effort, I know instantly that my mission has failed.

Unach wasn't kidding when she said the scouts had been increased. The area beside the canyon is dry and flat, so it's not hard to see the scouts stationed near and far, some only pricks of dark on the horizon. I can't fathom how to sneak by them, even if I were to wait for the cover of night, at which point Tayler would likely have given up on me. Then again, it won't be possible for Tayler to slip by, either. I doubt he would even try. And with the scouts roaming for a week now, he and any of his traveling party could be long gone.

I prop my elbows on the lip of the canyon and consider my options. The scouts, the time of day, a way to get a message . . . but no, none of those will work. And while I want to know more about Tayler, his township, and Baten, it isn't worth giving up all I have to sate my curiosity. I wouldn't know where to send a message, besides.

A memory niggles in the back of my mind. I try to grasp it, but it's made of dried leaves and sand and slips through my fingers. But staring into the great expanse of the canyon, I manage to grasp it at the last second.

We'll have to clear out the crag snakes.

I blink, backpedaling in my thoughts to Unach's lesson on monsters shortly after my arrival. Crag snakes live in the north, near the mountains. They only travel down toward Cagmar when prey is scarce.

"Crag snakes," I whisper. Which means I *do* know where Tayler's township is . . . or at least, the general area. I bite the inside of my lip. Someday I'll see Tayler again, and I'll learn more of Baten's story. I hope they can survive this never-ending drought, for the seeds Ritha gave me, and those I've collected from the canyon flora, will not make it into Tayler's hands. Not today.

After easing under the lip of the canyon, I allow myself a couple of minutes to rest and stretch my muscles before climbing back down the city. My shoulders feel rusted by the time I slip back inside, careful to ensure that I'm unseen, and my thighs shake with every step I take. I walk slowly to regain my strength, brushing against stone and metal walls to stay out of the way of trollis. I'm only just arriving at the Mid-divide when one of them blocks my path. I hug the wall closer, but he doesn't step around me. Confused, I lift my gaze.

My insides turn to water as I meet Grodd's sneering face.

"I saw you, little bird," he growls, and his meaty hand whips out, fingers enclosing my arm. He drags me down the corridor. I dig in my heels and try to twist free, but Grodd's grip won't relent. I fear he has more strength in his hand than I have in my entire body.

Horror melts through me as he yanks me across the market, drawing the attention of dozens of bystanders, toward the council's room. *I saw you*, he said. Not at the window in Deccor housing; he came from the other way. Then I realize he's wearing the garb of a scout.

He was on the surface, patrolling. He saw me pop up, must have watched me descend, then rushed through the city to intercept me.

I want to scream at him, to defend myself, to bite his hand, but that will see me punished. I cannot act out against anyone of higher caste than myself, which includes every trollis in Cagmar. I am utterly at Grodd's mercy.

Surely the council will see reason. Qequan is a brute, but he's reasonable. I merely have to wait.

I hold my breath when we reach the council's doors. Try to invite calm into my veins. The guards look confused when Grodd demands entrance.

"I've got an escapee," he says with an authority he no longer really has. "The council will want to know about this one."

The guards exchange looks, then whisper to one another. One surveys me and nods. He must recognize me. Were I any other human, they may have made Grodd wait. But they know Qequan has taken interest in me before. They know what I did during the last caste tournament. And so they open the doors to the long foyer and signal to the next set of guards to let Grodd through. When he finally jerks me into the council room and throws me onto the great fur carpet, my bruised arm starts to swell.

"We have a runaway," he announces with bold smugness.

The council isn't here in its entirety. Two of the Supra are absent, leaving only Qequan, Ichlad, and Agga. We've interrupted a meal or a meeting. A table set with food has been placed by the chairs. Qequan's heavy brow takes in the scene. His lips purse together. He's silent for several seconds.

I feel fear emanate from Grodd. But Qequan waves toward some servants in the shadows, and they collect the table and pull it aside. Qequan, Agga, and Ichlad take their seats.

"Runaway?" Qequan repeats, folding his fingers beneath his chin.

I stand, taking two large steps away from Grodd, and bow. "The Pleb is mistaken, sir. I was merely climbing the city."

"I've been scouting all week," Grodd says lowly. "I saw her climb out of the canyon and try to run. She scared when she saw me."

I gape at him. "That is a lie!"

Grodd's face brightens with a surge of blue blood. "You will watch your tongue with me, *human*!"

He seizes me again, by the same arm, and throws me back to the carpet. I gasp as pain explodes from my new bruises.

"That is enough," Agga says.

But Grodd puts a foot on my back, preventing me from getting up. "What's this?" he asks. I'm not sure what he means until he adds, "There's a bulge on her thigh."

My heart stops beating. *No.* Perg's knife.

One of the council members gestures, and a guard from the side of the room marches forward and indelicately yanks down the waist of my slacks, revealing my undergarments, the majority of my thigh, and the knife tied there. With a quick yank, the guard pulls it free. Grodd removes his foot. I scramble to dress myself and find my feet. My heart kicks into gear again, blistering within my chest.

I have no defense. It's illegal for humans to carry weapons. I might have been able to talk myself out of Grodd's initial claim, but I cannot save myself from this.

Qequan stands and crosses the room. Taking the knife from the guard, he examines it. "This isn't a slayer's blade. Where did you get it?"

I bite my tongue.

"I asked you *where you got it.*" His sharp demand carries all the power of a Supra. But Perg has suffered so much already. I will not give his name.

"I found it."

Qequan pats the flat of the blade against his palm and walks around the rug, studying me. "I don't believe you."

I stare at the fur beneath my feet.

"And where did you find it?"

"On the way to the south dock." I name the first place that pops into my mind. "Night shift. In the street leading past the food stores." I dare to lift my gaze, "I know it's illegal, but I've never used it. I was afraid for my life after —"

"*Silence.*" Qequan doesn't yell, but the force of his voice echoes between the walls. "I did not ask for your excuses, *human.* This"—he holds up the knife—"is against the law, and you know that, do you not?"

I swallow and drop to my knees. "I'm sorry. It won't happen again."

"No, it won't. Guards."

The guard who found the knife seizes my elbow, and a second one comes to take my other. Natural fear, cold and sticky, rises to my skin.

"A pity." Qequan strolls back to his chair. "I quite liked you, Lark. But I cannot tolerate untrustworthy humans in my city, now of all times." He turns and sits, flaring out his robes as he does so. "We will discuss whether it's exile or the canyon for you."

The guards haul me backward.

"Qequan, please!" I cry out, my vision blurring with tears. "I'm loyal to the trollis. I wasn't trying to flee the city!"

The trollis leader meets my eyes, and for a second I think he's been swayed, that he'll have pity on me, that my usefulness will outweigh what he sees as betrayal, or possibly even a suspicion that I'm connected to the humans who attacked the trollis band. But any trace of sympathy vanishes, and the guards drag me down a dark, narrow hallway that I recognize from when I first arrived. I know where it leads. The dungeon.

My hope fizzles out like a drowning candle wick, and I'm locked with the shadows, without a second chance to plead my case.

Chapter 22

After what must be a full night in this stony cell, I know I've been denied visitors. Azmar will wonder where I am when I don't seek him out. When he finds my quarters empty. He'll worry. I imagine him searching the city, asking around the south dock, maybe even approaching the human enclave. He'll find Unach, too, and ask her. Will Unach worry? Or will she shrug it off and expect me to show in the morning?

Is it morning yet?

I curl into myself on the floor. There's no bed in this cell, only a crude stone bench. Stone, rough and sharply hewn, composes everything but the ceiling. It leaves uneven red patterns in my skin.

I try to be brave. For hours I have tried to be brave. Bravery is one of the first things my father taught me. To remain stoic in the face of pain, to hide the hurt, to turn away when berated. But staring at the locked door, which I can barely see in the darkness, erodes my last traces of bravery. It slips away slowly, letting through shudders and lancing pain in my abdomen, then tears that spill over my lashes, half curving into my hairline and half pooling on the floor. Small, tight sobs form in my throat. The scent of bile clings to my sinuses.

Pressing the heels of my hands into my eyes, I cry as quietly as I can. I'm twelve years old again, muffling myself with a blanket, hoping no one hears me because I can't bear more punishment. But neither can I steal food from the kitchen and climb out the window, escaping into the desert beyond Lucarpo's borders. Despite what Grodd said, there is no escape from Cagmar. Not anymore.

Exile or the canyon. Either way, I'll never see Azmar again.

A sob breaks past my lips, and I drop one hand to strangle subsequent ones in the crook of my elbow. *Azmar, I'm so sorry.* He's the one sure way I could prove my loyalty to Cagmar, but I will never reveal him. I will not hurt him to save my own skin, even if the council chooses to throw me to the monsters. I am trapped between these walls for my own choices, not his. And I love him so dearly; I can't bear to imagine him harmed in any way. At least a sliver of peace settles in, knowing he'll be all right when this is over. Azmar will be all right.

I wish I could sleep, for dwelling on the place, purpose, and love I have found in Cagmar rips me to shreds, peeling my spirit away, one slender scrap at a time. It feels as though a fist clamps around my heart and slowly twists, never relenting. I think of Ritha, and it twists. Unach, it twists. Perg, it twists. And between each name and memory, Azmar surfaces, and the fist digs in its nails and squeezes, choking me with more sobs. It's like merciless clockwork, turning seconds to minutes and minutes to hours and hours to days and years, until I would rather jump into the canyon than spend one more second within these tortuous black walls.

My eyes peel open. I rub the crust from them and wince with an aching back. It's an effort to stand. Every part of me weighs a thousand pounds. My chest, tenfold. But I manage it. I'm dry to my bones, my water lost through weeping. No food or drink has been brought to me, though I'm not surprised.

I shove one foot in front of the other, walking to one wall, then to the opposite, until my body finds a rhythm in the pacing. I chew on my nails. Rip my hand away. Chew again. I try to piece my thoughts together, but I can't find a thread to hold them. So I pace, slipping in and out of memories, dazed.

When a soft tapping sounds at my door, it strikes my ears as thunder. I jump, limbs quaking, and hear a very soft "Lark?"

I run to the door, skinning the side of my knee on the bench, and press my hands against it. Have I finally lost my mind, or—

"Lark?" A little louder.

My stomach twists. "Perg?"

He shushes me. "I don't have a lot of time. Hold on." I hear scratching at the lock.

I find the thread and stitch my mind back together: fears, logic, worries, everything. "What are you doing?"

"Sh," he hisses, barely audible through the door. "There isn't much time. You'll have to climb out through Intra housing—"

He's breaking me out. Oh stars, Perg is breaking me out.

"Perg, stop."

The scratching halts. "Lark, they'll kill you."

"I can't leave." I can't leave Azmar behind. I have to say goodbye to him. Somehow, I have to say goodbye. "Have they ruled my death?"

He hesitates. "I don't know."

"Perg, I can't—"

"It's my fault." The scratching resumes. I can't tell if he's trying keys or a lockpick. "That's my knife."

"I didn't tell them."

"I'll get you out."

Every heartbeat is a hammer driving down on a spike in my core. I know it's hopeless, and yet still, "I can't leave, Perg."

The scratching stalls again. "Why not?"

I swallow against my dry throat. "I can't explain."

A moment passes, and I think Perg has left. But then, so quiet I have to press my ear to the door, he says, "I'll come with you."

I gape. "But, Perg—"

"If that will convince you, I'll come with you."

Somehow my body squeezes out two more tears, one from each eye. I press my forehead to the cool metal of the door and drag in a shaky breath. "Thank you, Perg. But I can't." My tears paint Azmar behind my eyelids. I can't abandon Azmar, even if the council will tear us apart either way. I can't bear him thinking I betrayed him.

Then the coolest ember of hope crackles. Maybe the council will let me say my goodbyes before it punishes me. Even my father let his prisoners say their goodbyes. Their last words.

Perg strikes the door, then curses. "Lark, if they catch me here—"

"Then go. Hurry."

"It won't be good, Lark. The humans attacked again this morning. Four scouts."

I fall to me knees. "Not Unach—"

"No. But it will be war. They say you're a traitor."

I grind my teeth. "I am no traitor."

"Let me help you."

"Perg, go. Please." I wipe my eyes. "Thank you. You are strong and magnificent, and you will prevail. You are my dear friend. But I will not be the reason for your downfall."

"Listen—"

"You will not fit through the windows." If nothing else, I have logic on my side. A trollis, even of Perg's size, can leave only by the bridge, the farms, or the docks. The first two will be crowded, and the last is too far from the dungeon. We'll be seen. And Perg . . . I don't know if he's strong enough to climb the entire city from the bottom, especially without someone to spot him. Even if I were to escape, I would have to do it alone.

I think I hear footsteps. Perg curses again.

"Good luck, Lark."

I hear no more voices, no more scratching at the lock. I am alone.

It's Ottius Thellele. My father. It has to be.

Only he could muster an army large enough to assault the trollis. Only he would have the power, the persuasion, to do so. He must be the human behind this.

I sit on the stone bench in my cell, my elbows pressing sore spots into my knees, my head in my hands. I don't have the strength to pace anymore. I've fasted for . . . I don't know. I should have asked Perg how long it's been. But then, I can't tell how much time has passed since he left. It can't be more than three days. I would be dead if it were more than three days.

A tender thought whispers, *Why did Perg come, and not Azmar? Why did Azmar not risk himself with the guards and promise to run away with me?*

I want to spit out the foul thought, but I'm growing so delirious with thirst and hunger I don't have the strength. It's a worm that eats through my heart, feasting on my fears and my worries.

How many trollis could I take down if I chose to run?

But how far could I possibly get, weak as I am?

When the door slides open, hinges creaking, I think it's a dream. That sort of half dream one has early in the morning, when she's not quite asleep anymore. But torchlight burns my eyes. I blink but have no tears to wet them. My stomach churns like I'm going to vomit, despite its emptiness.

Something hits my ankle. I try to see, but my vision blurs.

"Drink it. Now." The guard speaks with the lowest voice I've ever heard.

Drink? Fumbling, I reach down to find soft, bulging leather. It takes me too long to recognize it as a waterskin. My fingers tremble as I search for the mouth and uncork it. Warm water trickles onto my dry tongue. I choke with the relief of it. I feel each drop line the shrunken walls of my stomach. Mourn each drop that slides down my chin.

"Get up."

I squeeze the bag, sucking out every last swallow. My belly hurts. I find my feet. My legs feel brittle, but they hold me. Shielding my vision from the torchlight, I step into the narrow corridor outside my cell. The council must have ruled.

The guard isn't as cruel as his voice makes him out to be. He lets me walk on my own, instead of grabbing me like the others did. I try to find my courage. My body aches with the water, but it's slowly waking me up, granting me a little energy with every step. So much of this reminds me of my first day in Cagmar, begging the council to let me stay.

The light of the corridor slowly increases. We take a turn, then stairs. Another corridor. I feel cold, despite having had days to acclimate to the chill of a cell. Hugging myself, I blink as another guard opens a door to the council chamber, its even brighter light spilling over me.

The first thing I notice, after the light, is the silence. Eerie silence, like the calm before a dust storm, when even the birds and bugs fear to make themselves known. My vision clearing, I look to the council chairs; all five are full. No additional trollis stand guard along the walls. There's no—

My feet freeze midstep. Chills run through me as though the stone itself has opened and swallowed me whole.

Azmar.

Azmar is here.

He stands across the room from me, back rigid, hair coiled at the nape of his neck, arms folded. But when I meet his eyes, his arms drop, and the rigid expression on his face slackens. He doesn't speak. Doesn't move.

I wonder what I must look like. If it matches how I feel, it must be horrendous. For a split second, my heart leaps at the sight of him, but it crashes down again so quickly I stumble. If Perg knew of my arrest, surely Azmar and Unach knew as well. But Unach isn't here. As a Montra, her word carries more weight—

"Lark." Agga speaks, her voice sharp as a slayer's sword. "Are you or are you not in possession of this *trollis's* bloodstone?"

My lungs forget how to breathe.

No. No, no, no. How could she know? We'd been so careful. Did they root through my things while I was imprisoned, to find more evidence against me? Did Grodd? Did Unach's suspicions return?

My mouth works, but my voice stalls. My tongue tries to form the word *no*—

"Lark." The acoustics of the room carry Azmar's soft voice. "It's all right. They know."

My knees tremble. Shame, slick and bitter, swirls in my belly.

I wondered why Perg came for me instead of Azmar. I doubted, worried, feared. But Azmar *had* come. To the council. To clear my name when I would not.

The water hasn't worked its way through my body to allow me tears. Yet I feel them anyway, ghosts of sorrow and gratitude and shame trailing invisible rivers down my cheeks.

"Yes," I whisper, dragging my gaze from Azmar to Agga. "Y-Yes. I have it."

Ichlad's lip curls. He leans over Yog, one of the Supras, and whispers something. I don't need to make out the words to know it's vile.

Qequan's wide lips pull into an even wider frown. "Pitiful. Disgraceful. I can hardly stand to look at the two of you."

A hard lump swells in my throat. I want to cross the room. Run to Azmar, find solace in his arms. But the glares of the council pin me where I stand. Sour fear bubbles between my breasts, tempting me to push it away, to share it, but I swallow hard.

I wish Azmar hadn't confessed. I wish he'd protected himself. And yet I'm so relieved to see him. Stars, how did he say it? How did the council react? How long has he *been* here?

I finally manage a sliver of courage. "I-It isn't illegal—"

Agga snaps, "Do *not* cite trollis law to me, human."

"Illegal!" Qequan barks, slapping his hand on his armrest. "It shouldn't *have* to be illegal. Here I foolishly thought Posta was an anomaly, but it seems her disease festers in the city still!"

I bite the inside of my cheek at the harsh words. Posta must be Perg's mother.

Qequan swipes his hand as though he could erase me and Azmar from his sight. "Your filth will be dealt with after the war. I don't need our troops distracted by scandal." He focuses on Azmar. "Mayhap we'll streamline things and put you on the front lines."

I step forward. "No, please—"

Qequan stands from his chair and bellows, "Speak out of turn again and I will see your blood on the floor!"

I recoil at the power of his voice. Fear presses into my skin. *Let me have him,* it croons. *Let me remind Qequan what we're capable of.*

The temptation is wild and enticing. Gritting my teeth, I drop to my knees and bow. "May I please address the council in regard to the war?"

Agga snorts. "She presses too far."

"I think I know who leads the human army." I squeeze my eyes shut, euphoric with fear, waiting for Qequan's consequences.

He's silent for several heartbeats. "And here this worm has defamed himself to prove your loyalty."

"I am." I dare to raise my head. Glance at Azmar. "I am loyal. But I've traveled to every human township east of the canyon. I know only one man who could muster the forces. Who would dare to attack a city as great as Cagmar. His name is Ottius Thellele."

Qequan glances to Ichlad and Yog, his brow so low I can barely see his eyes. "And what good does this do us? You know his strategies?"

"I . . . don't. But I know his allies, and his temperaments." Though my father's allies easily could have changed in the last seven years. Nearly eight, now.

An idea strikes me. *If Azmar can sacrifice, so can I.*

I dare rising to a kneel. "My lord, Ottius is aware of my abilities and has coveted them for himself." My tongue feels like a sock in my mouth. "I-I believe I could earn his trust and wheedle information from him."

I shove my hands between my knees so that the council will not see them shaking. I stare at Qequan's chair, unwilling to look at Azmar, whose presence scorches like hot coal against my skin.

When the council doesn't respond, I continue. "You know what I am capable of, and yet I kept my word never to use it again on your people. I could have, when Grodd pulled me down here. I could have, when you dragged me away." I rush forward, not meaning to challenge them. "But I didn't. Between Azmar's . . . testimony, and that, surely you must believe me loyal to Cagmar. This is my home. I answer only to the council." I bow my head again.

I can hear Qequan's fingers drumming on his armrest. The muffled whispers of the council members. I bow for so long my legs start to tingle.

Finally Qequan says, "I'll play your game, little Lark. The army was last seen in the East Leagues. Say you gather this man's stratagems and deliver them to my messenger at the Pentalpoint by, oh, the twentieth, I might find it in my heart to show some mercy."

Agga scoffs. "A mere two days."

"And if you don't, I will do far worse than front lines to this creature." He gestures to Azmar. "And since you've shown such dedication to our little half-breed, he'll carry out the punishment."

My stomach clenches. *Two days.* If returning to my father isn't arduous enough, earning his trust and gleaning the information in so little time would be impossible. And yet I must make good on my offer now. For Azmar's sake. For Perg's.

I meet Azmar's eyes. They're golden and sorrowful, full moons above pained and pinched features. *I'm sorry,* I want to cry. *I'm sorry. I'm so sorry.*

The fist around my heart pulls, ripping it out fiber by fiber, unraveling every stitch of hope. Dizzy, I rise to half-numb feet. "I will do as you ask."

I hear a grunt from Azmar—words unspoken, frozen before he can earn more of the council's wrath. The fist starts to break the skin.

"Excellent." Qequan leans back in his chair. "You will leave now. We'll give you enough to see you there. And if the drought devours you, it's no leather off my back." He gestures with a finger, and Yog rises and knocks on the door I came through. Both guards enter.

Now. I'm leaving Cagmar *now*. To see the man I've spent years fleeing.

I'm leaving Azmar.

I turn toward Azmar. Take a step—

"I said *now*." Qequan taps his fingers.

My cracking lips part. I stare at Azmar. Of course they wouldn't allow us a goodbye. We disgust them. They hate us. Why would they let us have one more moment together?

I'm sorry, I mouth as tears blur my vision. Each guard takes me by a forearm. *I'm so sorry. I love you.*

Azmar reaches for me. I think he mouths, *I love you,* as well, but the guards pull me back and slam the door so swiftly I don't see him finish.

The fist rips my heart free. I am bloodless as the guards drag me away from the only family I can claim, equip me with minimal provisions, and usher me to the hot surface. Past the scouts, southeast, until I'm clear of the watch. Then they drop me onto the dry sand and leave me there to rot.

Chapter 23

I waste little time burning beneath the afternoon sun. Time will not mend me.

The horizon, an eternity away, expands to emptiness, save for some hills and rock formations. *Last seen in the East Leagues.* How long ago was that? Did Qequan send me to my death to make it *easier* on him?

I should never have climbed the city. I should never have let my curiosity and the need to sate my own desires draw me to Tayler and a township that was far, far north of me, if I guessed correctly. But that doesn't matter now.

Opening my little sack, I survey what the trollis gave me. No weapons, of course. Hunting is slim in these parts, but even so, it appears it won't be an option for me. Another waterskin. I drink from it carefully, knowing I'll need to ration. A day's worth of food, and that's only if I stretch it. Picking out a floral disk, I chew as I walk. At least after so long in the dungeon, I'm eager for the exercise.

I walk and walk and walk, loosening my knotted mess of a braid to shade my skin and arms. I see Azmar's pained expression every time I blink. Feel its weight on my heart.

The farther I walk, the angrier I become, the more absurd it all is, from the culture of Cagmar to my inability to claim a caste of my own, for if I could, Grodd would have no power over me. I hate him, and

I hate Qequan and his insufferable council, and I am *so angry* I could weep anew, but I don't, because water is precious. But apparently love is not. Life is not.

Is it so much to ask the gods, the almighty *council*, for an iota of happiness? Is joy something so fine, so light, that I cannot hold on to it for more than a few days? All my life it has flitted away from me, afraid of the curse within me. Azmar called it a blessing. I laugh into the nothingness surrounding me. The only people I have *blessed* have threatened to throw me into a canyon, murder me, exile me. Hurt my loved ones. Forced me to manipulate lawmen and farmers, bending them to his will, taking everything that was good for himself.

And I'm going back to him. My *father*. Now that I have Ritha's account, he is even more vile than I'd ever supposed. I feel as though I'm laying nearly eight years of hard-fought freedom at his feet, just to appeal to another tyrant, and it stokes my anger into the evening hours. The stars keep my course straight, though they offer me no guidance, no answers—nothing I can understand, at least. I walk and walk and walk, and inside I steam and fume and burn.

Anger is good. Anger fuels me. Anger keeps up my pace, one foot in front of the other, even after the sun sets and darkness consumes the world. Anger propels me forward when I trip over stones or dips in the dead earth. Anger keeps the sorrow and the fear at bay. Anger is my shield, and my crutch, keeping me warm when the temperature drops and the stars climb across the sky, almost like they're watching me, curious to see where I'll go. The shift, the space between them deepening, darkening, then lightening one, two, three shades.

I hear a voice far to the east, where the ground spans a black plain ribbed with periwinkle. A man's voice. How far have I walked? At my pace, fifteen miles at least. Is it so hard for Qequan to march his army here? Perhaps he wants to keep his advantage. Cagmar is a nearly impenetrable fortress.

"I said halt!" the voice bellows again. I don't heed it. I'm too angry to stop.

Sand slides under his footsteps as he nears me, the blade of a spear glinting in the light of a rising crescent moon. He grabs me by my bruised arm, and it makes me rage.

"Who goes there?" he asks, then stutters, "A w-woman? Where are you from?"

Through gritted teeth, I answer, "I'm Ottius Thellele's daughter. Do take me to him."

He hesitates. At least I know I have the right place.

"Or I will take myself," I spit. "Tell me your name, so I can relay it to him."

That startles him to action. He isn't gentle, but my womanhood apparently makes me less of a threat, so he isn't violent. Whether he knows of my existence is questionable. He won't know what I can do. My father liked to keep that our little secret.

We approach a sledge tied to two antelope. He keeps me between his arms and whips the animals forward. I grip the front of the sledge to stay upright, surprised at how awake I am. I force my rigid back to soften so the bumps in the ground don't crack it. My fingernails dig into the wood. So easy. I've been running nearly eight years, and it's *so easy* to go back. I merely had to wait for the last place I had found refuge to reject me and for my father to come to me.

Oh, Azmar. That lump returns to my throat, and stars above, I hate it.

We ride too long. I don't even see campfires until I'm nearly on top of them. The army, or at least this section of it, has erected canvas walls to help block the light, and their fires sit at the base of dusty holes. I'm not surprised to see so many awake. In the blistering heat, it's easier to travel by night. They may have only recently settled down to camp. The scout stops just outside the site, and I duck under his arm and walk into it.

"Stop right—" He reaches for me.

I spin around and slam my fear into him. He stumbles back. My pulse picks up, as it always does when I use my ability, but my anger flares so hot I barely notice the rest.

I wheel around and march through the camp. It isn't hard to guess where my father is. Three large tents occupy its south side. One of them is lit. My father is either scheming in that one or sleeping in one of the others.

I don't go unnoticed. Men—those still awake—stand, confused, ready to stop me, to call out to me, to draw their weapons. But I am impatient, and I am furious. I will not waste time on them.

Gooseflesh rises on my arms and back as I press trepidation into everyone who gets within six feet of me. They hesitate, they retreat, they reach for their weapons but do not strike. I'm only a woman, after all. But their rapid hearts tell them otherwise.

They part to either side of me, opening a straight path for that tent. A soldier mans the door. I send him backpedaling, like I'm a demon from hell itself, and tear aside the tent flap.

Seven men within. Conversation stops. I was right: my father is here. It's a shock to see his face again, but it's a shock somewhere outside my body, something I'll dream about tonight but am unable to feel now. He has new lines around his mouth and forehead, the latter of which deepen when he finds my face. I've never seen him so stupefied before. It makes me smile.

"Hello, Father." I let the tent flap fall behind me. "I've decided to come home."

My father and the men horseshoed around him stare at me like a phantom. I think my father forgot what I look like. Then again, I *would* appear different to him. I hadn't yet come into my full height when I'd run. I was still a child. I blossomed into a woman in Terysos. My face isn't as round as it once was. My hair is longer and bleached from so many days beneath the harsh sun.

But recognize he does. He schools his face—carefully, one muscle twitch at a time—so familiar, it's like the last eight years never were. He lifts his chin, straightens his shoulders.

"Calia, my dear." He speaks with both confusion and suspicion. "What an unexpected delight." He gestures to two men, and they push past me outside, likely to see if I brought anything or anyone with me. With my sudden arrival, my father doesn't know what to suspect. And he hates that.

He clears his throat, regaining a practiced calm with every breath. "I've been searching for you."

I raise my chin to match his. Is our eye level even? "I know."

His lip twitches. "Where have you been?"

I shouldn't be surprised to be interrogated. "Terysos."

"Lie." He grasps the table before him. I glance to see if there's a map on it—my father always loved to use maps like game boards, planning his conquests—but find only an open ledger, too far away for me to read. "Half the people here are from Terysos." He tilts his heads to his companions, as though I hadn't noticed them.

"Are they, now?" I have very little time to gain my father's trust. I have to give him anything I can spare. Easy facts, half-truths, flattery. "But I was in Terysos. How else could I have found your army?" Half-truth. I *was* in Terysos. When I was fourteen. Now for a fact. "But before that, I was in Cagmar."

"Cagmar?" one of the men repeats, like he's tasted something strange.

My father's brow shoots up once more. "Surely you jest."

"Not at all." I take another step into the room. Look around like it interests me, giving myself time to think. All tactics my father inadvertently taught me. Will he recognize them? "They keep humans as pets, just like you do."

The twelve-year-old me would throw up at the blatancy of my words. My anger fuels them, a dull simmer, but very much alive. I *have* run from my father a very long time. I caused him trouble. If I were to be perfectly compliant, he would suspect me more than he does already.

With a single gesture, he dismisses the rest of the men, who scrutinize me as they slowly wind their way out. My father says, "Come immediately if you hear any sort of struggle."

Ah, there he is. Cautious. Wise. He hasn't forgotten why he wants me. He remembers what I am. What I can do.

He bides his time until we're alone. The tent flap settles, and he steps around the table, strolls to my side, and seizes me by my hair.

I'm right. My eyes are level with his, until he wrenches my head to the side.

"Why, dear daughter," he hisses in my ear, "would you come back, after all the pains I've taken to retrieve you, hmm? Explain that to me."

I don't struggle against his grip. Fear has dulled and muted, an echo in my bones. Fascinating, how quickly I remember how to react, how to breathe, how to speak. It's been a second skin, all this time.

I feed him a sprinkle of truth. "Because I've been with trolls. And I realized that a life with you was better than life as a slave." As though life with him was anything but.

He holds me like that, my neck craned to the side, as though he's waiting for it to hurt. Then he releases me. I resume my posture as though nothing happened, keeping my hands at my side. I can rub the kinked muscles later.

Azmar, where are you now? In your room? In the dungeon? Are you angry, too? Do you hate me now? I remember him taking his own anger out on the training hall surfaces. I tuck the memory away like a prayer.

My father steps back. "You've riled my men."

I hadn't noticed, but now I hear quiet commotion beyond the walls of the tent. I bite the inside of my cheek to keep my expression dull.

He steps back like I couldn't possibly hurt him and leans against the table. "All right, then. Tell me about Cagmar."

And I do. I detail truths that will do little to help him, like the caste system. I tell him things I hope will dissuade him from attempting to conquer Cagmar and its resources, such as that every citizen in the city endures military training from ages twelve to nineteen, and how large their weapons are. I tell him a few names, including Grodd's, but many will never pass my tongue: Azmar, Unach, Perg, the council members'. He listens intently, asking a clarifying question here and there. In truth, I don't think I could give away any military secrets even if I wanted to, but I filter every syllable that exits my mouth anyway. Fatigue starts to work its way up my legs, but I continue to feed him with truth and fiction and anything else that could possibly endear him to me. Not as a father endears to a daughter. No, we never had such a bond. But as a soldier endears to his favorite sword.

"They eat monsters?" he repeats. I wonder what time it is, but I don't ask.

"Some of them."

He's been studying me this entire time, relearning my face, trying to read my mind, but now he watches me in a new way, and I cannot tell if it's good or bad. Then he saunters past me, opens the tent flap, and says to the guard outside, "Get me some rope." To me, he explains, "You'll sleep bound for the rest of the night. And every night, until you earn your place."

I try not to pinch my lips. I should have expected as much.

The guard returns with the rope. My father takes it in one hand and my arm in the other, then escorts me to the dark tent on the west. Which likely means he sleeps in the dark tent to the east. Farthest from the direction of an attack, should the trollis strike. Two men shadow him but keep a respectful distance.

Before we step into the tent, my father twists me around so my back presses to his chest, and with a jut of his chin, indicates a large, bearded man by a campfire about twenty feet away. "See that soldier over there?" His wet breath clings to my hair. The soldier is hard to miss—he might be the burliest man in the camp. "You make one wrong move, and I'll let him and his friends have their way with you. The men here grow anxious, Calia. They could use the sport." His grip tightens, rivaling even Grodd's. "And don't you *dare* use it on my soldiers again. If I feel even a whisper of it, I will ruin you. Do you understand?"

I don't know if he means torture, death, or the taking of my maidenhood. Unfortunately for him, I've already lost the last to his enemy. But I nod, keeping my face smooth. "I wouldn't dream of it," I murmur. "I want revenge just as much as you do."

He thinks I mean the trollis.

I don't bother specifying.

Chapter 24

Despite the fact that I've returned to my father's side, and that I sleep with my hands tied behind my back, my wrists nearly touching my ankles, I sleep soundly. Exhaustion—both from my long walk and my high-strung emotions—overwhelms everything else.

I feel a little more myself when I wake. I'm sore and hungry. My skin feels tight where the sun burned it. My mouth is dry. My rage has abandoned me, and it feels like a betrayal, my shield gone when I need it most. But when my father comes in to untie me, anger prickles at my back, reminding me of its allyship.

I clench my jaw as my joints reorient themselves. Massaging my shoulder, I say, "That was unnecessary."

"I'll be the judge of that." Otrius Thellele throws the bonds on the ground and hands me a piece of jerky. That's all my breakfast is to be, then, but at least he's feeding me. "Come. I've work for you to do."

Already. I chew on the jerky and stretch. The tent is used for miscellany, odd equipment that the army can't put elsewhere. A pile of belts, a few crates that might have foodstuff in them, two saddles, a bolt of cloth. I follow my father out, ensuring that I keep his pace. I am the obedient and repentant daughter. If that mask slips even a hair, both I and Azmar will suffer for it.

I'm led away from the main camp, only to discover a second, smaller camp just over a quarter mile away. There are roughly a dozen soldiers here and only one tent, though it's a high, round tent like the ones my father uses. The men busy themselves cleaning up: covering fires, rolling tarps, sheathing weapons. They glance my way when I arrive, but their glances don't linger, probably more my father's doing than mine.

Six of the men surround the circular tent, more heavily armed than any human soldier I've laid eyes on. At my father's approach, one of them pulls the door aside and allows us entrance.

I'm immediately assaulted by the scent of urine, thickened by heat. Nothing occupies the tent save for a trollis on his knees. My stomach lurches, and I hold my breath to keep my composure. I don't recognize him. He looks to be about Perg's age, with gray skin so rich it looks blue. His long black hair falls in a giant knot over one shoulder. He's completely naked. Red slash marks—from a knife or a whip, I can't tell in the low light—cover his person. Bile burns the base of my throat when I see deep blue holes in his shoulders. Someone has dug out the bone stubs.

The queen and the oak tree. *War.*

You hate the trollis. You hate the trolls. That is what he must believe, I remind myself. My thoughts try to superimpose Azmar, Unach, and Perg over this poor creature, and I mentally push them away. I cannot show sympathy. I must be as merciless as my father. He must learn to trust me. That is the only way to survive.

"This one's stubborn," my father ribs, as if we're talking about horseflesh and not one of the gods' own people. "He won't give up anything, even his own name."

The trollis lifts his eyes, first to my father, then to me. His brow twitches, and fear clamps on my belly. *He recognizes me.* All of Cagmar has seen my face, thanks to the caste tournament. Pressing my lips together, I silently plead with him to say nothing.

He glares.

"I want you to get him to talk," my father finishes.

My stomach tightens so severely I fear I'll lose my meager breakfast. I've come to a crossroads with my promises. I've sworn to Qequan that I will get battle information from my father. I've also given my word not to use my abilities against the trollis. But I will not garner my father's trust if I do not do as he says. I cannot stay true to both of these, not without talking to this trollis in hopes of convincing him to play along. My father will not leave me alone with him, I am certain.

The choice is easy to make. I choose Azmar. I will do whatever is necessary to spare him. Thus my father's trust trumps my promise to the council. Should this creature give any information that will hurt Cagmar, I will report it, then do what I can to counteract it.

My father says, "How many able trolls are in your army?"

I could tell him the answer, but that isn't the point of this exercise. He's testing me. Seeing if I still have the ability he indirectly gave me. Seeing if I will heed him as I did when I was a child.

I'm so sorry, I want to say, but the words must stay mute within me.

I push out a trickle of fear. The trollis and I recoil at the same time. He says nothing.

"How many." My father gestures to me. Hugging myself, I push out more fear. Cold sweat licks my palms and starts to form along my spine.

The trollis grits his teeth and turns away, resisting. He strains against the chains holding him. The depth of his skin pales.

I push.

He growls. "More than you have, louse."

My father waits.

The trollis shakes his head, obviously confused, and sends another scathing look my way. I focus on his stomach. He roars. "Five thousand."

He's lying. Cagmar isn't large enough to house so many. At best, they have half that.

My father's brows knit together. "And what is the tactic your generals will use in response to a frontal assault?"

A frontal assault would be difficult. Even if the humans managed to chop down the east side of the bridge, Cagmar wouldn't fall. Too many cords, beams, pressure points, and arches hold it up.

My father snaps his fingers. Ensuring I won't bite my lip or tongue, I push out more fear. My hands and shoulders tremble with it.

The trollis squirms. I can't tell if he wants to fight or run. He's too restrained.

He roars again. "We will pick you off one by one. You won't penetrate our walls. Our strongest will surface and slaughter you."

"Then we will goad you out into the open. Tell me, how could I best accomplish that?"

I'm starting to feel sick. Father asks more questions, and soon I'm on my knees, panting with my own terror. In the past, he always used me more subtly. He didn't want others to know they were being manipulated. He uses no such tact here.

After fifteen minutes, I cut off the fear. Blink sweat from my eyes. Cold flows from my erratic heartbeat and through my limbs. My belly and sinuses burn.

But it's satisfactory. "Well done, Calia." Ottius Thellele brushes his hands off and turns toward the door. "You've finally learned your place."

During the day the army moves northeast, farther from Cagmar. My father rides a horse—one of only three such animals among the men—and he has me walk beside him. We keep up a steady pace, but by the time we make camp for the night, I'm exhausted. My father must be itching to speak with the other war leaders, for he assigns a soldier named Dunnan to tie me up for the night, instead of doing it himself.

But this is a good thing. First, I must be gaining *some* trust if my father delegates the task. Second, *any* other man will be easier to fool than Ottius Thellele.

And fool him I must. I have just over a day to meet Qequan's messenger at the Pentalpoint. I need information, and my father admitted the men here were anxious for "sport."

As Dunnan leads me into a hastily erected storage tent, I bank on the assumption that not a single soldier here would dare touch me without his general's consent. Like me, none of them would risk his anger.

If my assumption proves wrong, I'm going to pay the price.

I'm not a practiced flirt, but I've seen it done. I understand the basic concepts of seduction: the goal is to make a man see me for my body only. Make him want it. When Dunnan drops the flap and sets his lamp aside, I lean into him, brushing my cheek against his.

"Ottius must trust you a lot, to handle me." I try to put a sexual inflection in my voice. It sounds stupid to my ears, but it gives Dunnan pause, so it must be doing its job. When I don't move, he grasps me by both shoulders and pushes me ahead of him. Grumbling to himself, he looks around, probably for the cot. It isn't set up.

At least he won't make me sleep on the dirt.

While Dunnan searches I pull my shirt forward and jerk it down as low as it can go, trying to show off a little more skin. I never had to use such a tactic on Azmar. But I force him from my mind. If I want to help him, I need to wrap this soldier as tightly around my finger as possible. Get him to do me a favor or . . . something.

He finds the folded cot and pulls it into the lamplight. His gaze catches on my chest, lingering for a couple of heartbeats, before he sets the cot up against the far wall, the only place where there's room.

I weave my hair through my fingers. "What rank are you?"

"Nothing impressive." He gestures toward the cot and pulls out a length of fabric. I wonder if someone took the rope for something else. Or if he couldn't find it.

Making a point of looking him up and down, I say, "That's not true." I do my best to saunter to the bed. I've never sauntered in my life.

His lip quirks. "Don't be trouble, Miss Thellele."

Matching his smile, I raise him a grin. "Call me Calia."

I hate that name.

I sit on the cot, as close to him as I can. Cross one leg over the other and run my fingers from my knee to my hip. He watches. I'm glad the poor lighting hides any rookie mistakes I'm making.

"Wrists."

Changing tactics, I try a pout instead and offer my wrists, leaning forward and squeezing my elbows together, trying again to emphasize my breasts. "Be gentle, Dunnan. I'm delicate."

Looping the cloth around my wrists, he asks, "How do you know my name?"

Because my father called for you in front of me. But he doesn't need to know that. "I've noticed you, is all." That sounded right. Like something Finnie might say to a boy she liked. But in my memory, Finnie is fourteen years old. I need to be careful.

His eyebrow rises, or the shadows around it do. "Oh?" He ties a knot around my wrists. I stroke his collar. When he leans forward to loop it behind my back—and he *definitely* leans too close—I swallow a gag and nip at his ear.

He pulls back. "Miss Thellele."

I run the inside of my foot up his calf, where he's not armored. "Calia."

"The general would not approve."

"Of what?" I blink at him. I try a coy expression. Rub his calf some more. Worried that I'm playing too dumb, I add, "He's not here."

A bud of fear sprouts behind my navel. *Please don't do it.* I could press a little fear into him if he does. Make him change his mind. As long as my father doesn't find out. But Dunnan should naturally fear Ottius Thellele.

He crouches down to knot the binds around my ankles. His knuckle grazes the side of my knee and draws downward. When he's finished, he plants his hands on either side of my hips. I fight the instinct to pull away. *Pretend he's Azmar. Pretend anything you have to.*

I lean closer.

"Calia," he says, a hint of tease in his voice. "The battle will be swift. Afterward"—he thumbs my chin—"we'll talk."

I want to laugh at him. Swift? And which side will make it swift? *My mate could crack your skull in the crook of his elbow, and he's only an engineer.*

I smile at him. Try to figure something to say that won't make him suspect me. With the job finished, he stands up and walks away, grabbing his lamp. He stops at the tent flap. I look up through my eyelashes at him. When he slips into the night, I let out a shaky breath.

I don't have time for *after*. I need to know *now*.

Working my jaw, I flop over on the cot. Pause. Twist my hands, then my feet. Smile genuinely, this time.

My plan *did* work. Dunnan was so caught up in me he wasn't focusing on the knots. They're loose. With a little wiggling, I'm sure I can free myself.

And if my father stays up as late as he did the night I arrived, his tent will be empty for several hours yet.

I wait an hour. I feign sleep, gently tapping a finger against the inside of my arm to keep myself alert. I'm checked on once. I don't turn to see if it's Dunnan or not, but lamplight flashes outside the canvas and the tent flap shifts. No sign of guards after that, though one could be standing at my door. I'll need to be as quiet as possible.

I twist one hand, then another, out of my binds. Sit up and gingerly work out my feet. It takes some effort. I'll probably have a bruise on my left heel in the morning. Free, I pull the cot out and wedge myself between it and the tent wall, then work up one of the stakes from the dry ground. Pressing my head to the earth, I peer out into the darkness. Only a couple of campfires remain. I guess it's nearing midnight.

Light emanates from the center tent, likely where my father meets with his men. I presume he sleeps on the other side, unless he's somehow humbled himself over the last decade. I scoff. Wait several minutes, surveying, before slipping out. I wish my hair were dark. It feels like a beacon, despite the new moon.

Needing to avoid the front of my tent and the campfires, I tuck my hair into my shirt and pad toward the lit tent, readying excuses in case any guards spot me. But they're murmuring to one another, heads turned away from me. Praise the stars. Behind the tent, I hear my father's voice. I freeze, listening. He's talking about disciplining men from Dorys. Not useful.

I sprint on my toes to the next tent. Don't bother checking the door. I slip in by raising a stake and dragging myself across the dust.

I can barely perceive anything within. I stub my toe on a cot. Swallow my reaction and move forward. It's simply furnished, which is to be expected for a traveling army. A cot and two tables take up the space, one narrow with an empty pitcher on it, and another in the center of the room with a drawer. I pull on the handle, but the drawer is locked. Cursing silently, I feel around for the keyhole—

Wait. I know this table. It sat in the front room of our house in Lucarpo. Though I can't see it, I know its top has a floral painting and a lily is carved into its front left leg.

I also know how the lock works.

Ducking beneath the table, I feel for the back of the drawer, but my fingers are no longer slender enough to reach over its lip. Holding my breath, I scramble across the dirt, searching for a flat rock, anything that could slip in and throw the latch for me. I find a tiny sagebrush and twist off a branch. Return to the drawer and shove it up. The latch is a long metal hook that extends nearly to the back of the drawer. After four attempts, I throw it, then discard the evidence of my effort.

Papers fill the drawer to the brim. I pull a book out from the top and carry it to the canvas where the light is strongest. Squinting, I see it's a book of pressed plants. A record of what grows where.

Rushing back to the drawer, I grab all that remains, fear dripping into my arteries as my mind tries to calculate how much time I've spent here, the noises outside, what I'll do if I'm caught. I don't have answers for the last.

I take the stack over to the better light. A leather bag of dice falls at my feet, sounding loud as the monster horn against the silence. I cringe, tilt the pages, squint. Carefully shuffle through, silent as a lecker. It's so hard to read, but I dare not take any and wait for daylight. Too risky.

I find something that looks promising, and I squat, listening for people. Encouraged by silence, I lift the bottom of the tent so unfiltered starlight can splash on the page. It isn't much.

I tilt the page, hold my face close. Read.

They're systematic, the attacks on the trollis. My father is goading them, trying to get them out of their city, thus the heads on pikes. And it's working. Cagmar has increased its scouts once already. And the more scouts outside the fortress, the more trollis the humans can pick off.

I wish I'd told Azmar about the converging constellations. About the signs. Then at least someone in Cagmar might know what's coming.

I shift pages. Find a map. It's difficult to make out, but I think my father intends to lead the trollis into a full-on battle so his army doesn't have to attempt a siege. Dwindle the numbers as much as possible, just like we did before the drought.

Pressing my lips together, my heartbeat loud in my ears, I put the papers back the way I found them, grab the dice bag, and shove it all back into the drawer. Push the latch to the right so when it closes, it locks. I don't know a lot, but I know enough. I know the army's path. I know where they plan to make their attack. I know a couple of their tactics.

And I know humans, my father most of all.

I'm due to rendezvous with Qequan's scout tomorrow night. If I run now, I'll arrive early, but most of my travel will be during the night, when it's cooler. I won't be able to get provisions. I'm not sure where they are, since I've never seen foodstuff in the other tents. But I can survive without food and water for a day. I've done it before.

My breathing sounds like grating slate to my ears, so I hold it when I slip out, replacing the stake and smoothing the dust. I stare at the lit tent between me and my cot, listening for guards. Someone passes on the other side of my father's tent. Maybe I can loop back around another way and avoid whoever it is. Scanning the subtle ridges of the parched landscape, I slink toward the shadows, imagining myself a beast from the canyon. I follow the shadows, surprised when my footsteps hush. I've stumbled upon a soft trail of sand, and I wonder if a river or stream used to flow here. Grateful for my luck, I quicken my speed. Following this, I'm moving away from my rendezvous, but once I get a good distance from camp, I can circle back and—

Men's voices touch my ears. I drop to my hands and knees, causing my hair to fall out of my shirt. It's so pale it reflects the starlight. Carefully tucking it away, I search for the source of the voices. It isn't hard, since one of them carries a lantern.

They're coming from up ahead, to the north. And they're getting louder. Pulse quickening, I search for cover, but there's nothing nearby but a riverbed. I hunker lower, listening to the steps. At least four men. But a scraping noise hums beneath the steps, like something dragging across the rough earth.

Biting my lip, I lift my head and squint. The lantern light casts a sickly yellow over the bunch, turning all but the front man into silhouettes. They carry a great, dark mass between them—the source of the dragging. At first I think it's a sledge, but as they near, I realize it's the trollis from the tent.

A shock shoots up my spine. I pinch my lips together. Where are they taking him? Is he still alive, or did they . . .

I don't have time to find out. The men walk straight toward me. Even pressing myself down into the sand, I'll be seen. Cursing inwardly, I carefully retrace my steps, tiptoeing as softly as I can until I wind back toward the lit tent where my father and his men are. I start to go south, even *more* out of the way of my rendezvous point, when I hear a soft sigh and a trickle of water. I freeze. Somewhere in the sagebrush, a soldier is relieving himself.

West, then. I pass my father's tent, too afraid to linger and glean more information. I'm confident that what I have is sufficient. I veer toward the storage tent where my cot is—

Guard.

Vile words push against my tongue. How is this so hard? My thoughts tumble over one another. The men need to rest at night, yes, but that's also when they're the most vulnerable. Though the center of the camp sleeps, guards will patrol its borders, ensuring the army isn't assailed in the darkness. I might try to outrun them . . . but if I stumble, if I hurt myself, I might not make the rendezvous, and then Qequan will believe me to be a traitor. I'll never see Azmar again.

My hands shake. *Focus on the guard.* It's not Dunnan; this soldier is too broad. He's circling the tent. He'll see me any second. I need to hide, and the only place to hide is *in that tent.*

I let a thread of fear trickle into him. I can't control *what* a person fears, but his mind will choose something—a sound, a smell, even the surrounding darkness—if he can't see me.

He stills. Turns and looks toward the southern horizon. I push a little more fear into him. Sweat beads along the curve of my back. My heartbeat strikes a little harder.

The man draws his sword. He's a fighter, not a runner. I clench my fists.

He heads toward the horizon. Perhaps to prove to himself there's nothing there. Regardless, I have my opening. Keeping my focus and the fear steady at his back, I tiptoe to the tent. Slip beneath, replace the stake. Step away from the cot to shake dust from my clothes. Smooth my hair. Draw slow breaths as I untangle my binds. Slip hands and feet where they belong, tighten the knots. Lie on my cot, listening. Worrying.

I hear the guard return. He doesn't enter the tent.

I don't fall asleep for a very long time.

Chapter 25

Today is the day I *have* to make my rendezvous with Qequan's scout. The option of sneaking away has come and gone, so I'm searching for any opening I can possibly get. My father has us marching northeast again. Judging by yesterday's speed, Pentalpoint will be closest around midday.

If I don't make the rendezvous, I fear the scout won't wait for me. And if I don't find him and deliver what little I know, I will never be allowed in Cagmar again.

My heart squeezes at the thought. Acting the part of the dutiful daughter, I help tie tents to sledges as the army prepares to set out at the cusp of dawn. I can't picture a life without Azmar. My mind refuses to piece together a future devoid of him, where I fail in my mission and spend my days looking west, toward the canyon, pining for him and the life we might have had.

Then again, a human and a trollis were never meant to have a happy life together. And yet part of me hopes that because I cannot truly picture a permanent separation, it must be an impossibility. It *must* be. I could not bear anything else.

When I see four soldiers crossing the dry plain, brushing their hands on their stained, faded-blue clothes, I pause. Were they the same men from last night? Dunnan lingers nearby. After securing a knot, I step over to him and ask, "Where were they?"

He side-eyes me, though I'm hardly flirting. "Set out the . . . troll."

My stomach turns. They killed him, then. Did they put his head on a pike, too, or something even more ungodly? Either way, I know they're using him as bait. I read my father's notes.

I desperately try to keep my face smooth, letting my hair shield my expression, and return to my work with the sledges. Bite the inside of my cheek.

I can't get the image of Azmar's severed head on a stake out of my mind. My eyes water, but when men come to hook up the sledge, I pretend I hurt my hand.

As before, my father tethers me to his horse. He's relaxed a fraction. He doesn't speak to me, which may be a good sign. No talk means no threats or demands. Maybe I'm playing my role better than I thought.

I scan our surroundings constantly as we march, trying to overlay the trollis map with the human one. Gauging the angle of the sun, wishing I had stars to direct me. Not only do I have to worry about escaping my father, but I can't get lost, either. I offer prayers to every god, including Regret, to aid me. My father notices my wandering eyes and remarks on it, but I tell him I'm watching for trolls.

I hate calling them trolls.

We stop for lunch at midday. I sit obediently near my father, keeping my nose pointed toward my rations but spying the soldiers around me. An idea strikes. While I could claim some privacy to go to the bathroom, Father will send soldiers with me. He did yesterday. But if I can make him uncomfortable, and if I *am* earning some esteem, my plan might work.

But I don't have a knife. I have to make do. This won't be pleasant.

While soldiers talk, a few packing up early, I gnaw on my thumbnail. Climbing Cagmar has worn down most of my nails, but my thumbnails have held on. I bite it at an angle, so it's sharp.

Then, checking to make sure my father's attention is elsewhere, I slip my hand down the front of my slacks, grit my teeth, and dig the point into the highest part of my thigh.

I try to hide my wincing. I dig a little harder, until blood slicks my thumb. Then I smear it across my fingers, pull my hand away, and clench my knees together, giving the blood time to seep through the fabric.

My bleeding is a week away, but no one here knows that.

Finally, I drop my plate and double over, groaning.

"What's wrong with you?" Father barks. "That's good food!"

"I-I'm sorry." I straighten, touch between my legs. My hand comes back bloody. "Oh no."

Revulsion strikes my father instantly. "You couldn't have done something?"

His tone is accusatory. He has no change of clothes for me, and the trollis council didn't allow me to take a spare.

"I just . . ." I try to let natural panic edge my voice. "I-I just need to take care of it."

I stand up, better showing the stain on my pants. My pulse radiates in the cut. I'll need to clean it out as soon as I'm able, so it doesn't get infected.

A few of the closer soldiers pale. One of them awkwardly withdraws a handkerchief.

My father snatches it and throws it at my feet. "Martos, watch her."

The youngest of the band frowns but begrudgingly gets up. Little provides cover out here, only a few scraggly trees and ditches, some sagebrush. I choose the farthest scraggly tree in the direction of the Pentalpoint. I'm halfway there when Martos whines, "What in hell are you doing?"

"I-I just need privacy." I show him my bloody hand again. He recoils.

Men.

I quicken my step. He quickens his to match. I slip behind the tree, which isn't nearly wide enough to cover me. I think Martos will turn around when I move to pull down my pants, but he only folds his arms and watches.

"Do you mind?" I wad up the handkerchief and remember what my father said about "anxious" men.

Martos shrugs.

Daring, I let the slightest shiver of fear pass from me. I don't even feel it, my own worry bubbles so strongly.

But Martos does. And thankfully, he turns around. Probably afraid of invoking Ottius Thellele's rage for ogling his daughter. Or he's disturbed by menstruation.

I rustle my shirt. Slip out of my shoes. Tiptoe away, keeping that trickle of fear steady, just as I did with the soldier last night. Just as I always did when Father brought in farmers and landowners to barter with, or anyone he wanted something from.

I don't want Martos to hear me run. There's a hill a short ways north. If I can wind around that, he won't see which way I went. I need to get distance between my father and myself. He has a horse, and—

A sliver of white crosses the sky overhead. I squint. An aerolass! I haven't seen one since I was sixteen. Like trollis, they have a build similar to a human's, but with great feathers stemming from their long arms, and wide tails like a bird's. Most of them have migrated away from here.

The ones that stayed were violent.

The stars, the gods, have heard my prayers. Or have they? The aerolass is so far away and alone. *Fight or flee.* If it's the second, then it doesn't matter.

Pushing my focus onto that aerolass, I ball up fear until my skin sweats cold and my knees clack together; then I shoot the fear out of me, sharp and fast as an arrow.

The aerolass's flight falters. It banks toward the army.

I start to run. I'm nearly to the hill when shouts sound behind me. I don't turn to see if the aerolass has attacked or if it's been spotted. I don't turn to see if my guard or anyone else has noticed me. I don't turn around for anything.

I run and run and run, slipping through any cover I can get, ignoring the jagged rocks and thorns that bite at my bare feet. I don't have time to put on my shoes. I don't have time to do anything but run, run, *run*.

My father will be furious. He'll send men after me.

With luck, I will never have to face them.

I don't stop running.

My heart burns my blood, my blood burns my muscles, my muscles burn my bones, and the sun burns my skin. I dash through every ditch, descend every hill, wind through every skeletal thicket and tree graveyard I find. I rush toward the Pentalpoint, looping around just in case Terysos, the closest human township, has its own scouts.

The evening is turning blue when I trip, skin my knees, and vomit over gravel and dust. I try to will my body to calm, to preserve its water, but it dry heaves and shudders, like I'm a wet rag wrung.

My stomach takes its time to settle. My muscles skip and twitch as though they're still running, and my wild, knotted hair sticks to my face. *Water. I need water.*

Light-headed, I stumble to my feet and look around. This is the place . . . or close to it. Isn't it? What if I guessed wrong? I can see the faintest indigo line in the north—the distant mountain range. I know this area fairly well. I should be close. And yet I doubt myself.

My hips creak as I stagger forward, searching, pulling sweat-slick hair from my face. My throat feels raw. My feet are shod—I couldn't keep them bare forever—but they thrum just off beat with my heart, swelling in their confines. The cut on my upper thigh radiates and chafes.

I wander for a quarter hour, every hair on my body standing with each sound, even if it's just the wind or a rare snake. Stars, what if it's too late? What if I missed the time? But what else can they expect? No roads lead from here. No signs, no designations. Only the stars, which haven't yet emerged.

I try to swallow and find I can't. My tacky tongue sits too large between my teeth.

I see movement to the southwest. Squint, wondering if it's an illusion. But it shifts against the night in the dying ripples of heat. Whether this is a trollis scout or a human soldier, I have so few options that I drag my feet toward it.

A few minutes pass before I realize it is indeed a trollis, and alone. I raise heavy hands to show I'm unarmed. Exhausted, I stop and wait for him to come to me. He holds a bow and nocked arrow in his hands. He's the shortest trollis I've ever seen, even shorter than Perg. His stout body still looks strong, his skin is the shade of night, and his large ears sit high on his head. I don't recognize him.

He stops eight paces from me.

I speak first. "Qequan sent you?" I don't recognize my own voice.

He keeps his distance. "What have you found?"

I lick my lips, though it does no good. "The army is trying to lure trollis out of Cagmar. They *want* the scouts increased, so they can pick them off. They plan to draw you out for open battle."

The trollis's expression doesn't change a hair. "Doesn't matter now."

My back straightens. "Doesn't matter? Has Cagmar mobilized?" Qequan's voice echoes in my memory. *Mayhap we'll streamline things and put you on the front lines.*

Azmar, please wait for me.

His eyes narrow. "Not for you to know."

I tell him everything else I found out, which isn't as much as I thought, once it's spoken out loud. I detail my father's map and his army, its supplies, and its weapons.

"I don't know if they're merging with another army or not," I confess.

The trollis frowns. "I'll pass it along."

Relief winds past my lips. "How far is the rest of your party?"

"You will not be attending me."

My gut drops to my feet. "Wh-What do you mean? Qequan promised. I got the information you need."

He squares his shoulders. "But we do not yet know if it's *true* information. My instructions were very clear. The council will reinstate you only if your findings prove correct."

I gape. Shake my head. Sputter. "B-But where am I to go? I've no provisions—" A cough squeezes my throat, and I turn away, but my coughing only emphasizes the scratchiness of my throat. I can't catch my breath.

Mercifully, begrudgingly, the trollis hands me a half-full waterskin. I take it and suck the liquid down. "Th-Thank you."

He squirms, as most trollis do when thanked. Handing back the waterskin, I beg, "Please."

"Go to your humans." He shrugs, uncaring. "Return when you fulfill your bargain with the council."

I shake my head. *What if my father's plans change?* But I don't speak it. I don't want to give this scout any reason to doubt me.

"I *can't*. Please." My tears are made of dust. "I had to flee them to meet you here. They'll know I'm loyal to Cagmar if I return."

He stiffens and looks past me. "You were followed."

Closing my eyes, I shake my head. "No. I-I don't think so. But I can't go back."

He steps away. "Then find shelter, human. If you follow me, I'll have to kill you."

My lips part, but the resolution on the scout's face doesn't yield. The trollis will not take me in. Not until . . . what? My father attacks? When will that be?

He walks away, leaving me standing there to face the night alone. And I do. I'm a statue, listening until his footsteps fade, watching until he vanishes.

Then find shelter. If only it were that easy. The drought has wracked this country. The mountains in the north might provide a cave, but they're at least two weeks' journey. I'll die before I make it there. And I'll die if I stay here.

I think of Terysos. But I'll be recognized. They know me. They drove me out. My father's army is not so far away that I wouldn't be reported. And I'd likely be tied up, unable to return to Cagmar even when my information proves true. I'm not hydrated enough to make it to another township. The next closest ones are Lucarpo, my hometown, and Dina, miles to the southeast. Too far.

Which means I must return to my father.

My jaw trembles. I bite down and start walking, my legs half-numb, half-ache. I'll have to march the entire night to catch up with the army before it sets out again. If it sets out again. I don't know, but I imagine they won't stay dormant long.

My tired mind threads through excuses, searching for ways to justify my absence. The aerolass scared me. The soldier threatened me. I got lost. All of them sound transparent. My father will see through my lies.

But if I must choose between his wrath and my death, I will choose the first. And so I remind myself, *I've survived him before.*

Chapter 26

My feet are bleeding by the time a scout finds me and escorts me to camp. It's near dawn. I'm exhausted. My body isn't really mine anymore. Everything feels far away.

The scout doesn't take me through the camp, but around it. A few soldiers meet him. They exchange words. I hear them, but I don't. I lean on the scout as we wait. I don't want to, but my legs are so weak, my stomach empty, my throat dry, my heart twisted to the point of shredding. I clutch at my chest as though Azmar's bloodstone hangs there.

My father will be even angrier to be awakened, given how late he turns in.

The soldiers return, each taking one of my arms. They escort me to my father's tent. A dim lamp glows atop the table there, the same one I pulled notes and maps from only thirty-six hours ago. Father's arms fold across his chest, his face a stoic mask.

That's the worst of his expressions. I avert my gaze.

"Wake up the men." His tone stings. "Might as well move out early."

The soldiers depart.

"Well, Calia?" He closes the distance between us quietly, like a cat, and I'm a mouse, trapped. "What's your story this time?"

I could scare him and run, but the truth has not changed. I have nowhere to run to. I'll be lucky if I'm fed today.

"I was frightened."

He laughs. It's a quiet, bitter laugh that oddly reminds me of Grodd.

"Oh, Daughter." He grabs a fistful of my hair and jerks me close. "Once again, I have to remind you what true fear is."

Bruises from those who should love you sting more than others. Deep and lasting, they bleed into your spirit, no matter how common they become. Something shatters with each strike, and it isn't always bone.

Fortunately, my father didn't break anything, though several of my ribs ache when I breathe. He spared my face, except for the side of my jaw, which was likely an accident. Clever men know to hit where clothes cover.

We march the next day. I'm allotted water, but without food and with a newly beaten body, I struggle to keep up and drag at the rope tying me to my father's saddle. After two hours, his exasperation wins out, and he has one of the soldiers toss me onto a sledge. I realize, as we grow close to the end of the day's march, that we're heading to the East Arrow, just as I'd told the trollis scout, a place nearly triangulated between Terysos, Dorys, and Lucarpo, where my father's plans indicated there would be a battle.

I lift my head as the sledge drags along. A spot on the mountains looks darker than the rest, but as I watch, I realize it's another portion of my father's army come to meet us. A portion that must have been working to draw out the trollis to the north. I ask the nearest soldier who they are, but he ignores me.

I look skyward, to the stars. A slip of light crosses directly overhead, then vanishes. My pulse quickens. It means something, surely. If only I knew what.

I count men when we make camp for the night, estimating nearly one thousand soldiers. When my father binds me—refusing me a cot— he says, "You're more trouble than you're worth. You want revenge?

Show me. I've a special place for you tomorrow, Calia. Prove yourself, and I'll let you eat."

He shoves me down and leaves, snapping his fingers. Two guards, including Dunnan, come inside the tent to guard me. Dunnan never meets my eyes. There will be no stowing away tonight.

And tomorrow, the battle will begin.

I do not leave my father's side.

He keeps my wrists bound by rough rope and totes me around like a dog on a leash as his men, and the men of a man named Lythanis, prepare for battle. They don armor, sharpen weapons, and assemble tents in practiced fashion, though there's only shelter to house half the soldiers. The trollis will be far better outfitted, yet I struggle to find relief in the fact. Most of the human soldiers have been coerced through desperation. They need food, water, and shelter, and they've been raised from infancy to believe the trollis are monsters. They have every reason to attack and no motivation to seek peace.

Surprisingly, my father lets me ride when we march, keeping me sideways and in front on him, holding my rope along with his reins. The lope of the animal hurts my bruises, but I try not to wince.

It's a short march, nearly to the place where I was supposed to rendezvous with Tayler. Lythanis barks at his men to line up. Where my father keeps his rabid anger in a steel cage, Lythanis wields his freely. No doubt my father has plans to help me cow the general if and when the humans earn their victory. He does not share glory well.

We ride behind the assembling soldiers. A few boys even younger than Tayler erect one of the tents where the dry ground inclines, allowing a good vantage point. Behind us, to the northeast, the ground slopes down toward a basin. To the southeast, it's flat and dry. A breeze, already hot from the rising sun, spins up a cloud of dust.

Lifting my head toward the dead city of Eterellis, where my kind once flourished, I see a dark line. Gooseflesh rises on my arms. The trollis scout insinuated that Cagmar already had plans to meet the humans in battle. Now they've unleashed their warriors.

I don't get long to look before my father gracelessly pulls me from the horse and presses me into the newly erected tent. Lythanis stands at its opening, talking to two more men. I don't see anything to denote rank, but they are alert and confident as they hurry to join the infantry.

It feels as though all the earth holds its breath. My father watches the army, distracted, and murmurs to Lythanis about numbers and strategies. I twist my hands, but the rope around my wrists tightens when I do.

"Look at them," my father says eventually, his lip curled. "Brutes and beasts. Uncouth, vicious. Do they even burn?"

Two hard lines form between Lythanis's brows. "See how well fed they are."

My father hums in agreement. "They eat monsters and have entire farms of fruit-bearing vines. My spies have told me."

I frown. Peer between the two men. Cagmar has advanced so quickly.

"Soon that food will be in our bellies." Lythanis rests a hand on the hilt of a narrow sword at his waist. He doesn't look like a man who misses many meals. I wonder where he's from but don't ask. I want them to forget I'm here. The trollis are close, and I will not stay with Ottius Thellele one moment longer than I must. I have no further rendezvous planned with Qequan; now that my words have proven true, how will I return home if I do not send myself?

A tug on my rope jerks me from my thoughts. Father reels me in like a fish on a line until I stand between him and Lythanis at the tent flap. He drapes an arm around my shoulder, and I see a short knife held casually in his fingers, too close to my collar for comfort.

"I've a special job for you, Calia," he whispers. Lythanis doesn't seem affected by my father's words or my presence, and I wonder if my father entrusted him with our secret. He must have. "Keep the toads from reaching the midline."

With his free hand, he draws a finger across the battlefield, indicating the center row of assembled soldiers. Keeping my nose pointed ahead, I nod. He's sparing his own hide, of course. The instant the battle appears lost, my father will mount and ride away. Will he take me with him? I'd rather die with the rest.

"When I'm finished here, we'll rebuild. Bolster the Thellele name. Send for your siblings and mother. Wouldn't that be nice?"

My half siblings and stepmother never knew me. I was a shadow in that house.

"Make you a little princess, hmm?" He taps the flat of the blade against my chin and smirks.

The trollis have arrived. They stop advancing two hundred yards away. Our numbers appear fairly equal. How many of us will be left when this is over?

Lythanis raises a spyglass to his eye, of finer make than the one the monster slayers use. It's gold and looks old. When he lowers it, I dare to ask, "May I?"

He hesitates. Glances to my father, whose arm still encircles my neck.

Lythanis hands me the glass. Exhaling, I lift it to my right eye and slowly scan the line. It's a cluster of gray and green, dotted with steely shields and leather jerkins.

My scan stops near the northern end. I extend the glass as far as it will go, turning it for the best focus. My heart rages so suddenly I fear my father will feel it. I hold my breath to keep it from sharpening.

The vision through the scope isn't perfect, but that's him. I know it's him.

Azmar.

Qequan kept his word. He put him on the front lines.

Tears pock my vision. I wrench the glass away to keep them from smudging it and blink quickly to hide them.

But my father notices. "What?"

I swallow a lump in my throat and pull up the easiest lies I have. "I don't want our people hurt. I don't want the trolls to take me again."

Lythanis raises a brow. He doesn't know about my stay in Cagmar, then.

My father straightens, but his arm, and the knife, remain. "The midline, Calia."

The only other men on horses are the two who were speaking to Lythanis earlier. I see them ride out front and yell something— encouragement, maybe. They haven't yet finished their speeches when a horn, higher pitched than the monster horn, rips through the morning air. The line of trollis charges.

Azmar, Unach, Perg. Stars, please protect them.

I've never seen real war before. I've read about it, heard stories of it, but never witnessed it. When the armies collide, it's loud and bloody and haunting. I turn away, but my father squeezes my shoulder and forces my face back. Forces me to see trollis and humans beat one another, scream at one another, run from each other. Paint the dust with blue and red and purple.

I hate this. I hate *him.*

"They're trying to flank us," Lythanis growls.

The moment my father steps forward to get a better look, I lift my bound hands and shove his knife away. Duck under his arm. Bolt out of the tent and twist northeast, away from the battle. He immediately screams after me, his bellows fading into the clamor of war.

Bruises on my thighs, as well as the cut I made with my fingernail, screech and pound with every step. My ribs sing their earlier torture. My pulse echoes in my collarbone. I pull up the rope between my hands.

I just have to outrun them and wait for the fighting to end. I just need to get away and hide—

Horse hooves sound behind me.

I sprint for the basin and its steep, sandy slopes. Only a little farther.

The pursuit grows louder. I dare to glance over my shoulder. My father is gaining quickly. A handful of men trail behind him on foot.

Digging in my heels, I spin toward him. I don't aim for my father, but his horse, when I push fear out of me. The animal rears. I don't wait to see if my father falls off. I run with everything I have. If I die running, I will die well.

I skirt a snake hole and a lone boulder. Sweat builds quickly on my skin. Weariness seeps into my limbs, reminding me I've not eaten in a day and a half. My pains become a single, unified pounding, an uncomfortable aura encasing my body.

I reach the basin. Barreling over its steep wall, I slide down, nearly losing my footing in the soft rust-tinted earth. Dust clouds burst around me. Dirt fills my shoes and coats my clothes. I cough, trying to expel it from my lungs. Take a few steps, cough. Dust clouds my vision. Rubbing it from my eyes, I focus on putting one foot in front of the other.

My father and his men descend just as quickly. He shouts something indiscernible. Even without horses, they're faster than I am and pierce through the cloud like phantoms.

Wheeling, I gather my fear like arrows and shoot.

One man gasps and falls. Another stops and draws his sword with a quaking hand, uncertain. Rage pools in my father's countenance. He continues on, slower, that knife clutched in his hand. Six men in total. Two of them charge me.

I dart south, trying to evade them. Both wield swords and chase me like I'm a prized boar. Changing directions, I come back around, pulsing fear into the other four again, trying to push them back. I'm so focused on driving them away that I don't notice one of my pursuers come around me.

His thick forearm clamps across my shoulders and yanks me back. My father shouts something. They all start shouting. I can't piece the words together. The blade levels at my chin. My pursuer's companion tries to help him, but I will die before I let them take me. Ignoring the blade, I push my fear into *him*, screaming as it chills my own blood in response.

My wail thins as my father and the other three men turn their backs to me, their focus drawn to the thick shadow emerging from the dust cloud.

My entire body goes limp.

Azmar.

Azmar.

Azmar came.

He was on the front lines. He must have seen me. Must have seen the cloud I stirred up.

He is a goliath compared to the others, well over a foot taller and twice as thick. His heavy, curved sword slices upward at one of the soldiers, sending him flying in a flash of red.

The man restraining me releases his hold. He and his companion run to intervene.

No. They will not have Azmar.

I limp after them. My skin cools as terror washes through me, spilling into them. They cower, leaving Azmar an opening to stab into another assailant, just as he notices the two others coming for him.

One, two on the ground. One cowering. Two approaching. Where is—

Pop! My neck makes a horrible sound as my head lurches backward, following the tug of my hair. I lose my footing and fall, tailbone slamming against the ground. The sun burns my eyes. A weight presses into my stomach. A hand tightens on my throat, cutting off my air.

My father's face hovers above me, red, with bulging veins. His knife glimmers silver.

"You bitch." He raises his blade. "I'll kill you, just like I killed your mother."

Fear floods every inch of me, so intense I cannot orient myself. I cannot find myself. There is only terror.

The knife comes down—

A shadow engulfs us. My father flies upward, five thick green fingers wrapped around his neck. His feet dangle above the ground. The utter rage on Azmar's face makes him nearly unrecognizable.

But before Azmar can crush my father's windpipe, before I can pick myself off the ground, I see him. The soldier who restrained me, bleeding from his arm. Coming up from behind.

I don't even have a chance to scream.

The soldier's sword comes up, then down, slashing across Azmar's back. Azmar wears only a tunic. He wasn't given armor. Qequan wanted him dead.

Blue blood rains over the ground.

"No!" I scream, launching to my feet. *"No!"*

The soldier stumbles with his own injuries.

Azmar releases my father and drops to his knees.

I don't know if it's my ability or their own fear that seizes them, but they run. My father and the soldier. They flee for their lives.

Azmar's palms hit the ground. His breaths come hard. Sweat drips from his nose.

Tears blur my vision as I rush to him. Indigo soaks his shirt. The cut is bad. Very bad. Bandages alone will do nothing to help him.

"Oh stars, oh gods." My hands shake. What do I do?

Azmar's elbow buckles and he falls onto his side. Falls, just like the star did last night.

Tears rush down my cheeks. I move in front of him, cradling his face. "Azmar? Azmar."

He lifts a trembling arm. Touches my hair. "Lark."

The sound of my name rips a sob from my chest. I pull off my shirt and crumple it in my hands. Hurry around him to press it into his wound. My breaths rip up and down my throat.

I rush to a fallen soldier and search his pockets and satchels. No medical kit. Nothing useful. But the belt, that might help. I unclasp it and pull it from his pants. Do the same to the next soldier before sprinting back to Azmar's side.

He's bleeding so much. It's already soaked my shirt.

"Hold on," I plead, threading the first belt around him, then the second, using them to put pressure on the wound and keep the wadded shirt in place. "Hold on, Azmar, please."

I check his clothing. His pockets are empty, except for one in his shirt. I reach in to pull out a stone. A dark stone with a faint blue shimmer.

Time stops.

Azmar took only two things to the battlefield. The sword allotted him, and my bloodstone.

Tears drip from my chin onto the dust.

Azmar's breaths grow weaker.

"No," I whisper. Plead. "No, no." I kiss his lips, and his eyes find mine. Their light still burns, but not for long. He will not survive without medical attention.

The sound of battle continues beyond the basin, yet has grown quieter. Is the end so near?

Azmar must return to the battlefield. To his people. But I cannot carry him.

It can cripple the strongest of men, I once told him as we sat on the bridge, gazing at the stars, *and yet it can strengthen the weakest of them, too.*

Strengthen the weakest of them.

I glance southeast, toward the battlefield.

"Fight or flee," I whisper.

"Lark?"

Pressing my lips together, I cradle his face and press my forehead to his, my tears falling onto his brow. "Fight or flee," I repeat. "That's how all creatures respond to fear. Azmar"—I choke on my own voice—"I need you to flee."

He meets my eyes. Confusion gives way to clarity.

There's an energy to fear. A desperation for preservation. A reserve of strength that only true terror can tap into.

It's Azmar's only chance.

But to channel so much into him, long enough to get him across enemy lines and into Cagmar . . . it will warp his mind, and his heart.

Our relationship will never be the same.

Crying, I press my bloodstone into his palm. Kiss him one last time. Stand. Back away, and take his sword with me, just in case.

"I n-need you to f-flee," I force out once more, sobs distorting my voice. "I need you to run back to the trollis."

Only they can save him.

It hurts when I push it out. It eviscerates my heart and steals my air, cuts into my every fiber like shards of glass. I shake with it, and when it hits Azmar, his body tenses. His eyes widen. His skin slicks.

He rises to his feet, new blood seeping into the makeshift bandage and dripping into his waistline. His veins darken, breath quickens, like my skin's peeled back to reveal a monster from the darkest depths of the canyon. His legs quake, like they've forgotten how to move.

I push harder, and my nails cut into my palms. I make him fear me more than anything else, even death.

And Azmar flees.

Fueled by that last reserve of strength, he runs. And I run after him, because I cannot let him fall before he reaches help. I cannot carry him. This is all I can do.

And so I chase him, across the basin floor and up its side, into a battlefield strewn with bodies, swallowing him in fear, sobbing, knowing that I am destroying everything we had.

Chapter 27

Cagmar feels colder than I remember. Even after Perg brought me a change of clothes and a fur, I can't get warm. I'm starting to forget what warmth feels like, and I returned less than a day ago.

The lights in the infirmary gleam too pale and shine with a strange sort of exhaustion I never noticed before. Casualties fill every bed, and any extra space has been stuffed with cots for the higher-caste injured. Others have been placed in their apartments, or even in the market. Azmar lies on a center bed on his stomach, his back stitched and bandaged and swollen. He lost a lot of blood, especially during his run. I know the medicine they've given him keeps him asleep, but I wonder if he would have awakened by now if left to his own devices. If the pain would keep him conscious.

With the doctors attending other patients, I dare to take his hand and hold it in mine. Is his skin too hot, or is mine too cold?

I want him to wake. I need to know he'll be okay, that he'll live. And yet I want him to sleep forever. If he never opens his eyes, he'll never look at me that way again, like I'm a morbid ghost, a repulsive monster, a living nightmare.

I lower my forehead to the cool bed frame. Ritha already treated my own injuries, but they come alive again. Pulsing reminders. *If you weren't like this, you wouldn't have these bruises.*

Azmar called my ability a gift. I don't think he could say so now. Not when it's been wielded so violently against him. But I didn't know what else to do. *It was the only way to help you. Oh, Azmar, please forgive me.*

My throat constricts. Gods above and below, I'm so tired of crying. I'll need my strength if I'm to prove to the council that I belong here. That I'm useful. I haven't spoken to any of the council members yet—they might not even know I've returned. But they kept their word; they have not yet revealed what's transpired between Azmar and me. If they had, I don't know if Azmar would have been treated.

I trace circles in his palm, watching his back rise and fall with each deep, quiet breath. Is he dreaming? Am I the subject of his nightmares?

I release his hand to wipe my palms over my eyes, banishing tears. I don't know what I'll do if he hates me now. I don't know if I could bear staying in Cagmar. But if I leave to seek out Tayler's township, I'll never be able to return. And if I never find Tayler, I'll die from exposure.

I don't know. I *just don't know.*

"Lark."

Startled, I whip around to see Unach behind me. She has a bandage around her left bicep but no other injuries. A sigh slips from me. "Unach, you're safe."

But her expression flattens. She glances at the other patients. Half are awake. "Come. Now."

Biting my lip, I spare a glance to Azmar. I don't want to leave his side, but I can't be here when he wakes.

After rising from the stool, I follow Unach out of the infirmary and toward the tribunal, which is presently empty. We pass through a dark, narrow corridor before she wheels on me.

"Why did you leave?"

I'm taken aback by her question. I hadn't considered explaining myself. My thoughts had been only for Azmar. "I . . . My father is the leader of one of the human battalions. I told Qequan I could get him information on their strategies."

Her gaze narrows. She hasn't regarded me so coldly since I first arrived. No, even then, her behavior wasn't laced with this sort of malice. "And that's why they threw you in the dungeon? Because you could *help* them?"

I shrink back. "H-He's my father, Unach. They thought I was a traitor."

She hums low in her throat. Steps to one wall of the corridor, then the other. "It's a funny thing, Lark. My brother was so beside himself when we heard you'd been arrested. I thought it peculiar. You weren't *his* servant, after all."

We're friends, I want to say, but the words stick to my throat like flour.

"And then he insists on speaking to the council himself." Her voice takes on a low timbre. "And then you leave. And he is miserable. Uncharacteristically so. Azmar is a level-headed trollis. It takes a lot to rattle him."

Fear, slick and oily, coats my belly.

She turns to me, her gaze a fire, and slams her fist into the wall. Were it not made of stone, it would have broken. "You *lied* to me, you little wretch."

She lifts her other hand. Half-embedded into her palm is Azmar's bloodstone, delicately wrapped in copper wire.

My heels fuse to the floor. "Wh-Where did you—"

"I took a tour of your room." Every word is a well-aimed dart. "You think I don't know what my brother's bloodstone looks like?"

She whips the precious stone away. I want to grab it from her, but my arms refuse.

"You disgusting little maggot." Her voice is little more than a whisper. It cuts me down to a stump. "I don't know what you did, but you are *nothing* to us. Nothing to me, and nothing to him. The only reason I don't denounce you to the city and feed you to a spreener is for *him*." She juts her finger in the direction of the infirmary. "How *dare* you? After everything we've done—"

"Please, Unach." I clasp my hands over my chest. "I love—"

She shoves me, and I stumble back, my shoulder colliding with the rough wall. The flames in her eyes have grown to a bonfire. Her mouth snarls like a feral dog's.

"If I *ever* see you again, I will break every damn bone in your body," she seethes. "I hope Grodd has his way with you. I hope you rot in the bottom of the canyon." She reels back and shakes her head. "You disgust me."

She turns her back and charges away, merging with the shadows, vanishing into Cagmar's maze. My fingers dig into the rocky wall beside me, desperate to keep me upright. I feel like I've been punched in the gut. I can't get enough air. My blood flows too thick in my limbs.

I've lost everything, haven't I? A jagged pain cuts from my crown to my ankles. *I've lost everything.* Crumbling on the spot, I hug my knees and weep into my shirt.

Cagmar's chill penetrates to my heart, and absolutely nothing can warm it.

◦⟡◦

I haven't been called to the south dock. My right to visit Azmar has been revoked, refusing me entrance into the infirmary. I haven't seen Perg since I first returned; he's with the army or scouts somewhere. Or perhaps he's found reason to despise me, too.

The next two days become the most miserable of my existence. I wish I were a child again, pinned under my father's thumb, naïve to the world around me, unaware of the trollis except for the occasional story. I could better bear disdain in that awful house than revilement here.

I fear most that Azmar will join the trollis in their hate. He has reason to. I've stripped him of his accolades. I've ruined his relationship with his sister. I've caused him grave injury. I . . . I used my *fear* on him.

Andru left me when he saw me use it on an enemy. How much worse must it be to be the recipient of my horror?

The horn blows. Not the low bellow for monsters, but the higher note for war.

Four days after the open battle, the human army has returned.

Cagmar is an efficient machine, trollis marching even through the winding hallways of the city, but they don't leave the strength of its walls. They wait, ready to rebuff the humans' strike.

I must defer to every single one, so it takes me a long time to reach Deccor housing and slip out the window, retracing the path that earlier led me to so much despair. But I want to see. I *have* to see.

My sore arms shake by the time I lift myself over the canyon lip. I'm sure trollis guards spot me, but I'm well known, and none confronts me. To the west, the human army is marching in. How does it not look any smaller than before? Surely my father didn't find reinforcements so quickly. There aren't enough humans in all of Mavaea to supplement his battalion.

I crawl back down the canyon, pausing at a bump in the rock to catch my breath. An all-out siege, then. Are my kind so desperate? What tactics will they use? Will they fight their way into the city, or try to chop it down?

Letting out a shaky breath, I lean my head back against the stone. They won't succeed. Cagmar is too strong. Even uprooting the Empyrean Bridge wouldn't see it crumble—it's too strongly embedded into the canyon walls. Yet how many people in the armies do I know? How many are just like me, or Ritha, or Wiln? Why must we kill one another?

If only I could scare them away, back to their townships. Back to the way life was. But there are too many, too many reasonable minds, too much scattered awareness. If I tried, they might respond by attacking each other, and I have no desire to dwindle the already floundering population of my own kind.

Opening my eyes, I peer down into the canyon, the endless depths below, and an idea creeps into my mind, so slowly I barely recognize it.

It plants itself, a ready seed, and digs in roots. They spread through my entire body, down the sides of Cagmar, and into the pit of the canyon.

I cannot scare an entire army.

But I know the things that can.

I've only been in the waterworks once, when I was running from Grodd. The place is just as dark and empty now as it was then. It takes me a beat to find the pulley system the trollis use to lower themselves down to the bottom of the canyon. I find a closet, identical to the one on the south dock, loaded with swords, harnesses, and ropes. I strap on all three, choosing the lightest blade and strapping it to my back.

I have to do this before the trollis leave the city, or before the humans enter it. I will not harm the citizens of Cagmar. And I hope this will do less harm to my own people than the wrath of the trollis would.

I step onto a plank held by a large hoist arm with massive pulleys and thick rope, all attached to the base of the city. I know it's made to support multiple trollis, but the way it sways with my weight makes my lungs seize. Steeling myself, I sit down for better balance, then slowly work the rope. It's similar to how the lifts operate, but the pulleys must be oiled or more complex, because it takes less strength to operate them. Makes sense. I have a long way to go.

I expected the darkness and have a lamp with me. I expected the exertion, which doubles because I work quickly. But I hadn't considered the temperature. The more I descend, the cooler the air becomes, until shivers of trepidation and cold merge into one, racking my body harder and harder as I drop. I hear the distant clicking of a tharker, a nonaggressive reptilian creature roughly the size of a man. Still I descend. A cool wind raises the skin across my shoulders and neck. I hear a croon of another beast, but I don't search for it. I don't try to scare it. I need it to find me. I need all of them to find me. After all, I'm the bait.

My sense of time fails me. I've been on this plank for both ten min-utes and ten days. I hear the river long before I see its rapids in my lamp. When I touch the ground, I have to remind myself how to walk. I hear a rushing that swallows my thoughts, and it takes me several seconds to realize it's the river; I've never seen a real river. Corpse-cold sprays of water tickle my legs. My own sour sweat sticks to my shirt. Chills twist my sinews and bend me like an old woman.

I turn the dial that feeds fuel to my lamp, until the light borders on blinding, creating a beacon. Its halo touches on a giant rib cage close to the canyon wall, half-crushed. Turning away, I shield my eyes from the light in an attempt to preserve my dark vision.

My spine aches. My stomach turns itself inside out. And I haven't even used my fear yet.

I hear clicks, croaks, breaths. *Come to me,* I think. I need to draw them in. I need to tell them I'm here.

So I sing. I sing an old song, part of the old bard's story that first told me of Cagmar and the oath that would see me in safely, a song of courage and promise. When I sing, my voice splits into a hundred echoes between the canyon walls, as though an entire chorus sings with me.

My love is true, my heart is yours
You deserve much more than I am
Four hundred suns, and I will come
A wealthy and affluent man
A canyon so deep, a canyon so wide
Monsters who feast upon flesh lurk inside
On his way to the glory of man
Crossing the bridge built by ten thousand hands

I feel the monsters coming. Their presence resonates under my skin, like worms in my food and breath on my neck. I sing the song again, taunting them, casting shadows by the light of my beacon.

They move slowly, stalking, glistening, hungry. I don't recognize most of them, despite all Unach's drilling.

Then, before they can attack, I reach out to them and push, push, *push*.

Fear floods the canyon, riding across the river and climbing up the stone. My skin rises in thousands of short peaks. My chest constricts. My lungs quit. But I keep pushing. I must reach all of them. I must horrify them. I must make them flee so far they will seek out the sun and the army that stands beneath it.

My heartbeats melt into one another. My bones rattle so violently I fall to my knees and hands. Hot streaks of urine coat my legs. The monsters howl and squall and bolt away. I push so hard, even the fighting ones turn back. Blood runs down my lips. Bile claws up my throat. But I follow them, pushing and stabbing, emitting as much fear as I can. I am their nightmare. I am their torment, their succubus.

They are my army. My monsters.

I push everything I have into them, until my heart arrests and muscles seize. Until I shatter into a million pieces, darkness rushes into every aperture and crevice, and the entire world snuffs out like one weeping candle.

Chapter 28

I dream of snow. It's a strange thing to dream, because I've never seen snow. It's one of those mythical story-time phenomena, just a fanciful thing to imagine.

The dream is reluctant to leave me as I wake, but consciousness wriggles through, eating away at it like moths. The first thing I feel is cold. The coldest I've ever been. Cold in my muscles, my bones. Even my eyes are cold, my lungs.

Then the pain. My heart hurts like it's collapsed and someone has built steel girders in my chest to keep me from falling into its brokenness. My breathing hurts, a deep and unusual pain that slowly beats away my dream and stirs me to consciousness.

I'm abnormally tired, like I could sleep forever and it still wouldn't be sufficient. Everything is dark, save for a dim, flickering light. I stare at its uneven lambency before recognizing it as a lamp. The rest of my unconsciousness falls away, and only then do I hear the angry river beside me. I can't see the sky. I've always thought of the canyon as a great maw, and now its jaws have closed around me.

I roll to my side, a weak groan pressing my throat. *Sleep. I just want to sleep.*

Something *thumps* nearby. The cold penetrating me makes it hard to turn my head. *Monster.* I didn't get them all. Of course I didn't. And now this one will consume me.

I'm almost too tired to care. If I can just fall back into my dream . . .

Thump. Thump.

I dig an elbow into the cold, moist earth beneath me. Mud clings to my clothes, skin, and hair as I lift onto an elbow and peer north. Shadows coat everything, but as the monster nears, my glimmering lamp catches its edges. It isn't the largest I've faced, but it's larger than I am. Memories of fear stir in my belly, but they're sleepy, too.

Then I notice its light. My sluggish mind can't recount monsters that glow. But the footsteps approach, and the creature takes on a greenish hue and bright eyes. Lifts its lamp.

"I thought it was you," it says. It sounds strangely like Unach.

My neck loses its strength, and I slip back into the muddy, blissful slumber.

When I wake again, I'm jerking up, up, up, on the waterworkers' plank. I blink, waiting for my senses to connect.

"—came out in droves," Unach is saying. She sounds like she's on the other side of a wall of water. "All breeds and species, even the ones that hunt each other. Utter insanity. I knew something was wrong. I knew it had to be you."

Ropes slide. Pulleys creak. Up, up, up.

She sighs. "I know you're good. I know you're useful. I know Azmar . . . loves . . . you, if he was willing to part with his stone. In truth, I thought he'd be a lifelong bachelor."

Something new and sharp hurts under the persistent ache.

I force my eyelids open. Force myself to look where the lamp highlights Unach's armor.

"If you were trollis, I would love you, too." She's so quiet. Maybe I heard wrong. "But you're not, so I can't. Either way . . ." Wind blows. No, that's a sigh. "I can't let you die. If you die, I'll lose my brother completely."

I try to respond. I don't understand my own words. My voice hurts, deep and raw. I'm so tired.

The plank halts. The lamp lifts. Unach reaches toward me. I feel a slap on my cheek.

"Wake up, Lark," she says.

But I'm gone.

I rouse sometime the next day, in my apartment, on my cot. Afternoon, judging by the sunlight prodding my little window. Ritha sews beside me. My chest feels like an anvil compresses it. Ritha hears me and lifts my head, offering water. It tastes strange. She's put something in it.

"I know what you did," Ritha says, feeling my neck. "Don't do it again. Your heart can't take it."

My heart. I press my hand to it. It smells like lavender.

"No monsters and no exercise for at least a week. It's like Wiln all over again."

I lay my head back. "What happened to Wiln?"

She tells me a story about the clockmaker's uneven heartbeat, how it seized on him once. He nearly lost his life. Did I nearly lose mine?

I swallow. "Is Azmar still in the infirmary?"

Ritha's lips pinch together. "I don't know, Lark."

"Perg?"

"I don't know."

"Unach?"

Ritha opens her mouth, hesitates. "She was here last night. I know she's not in the infirmary, nor with the scouts."

Scouts. "The war . . . ?"

"Over, for now." She gathers up her sewing materials. "The monsters fled. Trampled. Devoured, then scuttled back into the darkness. The trollis won the war without ever leaving the city." She shakes her head and clucks her tongue, as if she doesn't believe her own tale. "Now rest."

"Ritha." I point to the almanac on my small table. "Would you return that to Wiln for me?"

Ritha picks up the almanac and turns it over in her hands. Tilts her head in farewell.

She departs, and I fall asleep for a time. I wake a few hours later with a sore back and, one vertebra at a time, sit up. That ache still pulses in my chest, but it's softer now. Ignorable, with the right distraction.

Taking my time, I rise from the bed. My stomach growls. I find a floral disk on my little table and chew on it as I slip into the corridor. I keep one hand on the wall to steady myself and wait for the lift, unwilling to attempt any ladders. I'm nearly to the trade works when a familiar face crosses my path. I halt immediately, my chest aching anew as my pulse speeds.

Agga, from the council. She's broad and tall and looks at me with a narrow gaze. Hugging the wall, I lower my head.

"Good to see you finally, Lark." She sounds exhausted and waves a hand. "There's too much to do to keep up with the formalities."

Hesitant, I meet her gaze. I've never been this close to her before, and I can't help but gape at her sleeve. She might boast even more turquoise beads than Qequan.

"We know your information was true." She waves her hand again, as though it's inconsequential. "And, of course, we know only one person could have flooded our lands with creatures from the deep to drive off the humans. That noted, you may stay."

Air floods me. I bow my head again. "Thank you, my lady."

She scoffs. "Do not assign your human terms to me, child."

"My apologies." Agga begins to move past me, finished with our conversation. "Supra?"

She gestures impatiently.

"What about Azmar 937?"

Her wide lips turn downward. "He knows the consequences."

She leaves then, the train of her robe dragging behind her. I watch her go as I lean against a chiseled stone pillar. When I finally push away, another trollis hurries to me. He's a youth, a couple of inches shorter than myself, with broad shoulders and an abnormally thin waist.

"Lark?" He studies me with a sliver of skepticism.

I straighten. "Yes?"

"I've a message from Unach 935," he says. "Azmar is awake."

My body fights with my mind the entire way to the infirmary. I'm desperate for speed and barely remember to defer to the trollis as I go. But the faster I run, the more my chest hurts, and the more fatigue drips into my veins. I'm sweating by the time I arrive, and my skull hammers with my pulse.

I stand in the doorway, shoulders heaving with each breath. A nurse busies herself at the sink. Unach stands over Azmar's bed, speaking quietly to him. Azmar lies on his side, hair free and falling over the edge of the mattress, his eyelids heavy. He mutters something.

I take a step into the room, and his gaze shifts to find me.

His eyes widen.

I know what fear looks like. And even if I didn't, the way Azmar jerks back from me, hissing as his wound pulls, and struggles to clamber from the bed as his sister holds him steady is sign enough.

My body hollows. Unach sees her brother's distress and turns. Sees me.

"Lark—" she begins.

I grip the door frame. "A-Azmar, it's me." My voice quivers with my racing heartbeat. I dare to take a small step forward. "Azmar, it's Lark."

The glassiness doesn't leave his eyes. He reaches for a sword that isn't there. Teeth gritted, he tries to lunge for me, only to be stopped by his sister. His knee collides with the bed and knocks it over.

"Stop it!" Unach shouts, wrestling him down. "You'll kill yourself!"

My chest sears like it's been pierced with a hot poker, and all that I am wilts around the wound. Retreating into the shadows, half-blinded by my own tears, I mumble, "I-I shouldn't be here."

The sound of my own breaking is deafening.

I turn and run, but I don't get far before I'm desperate for air. Pain engulfs my head and chest. Tears wet my nose and cheeks.

I knew it would be this way. I knew it would taint him, change him.

But seeing the look on Azmar's face—the look of terror, the same across all the gods' creatures—made it real. Tangible. Engulfing.

I wish I hadn't come.

I wish I hadn't seen it.

I wish Unach had left me at the bottom of the canyon.

Chapter 29

I'm leaving.

After two days of forced rest and heavy misery, the choice is easy. I cannot stay in Cagmar, despite all the hopes I'd pinned to it. I cannot be where Azmar is and not have him. I cannot heal with the reminder of what I've lost waiting at the end of every corridor, around every turn, within every wall. Even in my little apartment, he haunts me. Once, he sat on my floor, guarding me from Grodd. Now he would not stand in the same room as me. I don't even have the excuse of pregnancy to tie him to me; my bleeding came, signaling the finality of it all.

Neither Azmar nor Unach has sought me out these past forty-eight hours, which only cements my sorrow. I have been utterly alone, save for a visit from Ritha, who misread my pain and increased my dosage of herbs. I swallowed all of them.

I rise from bed, feeling like a toddler just learning to walk. I am not entirely hopeless. Tayler mentioned crag snakes, and I have a general idea of where they nest. If I can find the crag snakes, I can find Tayler's township, and I'll be able to make a new home. Perhaps meet the Cosmodian and apprentice to her. I still have Ritha's seeds as an offering. And if they turn me away, or I'm mistaken in Tayler's location . . . I *could* strike out on my own, now that I know how the trollis eat. Stay near the canyon and garden, as they do. Or wander into the cooler parts of the mountains. Try to find water.

I'll need to be careful. I don't dare use my abilities should a creature of any sort decide to harm me. Not yet. My body has recuperated well, but I can feel in my bones that it isn't yet prepared to channel the fear my mother gave me. I cannot leave Cagmar with a blade, but I could fashion a sling. I've grown decent at using one, and I'll have plenty of time to practice.

Maybe I can coax double rations from the market, for the time I was away. Two weeks' food would be adequate. I know my father's map. I know how far I need to go. I only have to follow the canyon north.

I mournfully pack my few belongings, placing them into the bag the council gave me when they sent me into the desert. The one I had when I arrived is in Azmar's apartment, and I cannot bear to visit. If Azmar has returned home, he will not want me there. I cannot see fear on his beautiful face again. My last few fibers will snap if I do, and I must preserve what little, pathetic strength I have left.

I will survive this, somehow. I always survive, one way or another.

I stand in my room, surveying its stone walls, hugging warmth into myself. It's as though I never lived here, slept here. Yet I am very much like this chamber, empty, waiting to be filled.

I touch the lock on my door and blink back tears. I listen to my breathing and hum songs to myself. I leave my bag and slip into the corridor. I have a few goodbyes to attend to before I depart.

I go first to the human enclave. Ritha is unsurprised to hear that I'll be leaving. I invite her to join me, but she declines. "I have a place here. An important place here," she explains with an air of sadness. "Sasha is pregnant. Who will help her if I leave?"

I understand, of course. Colson is at work in the mines, but I'm able to greet Wiln and Etewen. We never were very close, so my leaving is easy, for them.

I'm on my way to Nethens housing when I catch Perg in the hallway outside military training. I call out to him, relieved to see him well, and wait for half a dozen trollis to pass before crossing to him.

"Lark! You're alive!" He grins.

I hug him, which startles him, but he embraces me back, releasing me quickly when a Centra swoops by. "I was going to say the same to you." I study him. "You seem well."

He shrugs, then winces. "A few injuries still. Old and new."

I gesture for him to follow me and guide him into a narrower, less crowded passageway. "Perg, I'm leaving."

His face falls. "You just got back."

A draining sensation tugs at my chest. Knitting my hands together, I ignore it. "I . . . I have to. I can't really explain, but there's a township I want to find. A human township. The one with the half trollis I told you about."

His features round. "What?"

"Baten, remember?" I place a hand on his. "He's *accepted* there, Perg. He's only a few years younger than you." I squeeze his fingers. "Perg, come with me."

His mouth opens, closes. His shoulders sag. "Oh, Lark . . . if you'd asked me two weeks ago . . . I think I would have."

I release him. "But?"

He offers me a half smile. "I'm a Deccor now."

"What? How?" The next caste tournament is nearly two months away.

"The war." He plants his heavy hands on my shoulders. "You should have been there, Lark. It was intense. Madness. Carnage."

My gut squeezes. The memory of Azmar's blood spilling onto the dust pushes to the front of my brain. I shove it down. Blink rapidly. That was the last time he loved me.

"I killed one of their generals," Perg explains. "The council promoted me."

I stiffen. "You . . . what?"

"Guess that fortune-telling thing you did for me was right." He misreads my shock. "I . . . I'm sorry, Lark. I know they're human but . . . it's war."

I shake my head. "N-No, it's just that . . ." My thoughts knot around each other. "Wh-What did he look like?" *Was it Lythanis or . . . ?*

Perg drops his hands. "Look like? Uh . . ." He shrugs. "He looked human. Um." He taps his foot. "He . . . oh, actually . . . he had pale hair, kind of like yours."

My heartbeat skips.

Lythanis had dark hair.

Perg killed my father.

It's so much to process. Stepping around Perg, I lean against the wall. *Ottius Thellele is dead.* The man who has haunted me all my life, who pursued me across half of Mavaea, who gave me the nearly healed bruises on my skin. My tormentor, my abuser, my cage.

He's gone. He is . . . gone.

"Lark?" Concern paints Perg's face. "Did you . . . know him?"

I meet his eyes. They look so human.

Perg has already loved me more than my father ever did.

"No," I lie. "No, I didn't."

Relief relaxes his features. "Good. But . . . already things are turning around for me." He grins, a touch of mischievousness in the expression. "I mean, now two castes can't mock me without a beating. And in a year, I'll be ready to compete for Intra." His grin fades. "So I can't—"

I pat his arm. "I'm happy for you. Truly. You've earned it twice over, Perg." My eyes moisten for so many reasons, and I don't want to examine any of them. I embrace him again, propping my chin on his shoulder. "I'm going to miss you, Perg."

He throws an arm around my shoulders and pulls tight. "I'll miss you, too, Lark."

I release him regretfully. I manage to wait until I'm around a bend in the corridor to wipe my tears. It really is goodbye, because we won't be able to write; no messenger service exists between the humans and Cagmar. And I don't even know where I'll end up. I don't know if I'll ever see Perg—my brother—again.

I'm so focused on keeping my face calm and dry that I run into another trollis when I enter the market. Backstepping, I offer an apology.

Turning, Grodd looks down on me and sneers. Fear pumps into my heart so quickly it stings. I retreat another step, then another.

"That's what I hate about rats," he growls, following me. "They never leave their nests, even to preserve their worthless lives."

A hand cups around my shoulder from behind. Perg. He must have followed me out.

"Is there a problem, *Pleb*?" he asks, his voice lower and bolder than I've ever heard it.

Grodd tenses. His tight fists make the veins in his arms pop out. His teeth will chip any second for how hard he grinds them. "No," he pushes between his lips. "None." He turns around like every movement pains him, and stalks back into the market as though on rusted joints.

I squeeze Perg's hand. If I allow myself to speak, I'll break into a blubbery mess.

He squeezes back. Nothing is certain but hope . . . and I hope dearly that somehow, someday, I will see him again.

Early evening hues filter through my tiny apartment window, colors of resolution, sorrow, and uncertainty. Standing in their glow, I feel like a stranger. Like I never was a part of Cagmar.

My gaze wanders to the natural crack in the stone behind my cot, where I had stowed Azmar's bloodstone. I wonder how long Unach searched for it, or if the glint of its copper wires gave it away. I yearn to hold it in my hands, but it's better that I don't. It would be cruel to Azmar to take it with me. It would be cruel to myself. Every time I looked at it would be like picking off the scab of a deep wound.

I take in a shuddering breath and hold it until my lungs hurt. Maybe, down there in the canyon, I tore my own heart out. Maybe I used so much fear on the monsters that I emptied the well. Maybe I can have a new start. One I won't ruin.

It's a nice lie. I'll hold on to it for a little while. I need every balm I can get.

The door creaks. I didn't bother locking it, since I only needed to retrieve my bag. When I turn, a shock like dry thunder runs from my heels to my skull, burning hot and cold beneath my skin.

Azmar.

He stands in the doorway, filling it, his corded hair pulled back. He's dressed in his usual simple attire. His shoulders hunch slightly, and a slip of bandaging peeks out from his collar.

I try to say his name, but my voice has turned to dust. My sore throat twists.

But the fear . . . There's no fear in his eyes.

"Lark," he whispers. I think I hear relief in his tone. But instead of warm hope blooming, a sapping dread pulls me down. I search his face, his stature, trying to read him. I can't.

My hands are shaking.

He steps in, closes the door behind him, and wipes a hand down his face. "I was so worried they'd hurt you. That you wouldn't come back."

Heat pricks my face. My eyes water.

Azmar sobers. Takes another step, then another. Reaches for me.

I step back, and a delicate fiber of fledging strength snaps like an old lute string. "I-I don't understand." I sound like a frog and shake my head like a madwoman. "I-I saw you in the infirmary. Azmar, you were so frightened—"

A tear burns down my face.

This time when he reaches for me, I don't move. His calloused thumb follows the tear's trail, erasing its passage. Then he cups my face. "I know. I wasn't . . ." He lets a hard breath out through his nose. Glances away, then back. "I wasn't entirely lucid. I . . . I needed to process. I was asleep for a while. Strange dreams . . ." His brow wrinkles.

"They w-weren't dreams."

But he shakes his head. "I knew what you were doing, Lark."

Pulling from his touch, I whisper, "It doesn't make a difference."

"Doesn't it?" He studies me before reaching into his belt for a few rolled-up parchments tied with twine. He hands them to me.

I hesitate. "What is this?"

"This came to mind this morning, before I was released. Read it."

I try again to read him, to understand, but I see only my own fears looking back at me, as though I've gone blind to everything else. Rolling my lips together, I take the papers in trembling fingers, slide off the tie, and unfold them, terrified.

Three different styles of handwriting cover the page, two blocky and one like angry scratches. The spelling of some words and the size of the letters tell me it's trollis penmanship. At the top of the paper, someone scrawled, *Azmar 937*. Dates line the left margin.

These first papers are fifteen years old.

Graduated rudimentary school with good marks, but hesitant in the field. Engages like a Pleb, the first line reads. The next says, *Holding back in practice. Ran extra drills until 1900. Little effect. Wrog has the idea to put him with the sixth-years. Beat some sense into him.*

I swallow. "These are your training records?"

"Part of them." Azmar reaches forward and takes the first page. A notation marks the center of the next one. "Read."

Thrust A937 into combat imitation with the sixth-years. Ordered several to gang up on him. A shock—he fought like a Supra. Turned into a right spreener and gave two of the boys concussions. Untapped talent here. Good breeding.

I look up to Azmar. "I don't understand—"

He takes the papers from my hands. "I was terrified, Lark. I thought my trainers were fed up with me and wanted me dead."

I pale. "That's terrible."

"Lark." He raises the paper before my nose. "I was *terrified.*"

A few seconds pass before realization dawns.

Fight or flee.

The walls of my apartment shatter, and I'm kneeling in the red dirt of the basin again, Azmar's blood pooling around me. *F-Fight or flee. That's how all creatures respond to fear. Azmar, I need you to flee.*

Azmar's gut response to fear is . . . to fight. That was why he lunged for me in the infirmary. He wanted to *fight* me.

"I knew what you were doing." He rests the papers on my empty side table. Takes my face in both hands. "You saved my life."

Tears pour freely. "Y-You saved mine."

He crushes me to him. I grab fistfuls of his shirt and sob into the linen, my own fibers breaking apart and restitching themselves. I am remade as hope burns away the last tendrils of fear.

A wet chuckle creeps up Azmar's throat. "I was terrified of you, Lark," he murmurs. "But I was more scared of losing you. I thought I already had."

I press into him, keeping my hands at his stomach. I don't want to worsen his injury. He probably shouldn't even be up. I think of the first time we embraced like this, in the waterworks, after Grodd dangled me out that window. How far we've come in so little time.

When I'm calm enough to speak, I confess, "I-I was going to leave."

"No." He drops to one knee, then the other, and looks me in the eyes. "Stay, Lark."

"The council knows. Others will know. Your life will be ruined. I n-never meant to ruin—"

He presses his thumb against my mouth. "No."

I pull back. "Denying it doesn't make it go away, Azmar."

His deep gold gaze scans mine. Several seconds pass. "Then I'll leave with you."

"No!" The admonition rings off the walls. I swallow again. "No. *Everything* is here. All your sacrifices, your education, your friends, your sister—"

"Calia Thellele." I've never heard my given name on his lips, and it shocks me to stillness. His voice is firm, his gaze unyielding. "All my life I've wanted change. I wanted some sort of progression in a city centuries-set in its patterns. I wanted something different. Something *exciting*. You appeared from the dearth, and you were all of those things. I will miss Unach, yes. I will miss her dearly. But I knew what I was doing when I gave you this."

He pulls from his pocket his bloodstone, fastened to the end of a thin chain. I gasp. When did he take it from Unach? Did she *give* it to him, after all she said about me? Azmar lifts the chain over my head, settling the bloodstone over my heart. And suddenly I'm whole again, all my forgotten and missing pieces fitted back into place.

I fall into Azmar, kissing him, almost knocking him over. I kiss him until I'm breathless, until our tears mingle and lips swell. Forehead to forehead, I whisper, "I'll miss Unach, too."

His arm winds around my waist and holds me close. I've become so unaccustomed to happiness that it hurts.

"She'll hate me for this," I mutter into his hair.

"She'll forgive you," he promises, tugging on his bloodstone. "She always forgives, in time."

We follow the canyon, walking largely during evening and night. This time of year, the relentless sun blisters even the thickest of skin. Azmar has a hammock he can nail into the lip of the canyon when we can't find cover to camp under. I'm convinced that a soldier or scout will spy us, or that a monster will brave the surface, but the journey is uneventful. For now, the battles are over. For now, I am at peace under the stars, with the first of the family a Cosmodian once promised me.

Two hundred miles north of the Empyrean Bridge, the canyon narrows and juts eastward, stretching to join the line of mountains that guard the northern border of Mavaea. I've never traveled as far as the mountains. My father's map listed no townships farther north than Ungo. But north we go, foraging in the mornings, resting in the afternoons, murmuring stories in the evenings, making love in the depths of night. I think of Azmar's confession, of his desire for change, and wonder how tedious he finds our travel. But he never once complains, even when our food stores run low.

On the eighteenth day, we find something unexpected in the early morning hours. Something we might have missed, had we passed it at night. A trail through the sagebrush, narrow, packed, and winding. Forking away from the canyon where the crag snakes lurk, toward the shelter of the mountains. I feel in my gut that this is it, the path to Tayler's home. A place that might accept me and Azmar. A place of hope.

We've only walked a quarter mile down the trail when I remark on the dimness of the day, as though the sun hesitates to rise. Azmar's footsteps stop. I turn to see what the matter is. His head is tilted up, watching the sky.

"Lark, look."

I look and see the most peculiar thing. A large, dark cloud creeps across the sky, smothering the sun and cooling the breeze.

A drop of rain strikes my cheek.

Acknowledgments

I am so very grateful to everyone who helped me with this book. Biggest thanks to my husband, Jordan, who quietly works behind the scenes so books can happen; my friend Leah O'Neill, who answered countless questions about civil engineering so Azmar would work as a character; and Caitlyn McFarland, who spent hours on the phone to help me get over the initial hump of writer's block and make this story really shine. I also want to thank Nancy Campbell Allen—it was a chat with her that made the idea for this story come alive.

This was one of those trickier tales. I absolutely adore this book, but I wrote the first two-thirds of it before *Star Mother*, so if you read the acknowledgments for *that* book, you'll know what I mean when I say this novel was sacrificed to the great breaking of 2019. It was hard to come back to, but I'm so grateful I did, because *The Hanging City* is now one of my favorite books in my collection. I hope everyone reading enjoys it!

Thank you to Marlene Stringer and Adrienne Procaccini, who got this project into the light of day, and to Jason Kirk, my reunited partner in crime, who helped polish this into something amazing. Thank you to the team of people who line up every sentence and place every missed comma. We all take legibility for granted.

Another special thanks to Tricia Levenseller and Rachel Maltby, who suffered through early drafts with incredible patience, especially considering that I didn't use spell-check.

Finally, my gratitude to God, who pulls me through dark times and rewards me with imagination and the ability to share it with the world.

I have so many more stories to tell.

About the Author

Charlie N. Holmberg is a *Wall Street Journal* and Amazon Charts bestselling author of fantasy and romance fiction, including the Paper Magician series, the Spellbreaker series, and the Whimbrel House series, and writes contemporary romance under C. N. Holmberg. She is published in more than twenty languages, has been a finalist for a RITA Award and multiple Whitney Awards, and won the 2020 Whitney Award for Novel of the Year: Adult Fiction. Born in Salt Lake City, Charlie was raised a Trekkie alongside three sisters who also have boy names. She is a BYU alumna, plays the ukulele, and owns too many pairs of glasses. She currently lives with her family in Utah. Visit her at www.charlienholmberg.com.